She changed her tack sudden him. He could smell her unmade-up skin was young blonde hair was, improbably, natural. that with every breath she took, her breasts pushed softly against him and she looked directly up into his eyes, her tongue moistening her lower lip. 'Be nice!' she said, softly. 'You look as though you could be!'

JAN MALCOLM

Roulette

GRAFTON BOOKS
A Division of the Collins Publishing Group

LONDON GLASGOW
TORONTO SYDNEY AUCKLAND

Grafton Books
A Division of the Collins Publishing Group
8 Grafton Street, London W1X 3LA

A Grafton Paperback Original 1989

ISBN 0-586-07440-6

Printed and bound in Great Britain by
Collins, Glasgow

Set in Times

PART ONE
London

1

It was the middle of the graveyard shift when the girl came in. Two A.M., and Ross Cavallo's eyes were gritty with sleep, his dress shirt beginning to stick to him with sweat, and his throat dry with the smoke of his own and other people's cigarettes. Two A.M. and still they came in, the rich, the bored, the idle, the greedy, all seeking a few moments' orgasm in the embrace of the whore Fortune.

He smiled as he moved unhurriedly across the casino floor, a practised smile that even reached his eyes, and not the most cynical punter guessed that behind the smile, Cavallo was thinking, 'Go home, you bastards, go home and let me go to bed.'

He thought of bed with longing – he had been in the casino for twelve hours and it would probably be another three before he could escape and drive through the still grey streets on his way home. The bed would be warm with Sarah's sleeping body, her breasts swollen and milky with feeding the baby, and she would come half awake and nuzzle into his arms like a child. What the hell was he doing here, anyway, being polite and charming to these mindless idiots who were too stupid to realize they weren't enjoying themselves as they strained anxiously over the roulette table, ludicrously dependent on the random tumbling of a ball.

Mrs Fielding put her hand on his arm as he passed. 'Ross! You haven't spoken to me tonight, you bad boy! I shall have to be cross!'

Her face had cost her a large fortune in cosmetic

surgery, and her dress was Gina Fratini, but her eyes were old, and beneath the gin and the 'Joy', her breath was like the stale exhalation from a cellar.

Cavallo raised her fingers to his lips and grinned at her.

'Stella, you're looking beautiful tonight. That's a new frock isn't it? Is Harry here? Come and have a drink with me in a minute, will you?'

He relinquished her hand and moved on. The Fieldings were not millionaires, but they could be relied on to drop their couple of hundred every week. It paid to keep them sweet, to cocoon them in a cosy intimacy that made them feel this was 'their' club – not a smoothly oiled machine for removing their money painlessly.

There were half-a-dozen American roulette tables under the eye of the pit-boss, Sandy McNeil, and as Cavallo glanced over, he saw McNeil stiffen slightly and move towards the nearest table. The dealer had just announced the winning number – 'Nineteen red, odd high,' and was paying out, and there was a slight commotion. It was Schaeffer, of course. He was perched on his chair like a malevolent raven, his heels on the rung so that his skinny knees in the rusty black dress trousers were almost beneath his chin, his claw-like hands hovering restlessly over his pile of chips and the plate of free bar-snacks which he had gathered to serve as his dinner.

'I had it on the number!' he was insisting, 'Right on the number! Somebody moved it! You're trying to cheat me!'

His nose was running with excitement and Cavallo noticed with distaste that he had made a mess of crumbs all over the layout.

The dealer, a girl called Candy who was quite new, looked at McNeil for assistance. 'It was a split,' she said, defensively. 'I saw it. Definitely.'

8

'Now, Mr Schaeffer,' McNeil said, 'you know the rules as well as I do – '

Schaeffer, one of the wealthiest men in London, was beginning to tremble with rage and his voice was rising above the quiet murmur of dealers' voices and the staccato rattle of the roulette balls.

'You're all in it! The whole thing's fixed! I know I put my chip on the nineteen! You just don't want to pay me, that's all!'

Cavallo stepped forward. 'What was the bet?'

McNeil tried unsuccessfully to smother a grin, 'Fifty pence on number nineteen, Mr Cavallo.'

'Seventeen pounds fifty, you owe me! You can't get away with it!' Schaeffer's ill-fitting false teeth clattered in his mouth and flecks of food and spittle sprayed the table as he continued his querulous complaint.

'Pay out,' Ross told the dealer. Then to Schaeffer he said, 'This is the last time, Mr Schaeffer, that we give you the benefit of the doubt. In future, the inspector's word is final, do you understand?' He glanced down at the mess of canapés, crisps and olives in front of the man. 'Bon appétit.'

The girl was still where he had first noticed her, over by the fruit machines at the foot of the wide marble stairs that led down into the casino. She had her back half-turned to him and one hand on the lever of the machine as he came up to her, but he was sure she had seen him approach, even though she continued to watch the machine until the orange, lemon and strawberry came to rest, her hand caressing the end of the lever almost absently.

'This machine must be gay,' she murmured, 'I usually hit the jack-pot.'

Cavallo scowled. He didn't like dirty talk from women,

and his marriage was too happy for him to be susceptible to insolent blondes in too-tight jeans. The jeans had a Cardin label on them, but they were still jeans, and the silk blouse she wore with them was so thin that she might as well have poured milk over her full, pink-nippled breasts.

Cavallo kept his face impassive. 'I'm sorry, madam,' he said, politely, 'but I'm afraid we don't allow jeans to be worn in the casino. It's a house rule.'

She turned slowly towards him so that he saw her face properly for the first time – a tangle of expensively messed-up hair, blue eyes with an expression of faint amusement, and a full-lipped mouth drooping at the corners with habitual boredom. Her voice was high-class, low-pitched, slightly husky, as she said, 'You know, an awful lot of men try to get my pants off – but yours is the most original approach.'

'I'm sorry,' he repeated stiffly, 'I must ask you to leave. You're not a member, are you?'

She stared at him a moment, frowning slightly, then turned back to the fruit machine. 'You're not going to be a pain in the ass, are you? *Actually*, I'm a guest of Johnny Pacelli's. You *may* have heard of him?'

Of course, he knew Pacelli. The brooding, petulant features that had appeared on a million record sleeves were to be seen almost as often hanging over the roulette wheel or the blackjack table, usually accompanied by a model or two or some minor television starlet. Cavallo couldn't stand the conceited little jerk, so that made it easier to say, 'It doesn't matter whose guest you are, I'm afraid. I can't alter the rules for anyone.'

She changed her tack suddenly, turned and came close to him. He could smell her perfume and see that her unmade-up skin was young and flawless and that the

10

blonde hair was, improbably, natural. She was so close that with every breath she took, her breasts pushed softly against him and she looked directly up into his eyes, her tongue moistening her lower lip. 'Be nice!' she said, softly. 'You look as though you could be!'

Cavallo looked down at her. She wasn't more than eighteen, he was sure. 'Save your talents,' he said, quietly, 'I can't afford high-class tail.'

Momentarily he read her intention of hitting him in the sudden widening of her eyes, then she was laughing and moving a step away as Pacelli came up.

'Come and protect me, Johnny! This man wants to take my jeans off!'

Pacelli was dressed in a suit of heavy cream watered-silk that had probably cost him a thousand guineas and made him, Cavallo thought sourly, look like a principal boy, especially against the marble and gilt and thick red carpets of the casino. Pacelli looked at him. He was only about five feet eight, so he had to bend his head back to do it, which rather spoilt the belligerent effect. He cultivated a lazy, drooping-eyed expression which was heightened by the half-dozen Scotches he had drunk so that he looked half asleep.

'Watch it, Cavallo,' he said, thickly, 'This is Dorrie St James, and she's with me. Get it?'

Cavallo could see Sandy McNeil looking over at them, grinning again like an idiot. He sighed. God, he was tired. He tried to speak patiently.

'I was trying to explain to Miss St James,' he said, 'that we don't allow jeans. It's nothing personal, but . . .'

'Oh, shit!' Dorrie said, 'This is beginning to be a bore.'

Quite calmly she began to unzip the front of her jeans, just as Khalid came into the casino.

He was a fat man, Giovanni Khalid, and, to those who

11

knew him only slightly, an apparently jovial one. He had a trick of creasing up the skin around his eyes which made people not notice the eyes themselves – cold, speculative and ruthless. Few living people knew his antecedents, which were Arab-Italian, or that he had been born and bred in Sicily. His credentials were in dollars, and he had been part-owner of the Olympus casino for nearly four years now, the London representative of a group of businessmen who preferred to stay quietly in the background. He left the running of the casino to Ross Cavallo, rarely putting in more than a token appearance, but as he came in now, he smelt the tension with an instinct born of generations of banditti, and the obsidian eyes went from the girl to Cavallo to Pacelli in a flickering assessment, even as he called out an exuberant greeting.

'Johnny! Great to see you! And Miss St James – how lovely you are, my dear! You still here, Ross? You work too hard, eh? If I had a charming wife like yours I would have been home in bed hours ago!'

And if I hadn't been here when you came in, Ross thought, you'd have fired me without a moment's hesitation. Aloud he said, 'I was explaining to Miss St James that we have a rule about jeans in the casino . . .'

Khalid waved him aside with little flapping gestures of his plump hand. 'Yes, yes – I know! But for Miss St James – who looks so exquisite in hers – we will make an exception, no?'

Pacelli grinned triumphantly, and the girl, leisurely fastening the zip of her jeans, smiled too, although with a shade of sympathy.

Ross, stiff-faced, stood aside to let them pass him on their way to the tables, but put a hand on Khalid's arm.

'Mr Khalid,' he said, quietly, 'if you want me to run

this casino, don't ask me to enforce rules that you are going to break.'

Khalid paused, his eyes following Dorrie's progress, and laughed silently. 'A lovely piece of ass, eh, Ross? You know who she is? Her papa is Sir Anthony St James – he's so rich he don't know what to do with the stuff. I tell you – if the girl wants to come in here with nothing but a daisy-chain round her fanny, it's okay by me. I make the rules, eh? So I break them – okay? You understand?' He punched Ross playfully in the ribs, his eyes as cold as if he had a stiletto in his hand, and turned away.

Cavallo made his way to his office and the drinks cabinet. Normally he drank very little except when he was obliged to entertain a punter, but the little scene had left a bad taste in his mouth and he wanted to wash it away with a large Scotch.

He had forgotten about Stella Fielding, but she saw him and came trotting after him, her husband Harry, who looked more like a bookie's runner than the successful businessman he was, firmly in tow, together with another man, a stranger to Cavallo.

'Ross!' Stella called, when she was still five yards from him, 'I want you to meet Jack Larcombe – the Right Honourable Jack Larcombe, MP.'

The man beside her was still young enough to flush at her over-loud introduction as he shook Ross's hand. Too young, Ross thought, to be an MP, or was that just a sign that he was getting old?

'Nice to meet you, Mr Larcombe,' he said. 'The bar's shut, I'm afraid – but come and have a drink in my office.'

He ushered them in to the private room with its deep carpet and comfortable armchairs, and turned to the

13

drinks cabinet. 'What are you having? Campari for you, is it, Stella?'

'Oh – just a beer, if you've got it, please,' Larcombe said, flushing again.

Stella Fielding laughed indulgently. 'He can't forget he's a Labour MP, can you, Jack? Go on – be a devil! There're no Chief Whips, or whatever they call themselves, spying on you! Have a Scotch or something!'

'No thanks, Mrs Fielding!' The young man's eyes showed an unexpected glint of humour. 'One of my constituents might see me and think I was being corrupted.'

'I've got lager, if that's proletarian enough?' Ross said. 'How's business, Harry?'

'Oh, mustn't grumble, mustn't grumble!' Fielding put a minute splash of ginger in his Scotch and tipped it down his throat, bringing himself one step nearer his incipient coronary. 'Got a bloody clever new thing on the market – sort of electronic cat door! Opens a flap when the moggy comes close enough!'

'For the man who has everything, eh?' Ross said, raising his glass. 'Cheers! Have you been at Westminster long, Mr Larcombe?'

'My first session. It's all a bit overpowering!' Larcombe admitted ingenuously. 'I mean – you wouldn't believe the amount of protocol – and all the (excuse me, Stella) all the bloody barmy bits and pieces you have to remember before you can even say anything. Well – it's all in a great British tradition, I'm sure – but I think we'd get on a bit faster without it.'

'Never mind, Jack! Now you're up here you'll be showing them a thing or two,' Fielding said, winking at Ross.

'Too bloody right I will! And I know you're laughing at

me, Harry – but, by God, it's time someone stood up and spoke out for the ordinary man in the street. Someone who knows what it's like to have your Dad on the dole and your Mum struggling to make ends meet.'

The young man was suddenly articulate and unabashed, and Ross could see how he'd got himself elected. But he couldn't resist saying mildly, 'Well said. But haven't you brought your reforming zeal to the wrong place?'

For a moment Larcombe looked taken aback, glancing round as though he were suddenly wondering what on earth he was doing here. Then he grinned at Ross. 'Know thine enemy!' he said.

Ross smiled back and raised his glass again. 'I predict a meteoric rise!'

Someone opened the door behind him and he turned, still smiling, to find Dorrie St James there. His smile faded. She stood with her head erect and her hands clasped behind her, but whether this was because of nervousness, or to emphasize the full curve of her breasts was hard to determine.

'I wanted to say sorry and I promise not to do it again,' she said in a low, humble voice to Ross, but her eyes were brimming with laughter as she looked up at him. 'Did nasty Mr Khalid rub your nose in it?'

She was a beautiful girl. Everything about her, from the clear, honey-pale skin and the glittering mass of hair, the cool, unafraid stare of the blue eyes, the white, expensively maintained teeth and the bored droop of the mouth, spoke of money. And power. Not just the power of her wealth, but the power of her vivid sex-appeal, which made Cavallo think suddenly of some jungle flower, brilliant and early-blooming, inviting helpless insects into the succulent moisture of its depths.

He felt a sudden wave of dislike which it was hard to

15

keep out of his face. 'Can I do something for you, Miss St James?' he said, coolly.

'You don't like me!' she said, in a silly, childish voice, and turned to the others. 'He doesn't like me!'

They laughed as though she had said something clever, and Harry Fielding said, 'Of course he does! How could he help it, my dear?' His slightly bloodshot eyes travelled helplessly to the transparent shirt and Stella Fielding's eyes hardened as she watched him.

'Aren't you going to introduce us, Ross?' she said, 'Although I must say I've often seen Miss St James in *The Tatler* at parties and things . . .'

Ross made brief introductions and was faintly amused to see the expression on Jack Larcombe's face. If he was as easily read in politics he'd never get out of the back benches. Without enthusiasm, he offered Dorrie a drink, and she accepted it and sat on a corner of his desk, her legs apart and swinging like a child's.

'You're the new MP for Brendon, aren't you?' she asked Larcombe, and the young man coloured again, gratified by her interest and made some halting remark about being flattered by her remembering. Cavallo was surprised – she did not seem the type to be interested in politics. But the next moment she was saying in a bored voice, 'Oh – I only noticed because you're a lot younger than most of the fogeys at Westminster. My father's been bringing them home in droves because he has a sudden yen to stand for Parliament in the next election. And I can tell you, there never was such a collection of dreary old farts.'

Stella Fielding tittered and Dorrie glanced at her with cool disinterest, then went on, 'Perhaps I'll get him to invite you. Oh – no, you're on the wrong side, I forgot.

16

What's a rabid Labourite doing in this sink of luxury and vice, anyway?'

Larcombe stuttered slightly. 'I – I'm only here as – as a guest. Of the Fieldings. It's not that I in any way endorse this sort of place. On the contrary – it seems a downright sin to me that money should be squandered in this way when a quarter of the population is unemployed . . .'

'Balls!' said Dorrie. She tossed back the rest of her drink and slid off the desk. 'What do you think the unemployed would do with the money if they had it? Invest it wisely for a secure future? Fill their homes with brown bread, classical music and literature? Think again, friend! There's only one thing people are basically interested in – and that's pleasure! And whether it's gambling, drinking or screwing, it all costs money!'

With a slight wave of her hand, she turned to go, then paused. 'Thanks for the drink,' she said to Ross, 'Sorry we don't hit it off – I must remember to tell Khalid not to have his next manager gelded.' And she was gone, leaving a faint drift of some musky perfume.

Harry Fielding guffawed, but Stella was not amused.

'Young people these days!' she exclaimed, 'I mean, the *language*! Well – it's not exactly ladylike, is it?'

Jack Larcombe said nothing, but he moistened his lips a couple of times as though they were suddenly dry.

Two-thirty, and the casino was still busy. Still the faces bent intently over the spinning wheels, impassive for the most part even when Lady Luck kicked them in the groin for the hundredth time. Still the cards slid slickly out of the blackjack shoe, the dealers' muted voices calling, 'Seventeen, card, no card . . .'

The crimson velvet curtains were snugly closed, the glow of the lights sparkling and glinting from the elaborate chandeliers shone on marble and gilt, on the heavy frames

17

of the original paintings on the walls – the Monets, the Claudes, the Sickerts. Silk and satin, cashmere and vicuna, diamonds and sapphires, made a slow-moving kaleidoscope of richness and colour, dazzling the eye and hiding all the ugliness, the fears, the perversions and the cruelty that lurked underneath.

Cavallo lit another cigarette and drew the smoke wearily down his raw throat. He made his way back to the roulette pit and noticed that a party of Arabs had taken over table five. He knew one of them, Tariq el Said – some sort of Saudi prince – and the others were all part of his entourage, so he went over, pausing on the way for a word with McNeil. 'How's table five doing?'

McNeil consulted his card. 'Winning eighteen grand,' he said, 'I don't think Prince Tariq is too happy.'

Cavallo shrugged. Eighteen grand to Tariq el Said was probably about five minutes' earnings on one of his oil wells. 'My heart bleeds for him,' he said to McNeil.

Tariq el Said glanced up at him, but did not return his greeting. He jerked his head towards the dealer. 'This girl is not lucky for me,' he said, 'I want a different one. Blonde. Where is that one – Suzie – that was here before?'

Cavallo smiled pleasantly. Normally he would tell a punter 'Nothing doing' if they wanted a change of dealer. But at three or four grand on every spin of the wheel, Said was entitled to ask for a Tahitian maiden in a grass skirt and get it. Not that he would – he preferred his women blonde, fair-skinned, blue-eyed and freely available. Biting into a smoked salmon sandwich with strong white teeth, the Arab gazed remotely round the casino while Ross had McNeil summon Suzie from the dealer's rest-room on his intercom.

'Cavallo!' Said was used to people jumping when he spoke and a momentary flicker of irritation passed over

18

his features when Ross finished what he was saying to McNeil before rejoining the Saudi.

'Who is that woman?'

Ross knew before he looked round that it would be Dorrie St James who had caught Said's eye. Of course. She was blonde and blue-eyed, like the two expensively dressed tarts who were sitting at Said's table. But, unlike them, she had that indefinable stamp of class, and that was what had caught the Arab's eye.

'Dorrie St James. She's a guest of Johnny Pacelli,' Cavallo said, and Said nodded.

'Introduce me.'

He was smiling, and Cavallo noticed how red the man's lips were, and how the harsh curve of his nose was echoed by the cruel curve of his mouth. Not a man to introduce to an innocent English rose. Dorrie St James, on the other hand . . .

He made his way to where Dorrie lounged, her face blank with boredom, against the back of Pacelli's chair. Pacelli was losing heavily and did not even notice Ross's approach.

'There's a gentleman who would like to make your acquaintance,' Ross said, formally. 'Prince Tariq el Said. May I introduce you?'

'What? Doing a little pimping now, Mr Cavallo?' Dorrie murmured, fluttering her eyelashes. 'I'm honoured. Tell your friend to take a run up his . . . No, wait a mo – I'll tell him myself.'

Suddenly irritated out of his habitual urbane politeness, Ross said quietly and savagely, 'You dirty-mouthed little brat. I'd like to thrash your bottom . . .'

As she turned away, he saw a sudden grin dispel the bored droop of her mouth. 'Whatever turns you on, Mr

19

Cavallo,' she said, and walked ahead of him to table five with a deliberate swing and bounce of her behind.

At four forty-five, Cavallo's BMW was travelling fast and silently through the empty streets towards home. The sky was beginning to lighten greyly, although a fine drizzle fell and the only things stirring were a few hardy cats and one or two stoically damp policemen. Through Chiswick, over Kew Bridge, and he was home, at the house on the Green, drawing up silently, closing the car door and quietly letting himself into the sleeping house, with his weariness suddenly overwhelming. It had been a long night, and one of the new cashiers had managed to mislay ten grand by putting some chips in the wrong tray. But – what the hell? He was home now and about to slip into oblivion. He opened the bedroom door, already loosening his tie, and felt himself at once cocooned in the familiar warm female and baby scents which to him meant Sarah.

She was asleep, and he didn't turn on the light, pulling off his clothes by the faint glimmer from the window. He lit a final cigarette almost without thinking, but extinguished it a moment later and climbed into bed with a faint sigh of relief.

Beside him, Sarah stirred and came half awake. 'Hallo darling. It's late,' she murmured.

'Yes. Bloody stupid cashier.'

'Poor you,' she snuggled her back against him, still drowsy, 'Anyone interesting in tonight?'

Sarah never came to the casino, but she had an unfailing interest in the rich and famous that Ross encountered. He found it funny and endearing in a woman of intelligence and education, and tried to remember when he could, although he had often pointed out to her that film stars and aristocracy were just as boring as anyone else when they bent over a roulette wheel with glassy-eyed concentration.

'Johnny Pacelli was in again,' he said, 'You know – the pop star.'

'*I* know. He's good-looking, isn't he? Was he alone?'

'No. With a bitch. A rich bitch. A spoilt rich bitch.'

Behind his closed eyelids, as he relaxed, ready for sleep, Dorrie St James's face swam up at him, the lips slightly parted, the blue eyes laughter-filled, and his memory filled in the picture with images of her breasts thrusting against the transparent silk of her blouse, the insolent swing of her behind, encased so tightly in blue denim. Unexpectedly he felt a tingling heat rising in his loins and stirred restlessly, annoyed with himself. Beside him, Sarah felt his erection and reached behind her, touching his stiff penis affectionately but lightly.

'God,' she said, with sleepy amusement, 'aren't you ever too tired?'

'No.' He nuzzled into the back of her neck where silky dark curls met soft skin, and pushed urgently against the slender curve of her buttocks. His hand slid round and cupped her breast, then gently explored her stomach and the soft warmth between her legs. She stiffened and moved a little away from him.

'Oh, Ross – I'm sorry, darling – but I'm so tired. I've been up twice with Thomas the Toad – and he'll be awake again at six.'

He kissed her lightly on one ear and rolled over. 'It's okay, sweetheart. I just felt horny suddenly. Go to sleep.'

Sarah lay staring into the darkness. She felt mean and ungenerous. It wasn't Ross's fault. She still loved him passionately after fifteen years of marriage, but since Thomas was born, four months earlier, she had been unable to feel any interest in sex. Perhaps it was just tiredness. Perhaps she would go and see the doctor and get a tonic or something. In the meantime, she could pretend, couldn't she? No need for Ross to live like a monk just because she felt about as sexy as a piece of cod on a slab. She moved closer and put a hand out to touch him. 'Ross?' But he was fast asleep.

He woke again briefly at six. Sarah was hunched in the chair by the window, her eyes closed, the imperious and demanding Thomas fastened to her breast like a pink leech, sucking loudly. Ross smiled and slept again.

In his private suite at the Hilton, Tariq el Said used one of the blonde prostitutes as detachedly and with as much pleasure as he would have used an unclean public lavatory. But as he ground his powerful erection vigorously into her professionally writhing body, it was of Dorrie St James that he was thinking. She had class, that one. And an insolent, provocative manner. He made up his mind to have her and, on the thought, emptied himself abruptly and with a grunt of satisfaction, rolled off the tart and gave her a shove. 'Out.'

'Charmed, I'm sure!' The woman hunted for her shoes, wiping herself briskly on a towel. 'Always a pleasure to do business with a gent like you, Your Highness.' But she was not really disgruntled. He paid handsomely and, if there were no frills, at least there were no perversions. The things she had to do for some of her clients would make a cat laugh. Now she could get some shut-eye in peace.

'Ta-ta, then. See you again,' she said, but the Arab only jerked his head at the door. When she had gone, he lay back amongst the tumbled bedding, staring into space. At home in Riyadh he had a wife – in fact he had two wives and might easily take a third. They were pretty and

22

young and they were obedient to his every whim. In his bed they were versed in all the most erotic arts, seeming to take pleasure only in serving him. And they were his alone. They could never walk in the streets half-unclothed as Western women did, so that all men's eyes might possess them. They lived in a seclusion that was becoming old-fashioned even in the Arab world, and no man would ever see Muhna's bronze-tipped creamy breasts, no one would ever see little Fatima's timid, biddable mouth, see her helplessly spread-eagled beneath him, as helplessly subject to him now as she had been as a bride of fourteen. But there were times when a man tired of willingness. Times when the glance of fear followed by the downcast eye sickened him and he hungered for more – for the thrill of the chase, the quarry that struggled and fought back.

Dorrie St James would fight back, he was quite sure. He smiled a little as he recollected her cool arrogant stare when he had invited her back to his suite for a night-cap. She was rich enough not to be impressed by his wealth and beautiful enough to need no reassurance from his flattery – but there were other ways to conquer a woman, and he, Tariq el Said, knew how to caress and excite tender flesh until it was all quivering ecstasy, and then to drive home to the centre of it with the fierce savagery of a striking scimitar. Yes, the English girl would be his. She might struggle a little, but he would have her. To his satisfaction, his recently exhausted organ rose again into a thick throbbing pillar. He rang for Kassim. 'The other woman,' he said, abruptly, 'and tell her not to speak.'

In a pleasant but modest flat just off the Bayswater Road, Jack Larcombe had not yet begun to undress. He was generally in bed by midnight and should have been

23

dropping with fatigue, but he was wide awake and restless. The events of the night seemed to whirl in his brain like a multi-coloured humming-top. He had gone to the casino with the Fieldings quite secure in his moral convictions, hoping to arm himself with ammunition against the rich and privileged who had been, he felt, his life-long enemies. Jack Larcombe's father had been a farm-worker on a big estate in Somerset. He had a tied cottage that was picturesque, rose-covered and barely habitable. He had worked long hours in all weathers, and by the time he was fifty, he was crippled with arthritis and looked seventy. Then part of the estate was sold and he was out of a job and out of a home. The family had moved to a small council house in Taunton, but Bob Larcombe had never worked again and his wife had taken cleaning jobs to eke out the dole money. Funnily enough, Bob Larcombe had continued to vote Tory till the day he died. 'It was good enough for my old dad and it's good enough for me,' he used to say. But his son, Jack, could date his conversion to Socialism back to one single day, one single hour in his life, when Colonel Pettit had told his father he was on the scrap-heap. Not making a special visit, even, but leaning down from his horse at the garden gate, the sympathy on his bland features and in his 'It's awfully hard luck, old chap,' so blatantly false that Jack wondered his father didn't spit in the landowner's face. And Primrose Pettit, his daughter – she had been there too, smirking at Jack behind her father's back, her hands too heavy on her mare's mouth. There had been a time when he had fancied her and had woven fantasies about them marrying and himself owning the estate, and he knew she fancied him – she was always ogling and smiling at him. There had been an embrace behind the village hall at a Harvest Dance, her egging him on a bit so that he pushed aside layers of fussy tulle and fumbled at her breasts. But when he had tried to go further and get his hand – and anything else she would allow – between her legs, she had drawn back, affronted. He realized she only wanted a bit of practice with someone anonymous and more or less sexy. The fact that he was a farm-hand's son only made it more of a thrill – but Primrose Pettit was saving the choicest parts for those that could pay for them with a ring and a piece of real estate. Besides, her breasts had been heavy and cold like unrisen dough – Jack had relinquished his dreams without much regret, and that autumn morning when they paused at the cottage on their way to a day's hunting, he positively hated her.

'The sodding, bloody bastards!' he stormed, when the Pettits were only a distant sound of ringing hooves on the frosty road. 'Why didn't you tell them, Dad? You should have knocked him off his horse, the sneering bastard!'

His father's face was grey, but he only shrugged and shook his head dumbly before he turned to go indoors, and Jack's mother said mechanically, 'What can't be cured must be endured, and I'll thank you not to use language, Jack.' She followed her husband indoors to give him comfort from her store of platitudes – a thin, wispy-haired woman who had once been pretty, and Jack stayed leaning over the garden gate, whose latch had been replaced by baler twine, staring blindly up the road. He made a sort of vow, in that moment, and the bitterness of it sustained him through years of work and study. He would be someone, one day. He would have a say in the way the country was run, and he would have a hand in bringing down all the rich, the titled, the privileged. And when he was someone, he would take girls like Primrose Pettit, screw them and toss them aside.

And here he was, not yet thirty, and one of the

youngest MPs in the House. It hadn't even been a safe seat, either, being a Liberal stronghold usually, but a combination of his fair, ruddy-faced good looks and his awkward charm, together with the fact that he was a local boy made good, had conspired to give him a narrow majority. He should have been over the moon – but, like many realized dreams, there was a certain sense of flatness and anti-climax. In a couple of days he was to make his maiden speech – a swingeing attack on the proposed cuts in super-tax, and he had gone to the casino to gather evidence of the wicked extravagance of the rich.

It was there all right. He was unable to distinguish Balmain from Balenciaga, but he was beginning to recognize the look of clothes that cost money, and he knew the icy sparkle of real diamonds. And then – the money thrown away on the spin of a wheel or the turn of a card – when there were old people not two miles away who huddled in bed all day because they could not afford to keep warm. And the food – the delicate canapés of crisp pastry and smoked salmon, the fingers of toast with caviare gleaming in dull richness. He thought of his mother, who had only had salmon out of a tin as a rare treat, and who had lived with a persistent cough for eight years which at last, and too late, was diagnosed as TB and killed her off quietly and without fuss. Thinking of her, he felt he should have stormed round the casino like Christ in the Temple, overturning the tables and denouncing the wealthy. But of course, he hadn't. He had been abashed, humbled, defeated by the sheer grandeur and magnificence of it all, conscious only of a stupid desire to belong – to be part of it. What had that girl said, that Dorrie St James? 'There's only one thing people are basically interested in – and that's pleasure.' Perhaps she was right, and perhaps the deserving poor, whose image

26

he carried like a talisman in his heart, would be just as corrupt and dissipated as the undeserving rich, given half a chance. The girl herself, Dorrie St James – wasn't she just another Primrose Pettit? He should be planning her seduction with cold-blooded cynicism, making use of his looks and position to screw a daughter of the aristocracy and make her atone for his parents' wasted lives. But Dorrie was as much like Primrose Pettit as a bird of paradise is like a hen. If she had given him a hint of encouragement he would, he knew, have rolled on his back slavering with abject delight and ready to lick her foot when she kicked him in the crutch. She was the most beautiful girl he had ever seen. Her eyes were a real, startling blue – not the faded grey that usually passes for that colour. Her hair was shining blonde down to the roots, glittering in a rumpled silk mass that made you long to touch it, and her face coupled the pretty discontent of a spoilt angel with the worldly wisdom and hint of eroticism of a Lilith. Her breasts – Larcombe shook himself away from contemplation of Dorrie's breasts and the thought of their warmth beneath his hand, and sat down at his desk, beginning to write with savage haste. But even as he formed the telling phrases, the vitriolic accusations, part of his mind was slowly undressing Dorrie St James and making love to her.

Dorrie paid off the taxi that had brought her home to Maida Vale and let herself in to her flat in Randolph Gardens. As soon as she was eighteen she had moved out of the family house off Cavendish Square, and there was still a palpable delight in shutting the world out behind one's own front door. Almost all the world. Her father had balked at the idea of her living alone until she had suggested sharing with an old schoolfriend. Not of course, that he had had Cy Coram in mind. He would have preferred the Hon Jessica Markham or Lady Claire Fitz-hughes, rather than Cy, who had been a scholarship girl and hadn't two pennies to rub together, as well as having some pretty weird ideas. But she and Dorrie got on fine. They had nothing in common except a respect for each other's privacy, and if Dorrie thought Cy's morning meditations and whole-food diet were bizarre, she tolerated them, just as Cy put up with Dorrie's untidiness and late nights.

It was nearly five A.M. Dorrie stripped off her jeans and shirt and dropped them on to the thick white carpet. She shivered slightly – the heating wasn't programmed to come on for another hour – and turned on an electric fire. She would have preferred coal or wood, but she could not be bothered with the thought of a servant fussing about laying or emptying it. Anyway – at least the electricity was instant. She stood, hugging her nakedness and letting the warmth play over her skin with a sensuous pleasure, staring thoughtfully into the imitation coals. Her skin still had a glow to it from the month in Jamaica that summer – not a deep tan, but just a suggestion of gold dust rubbed softly in, and the starry fairness of her hair was scarcely lighter than the curls that clustered below the smooth flat line of her stomach.

She stood for a moment or two, then shook her head with an impatient sigh and stretched voluptuously. She felt restless and discontented, longing for something that she couldn't name, that she hardly knew existed.

She had left Pacelli in the casino, too absorbed in his play to notice her go, and, on a whim, had accepted Tariq el Said's invitation to go on to a private night-club. He had asked her back to his hotel suite but she had refused, only to regret it later as she sat through an hour of boringly obscene floor show. She had felt Tariq's eyes on her every so often and had wondered with faint amusement what reaction he was hoping for. Shock? Maidenly English modesty? Or a sudden lewd abandon that would make her throw herself at him with outspread legs?

'What do you think of the floor show?' he had murmured, leaning close to her. He was, she thought detachedly, incredibly handsome, every woman's dream of an Arab prince, with those dark, hawk-like features and the powerful body that looked as though it would be as much at home on horseback as in his private jet. But her voice was cool as she replied, 'We have a farm in Devon – if I want to see animals coupling I can go there. Do you actually like it?'

He had smiled slightly and, taking her hand, had guided it beneath the table to the growing tumescence that pushed against his elegantly cut trousers. 'It is quite interesting,' he said.

His hand on Dorrie's wrist seemed light, but she could sense the steely strength in the long fingers and, meeting his eyes, she knew that this man was accustomed to having his way and would tolerate no defiance from man or woman. Around him were six or seven of his entourage – whether friends, servants or bodyguards she didn't know – dark, grim-looking men who seemed to speak little English, and the two blonde tarts who had been with him in the casino and who were holding a desultory conversation with only an occasional glance at the floor-show and a mechanical scream of laughter. It would be ludicrous to appeal to them. Besides – she could look after herself, couldn't she? She was Dorrie St James, brash, beautiful and eighteen years old, and she was a match for any man – even an Arab prince with hot black eyes and an erection that felt like the Post Office Tower.

She allowed her hand to rest lightly on him and saw his tongue moisten his lips and his breathing quicken. Beneath the fine silk cloth, his penis moved against her palm like a straining animal, and Dorrie, despite her annoyance, could not prevent a responsive warmth and tingling between her own thighs.

One moment longer she let her hand remain, caressingly, while their eyes held together, then, gently, with a little sigh that could have been regret, she withdrew it. 'Not here,' she whispered, and smiled. 'I have to go to the powder room.'

It was easy enough to find another exit and slip out, and she made her way quietly through several deserted back streets till she was able to hail a taxi.

She grinned now, reminiscently, as she thought of Tariq el Said waiting for her to return from the ladies' room. 'He can sit and play with himself all night,' she murmured. 'That'll teach him to take me for granted, cheeky sod.'

But she could not help recalling vividly the strength and power she had briefly touched, and an involuntary shiver of sheer animal randiness suddenly swept her so that she yawned and stretched voluptuously, straddling her legs to let the heat of the fire play on her most tender flesh, like a warm male hand.

The door opened and Cy came in, yawning and rumpling her short brown hair into something resembling a hedgehog. She regarded Dorrie sardonically.

'Worshipping at the shrine of the body beautiful?' she said. 'Well – carry on, don't mind me.'

'I shan't,' Dorrie said, unselfconsciously, sitting down on the rug in front of the fire and circling her knees with her arms.

Cy, dressed in a baggy night-shirt, also sat on the floor,

but cross-legged, fingertips on knees, and gazed into the middle distance.

'Om,' she intoned.

Dorrie giggled. 'Tiddley-om-pom!' she added.

Cy glared with mock ferocity.

'You'll get cold,' she said. 'Anyway – aren't you going to bed? It beats me why you don't end up a withered old hag with the hours you keep. But there you are with a skin like a milk-maid while I, early to bed and early to rise, seem to sprout a new zit every fortnight.'

'Well, I'll tell you a secret,' Dorrie said, solemnly, 'I think virtuous thoughts a lot. *Mens sana in corpore sano*, you know.'

Cy laughed and leaned back on her hands. 'And who were you thinking them with tonight? That little creep Pacelli? If he had a virtuous thought it'd choke him!'

Dorrie pouted, 'Oh – poor Johnny! He's quite sweet, really. A twit, but sweet. Anyway, I enjoy feeling I'm the envy of a million teeny-boppers.'

'I don't believe you,' Cy said, dryly, 'You never give a damn what anyone thinks.'

'Perhaps. Anyway – I haven't made myself a popular girl tonight! I left Johnny doing his brains (if he has any) at the roulette table, walked out on an exceedingly horny Arab, was cheeky to an MP, and . . .'

'And?'

'Oh – I can't remember. Yes – I was very rude to the casino manager, Ross Cavallo.'

'I wouldn't let that bother you. That's what he gets paid for – probably like water off a duck's back.'

'No,' Dorrie said, thoughtfully, 'No – it got through to him. He – he said he'd like to thrash me!'

Cy looked at her with faint interest. 'Seems he got through to you!' she commented. 'What was he like?'

'Oh – ' Dorrie shrugged impatiently, getting to her feet, 'how the hell should I remember? He was only the casino manager, for God's sake. D'you want coffee?'

'Dandelion,' Cy said, and resumed her meditative position, but it was a moment or two before she could lose herself. Her gaze travelled round the big untidy room with its pale carpet and walls, the big, original Hockney and the smaller Warhol, the honey velvet-covered Edwardian chaise-longue and the rare netsuke collection, the steel and perspex Italian table and the bronze chrysanthemums carelessly dropping their petals from a famille rose vase. Nothing should have gone together, and yet somehow it did, in a perplexing, beautiful mixture that was simply Dorrie.

In the kitchen, Dorrie filled the percolator and put the kettle on for Cy's revolting dandelion brew. She shivered, and picked up a cashmere sweater she had dropped there earlier, pulling it over her head, her buttocks protruding from beneath it with a bizarre and erotic effect. She leaned against the worktop waiting for the kettle to boil. It was not true. She remembered Ross Cavallo very well, and she could have given Cy a most accurate description of him, from the dimensions of his six-foot-two frame, to the dark eyes, a little tired, a little cynical, the nose that had perhaps been broken once, and the firm lines of mouth and chin. He had been polite – most of the time – but his mouth had shown the faint contempt he felt for her. Dorrie was used to seeing one particular expression in a man's eyes – a sort of speculative lust – and she had failed to see it in Ross Cavallo's. It piqued her – and it almost made her feel a little ashamed of herself. How annoyed her father would have been, with his ideas of 'noblesse oblige'. She could just picture the faint frown of distaste on his thin, highly bred face when she said 'Shit!'

'Dorian,' he would say (he was the only person to use her awful name, she thought), 'Dorian, a lady does not swear or raise her voice. The strongest language I ever heard your mother use was "drat!"'

Privately, Dorrie thought he must have been a bit deaf. She could remember at least one occasion, when a hunter had refused a fence, or one of the spaniels had piddled on the carpet, when her mother's language had been anything but ladylike. But, since her death on the hunting-field six years before, the vivacious, high-spirited Antonia St James had gradually been etherealized by her grieving husband, till even Dorrie was beginning to imagine her with tall white wings and an expression of sweet inanity. Dorrie smiled faintly, imagining a halo at a rakish angle on her mother's blonde head as she took a fence in style. Then her mind flinched automatically away from the vivid picture of her mother's horse, The Major, outlined against the sky in an untidy tangle of legs and reins, the sickening crash, the high, unending screams of a horse in agony, and her own thin, childish voice crying 'Mother! Mother!' to a white-faced stranger who would never answer again.

Dorrie shook herself, shoved the blonde tangle out of her eyes with an impatient movement and picked up the kettle. God – what was the matter with her this morning? She was getting as sentimental as the heroine of a Victorian melodrama. And all because some nobody of a casino manager had failed to respond visibly to her sex appeal. Forget him – what about the young MP, Jack Larcombe? With a sudden change of mood, Dorrie grinned broadly and poured coffee with a flourish, splashing a little on to her bare leg.

'Drat!' she said. Yes, if ever a man had his tongue hanging out, Larcombe had. Dorrie had almost felt his hot breath from five feet away. And why not? They were both young and healthy and he was really very good-looking if you liked that boyish, bucolic type. A nice body too – not terribly tall, but well-muscled and fit-looking. It might be fun to get to know him. Dorrie picked up her coffee and Cy's dandelion brew and bumped the door open with her behind.

Cy paused in the middle of an 'Om mane padme hum', and raised an eyebrow at Dorrie's outfit. 'Latest fashion?' she enquired. 'Pussy below the belt. Have you any idea how lewd that is?'

Dorrie shrugged and went back to the fire with her coffee. 'I'm hoping to set a trend. After all – boobs dangle everywhere these days and no one bats an eyelid. Can't you just see *The Tatler*? "For her coming-out ball, the Hon Felicia Ormskirk-Selby wore an ostrich-feather head-dress, a high-necked satin blouse, and the Selby diamonds tastefully entwined in her pubic hair . . ."'

'I didn't think they wore ostrich feathers these days,' Cy remarked, 'that all went out with the end of presentations.'

'Alas, yes!' Dorrie sighed, theatrically, 'What an opportunity missed! I might have got a chance at one of the Princes.'

'God help England!' Cy said fervently, and went back to her meditating. Dorrie finished her coffee and at last, reluctantly, went to bed.

It was still unmade from when she had got up the previous day – a tangle of sheets, underwear and paperback novels. She had fetched herself a breakfast tray and it was still there as well, an unappetizing array of egg-shell and old toast. She scowled and swore furiously, then remembered that there were no servants here – no one to pick up after her and make order of her chaos. That was the way she'd wanted it. She shoved the tray on to the

34

dressing-table which was a welter of make-up that Dorrie was always buying and rarely using, flicked clothes and books to the floor with one shake of the duvet, stripped off her jumper and climbed in. Six o'clock. One more thing before she slept. She leaned out and pulled the telephone towards her.

'Daddy? It's me. Are you awake?'

'Yes. Now.' Sir Anthony's voice was crisp but not unkind. However much he might deplore Dorrie's life-style, he adored his daughter and his heart lifted every time she bothered to contact him.

'Sorry – I forgot it was so early. Listen – I want you to do something for me . . .'

Sir Anthony suppressed a sigh. He never heard from Dorrie unless she wanted something, and it was usually something hare-brained.

'Yes?'

'Don't sound so snappish, darling! I don't want you to pawn the family jewels or anything! When are you having one of your boot-licking political sessions? Soon?'

'I am having a dinner on Friday,' Sir Anthony said, stiffly, 'for some of my friends who happen to be in the Government – if that's what you mean by boot-licking. I must say, Dorian, the way you express yourself is . . .'

'Sorry! Sorry! Abject apologies, dearest Papa! Now listen – will you be a kind aged parent and invite that new MP, Jack Larcombe?'

'Who? Oh, I know. Fellow's a Socialist, though, isn't he?'

'All the better – we'll convert him to capitalism and gracious living! Triumph for Sir Anthony St James and the glorious Tories!'

'We?' Sir Anthony repeated, dryly.

'Yes – I'm invited too, aren't I? I shall be your hostess

35

– and I promise you butter shall not melt in my mouth! You will be proud and amazed . . .'

'Very well.' Her father sighed, but she could hear from his voice that one of his rare smiles was in evidence.

'Eight for eight-thirty on Friday. Dress!' he added repressively.

'Oh? Pity – I have this idea for a new trend . . . But don't worry, I shall be in chin-high purple satin and a tiara.'

As he hung up, still smiling a little, Sir Anthony reflected that even if she were dressed in an enveloping potato sack, his irrepressible daughter would contrive to make every man present, from the butler to the ninety-year-old Earl of Ramsdean, aware that she was a beautiful and desirable woman.

Dorrie sighed with sleepy satisfaction, stretched her long golden limbs expansively, scratched at an irritating toast-crumb around her left buttock, and slept.

2

Jack Larcombe had spent the morning from ten A.M. in a small office in the dim recesses below the Chamber of the House of Commons. He was not established or important enough, besides being a member of the Opposition, to have an office of his own, and he supposed he should be grateful for the use of this one, shiny green paint, Ministry of Works desk and chairs, ink-stained brown lino and all. There was a secretary, too, from the Pool, a cool, dark-haired young woman with an efficient air and rather attractive slim legs. Her name was Natasha Troy. From her first firm handshake and modulated 'How do you do?' she had made Larcombe feel that he probably had manure on his boots and hay clinging to his hair, and, perversely, he found his West Country burr becoming more pronounced and his manners rougher whenever she was around.

This morning, he was supposed to be seeing constituents, but, so far, two who had made appointments had failed to turn up, and he fancied that there was a faint contempt on Miss Troy's well-bred face as they sat there in an awkward silence.

She broke it at last. 'Is there any correspondence, Mr Larcombe? Perhaps we could get something done before your next appointment?'

She was perfectly polite, but Larcombe seemed to hear the unspoken, 'Or are you going to lounge there all day waiting for people who don't turn up?'

Damn the woman – why did she have to be so cool and

self-possessed? He glowered at her for a moment and tried to imagine what lay beneath the crisp shirt and tailored skirt and the faint scent of White Linen. Were there breasts and genitals, or just a smoothly engineered female-shaped object, standard issue, MPs for the use of? His glower turned to a grin as he imagined unbuttoning the shirt and reprogramming Miss Troy to behave with lewd abandon, and to his astonishment, a faint answering smile appeared on her face and her pale cheeks flushed slightly.

'Well, sod 'em all!' Larcombe said, cheerfully, 'Let's get on with some letters, eh?'

'Quite so, Mr Larcombe,' Miss Troy said, in her best Cheltenham Ladies' College accent, but as she bent her head over her shorthand pad, the faint smile had broadened.

Larcombe got out his file, feeling pleased. Women were all the same, he should know that by now. No matter how high-class and frigid they looked, just give them the undressing stare and the slow grin and they melted. Magic! Another few weeks, the odd casual compliment, the occasional light physical contact, almost inevitable in a small, cramped office, and Miss Natasha Troy would be like putty in his hands.

'Dear Mrs Aldridge,' he began, 'I do appreciate the inconvenience to which you and the other inhabitants of Pegworthy have been put by the withdrawal of your bus service. It seems to me yet another example of the present Government's uncaring attitude towards ordinary people. I am putting your case to the Minister of Transport and I will certainly point out to him in no uncertain terms . . .'

Miss Troy coughed.

'What?'

'Certainly and uncertain – do you want to keep that?'

'Oh – oh, no, you're right. Thanks. Delete the certainly and put – er – '

'I will not fail to point out to him, perhaps?'

'Yes – yes, thank you, Miss Troy, that's splendid.'

She flushed and Jack began to calculate the time until he could put his hand up her skirt in weeks rather than months.

They worked on until quarter to twelve, pausing only for coffee – black for Miss Troy, white and sweet with a stodgy iced bun for Larcombe, and then his other constituent arrived, ten minutes late.

She was a small, wiry countrywoman in her late fifties, with an inimical grey stare, grasping her large plastic handbag tightly as though she feared London muggers even in the office of her Member of Parliament. She was a farmer's wife from near Dulverton, not far from Jack's own native village, and she had come to complain bitterly to him about milk quotas, apparently holding him personally responsible for agricultural policy.

'Us've built our herd up over years,' she said, leaning forward over her handbag and glaring at him. ''Tis the finest herd thereabouts, and you'm saying us has to get rid of ten milkers. Tidn't right, young man, and you knows it! And you'm a West Country man yourself – you ought to be ashamed. What be thinking of?'

'But, Mrs Bale,' Jack began, feeling rather helplessly as though he'd been caught scrumping apples, 'it really is nothing to do with me – the new regulations, I mean. It's all to do with CAP – you know, the Common Agricultural Policy. You see, we've been producing too much milk . . .'

'Too much milk, you says!' Mrs Bale was almost outraged, ''Tis the best milk in West Somerset, young

39

man! Us makes cream *and* butter from it, *and* feeds pigs on the buttermilk.'

'Yes – I'm sure it's marvellous milk,' Jack broke in hastily, aware that a certain element of farce was entering the scene, 'but, you see, there *is* a surplus – there's a butter mountain and a milk mountain and they're getting bigger all the time . . .'

'Not with our milk, they'm not,' Mrs Bale insisted stubbornly. 'Us has always got rid of every drop of ours. The Milk Marketing Board takes most and us sells what us don't use locally. 'Tis famous, our cream – look, I brought 'ee up a jar. You don't get cream like that in London, I'll warrant.'

She rummaged in her handbag and brought out a large jam-jar full of dark yellow clotted cream, almost butter-like in its thickness.

'Oh – thank you very much, Mrs Bale. That's really most kind of you.'

'That's all right, young man. Just you see us keeps all our cows, see?'

He could hardly keep from groaning aloud. How on earth could he explain that he had no power at all to prevent the Ministry from imposing quotas, even if it meant reducing Mrs Bale's herd by ninety per cent.

'I – I'm sorry, Mrs Bale. I'll speak to Douglas Jeffries, the Minister of Agriculture, but I'm afraid I have no actual power to say you can keep your cows . . .'

'Then you didn't ought to be here, young man, that's all I can say!' Mrs Bale gathered up her handbag and rose to her feet. 'What be the use of voting for a chap if he can't do what he's asked? Tidn't no good at all . . .'

The telephone rang, and Miss Troy answered it, her cultured voice effectively silencing Mrs Bale in mid-tirade.

'Yes? Who's speaking, please? Will you hold the line

40

one moment and I'll see if Mr Larcombe's available.' She glanced over at Jack, her eyes and voice cool and impersonal, 'Miss Dorrie St James. Shall I ask her to call back?'

Jack half-rose, his face flushing and conscious of a sudden quickening of his pulse. Then he subsided into his chair, reaching for the extension with one hand, and fiddling with the knot of his tie with the other.

'Hullo?'

'Jack Larcombe?' The low voice with its husky, mocking note of hidden laughter was unmistakable. 'This is Dorrie St James – we met last night.'

'Yes, Miss St James. What can I do for you?'

A soft chuckle. 'How stiff you sound! Is your collar too tight? Call me Dorrie and don't be so pompous! When I'm lying in bed with nothing on except a dab of scent I don't feel like being formal.'

Jack swallowed. He had never spoken to such an outrageous girl. Usually it was up to him with his bold stare and his quietly intimate remarks to make the woman blush with delighted embarrassment, but here he was, pink as a peony, stammering like a schoolboy on his first date. Struggling for composure and trying to close his mind to Dorrie St James's naked body and the hardly veiled invitation in her voice, he said, 'I'm so sorry, Miss St James – er – Dorrie. I have a constituent with me. May I call you back?'

'No-o-o,' on a long sigh, as though she stretched languorously, like a cat, 'No – I'm going to sleep again. I only thought I'd let you know my old man's inviting you to dinner on Friday. You can pick me up here at seven, if you like. Do you have a dinner jacket?'

'Yes. Thank you. That'll be fine. Friday at seven, then. Er – I'll see you then.'

'Mmm,' Dorrie said, and hung up.

41

Jack held on to the receiver for a moment, staring unseeingly at Mrs Bale, a faint smile on his lips. So, Miss Dorrie St James wanted a little amusement, did she? It was funny how these high-class women often went for men of his type. Perhaps they got tired of the unfailing politeness and cut-glass accents of the chinless wonders in their own set. They wanted something a bit rougher, but not too rough to bring into the drawing-room – a sort of Noble Savage. 'Do you have a dinner-jacket?' He should have said, 'No, but I can come in a clean smock and wellies.'

He turned to Mrs Bale with his most charming smile, 'Now, Mrs Bale – could I take down a few details of your case? I'm sure the Minister and I will be able to work something out.'

In a few minutes, the old lady's weathered face had softened considerably and when she rose to go, she gave Jack a nod of grudging approval.

'Us've always voted Tory, mind,' she said, as a Parthian shot, 'but us'll just 'ave to see how 'ee turns out. Good morning to you. And you, Miss.'

When she had gone, Jack grinned, stretched, and looked at his watch. 'Now then, my dear,' he said, in a broad Somerset accent, 'how would 'ee like a bite of summat to eat?'

Natasha smiled slightly and rolled a fresh sheet of paper into her typewriter. 'It's very kind of you, Mr Larcombe,' she said, coolly, 'but I'm afraid I'm engaged for lunch. I'll just finish these letters first.'

He stood for a moment, leaning against his desk, regarding her thoughtfully. She had an attractive face, really, if you subtracted the heavy-rimmed spectacles and the prim expression. A nice skin, too, the way it flushed that pretty pink, as it was doing now. No, Miss Natasha

Troy was not nearly as cool and invulnerable as she liked to think. He wouldn't have minded betting that if he slid his hand down the front of her shirt, he would find her heart pounding away like billy-oh, and the nipples of her nice little breasts all hard and eager against his fingers. He was half-tempted to try, especially when she raised her eyes and her flush deepened to crimson.

'Perhaps another time, then, Miss Troy,' he said, and grinned again, impudently.

As the door closed behind him, Natasha ripped the ruined letter out of her typewriter with hands that shook a little. That odious man! How dared he look at her like that, grinning as though it was only a matter of time before she became a conquest? He was so – so unpolished, so uncouth, even if he was an MP and had been to Cambridge. She found him absolutely repellent – especially the way he had practically slavered when Dorrie St James rang up. She, Natasha Troy, could never be attracted by a man like that, no matter how well-muscled his body or how charming his boyish, white-toothed grin. With a little sound that was almost a moan, Natasha put her hands to her breasts and pressed them against the aching nipples.

Jack Larcombe parked his Volvo carefully outside the flat in Randolph Gardens and locked all the doors. Even at three years old, it was the best car he had ever driven, and he looked after it with devotion. In his days as a Labour party agent and later at Transport House, he had felt it was rather sinful and against his principles to own a decent car, and for several years had driven everywhere in an ancient Morris Traveller, which had the one advantage that he could often mend it with string and safety pins when, as so often happened, it broke down. But, in the end, he found he was losing valuable time and arriving late at meetings and he noticed that some of the most humble members of the party were swishing round in Jags and Mercedes. The Volvo was one of the few concessions he made to his new life-style as an MP.

He went up the shallow flight of steps to Petrie Mansions, into the lobby of the house and was met instantly by a porter in uniform.

'May I help you, sir?'

There was a discreet consultation on the phone, then Jack found himself being politely escorted into the lift and whisked silently to Dorrie St James's front door.

It was opened, not by Dorrie, but by a shorter girl with a tousled mop of brown hair, either a long striped shirt or a short dress, and bare feet. She was munching an apple and she smiled at Jack, her plain, pug-nosed face wrinkling into an urchin-like charm.

'Hi!' she said, 'Come in. I'm Cy Coram, Dorrie's flatmate and worthy cause. Dorrie's getting dressed.'

He followed her through a hallway full of green plants and thick carpet, into the sitting-room, and sat where Cy indicated he should, on the chaise-longue.

Cy chatted casually to him as she poured him a drink, and he felt at ease with her at once, recognizing as he did that she was not a member of the monied aristocracy any more than he was. But the room – how was it that people were able to achieve that effect of careless luxury? It wasn't even tidy, but there wasn't a thing in it that didn't subtly murmur 'Money', in a way that his Bayswater flat never would, no matter how much he spent on it. It was warm, and there was a faint scent of coffee and bruised chrysanthemums and sensuous female essences. A fur coat, which he vaguely supposed was mink, had been flung casually on a chair, one sleeve trailing on the carpet, and a tray with used coffee cups and what looked like a pile of tights and panties, was balanced on some books on a delicate little side-table which he failed to recognize as Louis Quinze.

'Are you a member of CND?' Cy asked, handing him his drink and sitting down in an extraordinary double-jointed fashion on the carpet.

'What? I'm sorry – I was admiring your décor.'

She repeated her question, 'You *are* a Labour MP, aren't you?'

'Yes, but – no, I'm not actually a member of CND – though I do support them, of course.'

'How can you support them, if you don't join? Look – we're having a rally next Saturday in Hyde Park. Why don't you come? It's perfectly respectable – all sorts of eminent churchmen and politicians come along. It won't do your image any harm, you know!'

'Oh – it's not that! I'm not bothered by image, it's just – yes, okay. I'll come if I have time.'

'Some people will still be saying that when they drop the bomb on us,' Cy answered, dryly. 'Oh, well. Come if you can. Two-thirty. Here's Dorrie.'

Somehow he had expected jeans again, her hair in a tangled mane around her face, insolent and sexy. For a split second he did not recognize the sleek, expensively dressed young woman who posed for a moment in the doorway, regarding him with a half smile, her gilded hair shining in a coronet that made her look as regal as a princess. She was wearing a dress of a soft golden colour, in shot-silk organza, which Larcombe would have been horrified and outraged to know had cost over a thousand pounds at Giorgio Armani. Against the subtle colour of its off-the-shoulder bodice, Dorrie's skin gleamed with a faint bronze lustre, and the full, bustled, almost Edwardian skirts made her look as though she had stepped from the pages of a fairy tale. Her eyes rested on Larcombe, amusement gleaming in their blue depths, then she came forward, saying casually, 'What do you think, Cy? Too much gold? I don't want to look like a krugerrand. And am I formal enough for Papa and his dreary pals? Hallo, Jack!'

'You look superb, and you know it,' Cy said, dourly. 'Pity you don't dress up more often. Are you going now?'

'In a minute.' Dorrie's eyes were still on Jack. 'You haven't said you like my dress. Is it all right?'

She stood very close to him so that he could see the fine texture of her skin beneath the translucent powder, and smell the warm, musky sweetness of the perfume she wore.

'You – I think you're the loveliest creature I've ever seen!' he blurted out impulsively, and she smiled and patted his cheek with a swift, gentle gesture.

'Nice!' she said, 'Cy – fasten my necklace, will you?'

From a chair by the fire where she had casually dropped it earlier, she picked up a choker of pearl and topaz.

'One of these days you'll lose something, or have it pinched, the way you leave things lying about,' Cy said, exasperated. She did not envy Dorrie her wealth, but she came from a home where every object had had to be saved for, and was then cherished and looked after till it wore out.

Dorrie shrugged, her face tranquil and remote as a Botticelli madonna and stood while the jewels were fastened round her throat.

Jack stood tongue-tied, almost awe-struck, unable to equate this golden goddess with the brash, impudent enfant terrible of a few nights previously. He swallowed nervously and adjusted his ready-made bow tie, unable to think of anything to say and as ill-at-ease as a boy on his first date.

Dorrie moved past him with a soft frou-frou of rustling skirts and contemplated her face dispassionately in a mirror.

'I'm afraid you're going to find it all rather stuffy this evening,' she murmured, without looking round. 'My father is one of the old school and a stickler for what he would call "doing things properly". That's why I'm done up like a dog's dinner. He can't stand the sort of casual manners a lot of us use these days.' She gave a little laugh and touched an imaginary tendril of hair into place.

Cy met her eyes in the mirror and pulled a face at her, half-humorous, half-disparaging. 'Excuse me, won't you? I'm going to make myself something to eat.' She disappeared into the kitchen, closing the door behind her, and Dorrie finished her minute inspection and turned to face Jack, with a bright, meaningless smile.

'So, if in any doubt, when you're surrounded by about five dozen pieces of assorted cutlery and glassware, just glance over at me. And don't be intimidated by all the titles – there's absolutely no need for any forelock tugging.'

Jack drew in a sharp breath. He could feel the colour rising in his cheeks again, and it was not embarrassment this time, but sheer, bloody fury. So that was it! She was afraid that this rough country yokel whom she had invited on impulse was going to let her down with his lack of manners.

'Before we go,' he said, quite quietly, 'perhaps you could give me a few tips on how to behave. I mean – do I use one hand or two to pick up my soup bowl? And is it correct to tuck my napkin under my chin? Oh, and do tell

47

me,' his voice rose, 'please tell me, your high and mighty ladyship, do I use all the knives and forks or do I keep one for picking my fucking nose?'

He paused, almost panting for breath, and Dorrie gave a shout of laughter and collapsed into a chair in a foam of gold silk.

'Oh, marvellous!' she cried, 'You are human after all! I thought you were going to stand around in respectful silence all night, with your mouth open like a carp!'

Jack was still too furious to appreciate the fact that she had been teasing him. 'You little bitch!' he muttered, his big hands clenching into fists, 'Winding me up, were you? I suppose you think people like me were just put on this earth for your amusement – well, let me tell you, my Dad may have been just a farm labourer, but I'm more proud of him than I would be of the generations of effete parasites that you call your ancestors.'

'Hush!' With a graceful movement, still laughing, Dorrie rose from her chair and came over to him. She put a cool forefinger on his lips and looked up at him, her eyes half veiled by thick dark-gold lashes. 'Don't be cross! I'm sorry if I teased – but I only do it to people I like. And I *do* like you – that's why I got my father to invite you. Be friends, now!'

He still glowered, feeling awkward and unmollified, but terribly aware at the same time, of the beauty of the face upturned towards him, the lovely, half-sulky mouth with lips slightly parted, moist and tempting. She was very near him and beneath the low-cut bodice of her dress he could see the fullness of her breasts, almost to the nipples.

'Be friends!' she was whispering again, and her hands reached gently up and caressed the short fair hair at the back of his neck. The warm muskiness of her scent was in his nostrils and he reached for her blindly, covering the

48

soft, sweet lips with his own, thrusting his tongue in a twining ecstasy with hers, his engorged penis, grown painfully enormous, threatening to burst through the hired dress suit.

After a moment or two, she detached her mouth gently and smiled up at him. 'My goodness, Mr Larcombe,' she whispered, 'aren't we getting a little ahead of ourselves? In every sense . . .' Briefly she touched him, a quick, delicate caress on the tense straining of his erection, and he bit his lips on a groan of longing.

'Rule number one in the book of etiquette,' she murmured, looking solemn, 'No sex immediately before dinner. The soup grows cold – and it frightens the servants.'

'And – after?' he breathed, feeling that he would surely explode if there was not at least a prospect of possessing this creature of fire and ice, this princess – whore, this unattainable goddess with the tempting, wanton mouth.

'After? Oh – then comes the port,' she teased, 'and then – well, who knows? Now I shall have to repair my lipstick and we'd better go.'

Jack excused himself and went into Dorrie's bathroom where he splashed his face with cold water and tried to think of matters such as the previous day's Question Time.

The room was still slightly steamy and thick white towels were scattered on the floor around the deep pink, semi-sunken tub. There were huge mirrors with gilded frames, the floor was carpeted and the fittings were gold and ornate with Floris essences and Roger & Gallet soaps scattered in profusion. Jack allowed himself a faintly contemptuous smile, but when he re-entered the sitting-room, Dorrie said, 'I know the bathroom's like a ghastly tart's boudoir, but it came with the flat and I can't be bothered to change it.'

He grinned, helping her on with the honey-coloured mink. 'It is a bit much, isn't it? Makes mine look like a mediaeval torture chamber. But I liked the way it smelt of you. What *is* that perfume?'

She glanced at him with a half-rueful smile, 'Now you *are* going to think I'm a spoiled rich girl. It's one that Oscar de la Renta – you know, the fashion designer – had made for me as a birthday present. A lovely idea, wasn't it? He called it "Dorée" – "golden". It isn't on the market yet, so I'm the only one who wears it.'

Jack laughed. 'My God! You *are* spoilt! A rich pampered darling of fortune with everything she wants! And the added bonus of a double helping of beauty and charm so that everyone loves you as well!'

'Oh, no, they don't!' Dorrie protested, 'Look at that casino manager the other night – what's his name? Cavallo or something? He hated my guts!'

'What a ladylike way you have of expressing yourself! He was probably trying to restrain himself from ravishing you. Now – shall we go before I get carried away again?'

'Okay. And – joking apart, don't let all those Tory ministers get your back up tonight. Most of them are little pricks.'

They took a taxi to the Cavendish Square house and Jack was impressed but not overawed by the butler who admitted them. One or two of his friends when he was up at Queen's had had a similar background, and one, indeed, was active in the Labour Party and had declared his intention of renouncing his title when he inherited it. So Jack had rubbed shoulders with suits of armour and

William Morris wallpaper before, and, although he disliked the rich on principle, he could not help warming to the pleasant courtesy of Dorrie's father, Sir Anthony St James, who treated him as though he was at least a cabinet minister rather than a very junior back-bencher. He obviously loved his daughter, though he had the Englishman's dislike of showing his affection, but he could not help following the gilded, lovely figure with his eyes.

'You're looking extremely attractive tonight, Dorian,' he told her, and she smiled and gave him an affectionate kiss.

'Don't sound so relieved, Daddy dear! Did you think I'd come in my jeans? I'm on my best behaviour tonight – apart from introducing a dyed-in-the-wool Red amongst all your pet Tories! That should be fun!'

Sir Anthony glanced over to where Jack Larcombe was making polite conversation with the wife of the American Ambassador. 'He seems a pleasant enough young man. I don't imagine he'll try and overthrow the Government single-handed at my dinner table, if that's what you were hoping for.'

Dorrie heaved a sigh, 'Well, I'm sorry, darling, but your dinner parties are so stupefyingly dull. Half these old fogies use embalming fluid for aftershave. Couldn't you, just occasionally, have a minor rebel?'

'I had enough rebellions bringing you up, thank you,' her father said, indulgently. 'What I like now is good manners and polite conversation. Now, go and mingle, my dear, and try to remember what you learned at that very expensive finishing school.'

'Mostly the facts of life,' Dorrie said, dryly, but she went all the same and chatted charmingly to aged Lords, an uncontroversial Bishop and several tame cabinet ministers. No one who had ever twisted the tiger's tail, no matter how gently, was ever invited to the St James dinners. No Heseltine or Pym or St John Stevas, no matter how impeccable their breeding, was on the guest list, and, such was Sir Anthony's strict code of morals, even those such as Cecil Parkinson who had blotted their copybook in his eyes, or to whom the least whisper of scandal attached, were never seen at his table. In short, Dorrie reflected, swallowing a yawn, it was the biggest collection of boring old farts as one could wish to see gathered under one roof. She hoped that Jack Larcombe would do another of his nice little outbursts, although she knew her father would never invite him again. Perhaps when he'd had a few drinks.

Meanwhile she listened in incredulous silence as a woman in a too-young Bruce Oldfield dress with skin like frozen chicken, told her how much she loved Sir Anthony's dinners, and agreed with an inward shudder that the arrangements of pale-yellow carnations and stephanotis were 'sweetly pretty' against the deep crimson of the walls. She had spoken to her father about it before, but yellow carnations and stephanotis had been Antonia St James's favourite flowers, the ones she had carried on her wedding day, and her husband, with a touching faithfulness, would have no others.

Dorrie made her way round the large room, unchanged since her childhood, where the furnishings were a heterogeneous mixture of Indian curios, priceless antiques treated with the irreverence of long usage, pretty Coalport and Meissen china, two Gainsboroughs of earlier, vacuous-looking St James ladies, and a Reynolds which wanted cleaning. The whole place, Dorrie thought, with half-vexed affection, wanted doing over, the chairs covered with faded chintz and not entirely free from dog's hairs should be thrown out, and the once-beautiful carpet was worn colourless in patches. Still – it was homely, and 'done over' by a professional would lose much of its warmth and charm.

She reached Jack's side and touched his arm, hardly able to restrain her laughter at the mute appeal on his face. He had been talking to a retired Brigadier and to Lady Elwyn who had a country house on Exmoor.

'Good evening, Brigadier,' Dorrie said. 'You're looking younger than ever!'

'Eh? Speak up, my dear!' The Brigadier bent his stick-thin legs and poked his head towards her like a rheumy-eyed tortoise, but when she had repeated her remark three times, he smiled gleefully and carried her hand to his withered lips.

'Eighty-four next month!' he exulted, 'Not so bad for an old stager, am I? By Jove, if I was thirty years younger I'd give some of these young 'uns a run for their money! Eh? Eh?'

'Mr Larcombe is the MP for Brendon, Dorian, my dear!' Lady Elwyn informed Dorrie in her loud, neighing voice, 'Almost *our* MP! I was just asking him if he had a place near Exmoor – not one of those absentee Members, I hope!'

'No – that is, I don't have a house in the West Country yet. But I do visit it very often – I stay with my aunt.'

'Oh? Who is your aunt? Do we know her?'

Jack grinned slightly, 'I shouldn't think so. Her name's Perkins.'

He could have added that she worked as a school cleaner, but Lady Elwyn was already furrowing her boney brow and murmuring, 'Perkins, Perkins – no, I don't think – there was a Perkins, or was it a Purvess? But that was in Rhodesia, of course. Well, Mr Larcombe, you must come and spend a few days with us, next time you visit your constituency. We have excellent hunting, as you know. My husband will be delighted to mount you.'

'I shall look forward to that,' Jack said, poker-faced, but not daring to look at Dorrie, 'Thank you very much.'

'Not at all!' Lady Elwyn raised her upper lip and revealed long, yellowish teeth in an affable grimace, 'It's a pleasure to have the right *sort* of young man going into Parliament. I heard there was some talk of a Socialist being elected in the area! It wouldn't do at all! Council estates all over the moor, I suppose, and goodness knows what. Makes a mockery of the Election. Excuse me – there's Geoffrey Howe.'

'Never mind,' Dorrie murmured, 'I think it was a simply splendid Erection.'

'Eh?' said the Brigadier, 'Eh? What's that?'

The dinner was, from Jack's point of view, the best part of the evening. It was, like all the things Sir Anthony loved, English, unpretentious, and the best that money could buy. Salmon from the place on Dee-side, roast grouse with plenty of roast and boiled potatoes and vegetables, and huge trifles with thick clotted cream an inch deep on top. Jack ate with great appetite, sustaining a polite and uncontroversial conversation at the same time with Amy Blagdon, wife of some Permanent Under-Secretary for something or other, and Humphrey Manville-Walker, who sat opposite. Manville-Walker was the Member for some part of Birmingham, Jack recalled. He had been in Government for years, a small, Jewish-looking man with a clever face and a pleasant manner. He had never obtained, nor seemed to desire high office, but his presence was always being requested in the corridors of power and he was reputed to be one of the richest men in Britain. He seemed to know quite a bit about the new MP, and to be kindly disposed towards him, and when the ladies had left them to their port and Havanas, he came round and sat next to Jack, turning his chair sideways and putting a confidential hand on the younger man's shoulder.

'You know, we could use someone like you on the board of one or two of my companies,' he said. 'Full of energy and good ideas, and in touch with the working man. It wouldn't interfere with your constituency work, of course, and – let's face it, old man – we spend half our time in the Commons sitting on our arses doing sod-all, don't we? Anyway – just a thought. When you get bored and the novelty wears off, give me a ring, mm? You could expect about twelve thousand a year.'

With a final pat on the shoulder and the friendly wink of a dark, Levantine eye, he went back to his place, and shortly afterwards they rejoined the ladies.

'Have you had enough?' Dorrie murmured, with a slightly mischievous smile, 'or do you want to gather more damning evidence about the idle rich? I'm sorry there are no Royals here tonight – it's mainly politicals – or you could have stood on a chair and made a "down with the monarchy" speech!'

'I've nothing against the Royal Family,' Jack said, stiffly, 'and besides – I don't go around making a fool of myself when I'm a guest in people's houses, whatever you might think.'

'Of course you don't,' Dorrie said, soothingly, 'I think you'll go very far. Fancy – even Caroline Elwyn took you for a Tory! You should be flattered – it's not everyone who has the honour of being mounted by Lord Elwyn!'

'You're a terrible woman!' he grinned, 'How soon would it be polite to go?' He longed to be alone with her again, to take her in his arms and claim what she had –

surely – half-promised in those heady moments in her flat. Would the plain little friend have gone to bed? And would Dorrie let him stay the night? For a moment, as he gazed hungrily at her face she looked remote, ethereal – a little sad, even, as though in her golden dress and her crown of gilded hair, she belonged to some old fairy-tale of enchantment and long captivity. Then she turned to him again, the lovely, mutinous mouth touched with laughter.

'I ordered a taxi ten minutes ago,' she said, 'Let's go and say goodbye to Daddy.'

Sir Anthony accepted their explanation of a later appointment with his usual unquestioning courtesy.

'I'm glad to have met you, Mr Larcombe,' he said, 'and I hope we will have the pleasure of your company again. Incidentally, I shall look forward to reading your maiden speech next week.'

Jack flushed with embarrassed pleasure. 'Thank you, sir! I only hope it's worth reading – I doubt it'll make *The Times*.'

'He gets a weekly *Hansard*,' Dorrie made a wry face, 'Can you imagine anything more deadly dull?'

'On the contrary, my dear – quite fascinating. My daughter likes to give the impression that she is completely feather-brained, Mr Larcombe – but that is not the case at all.'

'I didn't suppose it was, Sir Anthony,' Jack said, and the two men smiled at each other with the beginnings of a cautious liking.

Dorrie yawned. 'Do come on, Jack,' she said, suddenly a little irritable. She wished she had not suggested he come to this dinner party. The silly impulse to shove a piranha into the goldfish pond had been a mistake. All the piranha wanted was to be accepted as a goldfish himself, and her father obviously found him a pleasant change from the pop-stars, motor-cyclists and prize-fighters that were her usual companions. Already he and Jack were looking conspiratorial. Those tolerant smiles meant that wild little Dorrie, the talk of the town, was in a fair way to being tamed, and if the tamer was a Labour MP, still – he was pleasant and acceptable and suitably appreciative of the grace and favour bestowed on him by his betters. Balls to that. Her father could wipe the approving smile off his face, and, as for Jack Larcombe – he could take a running jump up his own backside.

They got into the taxi and Jack leaned forward and gave Dorrie's address. He felt as warm and relaxed as a tom-cat by a fire, full of good food and wine and a prospect of sex with the most desirable woman he'd ever known.

'No!' Dorrie said, sharply, sliding open the glass again. The taxi driver sighed, not bothering to turn his head.

'Make your bleedin' mind up, miss. I ain't got all night.'

'Well, I have – and I'm not going home yet. Take us to the Olympus off Curzon Street.' She closed the partition and sat back, but not very close to Jack.

'Just a minute,' he said, mildly annoyed. The last thing he wanted was another couple of hours mingling with a crowd of people with more money than sense. 'I thought we were going back to your place.'

'No.'

'But – oh, come on, Dorrie. Aren't you fed up with crowds of people?'

'No.'

In the dim, reflected glow of the street-lamps, she looked cool and detached, her profile towards him, hardly seeming aware of his presence.

'Dorrie – I want to be alone with you – to get to know you better, to – '

'I know exactly what you want, Jack, and I could express it in one simple word of four letters – but tonight I'm a lady. And you, my friend, are my escort, so you can just contain yourself and stop coming on as though I were a bitch on heat.'

Her voice was quite calm and dispassionate, but Jack felt as though she had slapped him in the face. It wasn't as though he had received no encouragement from the bloody little tease – she'd as good as told him 'later'. Who the hell did she think she was – some sort of royalty who could push people around as she pleased?

He took a breath, half-leaning forward, about to stop the taxi and make a dignified exit. But – her perfume was in his nostrils and the memory of her pliant body and soft breasts against him made him hesitate. In the end he subsided and said, sulkily, 'Anyway, I haven't much money on me.'

She shrugged slightly. 'My credit's good.'

'Besides – you didn't like the place – you told me how you nearly got thrown out. You said, in your ladylike way, that the manager hated your guts.'

'Mmm. I wonder what he thinks about the rest of my anatomy?'

Jack maintained a stony silence until the taxi turned off the Mall and drew up outside the Olympus. For a second he contemplated staying in the cab and going home, but, even while he hesitated, Dorrie had the door opened for her by a uniformed commissionaire, and was half-way up the shallow steps to the entrance, and he was left to scramble after her, feeling a little foolish and as though he was attached to her by a lead.

'Good evening.' The young woman at the reception

desk in the vast, carpeted foyer, was polite and smiling. 'Are you a member, sir?'

Of course, he was not. And neither was Dorrie. They would have to go home after all. But, before he had a chance to open his mouth, Dorrie was saying smoothly, 'Yes. I joined last week, and Mr Larcombe is my guest.'

'Oh, of course, Miss St James. Would you sign the gentleman in, please? And you, sir – would you sign here, if you don't mind?'

Silent with rage, Jack took the proffered pen. The bitch had arranged it beforehand – it was no spur of the moment idea at all. Well, she could count him out, that was all. He would just remember a previous appointment and go. He glanced at Dorrie, scowling, and the cool remoteness of her face suddenly dissolved into a smile that lit the blueness of her eyes and made Jack's heart contract painfully.

'Only half an hour!' she murmured. 'Come on – it'll be fun!'

She reached for his hand and squeezed it, then put her arm through his so that he could feel the soft pressure of her breast against him. They went down the broad stairs, past the marble statuary of Greek gods and the vast, hot-house arrangements of flowers and plants, into the intimate, murmuring warmth of the casino.

Ross Cavallo was at peace with the world. He was on the early shift, so with a bit of luck, if nothing out of the ordinary cropped up, he would be home in an hour and leave Bob Haley, the assistant manager, in charge. Also, he had a day off tomorrow, and he and Sarah were going to take the kids to the zoo. Then they would have an early dinner at home, lounge around by the fire for an hour or so, and go to bed. Finally – and the memory softened the hard line of his mouth when he thought of it

– he had awoken earlier in the day to find Sarah back in bed beside him, naked, sweet and newly showered. The heavy smoothness of her thigh was over his so that he could feel the soft warmth of her pubic hair against him and her hand caressed his penis with a gentle, tugging motion that was bringing it already into urgent life. It was the first time for months that Sarah had initiated their love-making, and the first time she had seemed to want it as much as he did. He had left her alone as long as possible once Thomas was born, only taking her when his need became too overwhelmingly urgent to care if she enjoyed it or not. But he hated doing it – hated himself and almost hated her for her white, set face and averted head. This morning, though – that had been real enough, surely? The rigid tips of her full, milky-sweet breasts could not have been faked, nor the moist readiness of her vagina. It was only when he penetrated her, being as slow and gentle as he knew how, that he fancied her shuddering breath and arching body had something of pain in it, and by that time it was too late and his body carried him forward, thrust after thrust into hers, blind and deaf to everything until the shattering burst of released energy that was his climax.

He slept a little then, and when he awoke, she was still in his arms, her smile readily answering his own, her eyes unshadowed.

'That was nice,' he had whispered, kissing the tip of her nose, 'Let's do it again.'

'Soon. I must get up and make lunch. Lotte's taken Thomas into the Gardens, but she'll be back any minute. It won't do for "gnädige Frau" to be caught in the act with "gnädige Herr". Bad example for die Kinder.' She kissed him and got up, and he let her go, sure that this was the beginning of a return to the joyous love-making of earlier days.

So even the entrance of the mad, bad Dorrie St James, accompanied strangely enough by the new MP, did not ruffle his equanimity, and he greeted them with a professionally pleasant smile. If Khalid had not mentioned that the girl was now a member, he would not have recognized the tousled urchin he had met before, in this poised and gilded beauty. She might have stepped from the pages of *Vogue*, except that there was a living warmth and radiance about her that made even the most dried up old misanthrope in the casino turn his head and feel the nostalgic echo of a stirring in his loins. Even old Schaeffer raised his avaricious eyes from the roulette layout and gazed at Dorrie as though she were pure gold, quite forgetting to object when his fifty-pence chip was swept briskly away by the dealer.

'Can I offer you a drink while the bar's still open?' Ross said, pleasantly. 'I'm afraid Mr Khalid's not in at the moment – he had a meeting. But he asked me to give you his apologies and to say he hoped to see you later in the evening.'

'Thank you, Mr Cavallo – if you're sure you can spare the time?' Dorrie said, demurely. Both Ross and Jack Larcombe glanced at her sharply, but the lovely face was guileless, the blue eyes sunny and innocent. Jack thought, 'She can't bear anyone not to like her – she has to erase any bad impression she makes on people, whether she cares about them or not.' Ross thought, 'What's the brat up to?' as he ushered them into the bar, which was screened from the rest of the casino by banks of lush greenery and more discreetly fig-leaved statuary. A small fountain played into a little pool inlaid with gold and white mosaic, with a nubile nymph kneeling at the edge,

61

gazing raptly down at the collection of coins which people always feel impelled to drop into water.

'How pretty!' Dorrie murmured, and smiled her thanks as Ross held a chair for her. 'Thank you. Could I have a very small sherry, please?'

Jack went over to the bar with Ross, and was accosted by Stella Fielding who spent more time in the casino than Cavallo himself. He paused for a few moments' conversation, and to be introduced to her protégé of the night, a gay dress designer called Ludovic Bagel, while Ross took the drinks over to their table.

'Your good health, Miss St James,' he said, solemnly, lifting his small Scotch and water to her.

'And yours, Mr Cavallo!' She was equally solemn, but the corners of her mouth twitched with suppressed laughter. 'This is very kind of you – considering how abominably I behaved the other night.'

'Yes, you did, rather,' he agreed, 'but I'm used to that – I have children of my own, you know.'

A small intake of breath, and Ross grinned to himself. That had got through and drawn blood. For a second he could see a cutting and probably obscene reply trembling on her lips, then she mastered the impulse and turned the full blue battery of her gaze on him.

'You're quite right,' she said, humbly, 'I did behave childishly – and I'm sorry.'

'Not at all. As I'm sure Mr Khalid would tell you, that's what I'm paid for.'

Dorrie frowned, a small frown that nearly became a scowl, and took a swig of her sherry that nearly emptied the glass. The little encounter was not going as she had planned it. God damn it, she *knew* she looked her best tonight – she had seen it in the eyes of every man she met. Every man except Ross Cavallo, and he, far from being overwhelmed, was regarding her with what could only be called detached amusement. Well, she would continue laying on the sweetness and light for just so long, then it would be 'Up yours, Mr Cavallo,' and she would forget about him.

'How old are your children?' she asked politely, leaning forward in her interest and evidently unaware that the movement revealed almost the whole of her breasts down to a pink aureole of nipple.

'Let's see,' Cavallo did not avert his eyes, flushing with embarrassment, nor did he peer surreptitiously. He glanced at her bosom as detachedly and with just as much emotion as if she had been the marble nymph at the poolside, and calmly, with complete lack of interest, looked away again. 'There's Beatrice – she's not much younger than you, I should think. Then Ben – he's eight. And finally our newest, Tom. Or Thomas the Toad as Sarah calls him when he demands feeding at night.'

'Sarah's your wife?'

'Yes . . .' For the first time, Dorrie saw a softening in the lean, dark face, and there was a tender look in his eyes which made her unaccountably irritable.

'What's she like? Is she beautiful?' Even to herself, she sounded sulky and spoilt. Ross smiled at her, amused.

'You wouldn't think so. Most people wouldn't think she was half as beautiful as you. But to me, she's the loveliest woman in the world.'

Dorrie itched to draw back her foot and kick the man, but at that moment Jack Larcombe came back and she greeted him as though he had rescued her from intolerable boredom, bewitching him with smiles and enticing glances until he was flushed with pleasure. Cavallo excused himself and rose to go. He felt sorry for Larcombe. The poor mutt – could he not see that Dorrie was just playing games with him? She might or might not take him into her bed – but, as for her heart, Cavallo thought, that was probably the size and temperature of an ice cube. All the girl was after was an ego massage – she was so spoilt that she simply could not bear any man to be impervious to her, even a thirty-five-year-old father of three, deeply in love with his wife. Too bad. He could resist Dorrie St James even if he found her naked in his bed.

'Jack!' Dorrie said, 'Drink up before anybody else comes and bores me. I want to have a little flutter on the roulette table.'

She was lovely, leaning towards him and looking up into his eyes with that half-amused, half-affectionate glance. Jack, puritanical about money and gambling to the extent that he never had a bet on a horse or did the football pools, found himself following Dorrie like an obedient dog, first to the cash point, where he exchanged a fifty-pound cheque for two twenty-five-pound chips, and then to a roulette table. He had horrified even himself. Fifty pounds – and for a couple of pieces of plastic which he was about to chance on the random turning of a wheel. He must be mad. Dorrie accepted the chips with a casual smile and exchanged them for a very small pile of pink counters, which the dealer marked up on her chip tree as being worth ten pounds each. Everyone was very slick, very professional – the dealers in their elegant dark red evening dresses with a gold Greek key pattern round the hem, the inspectors who supervised every two tables and smiled pleasantly, wishing them good evening, the pit-boss, a young man with a Scots accent and a ready smile who even knew Jack's name – they were all prepared to take his money from him as painlessly as possible.

'Place your bets,' the dealer said, and hands reached

out from all sides, covering the green baize with a rainbow of plastic.

'No more bets.' It all looked so harmless, like a kindergarten game, and when the wheel stopped turning and the bits of plastic were nearly all swept away, who could feel that there was any harm done? Only – that had been ten pounds of Jack Larcombe's money, swept away with the rest, and when he thought how his mother would have gone out cleaning for hours to earn that much, he could almost imagine his own voice hoarsely calling 'Stop!'

'Damn!' Dorrie said lightly, and shoved two more chips on to the layout. The staccato noise of the little metal ball on the wheel seemed to fill Jack's ears, and when the dealer announced, 'Seven red, odd low,' he felt his heart begin to pound and his hands grow clammy with fear. Thirty pounds gone – for nothing – and Dorrie was reaching out for the last twenty, hardly looking to see where she placed it. Then a voice behind them spoke her name, and she glanced round, tossing the chips casually to Jack as she did so.

'You have a go this time, Jack – you might have better luck than me. Hallo, Prince Tariq.'

'Miss St James.' The Saudi bowed formally. 'I was so sorry you had to leave us unexpectedly the other night.'

'Oh – so was I, Your Highness. But I promised my governess I would be in bed by four. And she's very strict with me.'

'So?' Not quite sure whether he was being teased, Tariq el Said paused and stared at the English girl. She was indeed very beautiful – far more, even, than he had first thought. If a man once possessed that pale golden skin and the hair that was tonight like a royal coronet, then he would surely find a satisfaction that little Muhna and

65

Fatima and the rest could never give him. But – he had been too hasty the other night. He had wished to arouse her, and had forgotten how prudish English women could be, since he normally dealt only with whores. He would have to take more pains with this one – woo her gently, court her with flowers and fine speeches, startle her with his deep passion in the best manner of a smouldering Valentino. It was what some of them expected, little realizing there are few creatures as unromantic and earthy as an Arab sheikh.

'Miss St James,' he said, softly, allowing his eyes to dwell on her face. 'May I have the honour of taking you to dinner one night? It would give me great pleasure.'

'You hope,' Dorrie thought. Aloud, she said, 'Thank you, yes – that'd be nice. Give me a ring, if you like.'

Already she was half-turning away from him, back to the roulette table, and he bowed again and left her. Dorrie yawned and the yawn became a grin. Cheeky bastard! If he thought a meal out was going to buy a night in her bed, he could think again. She'd damn well take a chaperone and if he tried his party tricks she would freeze him with her best upper-class stare of outrage. Let him wait. Of course, he was undeniably attractive, and the cruel look about his eyes and mouth added to his sex appeal. A tiger is naturally more sexy-looking than a lamb, and Dorrie thought she could keep the whip-hand.

Jack had cautiously staked one of his remaining chips on the ten, and watched with a hollow feeling of inevitability as it lost.

'Bad luck,' Dorrie said, lightly, then she looked more closely at his face. My God – he really cared! It really was hurting him, losing that – what was it? Forty quid? What was an MP's salary, anyway? About sixteen thousand a year? Not riches – still, enough not to care too much about the odd fifty pounds. Then she remembered his background and made an effort to imagine what it would be like to be poor. It was difficult. Fifty pounds was – what? A few pounds of marrons glacés from Fortnum's? A silk scarf at Lord's in the Burlington Arcade? A bottle of scent or a couple of bottles of champagne? Dorrie gave presents casually and with a careless generosity, and those were the sort of things she bought. Never remembering birthdays or anniversaries, her friends and relatives were nevertheless often surprised on a dull day by the arrival of an extravagant gift, with a scrawled 'Love, Dorrie' on the card. It was hard to visualize a world where fifty pounds meant a lot of money. Poor Jack! She squeezed his arm. 'Come on – let's go now. You're not enjoying this, are you?'

Jack drew a breath and tried to calm his fluttering nerves. Dorrie must think him a fool, getting worked up over fifty quid. After all – he had a couple of thousand in the bank, and his salary was, he thought, enormous. He could not imagine ever spending it all. It was only the old 'workhouse' complex that had been drummed into him as a child that made him so panic-stricken about losing money. He smiled at Dorrie.

'Might as well do the lot in! What day is your birthday?'

'December the third.'

With a flourish, Jack put the last chip on number three. Other people, he noticed for the first time, were covering the table with bets – hundreds of pounds at a time. His small, ten-pound chip seemed to pale into insignificance. Stella Fielding came up behind him and poked him in the ribs, 'Didn't think I'd see you at the tables, you naughty boy! Are you having any luck?'

'No!' Jack laughed. He suddenly felt free and careless. He had staked the whole fifty quid and he didn't give enough of a damn even to stay and watch the ball tumbling round. 'No – this is my first and last experience of gambling. Too hard on the nerves!'

'Gets you, though,' Stella hitched herself on to a chair and took a stack of chips from the dealer. 'I always have green if I can. My lucky colour. And I always sit on this side of the table – somehow I never win on the other. Funny, isn't it?'

She placed her bets carefully, hunched over the table, her shoulders looking bony and old above the finely pleated silk of her lovely Jean Muir gown. Without taking her eyes off the baize, she scrabbled about in a little gold-woven clutch bag from Asprey's until she found her cigarettes and lighter.

'No more bets.' The ball seemed to leap and tumble and spin with a life of its own, round and round, with a dozen pairs of eyes fixed on it. It was mesmerizing, with an ancient, powerful magic, and it was impossible to walk away. The red silk-shaded lamp above the table seemed to throw into sharp relief all the straining faces below it, and in the seconds before the ball dropped, there was a curious similarity between them all, a fearful, hungry, excited look that made a mockery of their expensive clothes and jewels.

'Three red, odd low,' the dealer said, and began paying out the winning bets, starting with the lowest who had had splits, corners, six lines and so on. Jack felt an unaccountable thudding in his throat. He glanced uncertainly at Dorrie, 'Does that mean . . . ?' She laughed, pleased for him, 'Yes – you've won three hundred and fifty pounds. Hoorah! Let's have a drink to celebrate!'

The dealer was shoving a pile of chips at him, and he felt almost apologetic, as though he were being given something that he did not deserve.

'Beginner's luck!' he said, and the dealer smiled professionally.

Stella Fielding said, 'Why don't you leave it on? Your luck's in!' but Jack shied at the prospect.

'No fear! I don't think I'm the gambling type – I scare too easily!'

They took the chips to the cash-point, and, to Jack's secret astonishment, had them changed into real bank-notes without any problem, then they went back to the bar and bought a bottle of champagne of a fairly indifferent vintage at a very inflated price. But Jack didn't know, and he was too relieved and excited to care, and Dorrie was too pleased for him to say anything. When they had drunk several glasses and had got to the slightly tipsy stage where they were thinking of the most ridiculous things they could to toast, Stella Fielding came over.

'You look happy,' she said, pausing on her way to the bar, 'you should have stayed on the three, Jack – it came up again.'

She moved on, leaving Jack with a curious sour feeling of disappointment as though the champagne had suddenly gone flat. Trust him to back off when he could have made some real money.

Dorrie, watching his face, laughed. 'Cheer up! It's a mug's game, and you could have lost the lot! Now, I give you – the occasion of your being mounted by Lord Elwyn!'

They clinked their glasses together and Jack, looking at her golden, laughing face, felt a choking emotion rising in him which at first he did not recognize as love.

'Let's go home,' he whispered, huskily.

She said nothing, but stood up, smiling and stretching lazily, then, as she glanced idly round the casino, she gave a small exclamation, 'Help! There's my little friend

Johnny Pacelli. Let's avoid him if we can – he thinks I'm one of his groupies or something!'

They left discreetly, as Pacelli stood at the cash-point, and Jack, interposing his broad frame between the singer and any possible view of Dorrie, felt both protective and conspiratorial as they stole up the broad staircase and burst out laughing in the safety of the foyer.

'Oh, poor Johnny,' Dorrie said, 'but he's such a conceited little – bore!'

'Poor nothing! Did you see the amount of money he was changing into chips? Absolute bundles of the stuff! The pop business must be doing him proud.'

Dorrie frowned slightly. 'I didn't think so. He's popular, but he's always moaning on about this contract he has where he only gets a very small percentage. I remember because he was talking of going to court. Perhaps he did and has come to gamble away his winnings. Besides,' she grinned impudently up at Jack, 'bundles of the stuff to you might be peanuts to Pacelli! I expect you still barter with mangel-wurzels down in Somerset!'

They took a taxi back to Dorrie's flat, and Jack followed her to the front door, but when she had found her key, she hesitated, then turned and looked up at him, her two hands lightly on his chest.

'Don't come up tonight, Jack,' she said, softly. 'I know you want to – but – I – I don't want you to think I'm a – a one-night stand.'

He captured her hands in his and kissed the palms of them. 'I wouldn't think that. But I won't come up. I'll leave you to your innocent slumbers – for tonight anyway. Is it too much to hope for a chaste kiss?'

For answer, she tilted her face up to his, her lips parted and inviting, and he took the soft warmth of fur and silk and scented flesh into his arms, drinking in the heady perfume of her as he tasted the sweetness of her mouth.

'Oh, God,' he groaned, 'if I don't make love to you soon, I'll go mad.'

'Now then, Master Jack – "Patience is a virtue, possess it if you can", as my nanny used to tell me. Just go home and think of England and your glorious future as its Prime Minister!' She kissed him again lightly, and was gone.

Cavallo saw Dorrie and Larcombe go, and followed them leisurely across the casino. He still felt sorry for the young politician, who was so obviously falling hard for the girl, and hoped briefly that Dorrie got what was coming to her. He smiled to himself, remembering her efforts to charm him and found himself contemplating an image of her face which had an expression of wistfulness about it. Was his memory playing tricks? Probably. There was nothing very tender or wistful about Dorrie St James. It was only his imagination that had conjured up the picture of that admittedly lovely face, and endowed it with the expression of a lost princess in a fairy-tale. The sort of princess knights hacked their way through thorn forests to get to. The real Dorrie was as hard as nails.

'Good evening, Mr Pacelli,' he said.

Pacelli jumped and dropped one of his cash chips which Ross picked up for him. It was a five-hundred-pound one, and Pacelli had a handful.

'Shit!' the pop-star snarled, angrily, 'do you have to come pussy-footing up behind people like a fucking store detective? What the hell are you doing here, anyway?'

Ross stared at the man for a moment, not bothering to hide his distaste. 'I'm the manager of this casino,' he said, quietly, 'and among my duties is that of seeing that the

71

punters are not disturbed by the foul language of any undesirables. Do you get my drift?'

Pacelli swore again, but more quietly. 'Look – just fuck off, Cavallo. I'm only minding my own business. What's it to you? Don't you want people to use the joint?'

'If they can behave themselves, yes. Not if they're the cause of other people leaving.'

'Screw you, who do you think you are? All I want to do is place a lousy, stinking bet – not break in through the pearly gates and stick up the Angel Gabriel.'

Khalid had come in. Ross saw his bulky figure gliding towards them with his odd, graceful walk, his mouth smiling widely, his dark eyes fixed on them. He reminded Ross of an alligator.

'Hey, Ross! Not home yet? You're supposed to be on the early shift! Sarah will be telling me off – and you know how scared I am of angry ladies? Eh?' He laughed loudly and turned to the pop-singer, putting his arms round him in a friendly bear-hug, 'Johnny! Nice to see you! I thought you weren't coming in till later!'

Ross, still staring at Pacelli with undisguised dislike, saw a line of sweat on the man's upper lip and wondered if the little creep had been scared Ross was going to hit him. The jerk! What women saw in him, God alone knew – but, whatever it was, they paid well for it, judging by the amount of money he had to play with.

'I'm just going home now, Mr Khalid,' he said, 'Bob Haley's in charge. I'll see you on Sunday.'

'Good! Fine! See you then, Ross! You go relax, enjoy yourself with your lovely wife! Ciao!'

As Ross nodded and turned away, Khalid's arm, still round Pacelli's shoulder, tightened, and his fingers dug painfully through the silk Dior jacket. 'You stupid little prick!' he said, softly, 'You too doped up to get anything right?'

3

The October day was as crisp, blue-gold and perfect as any budding Keats could have wished, and London Zoo was at its best, with the animals posing affably in the unseasonable warmth and the smell at a minimum.

Beatrice and Ben Cavallo, exuberant as puppies, bounded from cage to cage, squealing and exclaiming, never pausing long enough to read the names of the occupants, and rushing back occasionally to round up their strolling parents and hurry them along.

'Slow down!' Ross protested, aiming a playful cuff at his son's head as he darted past, 'At this rate we'll be finished in five minutes.'

'Well, we want to see everything and then go back and have a good look at the ones we like best,' Ben explained, tugging at his parents' hands. 'Gosh – I don't know how you can walk so *slowly*!'

Beatrice, more gentle and considerate at twelve years old, took her father's other hand and walked beside him, only an occasional little spring in her step betraying her impatience to be running free.

'They're much older than us, Ben,' she explained, 'and you haven't got so much energy when you're older, have you, Daddy?'

'Very true, my pet,' said her father, with a rueful grin at Sarah. 'What with the rheumatics and tripping over my long grey beard, it's a wonder I can hobble along at all.'

'Oh, I didn't mean you were *that* old!' Bea said, hastily,

full of remorse in case she had hurt her parents' feelings, 'Not more than sort of middle-aged, really!'

'Off you go! You scamper ahead and get rid of some of that excess energy, and your mother and I will try and make it to that bench over there. Come back when you've had enough.'

'And stay together!' Sarah added, anxiously, 'And don't get lost!'

'Don't worry!' Ross took her hand and led her over to the bench near Snowdon's aviary. 'Bea's a sensible kid. Anyway – now that we're alone, I'm going to summon all my fast-decaying energy, drag you into the bushes and ravish you!'

Sarah laughed and rubbed her face affectionately against his sleeve. It was such a beautiful day, and Ross was the dearest and most wonderful husband in the world. The love-making would come right again, she was sure, but . . . She sighed and sat down heavily on the bench, and Ross looked at her, sudden concern in his face.

'What is it, darling?'

'Oh, nothing. Just a bit tired. I had to get up for Tom in the night again.'

'Poor darling – I didn't hear a thing. Look – couldn't you put him on to a bottle, so that at least I could give him a feed at night?'

'No! How could you, when you've been working half the day and most of the night? Anyway – I like feeding him. It's the last time I shall feed a baby – let me carry on a bit longer.'

Ross did not persist. They sat in a companionable silence, enjoying the warmth of the sun, but when Sarah closed her eyes, leaning against his shoulder, he studied her face with a stirring of uneasiness. She *did* look tired, and older than her thirty-four years. Her delicate skin had a fine-drawn, waxen pallor about it, like the fading petals of a magnolia, and there were harsh shadows beneath her eyes. Against the rich, dark background of the mink that had been his last year's Christmas present to her, she looked small and fragile, like a hurt woodland creature.

'Sarah!' he whispered, taking her hand, and holding it in both his own, 'Darling – what is it? You're not well, are you?'

She didn't open her eyes, but beneath the dark fan of lashes, Ross saw tears gathering, and saw her bite her lower lip as she struggled for self-control.

'I've got such a *pain*, Ross,' she whispered at last, 'Down here. Ever since Thomas was born. And – and I keep thinking it'll get better, but it doesn't.' Her eyes opened at last and fixed on his own, dark, pleading eyes begging him for comfort and reassurance. All the day's brightness seemed to die, and the sunlight became no more than the cold glare of a naked light-bulb. It seemed to Ross that he and Sarah had been sitting on that bench for hours, holding hands across a dark chasm that had suddenly yawned between them. Then, with an effort that was almost physical, he pushed the blackness aside, and smiled down at his wife's frightened face. 'You never did go for a post-natal examination, did you, silly? You go to the doctor first thing on Monday, and you'll see – it'll be something quite simple. You'll wish you'd gone weeks ago.'

'Oh, I know. It's just – I hate being poked about, even by Dr Colley who's known me for years.'

'Perhaps it'd be better if you went to the hospital out-patients? I mean – it'd be more impersonal, wouldn't it?'

'Oh – no! No, I wouldn't like that at all, Ross. Dr Colley's been my doctor since I was born – he knows all about me, and . . .' Her voice trailed away, and she sat

75

with her hands clenched between her knees, a picture of dejected misery. Ross knew what she meant when she said Dr Colley 'knew all about her', and he recognized the black, despairing mood that had suddenly engulfed Sarah. They were less frequent now, but at one time only anti-depressants and tranquillisers had helped her live with the terrible memories of her early life.

'All right, darling,' he said, gently, putting an arm round her and pulling her close to him, 'Of course you can see old Colley. It's only that he's getting a bit doddery now, and . . .'

'He's still a good doctor. I'll never ever forget how good he was to me . . .'

'I know. Now, don't worry. We'll go and see him on Monday. Come on – let's find the kids and go and have some lunch.'

The goldfish in the aquarium swam back and forth, their tails flicking with the regularity of a clock. Far from soothing the nerves, Ross found himself becoming more and more irritated by the vacuous, goggle-eyed faces staring out at him from behind the glass. Sarah had been closeted with that old fool of a doctor for half-an-hour now – what on earth was he doing? Ross had little confidence in Dr James Colley's ability, regarding him as a senile old fool, but Sarah would not dream of having anyone else.

The minutes and the goldfish ticked past. The waiting room was stuffy with an electric fire and smelt faintly of antiseptic and old outdoor clothing. Ross felt his eyelids growing heavy over last year's *Punch*. He had only had four hours' sleep, but he had insisted on coming with Sarah to the surgery, although she had protested that there was no need. There was no one else waiting. Most of the patients preferred to see the junior partner these days, and there were very few as loyal as Sarah who were prepared to come to the shabby, old-fashioned surgery off Goldhawk Road.

Sarah emerged at last, rather pale, and with her lips firmly compressed as though to stop them trembling. She avoided Ross's eyes, and went over to the electric fire where she made a great business of warming her hands. 'He wants to see you,' she said.

Ross went into the consulting room and found the doctor with bent head, busily scribbling notes and apparently quite unaware of his presence. Swallowing his irritation for Sarah's sake, Ross sat down quietly and waited, and, after a moment or two, the old man put down his pen and stared across the desk with faded grey eyes.

'Now, then,' he said, 'Have you ever heard the word "psychosomatic"?'

Sarah, in her turn, stared at the fish, sitting so close to the fire that she nearly burned her shins, and rubbing her hands together. Could it be true, what Dr Colley had told her? Was her pain something her mind was doing to her body? Had she not been punished enough, that she must now do without the joy of her physical love for Ross, because her brain had decided sex was dirty and frightening? She remembered her honeymoon, fifteen years before, and Ross's loving gentleness. He had made her feel like – oh, a queen, a goddess, a creature of fire and beauty. Over the years he had healed those deep wounds of her childhood until they seemed only faint scars, part of the landscape of her mind. And now Dr Colley was telling her that beneath those scars something had been festering for years. She was not healed, she was a maimed creature who could not even give her husband the physical love he needed. Silently, Sarah began to weep, the painful, suppressed tears that she had first shed more than twenty years ago, the night when her father had destroyed her life . . .

Arthur Dean was a solicitor, living in Chiswick with his wife, Marjorie, and their only child, Sarah. He was a big, bluff, hearty man with receding fair hair and a skin that flushed and perspired easily. He had not had the success he had hoped for in his chosen profession, mainly handling the seedier divorce cases, and neither had his own marriage been very successful. His rather eccentric tastes in love-making were not shared by his wife, who had quite early shown him her distaste and who tolerated the physical side of her marriage with an almost shuddering aversion.

Jovial and friendly to the people he met outside his own home, Arthur Dean vented all his spite and bitterness on his wife and child. They were much alike, small and thin and dark with huge, frightened eyes, and the more they cowered from him, the more he hated them and bullied them. Usually it was only his vicious tongue that they had to fear, his nagging and sneering and threats, but, more and more often as the years went past, he resorted to drinking, and then the two women were lucky to escape with a few bruises. Those nights when he came home an hour or so late, Sarah and her mother would sit there, pretending to listen to the radio in the little shabby-genteel sitting-room. Sometimes it was 'In Town Tonight' – 'Once again,' the announcer would say, 'we stop the mighty roar of London's traffic . . .' and then would come the sound of a key fumbling in the lock, and the two pairs of dark eyes would seek each other out, searching for a reassurance that neither of them could give.

'Bed, Sarah,' her mother would say, 'Quickly, now.'

And sometimes Sarah would go, hating herself for her cowardice, and lie tense between the chilly sheets, listening to her father's hectoring voice below, and the later, dreadful sounds from her parents' bedroom. Sometimes she stayed with her mother, and then her father would find an excuse for hitting her as well. Sarah hated him. She day-dreamed about his death as some girls dream of marriage, and she hated herself and her mother for their craven cowering beneath his tyranny.

When Sarah was twelve, the indiscriminate bashing and smacking suddenly became a ritual. He would find some pretext for punishing her and would put her across his knee and smack her bare bottom. The first time it happened, Marjorie Dean rushed forward and grabbed her husband's arm. 'Arthur! Please – no! Please – it isn't decent – leave the girl alone – Arthur!' She was weeping and clawing at him ineffectually and he swung his arm at her, hitting her in the mouth, so that she fell back, gasping and sobbing, then rushed from the room, holding her hands in front of her face.

Sarah soon learned that if she struggled, the pain and the humiliation went on all the longer. She used to lie as motionless as she could, sustained only by images of terrible retribution overtaking her tormentor.

Only a few more years, she would think, and then she could legally leave home. She would get a job, and a nice flat, and her mother could come and keep house for her. The beatings went on, became more frequent, until Sarah was nearly thirteen. She had gone to her room early and worked at her Latin homework in the icy cold until her hands were too numb to hold a pen any longer. She had heard her father shouting when he came in, and her mother's thin, conciliatory voice, rising in a trembling cry as his heavy hand fell on her bruised body. Sarah got into bed and lay with her hands over her ears. 'Let him die,' she prayed, 'oh, please, *please* God, let him die.'

She fell asleep at last, and woke sometime in the middle of the night when a shadow came between her and the light from the street-lamp shining through the thin curtains.

'Father? What is it? What's wrong?' She struggled into a sitting position, confusedly thinking that she had left undone some household task and he had come to shout at her about it.

'Hush! Nothing's wrong! Lie down – I just came to give you a little cuddle.'

His voice was different – hoarse and excited, and she could see his protruding eyes gleaming in the dim light. Uneasily, she pulled the bedclothes round her thin shoulders. 'I – I don't want a cuddle. I'm tired.'

He took a step nearer and she could smell whisky on him and hear his rapid breathing. 'Only a little cuddle. You must be nice to me.'

He had on his winter pyjamas, cream winceyette with a maroon stripe on them, and he fumbled at the cord and let them drop to the ground. Sarah could see his hairy, paunchy belly and, to her completely innocent and uninformed eyes, a dreadful thing, a huge deformity rising from his loins, swaying in front of him as he came towards her.

'Touch it!' he whispered, 'Would you like to? Go on – touch it!'

She shook her head dumbly, putting her hands behind her, then, as he pulled back the bedclothes, tried to beat him off, frantically pushing at his heavy body which crushed hers like a great stone. She cried out in terror, calling for her mother, but no one came, and in the end she was quiescent, only tears flowing in shamed silence

80

down her cheeks, as the man whom she would never call 'father' again thrust his heavy, engorged penis deep into her virgin flesh, again and again, painful and tearing, horrible, nightmarish, while he gasped and sobbed and murmured dreadful obscene things that she did not understand. And at last, with a great roar like a savage animal, he reached a climax and finished with her, rolling off her thin, aching body, and suddenly whimpering as though he realized what he had done. 'You dirty little bitch,' he moaned, 'what did you make me do that for? You're a dirty whore – you're no daughter of mine!'

But a few nights later he came again, and again, so that all Sarah's days came to be shadowed with the blackness of the coming night. She said nothing to her mother, and Marjorie, knowing but pretending not to, tried to tell herself that it didn't matter, that Sarah didn't care, and that, at least, Arthur was leaving *her* in peace these days.

Sarah's homework became erratic and she hardly ate. One or two teachers, already a little uneasy about the child's home life after seeing bruises on her arms and cheek, became more concerned, until one day her English teacher found Sarah in the book store-room, her teeth chattering as she tried to cut her wrists with a rusty razor blade.

The whole story came flooding out in a storm of hysterical tears and Sarah never saw her parents again. Dr Colley, summoned urgently to examine the child, took her to stay with him and his wife for a while, and two days later, Arthur Dean hired a car and drove it, with himself and his wife, over a cliff to their deaths. Sarah mourned neither of them. She could never forgive her mother for her failure, and her father's death filled her with guilty exultation. But there was shame left, and horror, and the guilt of feeling that it was somehow her fault, and Sarah never forgot how Dr Colley talked with her, hour after hour, comforting, reassuring, leading her back with gentle words until she felt she was a member of the human race again. She went to live with a maiden aunt after that, far off in the Yorkshire Dales, and the clean cold air and the austere, spinsterish household did their share in healing her, although she still had terrible troughs of depression and awful nightmares, and was still taking anti-depressants and tranquillisers when she was eighteen years old and met Ross Cavallo.

She had never expected to marry. The thought of the marriage bed filled her with trembling revulsion until she met Ross. It was like an awakening – like being dragged from a cess-pit and finding oneself clean and pure in a meadow of spring flowers, and Sarah woke and blossomed and made love and put on weight, and married and bore children and adored her husband. And now she had been told that it was all a pretence. That all the beauty and passion and delight of her marriage had been only a lovely robe flung over rotting, leprous flesh. That she was not, would never be, free of that ancient, contaminating evil. Silently, bitterly, Sarah wept.

Soon, Ross came back. He said nothing at first, only took her hands in his warm ones and pulled her gently into his arms, holding her close, his cheek against her hair.

'Oh, Ross – ' she lifted her face to him and it was wet with helpless tears, 'I'm sorry – I'm sorry! Please don't stop loving me, darling – I promise I'll get better . . .'

'Hush! Stop crying. Hush, darling . . .' He cradled her like a child and kissed the salt dampness of her face, 'Listen, Sarah – we'll go and see someone else. I know you think the sun shines out of old Colley's stethoscope, but he's not infallible. I don't believe you've suddenly got all screwed up mentally after fifteen years of happy marriage. You've always enjoyed making love, haven't you?'

'You know how much, but . . .'

'Well then, we'll see someone else.'

'Oh, *no*! Please, Ross – don't make me, not just yet! I can't bear to – to tell anyone else – oh, please!'

She was actually shaking with anguish, her hands grasping the front of his coat as though she was going to be dragged away by force.

'All right, darling – don't worry. No one's going to make you do anything you don't want to.' He soothed her, murmuring words of love and reassurance until the trembling stopped and she was in control of herself again. 'Come on – do your face a bit and we'll go and have lunch in town. What about "Le Soufflé" at the Inter-Continental?'

Sarah conjured up a tremulous smile and took a deep breath.

'Yes – that'd be lovely. I'll just give Lotte a ring and make sure Tom's all right. He shouldn't need feeding till after two . . .'

'Then leave him! You worry too much – Thomas the Toad is a natural survivor – it's Lotte I feel sorry for!'

Within half an hour they were installed amid the gently abstract dark red and gleaming glass decor of 'Le Soufflé', hesitating over the respective merits of Peter Kromberg's delicate 'feuilleté d'asperges au jambon de canard' or the dashing frothiness of the 'soufflé de saumon fumé à la ciboulette'. Sarah's eyes were warm and bright as they sought her husband's.

'You are the *nicest* man!' she said, softly. 'This was just what I needed and I love you very much!'

He took her hand and touched the fingertips gently to

83

his lips. 'I love you, too, darling. Just be well and happy, that's all.'

'I will be, I promise. I think I feel better already, you know.' There was an element of pleading in her voice, despite her smile. Ross knew what she was trying to tell him: 'Just let me be for a while. No doctors or consultants to intrude in the secret places of my body and my mind. Leave me in peace to heal myself.'

So be it, he thought. He loved and cherished his wife, and the idea of forcing himself on her was repugnant to him, but – it would be hard. He was no ascetic, and the physical side of his marriage had been one of the great pleasures of his life.

'Have you decided yet? What shall we drink – a Pouilly Fumé?'

They ate the lovely food, drank and talked and laughed, building an imaginary bridge across the chasm that was between them.

Larcombe had been in the Commons since ten that morning, wandering restlessly between the tea-room, the library and the smoke-room. He had a small sheaf of notes in his hand, somewhat creased and dog-eared, and a sick feeling in his stomach making him feel sure that when Mr Speaker called his name, he would throw up. Sometime that afternoon, during the debate on the cuts in super-tax, he was going to have to stand up and make his maiden speech – he, a farm-worker's son from Somerset, was going to say his piece in the Mother of Parliaments, where Gladstone, Disraeli and Fox had stood before him. 'Oh, God,' he muttered, and made his way to the lavatories again. A voice at his elbow as he washed his hands made him start, and he encountered the amused eyes of Humphrey Manville-Walker, whom he'd met at the St James dinner party.

'Dear, dear!' Manville-Walker said, with gentle irony, 'Jumpy today, aren't we? Oh – your maiden speech, I believe? Good luck – I shall come in specially to hear you!'

Jack groaned. 'Don't bother – I think I'm going to make an absolute balls-up of it!'

'Don't worry, my friend! Maiden speeches are always treated with special courtesy – you'll be congratulated from both sides, unless you do something deeply embarrassing or unparliamentary.'

'That's the trouble – so many bloody silly "dos" and "don'ts". If I get carried away, I'm liable to forget them all . . .'

'You won't get carried away. Believe me, the mood of the House for nine-tenths of the time is total boredom. It's very hard to get carried away in such an atmosphere.'

Jack dried his hands, and grinned a shade ruefully at the other man.

'You must think me very naïve. But – it really does mean something to me, fighting this Bill. If – if you'd been on the other side of the tracks, like me, you'd know the unfairness of the system, and you'd feel, just the same as I do, that the rich can't be allowed to get away with even more money.'

Manville-Walker's wide mouth curved into a faint smile. 'Save the rhetoric,' he said, 'for the floor of the House. And, believe it or not, my father was a rather hard-up Jewish tailor from Koblenz who died in Hitler's gas ovens. My mother brought me up in the East End of London by working in a sweat-shop, sewing clothes for rich women twelve hours a day. I, too, decided early on that it was unfair that some should have and some should have not – but my answer was to go out and grab a share of the cake for myself.'

'Oh – I'm sorry,' Jack said, confused, 'I didn't know – about your background, I mean.'

The other man shrugged, washing his hands as thoroughly and delicately as a surgeon.

'My dear chap – why should you? Not many people do. But don't delude yourself that all Socialists are St Georges, fighting for the poor – many of them are just as self-seeking and power-hungry as your average bloated capitalist. Anyway – how about some lunch? Are you engaged?'

'No – that is, I was just going to grab a sandwich in the refreshment room. I don't feel too hungry.'

'Nonsense. You'll speak all the better on a full stomach. Be my guest – I was just going to walk down to the Tate Gallery restaurant. Do you know it? Splendid English cuisine, and that rather romantic Whistler to look at while you eat – I guarantee that the veal kidneys Florentine will make you forget all about super-tax.'

And, after all, he made his speech to rows of green benches that were two-thirds empty. The opening speech had been made by the Chancellor of the Exchequer, hotly responded to by the Shadow Chancellor, then interest had slackened and Members had gradually drifted off to the tea-room.

'By God,' Larcombe thought, glowering round at his somnolent audience, 'no wonder they don't want TV in here. They wouldn't like the public to see how little they do for a living.'

The beginnings of disillusionment, sown in his mind by his talk with Manville-Walker, gave a harsh edge to his voice that made one or two members glance at him with a

86

passing interest. But it was only passing. They were all enthusiastic, these new fellows – full of fire in their bellies and thunder in their guts, sitting in on all the debates and thinking that they were going to change the course of events all by themselves. They soon realized that all the real governing was done by a very small handful of people at ministerial level and that the power of a back-bencher was non-existent.

One or two members closed their eyes, and more than one yawned pointedly. Someone should have told the new chap that one was supposed to avoid controversy and inflammatory matters in a maiden speech.

Jack saw the bored expressions, and that they were not confined to the Government benches, and he felt a sudden fury which reddened his face and made him clench his teeth.

'Some of my honourable friends grow weary,' he said, lowering his voice for a moment to an almost conversational level. 'Some of them close their eyes. It is not done, they think, to get so worked up in a maiden speech – it is not done, perhaps, to get deeply and emotionally involved, to really care about the poor people of this country. Well, let me tell the House, I *do* care! Let me tell them, there are people to whom our salaries as MPs would be like winning the pools, who work and skimp and save their whole lives with no holidays, no pleasure – no *dignity* as human beings. And there are other people, to whom this Government actually proposes giving even more money – people who live lives of such idleness and luxury that the man in the street simply would not believe the vast sums of money they spend, simply on pampering themselves. I've seen it myself – and I tell you, it's a wicked sin and shame for a woman to spend a thousand pounds on a dress, or a man to squander thousands at the gaming table, while there are people in want throughout our country. We need new hospitals! We need new schools! We need better care for the old and infirm! For God's sake, let it not be said of this country, "to those that have shall be given, from those that have not shall be taken away".'

He sat down, and there was a token 'Hear! Hear!' or two from the Labour benches. Why did he feel that he had been ridiculous? That he had ranted when he should have drawled, and grown hot when he should have stayed cool? He felt himself trembling with reaction, and hardly heard the witty little speech with which a member of the Government replied to his own. But he felt that they laughed at him, and as soon as he could he rose and hurried out of the Chamber to walk on the River Terrace.

It was nearly seven o'clock. The murky waters of the Thames were transformed by darkness to black silk, jewelled with the reflection of a thousand lights. Jack walked quickly up and down, and cursed himself for getting carried away. He should have been calmer, he told himself, and dissected the upper classes with the detached skill of a surgeon, not gone for them with a bludgeon. His speech should have been better prepared – he had worked harder on speeches for the debating society at Queen's. But – since last week, Dorrie had intruded on all his thoughts. He had rung her several times over the weekend, but there had either been no reply, or Cy Coram had answered to say Dorrie was out. He was longing to see her again, and he could hardly sleep for thinking about her, or day-dreaming like some lovesick yokel about becoming rich and important and getting married to her. Would she ever consider it – or did she find him as ridiculous as those sneering fools in there? With an impatient shake of his head, he went in from the terrace and went back to the tea-room for tea and Ryvita and cheese. He passed Michael Foot in the corridor and hesitated, not sure whether to speak, but the ex-leader smiled at him, kindly if a little vaguely, 'Good luck – um – in your speech – '

'I've already made it,' Jack said, awkwardly, reddening. Foot was contrite.

'I say – I'm awfully sorry I missed it! How did it go?'

'Not too brilliantly, I'm afraid. Got a bit carried away.'

'Don't worry about it, my dear chap! You know, even Fox stuttered and stammered at the beginning of every speech – and Parnell and Cobden both made complete flops of their maiden speeches. Anyway, I'm sure you did very well – I've heard great things of you, believe me, great things!'

He moved on, with an affable smile and a wave of the hand, leaving Jack feeling disproportionately grateful for the great man's attention, though still not sure whether Foot really knew who he was. Still, his words had made Jack feel more cheerful. Perhaps his speech had not been so lousy, after all. In the tea-room, he spotted two Honourable Members who had been present while he spoke, and who were conversing with animation, heads close together. One of them was a senior statesman, a man of tremendous dignity, with a leonine head and a distinguished political and academic career, and the other was a junior back-bencher of impeccable background and the bluest of blood. Jack edged nearer to them, tea in hand, as eager as any actor mingling with the theatre crowd to find out what his audience had thought of him. The younger man's voice suddenly became quite clear: 'He took Eleanor into the Stranger's Bar and they both got drunk – *absolutely* blind, old boy! They were quite incapable, so we locked them in for the night and the security staff spent the time walking along the terrace, peering in at them, and they were stark bollock-naked! Yes, I promise you, my dear!'

The elder statesman threw back his head in a delighted bray of laughter, and Jack turned away, wondering if the country was being run entirely by dissolute fools. He suddenly felt like a drink, and, abandoning his untouched tea, he went out, intent on a large Scotch in one of the seven bars.

'Mr Larcombe!' A light touch on his arm made him look round, and Natasha Troy was there, cool and efficient-looking in her tailored grey suit.

'Yes?' He was brusque, almost irritable, supposing that she wanted to ask him some trivial question about the letters she'd typed for him. She was a pale, frigid-looking woman, as unlike Dorrie as anyone could be, and he always felt that she was sneering at him. 'What is it, Miss Troy?' he said.

A faint stain of pink came over her cheeks. She looked down at the bundle of papers she was carrying and fiddled about, rearranging them.

'I just wanted to congratulate you on your speech, Mr Larcombe,' she murmured. 'I – you were very eloquent. One of the best maiden speeches I've heard.'

'You heard it?' Jack said, stupidly. He could not hide a delighted grin as he looked at Natasha Troy's dark, bent head. 'You must be about the only person who did, then! Everyone else was asleep!'

She looked up at him, smiling rather shyly, and he noticed how much smaller she was than he had thought. 'Oh, I'm sure that's not true! Anyway, there was a reporter near me in the Stranger's Gallery, and he was making copious notes – I'm sure you made an impression.'

'Miss Troy!' Jack said, impulsively, and full of a sudden

gratitude and good-will, 'I suppose you wouldn't like a – a sort of late supper, would you? After the vote? I'd be most grateful if you'd keep me company – I was a bit too nervous to eat much at lunch-time today!'

She hesitated, but the boyish smile and the ingenuous admission were irresistible. 'I'd like that,' she said. 'If I go home and change, I can be back here by ten – will that be all right?'

'Fine! Great!' Jack said, heartily, then, with memories of Dorrie's exotic gold dress, he added, 'Nothing too posh! I – I mean, I wasn't thinking of the Savoy or anything!'

For the first time since he had known her, he saw a gleam of mischief behind the heavy spectacles, and a previously unnoticed dimple appeared briefly in Miss Troy's left cheek. 'Fish and chips will be fine,' she said.

In the end, they ate at Flanagan's in Baker Street, sitting at a converted Victorian sewing-machine table, and gorging themselves on game pie and treacle pudding. Miss Troy, Jack noticed with approval, had a hearty appetite that one would not have imagined from her slender appearance. She had left off her glasses, and with them much of her secretarial manner, and now she seemed like any pretty, rather shy girl being taken out for the evening. She didn't talk a lot, but she encouraged Jack to talk, and she laughed at his jokes and, in short, made him feel that it hadn't been such a bad day after all. The time passed quickly, and although it was midnight when they'd finished, Jack was unwilling to bring the evening to a close.

'Have you ever been to a casino?' he said. 'There's quite a good one just off Curzon Street – the Olympus. Would you like to go in for half-an-hour?'

'Oh – I don't think – don't you have to be a member or something?'

'Yes. I joined the other night. I don't know why – except that I'd just won three hundred quid and it seemed like a good idea.'

They laughed and Jack hailed a taxi to take them the short distance to the Olympus. He felt expansive, sophisticated, a man of the world, and he wanted to show someone – he was not sure whom – that Jack Larcombe was not hanging round after Dorrie St James, and that there were plenty of pretty women eager for his company. And Natasha was pretty tonight. In a dark red Liberty silk dress with a discreet gold necklace, she looked elegant enough to take anywhere. He had, Jack told himself, been making a fool of himself over Dorrie St James, and it was high time he stopped and took advantage of the other fish in the sea.

Natasha had never been to a casino before, and it gave Jack an unexpected pleasure to be able to instruct her on what to do, and her delighted gratitude when she won a little money, made him feel as though he had arranged it specially.

Then Dorrie came in. In a second, the bright gaiety of the evening turned to tinsel. Natasha was a sallow, too-thin girl with an over-severe hair-do, and an aching lump of longing gathered in Jack's chest like a physical symptom.

She drew all eyes, as though a bird of paradise had suddenly flown in, in her short dress from Avantgarde, covered with blue and silver sequins from throat to hem, a sequinned bandeau round her hair, which was loose tonight, a cascade of spun gold round her shoulders.

And round her shoulders, also, lightly but with an unmistakably proprietary air, was the arm of the Saudi prince, Tariq el Said, as he ushered her forward amongst the small crowd of his retinue.

Dorrie bore his arm with cool composure, almost as though it was something she was wearing, and, when she saw Jack, she shrugged it casually off and made her way towards him, smiling.

'Hallo, Jack! What are you doing in this wicked place? And how did your speech go?'

'Passing through,' Jack said, 'and OK, thank you. This is Natasha Troy – Dorrie St James.'

'Hi!' Dorrie grinned briefly at the other girl, and was about to say something when Tariq came over.

'Dorrie! Will you come? I don't wish to begin playing until you are there.'

He ignored Larcombe and Natasha, frowning impatiently at Dorrie, a tall, autocratic figure in his beautifully cut Western clothes. Dorrie laughed and made a mock bow, her hair swinging forward in a scented cloud. 'At once, my Prince,' she said, humbly, 'I suppose it's *lèse-majesté* if I don't.' She winked at Jack and blew him a brief kiss, then turned and accompanied Said to his usual table, not looking round again, but with her sequinned behind seeming to convey an insolent message.

'It's getting late,' Jack said, heavily, 'Shall we go now?'

'Yes, all right.' Natasha's voice was also subdued. How strange that a few minutes before she had felt like a pretty, charming woman, enjoying an evening with an attractive man. And now – she was twenty-nine, and she felt middle-aged and dowdy, her silk dress fading to a safe 'niceness' beside the outrageous glamour of Dorrie's, and her colouring to that of a farmyard hen. She was Miss Troy, the secretary again, efficient, quiet and – oh, utterly sexless.

'It's been a most pleasant evening – I *have* enjoyed it,'

she said, brightly, as they went up the marble stairs. She glanced at the statues of Greek gods and compared their physiques unfavourably with Jack's. She could not help a sudden fervent desire to see him undressed and, with the thought, she shivered, despite the scented warmth of the foyer.

'Cold?' Jack said, absently, and put an arm briefly round her shoulders not even thinking about it. He fetched her coat and helped her into it, but there was no intimacy in the action. His mind was so full of Dorrie that he might have been alone. She had seemed so warm and loving towards him the other night – he had been so sure that it was the beginning of a deep and passionate relationship, that he could hardly believe that the girl who had paused to greet him so briefly was the same soft, ardent woman he had held in his arms. And she was with that Arab – one of the world's richest men, as Stella Fielding had pointed out to him – and one with a reputation for womanizing second to none. Why? Why? He almost groaned aloud as he pictured her in the Arab's arms, in his bed . . .

The doorman called a taxi for them, and Jack sat beside Natasha in gloomy near-silence all the way to her flat, which was in Leinster Mews, not far from his own flat. She made polite conversation for a while, then she, too, fell silent until the taxi drew up, when she turned to him and asked, diffidently, if he would like coffee.

'What? Oh – all right. Thanks.' Anything was better than lying awake, his imagination running riot.

Natasha's small flat was impeccable, like herself, with cool, clean colours, the odd vivid accent of a scarlet cushion or a brilliant reproduction, and not a single thing out of place. She excused herself for a moment to make coffee, turning on an electric fire, although the room was warm, and leaving Jack sitting on the sofa, staring into space and barely conscious of his surroundings. It was nearly two A.M. He had been stupid to come in for coffee he did not want with a girl who did not interest him. Perhaps he could make some hasty excuse and go. He stood up and wandered restlessly across to Natasha's bookshelves. They contained a few classics, some histories – Macaulay and P. D. G. Thomas, one or two biographies of politicians, Ramsay Muir's 'How Britain is Governed' and, astonishingly, the 'Kama Sutra' and Anaïs Nin's 'Erotica'. He had picked up the latter, grinning incredulously, when Natasha brought the coffee in.

'Hardly your line, I should've thought,' he said, indicating the book. She glanced across, quite cool and unembarrassed, seeming far more assured here in her own flat than she had been all evening.

'Oh? And what is "my line" should you think?' She put the tray down on a low table by the sofa, and smiled at him with raised eyebrows.

'Oh – I don't know.' He put the book back and went over to the sofa. 'Cool efficiency, I suppose.'

'Really? Sit down and have your coffee.'

She handed him a cup, then sat down beside him, almost but not quite touching, and began to sip her coffee thoughtfully and in silence.

Glancing down, Jack noticed that she had taken off her shoes and that her feet and legs were bare beneath the red silk of her dress. She had small, white feet with delicate, painted toe-nails, and the sight of them naked on the soft carpet was oddly disturbing. Her legs were very slim and smooth, and so close to his own that he only had to move a fraction of an inch to touch them.

'Do you like working at Westminster, Natasha?' he

asked, making the question an excuse to move slightly towards her. Their legs were touching now, and she made no attempt to move hers.

'Yes. There are times when it's – very enjoyable,' she said, quietly, not looking at him. She leaned forward with her coffee cup and put it on the table, then crossed her long, slender legs. They were both against his own now, and the movement had caused the red silk to slide up above her knees. But still her profile was cool and detached as though she was about to take dictation. Jack almost expected an indignant rebuff when he put his hand gently on her knee.

'You have really lovely legs,' he said, softly, watching her face and prepared to withdraw at once at the first sign of alarm. But she said nothing, only moistened her lips with the tip of her tongue. He noticed now that she was not wearing a bra – had she discarded it with her tights? – and the nipples of her small, firm breasts were pushing against the red silk, hard and pointed. Slowly, he moved his hand further up her leg, his thumb gently rubbing the smooth skin inside her thigh. Her breathing quickened, and she suddenly clenched her legs together, trapping his hand between them and putting her hands on his wrist.

'Wait!' she whispered, 'Not here! Let's do it properly.'

He followed her into the bedroom, excited and bemused at the sudden change in the cool little secretary, and watched as she turned on the bedside light.

Natasha Troy was not a virgin. Beneath the cool, calm, exterior, she was a deeply sensual and passionate woman, and she was as hungry for Jack Larcombe as a gourmet for a feast. But to be savoured and lingered over, extracting the maximum enjoyment, not gobbled down in a quick five-minute session on the sofa.

'Come here – let me take your clothes off,' she commanded.

'Shouldn't it be the other way round?' he said, teasingly, but she shook her head impatiently.

'No. Do as I say.'

Nevertheless, he took off his shoes and socks, and hung his jacket on a chair before standing passively, smiling at the small, imperious figure who was swiftly unbuttoning his shirt. Her fingers scarcely touched him, but her eyes explored the muscles of his bare chest avidly, and once again her tongue moistened her lips. Then she unzipped his trousers, again avoiding any contact with his body, until he was standing in his briefs, his penis by now rigid and throbbing, pushing painfully against the tight material. Deftly, she removed the briefs, still not touching his skin, and when he made a move towards her, she stopped him with a gesture.

'Wait. Not yet.' For a moment she prowled round him, feasting her eyes on his naked body and the thrusting erection of his flesh. In a few years he would run to fat, but now – oh, now he was superb, and she, Natasha Troy, would have the enjoyment of him.

'Now – lie on the bed, and let me love you,' she whispered huskily. Jack hesitated. He was used to taking the initiative, but in the end the very novelty of the situation excited him and he did as she asked, lying on top of the bedclothes in the warm, quiet room and watching as Natasha unbuttoned the front of her dress and let it slip to the ground. She was naked beneath it, slim, but delicately made, with small breasts and hips wider than one would have imagined. Jack groaned a little, and held out his arms, but she shook her head, her face as serious as some high priestess at an initiation rite. 'Wait. Just lie still.'

He lay, and she bent over him, till her breast was almost touching his lips and he reached hungrily, taking the nipple into his mouth and pulling on it feverishly until she moaned with mounting desire.

Then she pulled herself gently away and began to explore his body with her mouth and tongue, gently licking and kissing his chest, his neck, his shoulders, his belly, his thighs and, coming at last to the violent upthrust of his erection, she put her mouth over it and gently massaged the tip of it with her tongue, her lips pulling gently at the foreskin in a slow, sensual rhythm. Fireworks seemed to explode in Jack's brain – he had never, ever, had such things done to him, and the aching ecstasy of it, rising to an unbearable height made him cry out and gasp, 'No – I – I can't – '

'Yes – hush – wait one moment longer – '

She stood up, astride him, her own genitals swollen and engorged with excitement, and parted the lips of her vagina with her fingers in a gesture of unselfconscious eroticism. Slowly, with a sinuous movement, she lowered herself on to him, pulling his hard penis firmly away from his belly and guiding it into herself, intent now on her own pleasure as she allowed first the tip alone, then, very gradually, more and more of him to penetrate her, her breathing becoming a sharp moan as she slid up and down on the thick, thrusting column of him. He clutched at her buttocks, driving himself deeper and deeper into her, and his climax, when it came, seemed to go on forever in a cataclysmic, relieving rush, just at the same time as she, lips parted in a wordless cry and legs convulsively tightening around him, achieved her orgasm.

They lay quiet for a long time afterwards, she sprawled across him as though she had fallen in battle, both of them motionless in the aftermath of passion.

At last, Natasha stirred, opening her eyes with a dreamy smile. She leaned over Jack, cupping the warm limpness of his penis in one hand and kissed him on the lips.

'Was it good, darling?' she whispered, 'I wanted so much for you to enjoy it.'

He smiled and put an arm round her, pulling her down with her head on his shoulder, the warmth of her breasts, belly and thighs against his side. He was filled, still, with an incredulous pleasure and presently, in her palm, she felt him stirring again.

4

Dorrie was bored to the point of weariness. Dinner had been fine, although the Hilton would not have been her own choice for eating. But Tariq always stayed there, in the same suite, and they knew his likes and dislikes. When he suggested coming on to the Olympus, she agreed readily, fed up with being surrounded by the prince's dead-pan entourage – but roulette was boring, she thought. She could not understand the almost sexual thrill that people got from it – even Jack Larcombe, for all his puritanical ideals had had his breathing quickened by winning three hundred pounds. And he had come back tonight with that mousey girl, whatever her name was. If he was not careful, he would be hooked just as firmly as people like Stella Fielding who spent more time in the casino than she did at home.

Tariq el Said, too, was a fanatical gambler. He had a table to himself, always number five, and the maximum fifty pounds a spin rule was ignored. Three or four thousand were gambled on each spin of the wheel, and although sometimes he won, more often he lost – at times as much as a quarter of a million in one evening. Why did he do it, Dorrie wondered, watching the hawk-like face in detached boredom as the wheel spun and another four thousand went into Mr Khalid's coffers. Was it because the roulette wheel was the only thing left for Tariq el Said with an element of surprise and excitement in it? Everything else could be bought, except the favours of Lady Luck, and she was as capricious and wayward as . . .

Dorrie smiled. Perhaps that was why Said was pursuing her. He had been piqued by her disappearance from the night-club, and attracted by her lack of interest in either himself or his money – but she was quite sure that if she slept with him he would toss her aside like a used Kleenex. Well, she would give him a run for his money. He was an attractive, powerful-looking man, with a tigerish aura of sexual potency – but Dorrie was no tethered lamb. She had claws of her own. Meanwhile, the wheel spun, Tariq's dark face was bent intently over the green baize, and Dorrie was sitting on the delicate Louis Quinze chair like a piece of left luggage. She was bored. Bored with the roulette, bored with the casino – and Ross Cavallo was nowhere in sight.

She got up and wandered idly, pausing for a moment at the blackjack table and exchanging a few words with some people that she knew.

'Dorrie, darling!' the Honourable Esmé Fry screamed at her in that peculiar high-pitched whinny beloved of so many of the upper classes. 'Look, Roger! It's Dorrie – we haven't seen her for simply *ages*, have we? And don't you look *stunning*, Dorrie – what a *super* frock – isn't it, Rog?'

Roger, Lord Harrington, raised cloudy, stupefied eyes from his cards, and made a half-hearted movement to get up, nearly falling off his chair as he did. He smiled apologetically at Dorrie, his mouth loose and wet. ''Lo, Dorrie,' he mumbled, 'Sorry – not too sparky tonight.'

'Sparky?' Esmé shrieked, 'My God – you're pissed as a newt, Roger – look at you! Isn't he awful, Dorrie?'

Dorrie regarded Harrington with contempt, not unmixed with pity. He was only twenty-two, but he looked fifty, with his yellow, unhealthy skin and bleary, unfocused eyes. He had been heavily fined on more than one occasion for minor drug offences and it seemed now only a matter of speculation whether he would be arrested, take an overdose, or wrap his car round a tree under the influence of drink and drugs.

'Pissed, my arse,' Dorrie said, quietly, 'He's doped to the eyeballs, you idiot. Why don't you try and get him off that stuff?'

'Oh, Dorrie, honestly! He's only had the teeniest bit of coke – the merest sniff – he's really reformed, you know. He went to this *lovely* place called Leysholme Park, in Yorkshire, and they did *wonders*, you know.' Esmé's lower lip quivered childishly beneath her rabbity teeth and she turned away from the blackjack and put an appealing hand on Dorrie's arm. 'Don't tell anyone he's back on it again, will you, darling? His father won't have anything to do with him unless he stops, and poor old Rog won't have a penny. I *try*, Dorrie – I really try to keep him away from it, but – oh, God! He's so cunning, you wouldn't believe.'

'Poor old Esmé!' The contempt had left Dorrie's blue eyes and only pity remained, 'I don't know why you stay with him – it must be like having a baby.'

Esmé looked away, blinking rapidly. 'We *were* having a baby,' she confided in a low voice, 'and I thought it would – you know, buck Roger up a bit. But – the parents made me have an abortion. They said it would be deformed or – or born with a habit, poor little thing. Oh, well – I suppose it was for the best. I can't really see Roger pushing a pram, can you?' Then, as though ashamed of her confidences, a mask of brightness seemed to descend over her face, and in her usual piercing tones she said, 'Oh, look – there's Chucky Berners! Chucky! Chucky, darling! Come and help Roger turn his cards over – he's quite blotto!'

Dorrie moved away, a little sickened, a little depressed,

wishing she had not stopped to speak to Esmé. What a lot of boring misery there was in the world – and how eagerly people poured their sufferings into one's ears – as if she, Dorrie St James, could do anything to help or even comfort. She felt irritated and annoyed, more bored than ever, and, with a perverse desire to tease someone, she looked round for Ross Cavallo again.

There was still no sign of him – the assistant manager, Haley, seemed to be in charge, and Dorrie had no wish to talk to him – an unctuous fellow with too many teeth showing in an ever-ready smile, but she paused to ask him idly if Mr Cavallo was around.

'Why, yes, Miss St James,' Haley said, eagerly, 'he's in his office – but he's awfully busy tonight. Will I do instead? How can I help you?'

Dorrie gave him a cool, unsmiling stare. 'No,' she said, 'you will not do. Never mind.' She drifted unhurriedly away, ignoring the man's stuttering reiteration that Mr Cavallo had not wanted to be disturbed by anyone, and opened the door of Ross's office. The thought of how she would irritate him until he lost his professionally even temper made Dorrie smile, and she was on the point of saying, 'Now you mustn't sit in here playing with yourself all night, Mr Cavallo.'

He was sitting at his desk, surrounded by paper-work, but he was not working. He was staring into space, an expression of such bleak unhappiness on his face that all the mischief went out of Dorrie and she was only able to say, in a small voice, 'Hallo!'

Immediately, the naked expression was banished from the dark eyes, and he rose to his feet.

'Miss St James,' he said, neutrally, 'I'm sorry – I'm rather heavily engaged this evening – I'm in the middle of doing the profit plan. But Bob Haley will look after you.'

'Ugh. No thanks – he's a creep. I came in to see you. And you were doing bugger all except sit and look miserable. What's wrong?'

She could see she was trespassing. He was not likely to pour his troubles out to her like Esmé Fry, and she was not surprised when he said lightly, 'An excess of paper-work, no doubt, and the realization that Mr Khalid would like me to double the takings of this place every quarter. Still, since you're here, I'll make it an excuse for a break. Would you like a drink?'

'Mm. A large Scotch.'

He looked faintly amused, but made no comment as he poured her drink and his own.

'Are you here with Jack Larcombe?' he asked, raising his glass in a brief salute.

'No.' Dorrie sipped, stared down at her drink, then up at Cavallo with something of defiance in her eyes. 'No, tonight I'm accompanied by Prince Tariq el Said and a cast of thousands.'

He grinned. 'And you feel like an extra in *Lawrence of Arabia*.'

'Oh, exactly!' Dorrie laughed aloud, showing her white even teeth, the sulky droop of her mouth vanishing, 'That retinue follows him round everywhere – and they're all completely deadpan and never say a word. Honestly – if I ever sleep with His Highness I expect they'll all stand round the bed!'

He frowned. 'Why do you say that? If it's to shock – you're too late, Queen Victoria's dead. So you're the mad, daring Dorrie St James and you sleep around a lot – so what? No one cares a damn, and all it's likely to get you, in your own earthy terms, is a dose of the clap.'

She didn't answer for a moment, sitting with her head bent over her glass so that a curtain of hair hid her face from him. He made her feel like a child, rebuked for showing off, and, ridiculously, uncharacteristically, she could have wept. Perhaps it was the time of month. She took a deep breath and raised her head, her smile as insolent as ever.

'Good Lord – do you take me for a fool? No one sleeps with me without a medical certificate!'

'Really. Will you excuse me now? I do have a tremendous amount of work to do – besides, I'm sure Prince Tariq will be looking for you. He has a profound belief in the lucky mascot powers of a dumb blonde.'

'My *God*, you're rude to me! I bet you're not supposed to be rude to punters!'

'That, my dear, is one bet you'd be sure of winning. I am unfailingly polite. Now bugger off!'

'If I told Mr Khalid what you'd said . . .'

'Quite. But – noblesse oblige, don't you think? Now – back to the harem and let me work.'

He came round the desk and put a hand lightly on her shoulder, reaching forward with the other hand to open the door for her, and Dorrie suddenly turned, impelled by a mad impulse, put her arms round his neck and her open lips against his. For just a second, as his hands involuntarily tightened, pulling her against him, and his muscular body seemed on the point of responding to her, she had the strangest feeling of being in a place that had long been familiar to her. Then, with a convulsive movement, he had shaken her off and opened the office door.

'Get out,' he said, his voice level, but his eyes on hers almost black with anger, 'and if you ever do that again, I'll have you barred from his place, I don't care if your father's the King of England.'

Dorrie's eyes were suddenly filled with tears of fury, pain and humiliation. She could have screamed and struck out at him in her bitter rage, and she sought for words, any words, to wound him.

'You make me sick, Ross Cavallo,' she hissed, 'with your "holier-than-thou" attitude! You're only mad because you enjoyed it! Yes, you bloody did – I *know*, I can tell! If you hadn't been too fucking scared to get it up, you'd have screwed me right there on your office floor! And, who knows – I was so bloody bored I might just have let you! As it is – it will have to be Tariq – and his whole sodding entourage can have a go as well!' But she was talking to a closed door, and after a second during which she was on the point of hitting the door, she drew a gasping breath and escaped to the powder room where she sat and wept for ten minutes, too miserable even to know why she was crying.

Back at his desk, Ross Cavallo too took a deep breath and ran his hands through his hair. He felt more shaken than he would have admitted, and when he remembered the feel of that soft, ardent body against his own, the slim arms round his neck and the warm intoxication of a mouth pressed hungrily to his, the tongue tempting him like a hot, sweet serpent, he knew he had been within an inch of madness. And madness it would have been. He could hardly have faced Sarah with the knowledge that he had made love to another woman – he could imagine the dreadful, wounded look in her eyes and the way she would blame herself and say that she had failed him. Damn Dorrie St James – she was so determined that every man she met must come whimpering after her as though she was a bitch on heat. She was the most bloody-minded, spoilt, arrogant little tart he had ever met. And yet – there had been tears in her eyes, he could have sworn, and when he had pushed her away from him, she had a bemused expression, a soft warmth in her face that was quite uncharacteristic – almost as if . . . Abruptly, Ross shoved Dorrie's image from his mind as roughly as he had shoved her body from his arms and bent his head once more over his profit plan.

Tariq el Said raised his head as Dorrie returned to the roulette table and stared at her. 'Where have you been, Dorrie?'

Dorrie stared back, incredulously. The sheer arrogance of the man! He really thought she was part of his harem and had to stay where she was put until he required her. Smiling sweetly, she said, 'None of your damn business, Tariq, old boy.'

She saw anger spark in his dark eyes, but his face remained impassive and he only shrugged slightly as he turned back to the table.

'If you don't mind, I'd like to go home now,' Dorrie said, coolly, 'but please don't interrupt your game – I can easily get a taxi.'

'My dear, of course you will not,' he said. He was very polite, very formal, and had not put a hand on her all evening. He rose now, with a word to his entourage and bowed slightly in the direction of the dealer.

'You wish to go straight home at once?' he said to Dorrie, 'or would you wish to visit a night-club?'

'No, I would not,' Dorrie said, feelingly.

'Ah – I did not mean the one we visited last week. It offended you, did it not? I am sorry. That was a mistake.'

'What we call a tactical error, Your Highness. Showing your hand too soon. If hand's the right word.'

'I thought perhaps Annabel's?' Tariq suggested.

'Annabel's?' Dorrie was amused. 'No – I can't see you on the disco floor, Tariq. Anyway, I'm tired. I want to go to bed.'

There was, Dorrie thought, something vaguely ludicrous about the motorcade of black cars that swept through the streets back to Maida Vale. She travelled in front in the vast Silver Ghost, in comparative privacy with only Tariq, the chauffeur and one bodyguard. The rest of the retinue followed in assorted Jaguars and Rovers at a discreet distance.

'Do you really have to have all these people following you about like a circus?' Dorrie asked. 'It would drive me up the wall.'

'But of course. It is absolutely necessary. Only a short time ago one of my relatives was kidnapped in this country – and a ransom of two million pounds was paid for him. We are wealthy people, my dear Dorrie, and we accept that wealth has its drawbacks as well as its privileges.'

'Well, my father's quite rich – but I'm damned if any of our family would go around with a hundred heavies.'

He shrugged dismissively. 'When I speak of wealth, I mean real wealth. Your father owns – what? The house in London, a manor house in Devon, Ash Friars, sixty per cent of a company called St James Holdings which has assets of two hundred million pounds, and various other stocks and shares and other smallish properties.'

Dorrie gaped. 'How on earth do you know?'

'I make it my business to be well-informed. Please do not be offended. My investigations uncovered nothing at all detrimental to you or your father. It is merely a precaution that I take when I commence a relationship with anyone.'

'I think you have a damned cheek!' Dorrie said, 'How would you like it if I investigated you?'

'But – why should I care, my dear? You are more than welcome – though I think you will find it difficult. Even I

108

do not know the value of all my assets – and of course they increase daily.'

'Smug bastard!' Dorrie muttered, but she knew that Tariq's arrogance and his assumption of the power that his wealth gave him, really were based on riches that would make the St James fortune seem like a hand-out from the DHSS.

'Anyway,' she added, rather peevishly, 'I'm not having my flat invaded by your Rent-a-Crowd, so if you want coffee, you can come up by yourself or not at all.'

'Of course. You will have no objection to two of my men waiting outside your door? Merely a precaution.'

'I don't care. They won't have to wait long.'

In the hallway of Dorrie's flat, a heavy, unfamiliar sweetness hung in the air and when she opened the door to her sitting room and switched on the lights, she stood for a second, staring.

'What the *hell* . . .' she said.

The room was full of roses. Red, pink, orange, yellow, white, they stood in vases, bowls, buckets and jam-jars and a swathe of them lay on the sofa, their crisp petals already softening in the heat, mute witnesses to Cy's inability to find anything else that held water. The whole scene was so odd and surreal that for once Dorrie could find nothing to say.

'I hope you like this small token of my esteem,' Tariq said, watching her astonished face, and at his words, she suddenly dissolved into helpless laughter.

'Oh, God!' she hooted, collapsing on to the sofa in a welter of petals and florist's paper, 'A small token of your esteem – oh, Tariq, you're absolutely – absolutely – oh! a collector's piece! Oh, help, I'm being attacked by a wild rose! Help me up, Tariq – you're really wonderful!'

Understanding neither her laughter nor her words,

except for the last ones, and not realizing that Dorrie meant he was a source of wonderment, Tariq smiled cautiously and helped her up, keeping hold of her hands in his own.

'You like it?' he asked.

Dorrie regarded him solemnly. 'Tariq – I promise you, I shall never forget it.'

'Oh,' his smile broadened, 'it is nothing – too little to speak of. I can give you far more than a few flowers.'

'Oh, hush, don't! Oh – I ache with laughing. Don't mind me, though – ' she struggled not to giggle any more, 'I just have a funny sense of humour.'

Tariq was a little perplexed, but not much. Arab girls giggled, too, behind their hands and behind their veils. He had found, however, that in bed with him they did not giggle. Quite gently but firmly he pulled at Dorrie's hands until she was in his arms. She was, by Arab standards, indecently exposed, with her bare throat, chest and shoulders, her long legs covered only in the sheerest nylon below the zig-zag sequinned hem of her dress, but, although Tariq disapproved as a good Muslim, as a man he found the bare smooth flesh exciting and desirable. But – he must go slowly this time. He had learned that English women were in some respects the opposite of their Arabian sisters, and that a sexually permissive exterior often hid a basically frigid nature. So the kiss he gave her was quite gentle and undemanding. Dorrie found it oddly touching. She had been prepared to fight against rape, and here was Tariq being – well, respectful was the word that came to mind. The wounds that Ross Cavallo had inflicted on her ego were salved by the balm of the Prince's attentions and, with this unexpected gentleness, she regarded Tariq el Said with new eyes, and began to return his kiss with interest. The Arab felt the pliant young body pressed against him with the pleasure of a connoisseur. He had had more women than he could remember, but rarely had there been one whose possession promised as much pleasure as this one. He would savour her as one did a perfect ripe fruit, slowly, not wasting a drop of enjoyment, and he would give her pleasure, too, for he was not an ungenerous man, and a fulfilled woman, besides, gave back more pleasure than she took. Slowly, without removing his mouth, he slid his hands down to cup the woman's buttocks, pressing her against himself so that she might feel how great and hard he had grown, and how much delight she would have when once that princely organ thrust inside her.

Dorrie removed her mouth from his quite gently, and regarded him quizzically. 'You really only think of one thing where women are concerned, don't you, Tariq? You're the most single-minded person I ever met.'

He smiled suddenly, white teeth gleaming against red lips and dark, bearded face. 'We have a saying: "al insann tawkum wa rraghba" – "man is all passion". Who am I to deny my nature? You are a very beautiful woman, and I – I am not unpleasing, I believe. I can give you much pleasure in bed, trust me.'

'I am really tempted, believe me,' Dorrie assured him, 'I expect it would be a unique experience . . .'

Cy came in then, rubbing her eyes and frowning sleepily.

'Blimey O'Reilly,' she muttered, 'Rudolf Valentino. Sorry, people – didn't mean to interrupt. I'm going for a pee. By the way – some flowers came.' She disappeared towards the bathroom and Dorrie detached herself from Tariq's arms.

'My duenna,' she explained, regretfully, 'she is really very strict, so I'm afraid you'll have to go now.'

Tariq was disappointed, but not terribly surprised. The English were a strange and unpredictable race, and the members of its aristocracy were more eccentric than the rest. Perhaps Dorrie really was more protected than he had thought, and perhaps the siege would be long and hard. But – was he not the descendant of Abdul Aziz, who had taken the Musmak in Riyadh with a handful of followers? The chase gave added savour to the quarry, and he, Tariq el Said, was as well equipped for the hunt as the finest, most predatory falcon.

'Yes, I will go now,' he said, softly, still holding her, his eyes fixed almost mesmerically on her face, 'but I will come again – and again. I am Tariq el Said, and that which I desire I always get. Always.'

'Really?' Dorrie twisted from his arms and laughed up at him, 'but perhaps this time you've met your match, my Prince!'

Cy came out of the bathroom. 'And if you thought of having a bath,' she said, sourly, 'don't. It's full of bloody roses.'

The Cavallos were walking, as they often did, through Kew Gardens, wandering along deserted paths as the violet mists of an autumn afternoon drifted lower through the treetops and wintering geese called plaintively from the lake. It was Lotte's day off, so Ross pushed the sleeping Thomas in his pram, while Beatrice and Ben ran ahead, their voices thin and distant in the still, damp air.

'I love these afternoons.' Sarah, her arm through her husband's, rubbed her cheek against his shoulder, 'I love the soft mistiness of autumn, and the smells of wood-smoke and chrysanthemums and – and the sort of calm sadness of it all!'

Ross smiled down at her. 'What an imagination! What

I like about it is getting inside afterwards and getting warm again.'

'That must be your Latin ancestry – your body was obviously designed to soak up the sun.'

'Well, with a mother from Inverness and a father from Milan, I should be adaptable to all climates. Given the choice, though, I think I'd choose the sun.'

'Would you really?' There was a trace of anxiety in Sarah's dark eyes, 'Would you like to move – to go to a warmer climate?'

'I don't know. Yes, sometimes – wouldn't you?'

'No!' she said, vehemently, 'No – I love it here! I love our house, and – and Kew Gardens. I love days like this, and days when we walk by the river and it smells of plum-cake just like in *Wind in the Willows*. I like winter afternoons when the pavements are frosty and you get glimpses in at people's windows of Christmas trees and fires, and summer days when we bring picnics in here and lie on the grass . . .'

'All right! All right!' he laughed, 'You've convinced me. I like it here, too – but I don't much mind where I live, as long as it's with you! So, don't look so worried, sweetheart – we'll stay here for ever if you like.'

He took his hands off the pram for a moment and put them on her shoulders, bending his head to kiss the cool dampness of her mouth. 'Darling Sarah! I could never do anything to hurt you.' It was true, but even as he spoke the words, the image of a golden face with mocking blue eyes came suddenly into his mind.

'Daddy! Mummy! Somebody will see you!' Beatrice said, horrified, and Ben, less inhibited, yelled, 'Mum and Dad are snogging!' and whistled loudly and piercingly.

'Any more of that, my lad,' Ross said with mock

ferocity, grabbing his son and swinging him in the air, 'and I'll toss you in the lake!'

Ben screamed with delight, thin arms and legs waving, as Ross flung him up and caught him again.

'Daddy!' Beatrice muttered, pulling at his coat, her face pink with embarrassment, 'there's a lady watching you!'

He half-turned, still grinning, and saw Dorrie St James. She was leaning with her back against a birch tree, her hair, spangled by the mist, taking on a sheen that matched the tree's silver bark. She had on jeans and a pair of Manolo Blahnik boots, a gold and wool polo-neck from Ralph Lauren, and a disreputable sheepskin coat, her hair was a tangled mass of strands like gilt candy-floss and her only make-up a dark pencil line that emphasized the deep blue of her eyes, as she watched the Cavallos.

The smile left Ross's face and he said nothing for a moment, only staring at Dorrie as though she were a mirage.

'Hullo!' Dorrie said, at last. She looked sulky, like a small girl at a party to which she hasn't been invited.

'What are you doing here?' Ross said, his voice so cold and unfriendly that Sarah glanced sharply at him.

'I often come here,' Dorrie replied, her eyes meeting his and daring him to accuse her of lying. She kicked the heel of one boot against the tree-trunk and stuck her hands in her pockets, 'Do you?'

Sarah, by nature a peace-maker and mediator, sensed Ross's irritation and felt sorry for the girl.

'Yes,' she said, smiling, 'we live on Kew Green, so the Gardens seem almost like our own. Ross – aren't you going to introduce us?'

'This is Dorrie St James,' Ross said, stiffly. 'This is my wife, Sarah, and my children – '

'Beatrice, Ben and Thomas the Toad,' Dorrie said, smiling suddenly, 'Hi, kids!'

'How do you do?' Beatrice said, formally.

'Is that your own hair?' Ben asked, 'Only Lotte has a wig like that. She let me try it on.'

'I bet you looked a scream,' Dorrie said, 'but I'm sorry I can't oblige. It's growing on me.'

'Ben – don't be so rude!' Sarah scolded, 'I do apologize, Miss St James – his curiosity is outstripping his manners at the moment.'

'That's okay – I like kids like that. You know where you are with them.' She came over and peered into the pram with a detached interest not unlike Ben's. 'Thomas the Toad,' she murmured, touching a warm, downy cheek with one finger. The baby opened round dark eyes and stared, before exposing two small teeth in a wide yawn and sleeping again.

Ross moved the pram with a faint air of impatience and Sarah wondered again at the loss of his usual good manners. She had heard him mention this girl as a punter at the casino, and she knew that he liked to keep work separate from his home life, but – she seemed a friendly enough girl. Rich and spoilt, no doubt, but perhaps a little lonely as well. There was really no need for Ross to act as if she were a leper or something. Sarah smiled again, warmly. 'We're going home for tea in a moment. Would you like to join us? It's only tea and cakes by the fire.'

'Oh,' Dorrie said, doubtfully, 'are you sure? I mean – I don't want to butt in or anything . . .' She glanced at Ross and saw the corners of his mouth turn down in an expression of wry amusement, as though he suspected that that was exactly what she did want. Then he said, starting to push the pram again, 'You may as well. My wife's never happy unless she brings home some waifs and strays from a walk.'

'Ross!' Sarah said, but Dorrie grinned.

'Good – I feel a bit waifish today, I must say. Father's gone down to the country, and my flat-mate's gone to Greenham Common, so I'm all alone.'

'Touching,' Ross commented, dryly. 'Come on. It's getting late and we'll be shut in.'

'Come on then, kids. Race you to the entrance,' Dorrie cried, dashing off across the grass, kicking up leaves as she went, as though she were ten years old and not wearing boots that had cost over two hundred pounds. Ben tore after her, entranced and yelling gleefully, but Beatrice took hold of the pram with one mittened hand, and put her arm through her mother's. The faint frown above her dark eyes made her look like her father, Sarah thought.

'Why did you have to invite her to tea, Mummy? I like it to be just us. *And* there won't be enough crumpets to go round, I bet,' Beatrice said. Ross said nothing, but he echoed his daughter's sentiments. The last person he wanted in his house was Dorrie St James. He wanted the rooms to be free of her presence so that at home, at least, he would never be reminded of the slender, voluptuous body that he had held for an instant in his arms. As a person he found her rude, spoilt, a badly behaved super-brat too used to getting her own way. But sexually, there was no denying her attractiveness, and he could not pretend that the thought of possessing her, even in the crudest, most transitory fashion, had not entered his mind. But he could live with that – he rarely saw the girl, and the casino was not conducive to intimacy. But Sarah – dear, sweet, generous Sarah, was going to befriend the brat, he could just see it, and have her hanging round the house, a tempting cream cake for a man on a diet. He quickened his pace, resolving at the first opportunity to tell Dorrie St James to keep far away from the Cavallo family.

'Ross?' Sarah's voice was uncertain, 'Ross – you're not angry, are you? I'm sorry if you don't like her – but I thought she looked a bit sad and lonely, that's all.'

'Dearest Sarah! Save your sympathy for cuddly pathetic things like she-wolves and sharks. Dorrie is about as sad and lonely as – as Lucrezia Borgia!'

'Now, don't be so horrid! How do you know Lucrezia Borgia *wasn't* sad and lonely? Anyway – it's only tea. Judging by the antics of the people she goes round with, she'll find it very tame and boring and never come back!'

When they reached the house, Dorrie and Ben had beaten them to it. There were two coats flung over the banisters and laughter from the playroom upstairs.

'They're playing with Ben's train-set,' reported Beatrice, incredulously, 'and that girl's wearing the station-master's hat. Ben must've gone mad – he doesn't let *anyone* wear it!'

Ross sighed for his susceptible son. So Dorrie had added another heart to her collection, even if it was only eight years old. He gave Beatrice's dark ringlets a gentle tug. 'Come on, my sweetie – shall we get the tea ready while Mummy feeds Tom?'

Sarah sat by the fire and put Tom to her breast, feeling, as she always did, the most intense love and pleasure as the little questing mouth captured her nipple and sucked at the generous out-pouring of her milk. Her eyes grew warm and dreamy, and the firelight played on her too-thin face, softening the features and lending them beauty. It was like this that Dorrie saw her when she came in, and

117

she stood just inside the door, watching, the station-master's hat still perched absurdly on her tumbled hair.

Sarah looked up, saw her and smiled. 'Come and sit down by the fire. I hope Ben hasn't been a nuisance?'

'No – he's great. I like him. You're lucky, aren't you?' She did not specify in which way, but Sarah nodded. 'Yes.'

There was silence for a time. Both women stared into the leaping flames. From the kitchen on the other side of the big hall came the faint sound of plates being rattled, voices and laughter. Thomas finished feeding, and his head lolled sleepily back, mouth open, a picture of blissful satiety.

'Come on, you old drunkard,' Sarah said, propping him against her shoulder, 'you can't go to sleep till you've got your wind up.' She rubbed his back gently and there was a small and genteel belch. 'Good boy!'

Dorrie laughed. 'When do you stop saying "Good boy!" and start saying "Manners, Thomas!"'

'All too soon!' Sarah smiled. 'I wish this age would last a bit longer – they're so adorable. Here – would you like to hold him for a moment?'

It was the greatest favour Sarah could imagine confer-ring on anyone. She could not believe any woman might lack the almost painful maternal feelings that she pos-sessed, and holding the tiny, warm body, putting one's lips against the soft, downy head, was the deepest physical pleasure she had ever experienced.

Dorrie was horrified. She always kept well away from family babies, and even as a child had had more affection for horses than dolls. But she realized from Sarah's expression that she was being accorded a high honour – it would be churlish to refuse. She took the child gingerly, and when Ross came in with Ben and Beatrice and a trolley full of tea-things, he almost laughed to see her sitting stiffly, regarding her burden as though it was a small but rather dangerous wild animal.

'He doesn't actually bite, you know,' he said, sitting down by Sarah and grinning rather nastily at Dorrie, 'and if you hold him as far away from you as that, you're going to drop him.'

'Ross! Don't frighten the poor girl!' Sarah said, as Dorrie anxiously clutched the baby to her, all her usual poise deserting her. She was not so brash as he had imagined, Ross thought, and the way she clutched the baby was rather touching, like a child looking after a baby brother.

Then Tom gave another burp and sicked a mouthful of milk over Dorrie's Ralph Lauren sweater.

'Shit!' said Dorrie.

The Cavallos exchanged glances and Sarah rose to her feet.

'I'm so sorry,' she said, scooping Thomas up with an expert hand. 'How very anti-social of Thomas – and on your lovely sweater, too. Do you want to come and sponge it off?'

'No, it doesn't matter – if you don't mind me smelling of baby-sick. Obviously his way of telling me I'm not wanted.'

'Oh, no – he does it quite indiscriminately,' Sarah said. 'Will you excuse me a minute – I'll just change him and put him to bed. Bea, darling, would you pour the tea for me?'

Beatrice, flushed with pride, poured milk and tea with painstaking care, and handed it round.

'You might offer the sandwiches and cakes, Ben,' she said, with an air of virtuous martyrdom, but Ben, sprawled on the floor in front of the blank television, hunched his shoulders and ignored his sister.

119

'Dad – can we have "The A-Team" on?' he asked, one hand reaching for the knob.

'No, of course not. We have a visitor.'

'Shit!' Ben said, experimentally, glancing at his father. Ross scowled.

'I take it you don't want any tea, Ben?' he said, coldly.

'Yes, Dad. Sorry, Dad.' Humiliated when he had wanted to seem sophisticated in front of Dorrie, Ben turned his back and studied the books that lined one side of the room, so that no one would see the childish tears, so shaming at the age of eight.

'Sorry,' Dorrie muttered. 'My fault.'

'Yes,' Ross said, and regarded her with unconcealed dislike. 'Have a sandwich.'

Beatrice handed her a plate of sandwiches, then took one herself and sat beside her father, nibbling with small precise bites and staring at Dorrie unblinkingly.

'Marigold Chatham,' she offered, 'she's in my form at school, when *she* said *that* word, her father washed her mouth out with soap.'

'That'll do, Bea,' Ross said.

'It was coal-tar soap, as well,' pursued the little girl, still staring coolly at Dorrie.

'Beatrice!'

'Well,' Dorrie said, meeting the inimical stare and forcing herself to smile cheerfully, 'that must be the trouble. We never had coal-tar soap in our house. I did once get spanked with a riding-crop, though,' she volunteered.

'*Did* you?' Beatrice was interested despite herself, 'What for? For swearing?'

'No . . .' Dorrie grinned reminiscently, remembering her nine-year-old self exposing the secrets of her anatomy to a young cousin in exchange for a glimpse of the funny limp wormy thing that boys thought so special. Lady Antonia had yelled with laughter, but Dorrie's father had given her the only severe beating she had ever received from him, so great was his dislike of what he considered to be licentious behaviour. 'No – I can't remember. I was a very naughty little girl, I expect.'

'Well, perhaps you were just spoilt,' Beatrice said, kindly. 'Do you want another sandwich? Or would you like a Maid of Honour? We get them round the corner and they're really delicious.'

'Thank you.' Dorrie took a cake and bit into flaky pastry and curd filling, 'Mm – they are nice. Are they your favourites?'

'Yes – though I like chocolate éclairs as well,' Beatrice said. 'What do you like best?'

'Let's think. Yes, I know. Our cook at home in the country makes lovely meringues – when she's in a good mood, that is. They're not like those white, shop ones – they're very pale golden and she puts Jersey cream in them.'

'Gosh – delicious!' Beatrice said. Ben, his tears forgotten, had turned round and was regarding Dorrie with something like awe.

'Do you have a house in the country, as well as in London? *And* a cook?'

Dorrie looked suddenly rather embarrassed. 'Well – yes.'

'And I bet you had a pony when you were little, didn't you?' Beatrice said, eagerly.

'Yes, I did. I've still got him, actually, although I'm too big to ride him now. He's enjoying his retirement and growing fat and lazy.'

'What's his name? And what colour is he? Did you ever

121

go hunting on him – and don't you feel sorry for the poor old fox?'

Beatrice put down her cup and plate and went to sit, both literally and metaphorically, at Dorrie's feet, while she recounted tales of a rather bad little girl and her pony, and Ben came over and leaned on the back of Dorrie's chair, hopelessly enthralled.

She really, Ross thought grudgingly, seemed to have more than her fair share of charm. He seemed to be the only member of the Cavallo family not to have succumbed to it. Even Sarah, when she came down from settling Tom, seemed as spellbound as the children, laughing and exclaiming at Dorrie's anecdotes as though she was a schoolgirl again, giggling in the dormitory.

Sarah had never had a close friend at school. The consciousness of the deep gulf between herself and other girls had made that impossible and, since she had been married, Ross had been the only companion her shy nature had needed. She was always befriending people – old people, sick people, people in trouble, and bringing them home for food or money, a bed for a few nights or simply tea and sympathy, but she had never known anyone like Dorrie – so golden and vital, so full of the confidence of generations of wealth – and yet so ingenuous, almost childlike in her desire to please and be liked.

Ross looked round at the cheerful, laughing group, and marvelled again at the ease with which Dorrie could make people like her. He drained his cup and stood up abruptly.

'I must go and get ready for work. It's getting late.'

Dorrie looked up, almost guiltily and met his dark eyes fixed sardonically on hers. He looked unfamiliar today, with his family about him, and with an Arran sweater making his face look dark, almost foreign. But his cool expression was as familiar as ever. It said, 'Get out, Dorrie St James. You're not wanted here.'

She got to her feet hastily. 'It *is* late – sorry, I didn't mean to stay so long. I'd better go now.'

'Where's your car?' Sarah said. 'Is it parked nearby – it's so dark now.'

'No – I came on the tube. It's easier than coming through the traffic.'

Ross, preparing to bid Dorrie a brisk farewell, cringed, knowing what was to come next.

'Ross!' Sarah said, her face lighting up as the idea came to her, 'You could drop Dorrie off in town, couldn't you, darling? Then you wouldn't have so far to go, would you?'

'Oh, no – that's all right,' Dorrie muttered. 'Really – I like the tube. You meet all sorts of odd people.'

'Some of them more than odd,' Sarah said. 'No – do be sensible. When Ross is going in anyway, it would be silly not to go with him.'

Dorrie glanced at Ross doubtfully, and he shrugged and summoned a faint smile. 'At your service, Miss St James,' he said, 'I'll be leaving in about an hour. Now – if you'll excuse me?'

'Sit down and have another cup of tea, Dorrie,' Sarah said. 'Tell me – is it true you know Johnny Pacelli?'

'Oh!' Beatrice's eyes grew starry. This was almost better than ponies. She had three posters of Pacelli on her bedroom wall.

'Oh, yuk!' Ben made retching noises, 'Oh, blimey – now we're for it! Old Bea is soppy about him – *really* soppy!'

'Shut up, Ben, you pig! I am not!' Beatrice grew scarlet, 'I just happen to think he's quite nice. He is, isn't he, Dorrie?'

123

Dorrie hesitated. No, she wanted to say, he's a conceited little prick and not worth a single sigh from you or any other little girl. But that would have been too brutal.

'Yes,' she said, 'he's very charming and talented. I go out with him occasionally. Would you like me to get you his autograph?'

'Oh – *would* you?' Beatrice gasped, 'My friends will be *green* with envy!'

When Ross came back, shaved, showered, immaculate in his dinner jacket, the children and Sarah took their leave of Dorrie with real regret.

'Come and see us again, *soon*,' Sarah said, meaning it, and Beatrice and Ben echoed her words enthusiastically.

Ross opened the door of the BMW for Dorrie without speaking, and was still silent when they reached the Chiswick roundabout. Then, 'You must be quite pleased with yourself,' he said.

'What do you mean?' The charm, he noticed with satisfaction, had gone. The voice was that of a sulky child again.

'I mean, the way you had my family eating out of your hand. Almost all of them – Tom seems to share my sentiments about you. Do tell me – I'm really interested to know – why was it so important to you to be liked by an obscure family with neither wealth nor title to recommend them? You take the trouble to come all the way out to Kew – and don't give me that stuff about often coming. One thing years of casino management have given me and that's the ability to tell when people are lying. But why? Surely your pride can't have been hurt too much by my rejection of your flattering advances? Surely not. There must be enough men who think the sun shines out of your charming little ass for it not to matter if one middle-aged family man thinks you're a cheap tramp?'

He glanced at her, but she said nothing, only seeming to huddle into her sheepskin coat, her gaze averted, biting on the side of her thumb.

'However,' Ross pursued relentlessly, 'if the collection of yet another scalp means so much to you, and you think it would be fun to have me lying at your feet – don't bother. I happen to love my wife and family very much. Also, I would prefer it if you didn't accept Sarah's invitation to come again. I can hardly feel you would be a suitable influence on the children.'

He had been deliberately wounding, choosing words to hurt, driven by what he told himself was his intense dislike for the girl, and also by some obscure sense of danger that she represented. She still had not spoken. He looked at her again, bracing himself for the stream of vitriol that he was sure would be forthcoming, but she was still huddled, her head averted – only the light from the street-lamps reflected from a wetness on the curve of her cheek. If she had cried aloud, or sobbed pathetically, he would have shrugged and ignored it. It was only the silence and the surreptitious attempts to wipe away the flowing tears that made him suddenly feel as brutal as if it had been Beatrice he had hurt. He was going over the Hammersmith flyover, and it was a few moments before he could find a place to stop, but when he did, he put a hand gently on her shoulder. She looked round at him, bewildered, her face streaked with black where her eye-pencil was smudged with tears, her mouth drawn childishly down with weeping.

'I'm sorry,' Ross said, 'Please don't cry.'

Angrily, she shrugged off his hand. 'Oh – don't bother. Don't take any notice. I expect I deserved it, anyway – I expect it's true, what you said, and you probably think I'm just putting on an act – blubbing so you'll feel sorry

125

for me. Well, I'm not. I never cry, no matter what. I did come to find you – but only because I wanted to apologize for last night – and – and then – I liked your family – really I did. They were so nice . . .' Her voice shook and she bit her lip fiercely, not trusting herself to say more. How could she explain, anyway, about the pleasure she had felt with his family? How could she tell him about her own solitary childhood, with no brothers and sisters, a father who was loving and remote, and an adored mother whose affection seemed as casual and unconcerned as if Dorrie had been a puppy? She fumbled angrily in her pockets for a handkerchief and Ross handed her his own, in silence, watching her, the stern lines of his face softening into a kind of tenderness. She was only a child, really – as vulnerable beneath the street-wise exterior as any kid. He had been a brute – and a fool, too, to be afraid of what this weeping child could do to him. Safe, out of danger, he reached out a hand to push the mass of damp, tangled hair back from her face. It was a mistake. As his fingers encountered the soft, living warmth, brushed the curve of her cheek and, finally, cupped the perfect shape of her head, turning it towards himself, a sort of madness took him, and he had bent towards her mouth before he was fully aware of what he was doing. He felt her quickly indrawn breath, and her lips trembled and parted beneath his as he kissed her, tasting her mouth, breathing in the sweet warm scent of her, half-dizzy as her arms went round his neck. He could feel the warm pressure of her breasts against him, and, without moving his mouth from hers, he put his hand inside her sweater, pushing aside the silk chemise she wore beneath, and cupping the softness, caressing the hardening nipple until she groaned, suddenly arching her back with longing. He took his mouth from hers and covered her face with

126

kisses, her temples, her cheeks, her hair, her eyes, breathing her name as he did, while his arm encircled her and his other hand stroked and caressed, touching her body with an ardent gentleness, from the tips of her breasts to the tender flesh of her belly and down, so that she moaned softly with pleasure, to the soft curls that covered her mound of Venus and the labyrinth of delight that was there for him to explore. It all lasted for no more than a few minutes before Ross, with a super-human effort, tore himself away from her. He gripped the steering-wheel with one hand, breathing as though he had been running, while his other hand covered his eyes, the knuckles white as he tried to force sanity back into his mind.

'My God,' he breathed, 'what the hell am I doing?'

Dorrie, still trembling with fearful joy, reached out to him and he flinched from her as though her fingers burned him.

'For God's sake, don't touch me,' he whispered. 'Don't you see – don't you see, this is what I was afraid of? This is why I didn't want you to come near me?'

'I'm sorry, Ross,' she said, in a voice so small and woebegone that he almost laughed, almost took her in his arms again.

'Hush – don't be. It was my fault, for thinking I could resist you. Who could resist you, Dorrie? Now, I shall drive you home, your virtue almost unsullied, and I shall go soberly to work, and we shall not see each other again.'

'But – but Ross!' Her voice was still tearful, 'Ross – I – I *love* – '

'Be quiet!' His voice cut across her words like a whiplash, 'Don't say that – don't ever say that. Just – go home, Dorrie, if not for my sake, then for Sarah's sake and the

127

children's, and forget about this. It was only a moment of madness.'

'And – and can't I ever go to your house again? Couldn't I just go and visit sometimes – when you're not there?'

He sighed. Her presence would be there – her perfume in the air, her name on his children's lips. The spectre of her would lie in his arms at night, like a golden wraith, haunting him. But he felt all at once too weary to argue. 'All right,' he said, 'but only when I'm not there.'

They did not speak again while he drove her home to Maida Vale. He was cursing himself for a fool, wishing to God he could undo the events of the last minutes. He felt he was like a man who has casually tried a powerful drug, secure in his immunity, and finds himself hooked, hopelessly addicted. He knew he would never be able to forget the intoxication of her kisses, the promise of delight that her warm body had held. And yet – an affair with Dorrie would be such a betrayal – not just of Sarah and the children, but of all the values that he had adhered to through years of exposure to the cut-throat world of gaming. He could not do it – he would not do it. It would be hard to resist – doubly hard now that he and Sarah were not making love any more – but there was a grim, Calvinistic streak in him, inherited from his Scots ancestors, that made him determined to endure. It was, besides, only a physical attraction of the most basic kind – even if it was stronger than he had ever felt for any woman. And on her part, too, he could be sure that there was no deep or lasting feeling. Surrounded as she always was with other men, the brief incident would soon only be something to be recalled with embarrassment – or giggled over with her friends. He winced slightly at the thought, but, after all, he had only himself to blame.

He stopped outside her flat and waited for her to get out, staring straight ahead, both hands on the wheel. When she did not move, he said, curtly, 'Go on. I'm late for work.'

'Ross?' she whispered, 'Must we really never see each other again?

'Dorrie – for God's sake, don't torment me. Just go. I know we can't avoid seeing each other if you come to the casino – but – just stay aloof, will you?'

'I'll try,' she said, almost inaudibly.

'And – another thing,' he turned to look at her and she saw how bleak, almost haggard his face was, 'I know I have no right – it's none of my business, but – Tariq el Said – don't get involved with him.'

Stung out of her miserable apathy, Dorrie turned on him. 'I suppose you'd like me to take the veil? You don't want me yourself, but you're damned if any other man will have me! Well, you're right – it *is* none of your damned business!'

'I know,' Ross said, soberly, 'I'm sorry. It's only – I've heard a few rumours about him – he's a cruel man. I don't want you to get hurt.'

'Oh, bloody noble! Don't want me to get hurt – not by anyone except you, you mean! Or perhaps you just don't like the idea of any other man screwing me. You'd like me to be like Snow-bloody-White, shut up in a glass coffin for you to dream about! Well, bloody hard luck, because – '

'*Shut up!*' He reached out and grabbed her shoulders, shaking her so that she gasped, 'You stupid little bitch! Have you no self-respect at all? What are you trying to do to yourself?'

'Get off. Let go of me,' she sobbed, pulling away from him, 'What do you care? Anyway, I – oh, *shit!*'

She pushed open the door of the car and flung herself out, stumbling up the steps and into the house, pushing blindly past the porter and into the lift. Cy, just returned from Greenham Common and unloading her rucksack in the middle of the carpet, stared in astonishment at her friend's distraught, tear-blotched face.

'What on earth's wrong?'

'Oh, for God's sake!' Dorrie yelled, pausing and looking wildly about her, 'Can't we get rid of those *fucking* roses?'

5

Cavallo drove fast to the casino and flung his keys to one of the porters to park the BMW. It was early yet – not quite eight o'clock, and only a few of the regulars were already at the table. Schaeffer, his plate of free bar snacks and cup of coffee at his elbow, Stella Fielding, hair and face immaculate after an afternoon at the beauty parlour and yet another expensive new gown, some provincial businessmen unwinding after a day in the conference hall, and the usual group of Chinese, quiet and self-contained, rising politely to their feet as he paused to say good evening, then returning with the fanaticism of their race to their gambling.

Bob Haley came over, full of importance and a desire to please. He lived for his work and could scarcely be persuaded to go home at the end of his shift. The world of gaming, long since grown tawdry to Ross Cavallo, seemed to Haley to be full of a bright Hollywood glamour that would never grow dim.

'Fairly quiet, so far, Ross,' he volunteered, 'but it's sure to liven up later. Mr Khalid told me there was some talk of Sean Connery looking in!'

'Oh?' Ross, not listening, glanced at the figures, 'Ten grand on table three already tonight? Who was that – a regular punter?'

'Oh, yes – Mr Pacelli again. He's been having a run of bad luck lately, hasn't he? But I suppose it doesn't mean much to him, the amount he must make.'

'I suppose not,' Ross said, slowly, staring at Haley, 'And I suppose it was cash?'

'Oh, yes!' Haley laughed a little, pleased to show off his inside knowledge of the rich and famous, 'Yes, Mr Johnny Pacelli has a bit of a fetish about that, doesn't he? He likes to use cash rather than cheques.'

Ross shrugged and turned away to go to his office. As eccentricities went, Pacelli's was mild. He had punters who thought it was unlucky to hear the ball drop in the wheel and would crouch in the vestibule, fingers in ears, during the spin. He had a punter, one of the richest men in London, who always arrived with a Co-op carrier bag stuffed with bank-notes. He had many punters who would refuse to play if they could not sit at a particular table, on a particular chair, using their favourite colour chip. No – Johnny Pacelli's quirk was by no means abnormal. But the amount he was losing on the tables was. At this rate, Ross calculated, even if he had got three golden discs, he would be broke within a year. Who cared? The man was a conceited jerk, and deserved everything that was coming to him.

Cavallo paced restlessly around his office for a few minutes, picked up the photo of Sarah from his desk, then poured himself an uncharacteristic Scotch, and lit a cigarette. The profit plan was on his desk, neatly typed with three copies by his secretary, Leila. He picked it up and glanced at it, frowning faintly. It was good. The figures for the last year were well beyond his projected ones, and there was no reason why they should do less well in the year ahead. Khalid should be delighted – they were, Ross knew, making more money than Crockford's or Aspinall's. It was only some sixth sense that made him feel very slightly uneasy.

There was a tap at the door and Haley stuck his head

round, apologetic and uneasy, 'Sorry, Ross – er – I'm not sure what – er – what the procedure is. It's that snooker player – you know, the one you barred. He's at reception, demanding to be let in. He's getting rather abusive, I'm afraid.'

Cavallo sighed. 'Look, Bob – I barred him because he's a drunken sot with a mouth like a blocked drain. I know he's on telly just about every night and he thinks we should lie down and let him walk in over our faces. But just go out there and tell him in the nicest possible language to sod off. And if he doesn't, take Harry with you and have him forcibly removed.'

Haley disappeared, making anxious clucking noises, hating to offend anyone who was a celebrity, and not wanting an unseemly brawl to develop in the foyer, in case Mr Connery should appear.

Ross grinned faintly and returned to his study of the profit plan.

'Dorrie?' Cy tapped gently on the bedroom door.

'Go away.'

'I've brought you some coffee. Real, not dandelion.'

There was no reply, so Cy shoved the door open and went in. The room was a mess, as usual – expensive clothes dropped casually on the floor, a long double string of pearls that had been a present from Sir Anthony, lying in spilled talc and hair-grips on the dressing-table. Dorrie lay on the unmade bed, still in her sheepskin coat, her hair tangled and damp and her face still wet with tears. How on earth, Cy thought, enviously, could anyone manage to cry so much without getting red eyes and a scarlet nose? Dorrie just looked like a flower that had been rained on. So it was with rather more acerbity than she had intended that Cy said, 'Come on! Don't lie there like the last Act of Hamlet. Drink this, and try a bit of stiff upper lip. What's wrong – did someone make an improper suggestion?'

Despite her tears, Dorrie almost giggled. 'Oh, shut up, Cy – you are a fool. Oh – God, what a stupid mess.'

'The room? Yes – it could do with a spring clean.'

'No, idiot. Me. Oh – Cy, you wouldn't believe – of all things, I have to go and fall heavily for the one man I can't have.'

Cy was unimpressed. 'Why can't you? Is he a priest? Or dead? Otherwise I can't see you giving up that easily.'

'No, worse. He's happily married – and – and I've met his wife and we really liked each other – and he has these nice kids – and – '

'And I take it he has no interest in you,' Cy said, dryly, 'which no doubt explains why you fell for him – it's such an unusual experience for you.'

'No – I don't know. That's what I thought – that I just wanted to see if I could get him interested. But – when he touched me, I – oh, I can't explain it. It wasn't like anything I've ever felt before . . .'

'When he touched you? I suppose after struggling manfully against his emotions he decided a bit on the side wouldn't be a bad idea after all? And that his wife didn't really understand him? You are an idiot, Dorrie.'

'No, I'm not!' Dorrie said, angrily, 'And it wasn't like that at all! He – never wants to see me again! He – he shook me, Cy! Oh, God – what shall I do?' Her face crumpled again, and she fumbled blindly for Ross's soaked and mascara-stained handkerchief.

Cy sat down on the foot of the bed and crossed her legs beneath her, running a hand through already rumpled hair as she stared at her friend in perplexity.

'Blimey O'Reilly. You do get into some situations,

don't you? Drink your coffee and calm down. Look, Dorrie – I don't mean to be brutal, but – this is a new experience for you, isn't it? I mean a man who says "I could not love thee, dear, so much, loved I not Honour more." Are you sure there's not a bit of hurt pride – and a touch of wanting what you can't get? Don't get mad. You see – girls like me, ordinary, plainish girls, are used to swooning over people who wouldn't look twice at us. But you – well, at risk of swelling your head, I must say you are an exotic and beautiful creature. So you can't take it when someone says, "Thanks, but no thanks."'

Dorrie drew a deep, tremulous breath. 'Perhaps you're right, Cy. And this man, we – I thought we hated each other. Only – I didn't seem able to keep away.'

'Well, kid. You're going to have to, I'm afraid. I know you're a wild, bad girl – but I somehow don't see you as the femme fatale, breaking up the happy home.'

Dorrie shook her head slowly, staring down into her coffee mug. 'No. No, I'd hate to do that.'

'What you want to do,' Cy said, 'is take your mind off him. Why don't you give that Jack Larcombe a ring? He seemed a genuine sort – and good-looking, too.'

'I might do,' Dorrie said, listlessly. 'He won't be in, anyway. He's usually at the Commons till after ten. And – oh, hell, I forgot to see if there was anything about his maiden speech in the paper.'

'There was. I cut it out for you – a bit in today's Agenda page in the *Guardian*. Quite flattering, really – for the *Guardian*. Anyway – you'll have time to get changed and then give him a ring. Tell him you want taking somewhere lively. I bet he'll jump at the chance.'

'Oh, I don't know. I feel like a dead cat. I think I'll have a bath and go to bed.'

'You won't sleep. I bet you didn't get up till midday.

You'll just toss about and fret yourself silly over this Ross Cavallo.'

Dorrie stared, open-mouthed. 'How did you know? I never mentioned – '

Cy grinned. 'It's what you don't say, my sweeting. Now – go and run a bath – the roses in there have gone to Great Ormond Street – and Auntie Cy will see if she can get the House of Commons on the blower.'

Five minutes later she carried the extension triumphantly into the bathroom where Dorrie wallowed in scented froth, and handed her the receiver.

'Hallo? Jack? Oh – I'm sorry to bother you at work. How are you? Congratulations on your speech, by the way – it seemed to go down well. Listen – are you free later? I thought we could go out. Good. Okay – just after ten'll be fine.'

She had not even identified herself, but the light, slightly husky tones were more instantly recognizable to Jack than his own mother's would have been, even with the unfamiliar wistful note that made him want to rush to her side and drive away whatever had made her sad. He hung up, then redialled almost immediately.

'Natasha? It's me. Look – I'm awfully sorry, but something's come up and I'm going to have to go to a meeting. What? Well – I don't want to disturb you later – God knows what time it'll be. We'd better leave it tonight. I know – I'm disappointed, believe me. See you tomorrow? Take care.'

Cy said, 'There! Quite painless, wasn't it? Where are you going?'

'I don't know.' Dorrie lay back in the water and flicked bubbles idly over her breasts, 'Nowhere quiet and intimate, anyway. I don't want to end the day fighting Jack Larcombe off.'

'Do you have to fight him off? Some nice cosy sex with a clean young man is just what you need to relax you.'

'Thanks. Now I come to think of it, that Waldo of yours reminds me of a mug of Horlicks – pale, bland and soporific. I'd prefer something a bit more stimulating.'

'Suit yourself – I wasn't offering you Waldo, anyway. Besides – he may look dreamy, but he's quite nice in bed.'

'So's a teddy bear,' Dorrie commented. 'Here – scrub my back, will you? I feel lazy.'

'Yes, milady – and what clothes should I lay out for milady? The spangled G-string and two pink tassels tonight?'

'No, nothing so formal,' Dorrie said, sitting up and presenting her back to her friend. 'Go on – scrub.'

At ten-thirty, Jack Larcombe knocked at the door of the flat and was admitted by Cy. She gave a faint scream when she saw him and dissolved into laughter.

'What's up?' Jack said, ready to be affronted, and glancing down to make sure his fly was zipped, which made Cy laugh all the more.

'Oh, nothing – I'm sorry, Jack! It's not you – just come in and you'll see!'

She led him into the sitting-room, still scented and littered with dozens of roses, some of them wilting already.

'Oh – I see.' Jack looked ruefully at the dozen cellophane-wrapped red roses in his hand, and grinned reluctantly at Cy. 'Coals to Newcastle, eh? Where on earth did this lot come from? No – I can guess. The Sheikh of Araby, right? Doesn't do things by halves, does he?'

'No – it's a bit ludicrous, really. I'm expecting a train of heavily laden camels any day now.'

He grinned again. 'As long as he doesn't plan on Dorrie joining his harem.'

Cy shrugged. 'No – I don't think she's that keen, frankly. She'll be out in a minute – d'you want a drink?'

'Thanks. Scotch and soda, please.'

He sat and watched Cy's small neat figure as she pottered about with drinks. She was a nice kid, he thought, and untemperamental. She would have to be, to live with Dorrie.

'I haven't forgotten about your rally on Saturday,' he said, 'I'll try to get there.'

'It's not "my" rally,' Cy said, rather caustically, handing him his drink, 'it's "our" rally. The bomb won't discriminate, you know. Like the quality of mercy it will drop on the just and the unjust alike.'

'Okay! Don't bite my head off! I'm not Lady Olga Maitland in disguise! I promise, unless Her Majesty actually asks me to form a Government on Saturday, I shall come and sit humbly at the feet of Monsignor Kent.'

'Good. And get some of your cronies to come along, too. It's about time the Labour Party stood up to be counted.'

'Yes, ma'am,' Jack said, with mock humility, and was about to ask if Cy numbered Attila the Hun amongst her ancestors when Dorrie came in.

'Hullo, Jack,' she said, briskly, 'Don't gape, my child – it's most unbecoming, and also hard to tell if it's admiration or horror. If the latter – you're excused duty, and I shall just boogie on down to the night-spots all on my own.'

'Well,' Cy put in, as Jack remained dumb-struck, 'you do look a bit bizarre, to say the least.'

'I feel bizarre. I *am* bizarre. No knowing what strange

138

and exotic things I shall get up to tonight. Or do I mean erotic?'

She executed a few dance-steps, humming the tune of a pop song and adding her own bawdy words. To Jack, she seemed brash, bright, hard and brittle, a Christmas tree ornament that looks like Fairyland and crumbles into sharp splinters. Only Cy, because she looked for it, could see the pain hidden in those brilliant blue eyes.

Dorrie was wearing a brief pink mini-skirt, a tiny square of fabric from Joseph Tricot, and with it, a black ribbed vest which clung as closely as a lascivious lover to her breasts, plunging deeply between them and scarcely covering them at the sides. Her legs, in their black, fish-net stockings and gleaming black, pink and silver Manolo Blahnik sandals, seemed longer than ever, and she had a mass of chunky assorted beads round her neck, which looked to Jack as though they'd been strung together by primary school children, but had actually cost a couple of hundred pounds at Joseph's in Sloane Street. This was not the worst of it, in Jack's view. Dorrie's face was made up as though she were going to take part in some exotic stage show, her eyelids striped in gold and pink and blue and lined with black, and her hair a wild tangle sprayed bright pink all over and spangled with silver.

'I thought perhaps we could go to the Stranger's Bar at the House of Commons for a drink first,' she said to Jack, straight-faced.

'Dorrie – do behave!' admonished Cy. 'She's only teasing, Jack. Really – I don't know if you look more like Tina Turner or a stick of candy-floss, Dorrie. Where on earth are you going like that? You'll even raise eyebrows at Annabel's or Garden's, I should think.'

Dorrie stuck her tongue out. 'Well, Jack? You haven't said a word. Do you want to take me out, or not?'

139

'Of course I do,' Jack said, hastily, 'and I think you look – um – very – very nice and – unusual. But I'm afraid I'm not exactly dressed to match – I came straight from the House.'

'That's okay. I could do your hair to match mine, if you like? No? Well, perhaps not. Anyway – not to worry, my poppet, we're going somewhere quite private where it'll probably be so dark neither of us will be seen at all.'

Cy groaned. 'Dorrie! You're not going to Tubby Dorset's party, are you?'

'Why not?' Dorrie said, airily, 'Just button it, Cy. Come on, Jack – we'll leave Cy to her chaste couch and her Horlicks.'

She snatched up a white fox jacket and flung it round her shoulders. 'We'll take my car,' she said, 'in case we have to leave in a hurry.'

'What she means,' Cy said, acidly, 'is that Tubby Dorset's last two parties have been raided by police. Oh, well – you've been warned, Jack.'

Even Jack had heard of the notorious Viscount Theodore 'Tubby' Dorset, the heir to the Marquess of Inverewe. He was constantly in the columns of the less salubrious papers under headlines such as 'Peer's Son in Nude Dash down Piccadilly' or 'The Viscount and the Vicar's Wife', and, as he approached his mid-thirties, his exploits seemed to lose some of their youthful panache and to seem mere sordid debauchery.

'Don't look so worried!' Dorrie said, patting Jack's cheek lightly as they went down in the lift, 'I promise you won't be forced to sniff coke or have sex with the family beagle! And if it's a real pain in the ass, we'll come home again. Here – let me give you a little hug – but no kissing or you'll spoil my make-up.'

She put her arms round him and squeezed, rather like

a child, smiling up at him in a coaxing, irresistible way. She was still hugging him when the lift doors opened and the porter regarded them with a tolerant grin.

'Evening, Miss St James.'

'Hi, Mr Perks. Could you bring my car round, please?'

'A pleasure, Miss.' He caught the keys she tossed him and went out of the swing doors.

'Don't you do anything for yourself?' Jack enquired, 'We could easily have got your car out – or gone in mine.'

Dorrie shrugged. 'It's his job, anyway – and he's not exactly overworked.' She could not be bothered explaining to Jack how much the old man enjoyed bringing the car round for her. He would only think she was being patronizing. They stood at the entrance without talking and in a moment or two there was a full-throated roar which throttled back to a quiet throb as a Daytona Ferrari drew up at the kerb.

Jack groaned. 'Oh, Lord! I might have known. Can't we just get a taxi?'

Dorrie grinned impishly. 'Oh, no, you don't. And don't be so rude, either – I drive it very well.'

'Famous last words of all women drivers,' commented Jack, but he could not help a tiny stab of envy as he looked at the sleek, elegant lines of the car. What on earth must it have cost? At least £50,000 he guessed – just for a kid of eighteen to show off in. Her father must be mad.

'Stop grumping and get in,' Dorrie ordered, 'or do you want to make a point and arrive at the party on a haywain? Come on – you won't compromise your principles any more by a ride in my beautiful Ferrari than you do by driving that rather ugly Volvo. Admit it – even your Volvo is rather out of the reach of the ordinary working-class man, isn't it? So, what's the difference?'

She got in, smiling her thanks to the porter, and Jack slid in beside her, wondering how it was that Dorrie could so easily make him feel like a boorish clod. And she could drive, he admitted grudgingly. There was no showing off or speeding, but her reactions were fast and skilful and her slim hands on the wheel were as light as he imagined they would be on a horse's mouth.

Viscount Dorset, being under a temporary cloud and banned from the family's London home in Kensington, had taken a house in Brondesbury, where he was electrifying his respectable neighbours with the noise of his parties, his sports cars, and his minor pranks like driving a coach and four at top speed round the block at three in the morning in a state of heavy intoxication. There was a lot of noise already, sixties rock music and shrieks of laughter, when Dorrie and Jack arrived, and a shadowy figure clinging to a bare tree in the small front garden and muttering, 'Oh, my God, oh, my God,' bore witness to the amount of liquor that was being consumed.

Tubby Dorset himself bore down on them as they pushed open the unlatched door, and swept Dorrie into an exuberant hug. 'My darling Dorrie! You look divine – I could eat you! May I take you upstairs and ravish you now, or would you like a drink first?'

'A drink, please,' Dorrie said, firmly. 'Tubby – this is Jack Larcombe.'

The Viscount offered a limp hand and at the same time squeezed Jack's biceps. 'You're rather divine, too!' he said, with a mocking leer, 'I may ravish you as well when I'm a bit drunker!'

Jack laughed uneasily and felt himself reddening. Dorrie took his hand. 'Don't take any notice, Jack. Tubby has a warped sense of humour. Have you got anything to eat here, or is the refreshment all liquid?'

'My dear! You are joking! No expense has been spared – mountains of stuff has arrived from Fortnum's – the tables are groaning – *do* help yourselves! Mm! You're sweet!' he added, pinching Jack's cheek as he turned away.

Dorrie smiled, 'He's a fool, isn't he?' but Jack was not amused.

'That sort of thing makes me feel a bit sick, actually,' he said, stiffly.

'Oh. Well, all right. Let's go and find the food. I'm hungry.'

They pushed their way through crowds of people, some of them shouting inanities at each other above the noise, others swaying and bobbing in a semi-mesmerized response to the beat of the music. On the stairs a very young-looking girl in a blue lace frock was being fed ice-cream by a drunk young man who kept spilling it on to her chest and wiping it away with his hand. She looked unhappy but passive. People greeted Dorrie enthusiastically as she passed, in voices that seemed to Jack to be parodies of P. G. Wodehouse novels.

'Do they all speak like that, all the time?' he muttered to Dorrie, as they reached the buffet table and helped themselves to smoked salmon sandwiches and rolled chicken breasts. Someone, Jack noticed with disgust, had stubbed out a cigarette in the middle of an elaborate trifle.

'What do you mean?' Dorrie said. 'Oh – quails in aspic. I loathe aspic.'

'Your lot, I mean. Do they really talk like Lord bloody Haw-Haw all the time?'

'They're not "my lot". And yes, I suppose they do, some of them. It depends how they were brought up – some are more affected than others. But they can't help

143

it, any more than you can help those rolling "r's" and the way you sometimes say "oi" for "i".'

'Do I? I thought Cambridge had got rid of that.'

'Well, it hasn't. Anyway – you must have met quite a few of what you call "my lot" at Cambridge, so don't act as though it was a new species you've just discovered.'

'I didn't mix with them much at Cambridge. No money and no influence. So I've never come across them en masse before.'

'I can just picture you at Cambridge,' Dorrie said, rather nastily, biting into a sandwich, 'I bet you were earnest and hard-working, a member of the Fabian Society, with a pin-up of – of – Shirley Williams on your wall!'

'She's SDP, not Labour,' Jack said, 'And you're wrong – I had quite a lot of fun at Cambridge – '

'Singing "The Red Flag" very loudly?' Dorrie suggested.

'No – don't be silly. Socialists can enjoy themselves just as much as anyone else . . .'

'Sounds like a good slogan for the next election.'

'I wish you'd stop interrupting! All I'm trying to say is . . .' he stopped, unable to remember what he had been trying to say and Dorrie laughed, selecting a cheese straw from a delicate pastry basket and pushing it into his mouth.

'You're trying to say that you only enjoyed yourself in a godly, righteous and sober way. *À bas les aristos!* No one from the working classes ever gets drunk or makes a fool of themselves, right? I like you, Jack – but don't be such a pompous twit!'

Without warning, she shrugged off her white fox jacket, dropping it carelessly over a chair, and joined the throng of dancers, gyrating and hip-swinging, her pink and silver cascade of hair shining with a surreal effect beneath the stroboscopic lights that had been rigged up. Jack made a movement as though he would follow her, then changed his mind. Damned if he was going to make a spectacle of himself. He was twenty-eight years old and a Member of Parliament – he was not going to wiggle his behind for Dorrie or any woman, even if he was a pompous twit. Someone had given Dorrie a glass of champagne and she was quaffing it like lemonade, without pausing in her dancing. Jack looked tentatively round for something to drink and, as if summoned telepathically, a waiter appeared at his side with a tray of glasses. Jack accepted one, smiling his thanks, impulsively wanting to tell the waiter that he, Jack Larcombe, was not one of your upper-class idiots. He was on the side of the workers. But the waiter's answering smile was faint and professional. He was, as is so often the case, a greater snob than his employer.

'Hallo!' said a small, fluting voice beside him, 'You look lonely. Would you like to dance?'

It was the young-looking girl in the blue lace frock, now separated from her drunken companion, though still bearing ice-cream stains across her front.

'No, thanks,' Jack said, but smiling to show that it was not a personal rejection, 'I'm not very good at this sort of thing. Would you like me to get you a drink? You – you are old enough to drink, aren't you?'

'I'm almost eighteen,' she said with dignity, 'and I should love some champagne. I'm Tara Hensham, by the way. Who are you?'

She drank several glasses of champagne, her small beaky nose becoming quite pink in the process, and persuaded Jack at length on to the dance floor, where she pressed her thin little body earnestly against his and told him of her intention of taking a lover as soon as possible.

'I thought Timmy might do, as I've known him all my life,' she said, 'but he got so hopelessly drunk that he passed out on the stairs before we even got up them. But I should think he'd be quite interested. He did *fondle* my breasts a lot after he'd dropped ice-cream down them – I should think that shows interest, shouldn't you? Or would it just be a fetish?'

Jack was saved from pursuing this interesting subject by Viscount Dorset's announcement of a champagne race. He lined up competitors, most of them quite drunk, opposite each other, each armed with a well-shaken bottle of champagne and at a given signal they hurried to uncork their bottles and spray their opponents.

'What a waste of good wine,' Jack muttered. 'What on earth must that lot have cost!'

'Oh, heaps, I expect,' Tara Hensham said vaguely. Her father was a duke, doing a booming business with his stately safari park and his mediaeval banquets. 'Cost' was not a word Tara was familiar with. She had a few more drinks and asked if Jack would care to deflower her.

'It's too shame-making, being a virgin at nearly eighteen,' she confessed, her speech a little slurred, 'I mean, one feels so left on the shelf, do you know? Why don't we go upstairs and do it now? It won't take long.'

'I wouldn't, if I were you,' Dorrie said, taking Jack's arm suddenly. 'Somebody's having a bad trip in one bedroom and seeing giant spiders crawling up the walls. At least ten people are rutting with drunken gusto on all the available beds and several more have been disgustingly ill along the corridors. Not a pretty sight. Besides, Tara, you little whore, this is my escort for tonight. Piss off, like a good child and go and find an Action Man to practise with.'

Sulking, Tara drifted off, and Jack said, 'You needn't

be so nasty to the poor kid – you haven't shown much interest in me tonight.'

'I didn't want to cramp your style, Jack darling. Sorry if I interrupted something promising – did you want to screw that tiny stick-insect? I can call her back . . .'

'You know I bloody didn't,' Jack said, exasperated, 'Don't be stupid.'

Dorrie sighed. She looked suddenly tired and her brilliant hair and make-up looked as though they belonged to an actress after the curtain has fallen. 'Let's go, shall we?' she said, flatly, 'You're quite right – the upper classes at play can be particularly repugnant.'

She pushed her way to the buffet table, by now resembling the aftermath of a jumble sale, to retrieve her jacket, pausing on the way to offer farewells and thanks to Tubby Dorset who, with several cronies, was engaged in debagging the waiter.

'*Not* going, surely, my sweetest?' wailed the Viscount, 'But I have the most glorious idea for a game – I want you to judge it! It's called Cock-a-Doodle, and we men have to decorate our little Willies . . .'

'Sorry, Tubs,' Dorrie said, 'it sounds enthralling, but I must get my beauty sleep.'

'And what about your friend? I wanted him to join in! He's sweet!'

'Tut, tut! Have you forgotten, he's a *Private* Member?' Dorrie said with severity. 'Toodle-pip, old chap! Thanks again.'

It was two A.M. when they returned to Dorrie's flat. She did not invite him in, and gave him the briefest of kisses before leaving him. She was doing her Ice-Maiden stuff again, Jack thought, leading him on with her bawdy language and her revealing clothes, then dropping a freezing plate-glass barrier between them. He wished he

147

had not come tonight. Did she think he was a dog to come running when she whistled? Next time, he would show her. Next time he would tell her to drop dead. But he knew he would not. He was as much in love with her as ever. It was late, but not so very late. Would Natasha be asleep yet? He backed the Volvo, turned it, and drove off towards Leinster Mews.

Cy was still up when Dorrie went in. 'Thank God!' she said, 'I've had a bunch of marauding Arabs here, determined to carry you off! And His Royal Highness on the blower every hour, wanting to know if you're back yet. I can tell you – Waldo went home in disgust. He said it was like making love in the Central Telephone Exchange. There it goes again.'

Dorrie picked up the receiver, 'Yes?'

'Dorrie – where have you been? I have telephoned all evening. Will you join me at the casino, please? I will send a car for you at once.'

'Tariq,' Dorrie said, sweetly, 'I'm tired. I'm going to bed. I am not your personal property. Now, I don't know the Arabic for it, but I'm sure you'll get the gist when I tell you to go and take a running jump up your own backside. Goodnight.' She depressed the receiver rest but did not replace the receiver. Then she took a long shower, the warm water on her skin inevitably recalling Ross Cavallo's touch, like the faint memory of a dream, drank a large glass of Scotch to augment the stupefying effect of the champagne she had drunk, and lay awake for hours, sick and dizzy, until at last she fell asleep with the dawn.

A week later, Sarah Cavallo rang Dorrie and asked her to come out to Kew. 'Please come,' she said, 'the children are on half-term and the weather's too awful to do anything very much. We've exhausted the museums and

148

things and tempers are getting frayed. You'd really be doing an errand of mercy if you came. Can you be bothered?'

Dorrie's heart had leaped at the first thought of going to Ross's house, perhaps seeing him again. She had stayed away from him, not even going to the casino. She had been out with Jack Larcombe for dinner, with Tariq el Said, and even with Johnny Pacelli, and by odd coincidence they had all wanted to end the evening at the Olympus. But she had refused point-blank, as wayward and capricious as a spoilt child, and, because she did not care whether she ever saw any of them again, and because she was beautiful and, when she wished, charming, they accepted all her moods and came back for more.

'I don't know,' she said, cautiously to Sarah, 'Will Ross be there?'

'No – he's at the casino from one o'clock today – why? Does it make a difference?'

Dorrie could hear the amused surprise in Sarah's voice. 'Yes,' she said, feeling she had to get certain things sorted out straight away, 'I'm afraid it does. I know he's very polite and all that – but he doesn't like me very much, you know. And he thinks I'm a bad influence on the children.'

'Oh, no – don't be silly! Ross isn't like that – you're imagining things!'

'Perhaps. Anyway – I'm a bit scared of him, so if you don't mind I won't come while he's around.'

'Okay,' Sarah laughed, 'though you don't seem the type to scare easily. Come about two, then, and spend the afternoon – if you can bear it, that is!'

Dorrie put down the phone and found that her hand was shaking. For an instant, she almost rang back to tell Sarah that something had come up and she couldn't make

149

it. She was afraid that she would give herself away – would Ross's wife see the hunger in her eyes when his name was mentioned, as it inevitably would be? Oh, God – it was all such madness. When – at what exact point – had she started to feel like this about Ross Cavallo? She was Dorrie St James and she had been out with movie stars, politicians, the cream of the aristocracy, men of wit and charm. But none had stirred her heart in the way that a faint, reluctant smile on one particular dark face did. Even his looks were not the type that Dorrie usually admired – his face in repose could look grim, and in anger savage, and it was only his smile that saved his features from an inherited Scots dourness. His nose had a slight crookedness in it, perhaps had once been broken. He was tall and well-built – but so were dozens of other men.

For the first time, Dorrie realized that the phrase 'falling in love' was an exact one. You went along, foot-loose, cocksure, pleased with yourself and with life in general, and, all of a sudden, wham! you were lying at the bottom of a big pit without the least idea of how you got there. All those stupid, trite phrases, so misused that they seemed completely worn out, suddenly leaped into vivid life for her. Loving Ross was like hunger, like madness, like being on fire, like drowning. She lay awake, no matter how late she went to bed, and tortured herself with the memory of his hands on her body, his mouth on her own. Once or twice she had reached for the telephone, full of an unbearable longing to hear the sound of his voice, but she knew that if she spoke to him she would be unable to stop herself from pleading with him to see her. And she would not do that. She still had some pride, even if it was only a tattered remnant. But she had been unable to refuse Sarah's invitation. The longing to be where he had been, to talk about him, no matter how impersonally, to touch his possessions, was too great. She would go.

She drove over to Kew at speed, carving up the traffic with careless ease and a casual, vulgar motion of her fingers to angry, hooting motorists, and only by some sixth sense escaping a radar trap.

'Oh, boy!' Ben shouted, racing out of the house and gazing with stunned joy at the Ferrari, 'Oh, grief! Is it yours? I mean, *really*? Not borrowed or – gosh, I didn't think girls drove cars like this!'

'Ben – you are a chauvinist pig,' Beatrice said, coming out to join her brother on the pavement. 'Girls can drive anything, can't they Dorrie? Anyway – don't be so bad-mannered – you should ask Dorrie to come in.'

'Here!' Dorrie grinned at Ben and tossed him the keys, 'Have a poke round, and lock it up when you've finished. There's some stuff in the back you can bring in as well.'

They went up the path to the mellow, greystone house, its walls half-hidden behind a curtain of wisteria which dripped lilac blossoms in the summer. Sarah met them at the door, as eagerly welcoming as though Dorrie was an old friend.

'Hallo! How nice of you to come! We're all feeling fed-up and Thomas is teething. You look like a spring day!'

She was wearing a fine white wool Escada trouser suit with a pleated silk blouse beneath it, her golden hair brushed and loose, a bright note on the grey, drizzling afternoon.

'I wish my hair was like yours,' said the dark little Beatrice when Dorrie had been installed in front of the fire, 'd'you suppose if I bleached it, it would come out that colour?'

'I wouldn't do that,' Dorrie said, taking a silky brown lock between her fingers. 'It's pretty hair – so lovely and

151

shiny. When I was your age, I wanted to be dark, because all my favourite heroines like Estelle in *Great Expectations*, Cathy in *Wuthering Heights*, Scarlett O'Hara – they were all dark. It seemed far more romantic than being an insipid blonde. I remember trying to dye it with black ink – what a mess! It didn't do anything to my hair, but my face was blotchy grey for days.'

She was talking, laughing, chattering with an unnatural, girlish vivacity, knowing that if she did not, she would find herself mentioning his name, just for the bitter-sweet pleasure of hearing them talk about him. She wanted to prowl about the room, touching things, looking at things. The unfinished game of chess on the low table in the bay window – had he been playing? The books lining one wall – which were his favourites? Did he have the same tastes that she did? The bronze chrysanthemums in a copper bowl – had he bought them for Sarah? She seemed to feel his presence about her with a vivid intensity that was almost unbearable. It had been a mistake to come. And these, his women-folk, these two dark, sensitive faces that responded to her own with such pleasure – surely they could sense the tension in her? It was a relief when Ben came in, his arms full of the packages from the car.

'Did you mean me to bring all this stuff in?' he asked.

'Yes – I brought some presents to cheer you all up. Have a rummage!'

'Oh, Dorrie! How awful! You shouldn't have done that!' Sarah cried, her eyes round as she looked at the expensively gift-wrapped packages.

'Why not? It's fun! More fun than getting something on birthdays and Christmases, don't you think? Do open them!'

Sarah and Beatrice hesitated, but Ben plunged eagerly forward and found a parcel with his name on it. Inside, there was a magnificent kite, scarlet and gold with dragons and streamers and a long glittering tail. Ben could hardly stammer his thanks.

'It's *super!*' he breathed, 'Mum – when can we fly it?'

'Perhaps Daddy will take you to Richmond Park tomorrow,' Sarah said. 'It is a beauty, isn't it? Dorrie – how naughty of you to spend so much!'

Dorrie shrugged and smiled. She hoped Sarah wouldn't think she had been ridiculously ostentatious. Cy often reproached her for extravagance, but it was hard, when you had always been rich, not to spend money just as you pleased.

There was a fat, lavishly illustrated book on horses and ponies for Beatrice, which she seized with a crow of delight and carried off to a corner from which she excitedly regaled them with hitherto unheard-of facts about spavins, martingales and numnahs. There was a furry seal for Thomas from 'Tiger Tiger' and for Sarah a long silk scarf in soft shades of jade, slate and blue. Finally a large box of chocolate truffles was unwrapped and pounced on.

'But what about Daddy?' Beatrice said, suddenly, through a mouthful of truffle, looking up from her book.

'He isn't here!' Ben said, callously, helping himself from the elaborate box. 'Anyway, he can share my kite.'

'I – I'm not very good at choosing things for men,' Dorrie said. She was not the blushing type normally, but she could feel her cheeks grow hot. Sarah, noticing, thought Dorrie was embarrassed at forgetting Ross, and hastened to reassure her.

'Good heavens – I should think Dorrie's spent enough already! And we'll keep all the rum truffles with the dark chocolate for Daddy – they're his favourites.'

'Really?' Dorrie, stupidly pleased, was grinning like a kid, 'Oh, I'm glad!'

The drizzle had increased to a steady downpour, and the wind got up and hurled careless handfuls of gold leaves across Kew Green. The two women and the children talked and played board games, made toffee in the kitchen and toasted crumpets for their tea.

Lotte, the German au pair, brought the baby down for Sarah to feed, and Dorrie watched with a new hunger as Ross's wife put the child to her breast, her dark, curly head bent over him tenderly, like an archetypal Mother and Child. Dorrie, who had always felt about babies rather as if they were invaders from outer space, felt her own breasts tingling and aching with a sudden longing to have a child of Ross Cavallo's suckling them. If she only could bear his child, she thought it might make up for having to live without him. Sarah, looking up, caught Dorrie's expression and decided she had been wrong about her. The younger girl did have a maternal instinct after all – she was just a little unused to babies.

'Would you like to hold him again?' she suggested, 'He promises not to be sick on you!'

'I wore white especially,' Dorrie said, holding out her arms.

'I'll just go and see if Lotte's done his bed,' Sarah said, 'I won't be a minute.' She hurried away, leaving Dorrie in anxious charge of the baby.

His eyes, closed at first behind their delicate, dark-lashed lids, opened after a moment and stared up at Dorrie. She hoped desperately that he would not begin to cry at finding himself in a stranger's arms. His eyes were changing from a very dark baby blue to brown, and they were as shiny and bright as new conkers, the whites clear and unclouded. They regarded Dorrie solemnly for a moment, then a hand like a plump starfish waved uncertainly in the air and fastened on Dorrie's hair. Tom smiled, and Dorrie's heart missed a beat. He was so small, so perfect, so confident in his expectation of goodness and kindness. How could she ever have found babies boring? Sarah returned to find her youngest child and her visitor gazing at each other with besotted smiles.

'He's sweet,' Dorrie said, trying to speak lightly, and dropping a kiss on the warm little head before she handed him back. 'He's like Ross, isn't he?' she couldn't help adding.

'Yes!' Sarah agreed, 'but you're the only other person except me to see it. How clever of you!'

It was nearly time for the older children to go to bed, and they begged Dorrie to come again soon and visit them.

'You could come and fly the kite with me and Dad,' Ben offered. 'I bet you're quite a good runner for a girl!'

An improbable picture of herself and Ross, hand in hand beneath a blue and white sky, running and laughing as they flew the kite, came for an instant into Dorrie's mind, and was as quickly dismissed. Such ideas were best stamped on as mere wishful thinking. And besides, whatever it was that had leaped into sudden being between herself and Ross, she could not imagine that they would ever laugh together.

She said goodnight to Beatrice and Ben and they finally disappeared after two or three return visits on one excuse or another. The last time Ben reappeared, it was to say, 'Will Dad be home soon? Will you get him to come up and say goodnight?'

'Yes, all right,' Sarah said, 'if you're still awake. I don't suppose he'll be long.'

'I'll be awake,' Ben assured her, 'Did I kiss you goodnight?'

'Only about fifteen times. Now go!' Sarah tried to look fierce and Ben finally vanished.

'I must go,' Dorrie got to her feet in sudden panic. She longed to see Ross again – but if he came home and found her here, he would think it was deliberate. And if he looked at her with that expression of icy contempt that she had once or twice seen on his face, she would burst into tears and give the whole game away.

'Oh, no – please stay a bit longer,' Sarah said, 'we'll have some coffee.'

'No, really – I have a date, I'm afraid,' Dorrie said, 'with an importunate Arab prince. He'll probably have me hung, drawn and quartered if I don't turn up! I think he's almost had enough of liberated Western women!'

'Oh, of course you must go!' Sarah was contrite, 'It was awfully kind of you to come.'

'I've had a lovely time,' Dorrie said, truthfully, 'It was nice, being with you all, and the kids are great!'

'You cheered them up. They were feeling a bit low, I think, because I was going to take them up to my aunt's in Yorkshire for a few days this half-term. But – oh, I don't know, I haven't been feeling very well lately, and the thought of the long drive, or even a train journey . . .' She shrugged, her thin face suddenly shadowed by her own private thoughts, 'Well, I just couldn't face it. Bea and Ben were very good about it, though – they haven't made a fuss at all.'

'They're good kids,' Dorrie agreed, almost absently. She picked up her handbag and stood, passing the soft leather strap between her fingers, a faint frown ruffling the straight line of her brow. She had an idea – a marvellous, tempting idea. There was no harm in it, surely? It would hurt no one, and would give pleasure to several people. Before she could give herself time to think further, she turned impulsively to Sarah and said, 'I'm going down to Ash Friars for a while this week – that's our house in Devon. D'you think the children would like to come for a few days? I promise I'd look after them – or, at any rate, my old nanny would – she'd be delighted to have kids in the house again. And then, either I could put them on the train – or, if you felt up to the drive, you could come and collect them – perhaps stay the night. Do say yes!'

Sarah laughed. 'Do you often regret these mad impulses of yours, Dorrie? I bet they get you into trouble sometimes! Look – you're being very sweet and generous – but perhaps you'd better think it over. You might change your mind in the cold light of dawn.'

'No, I shan't. Please, Sarah! It'd be fun for me, too. They can ride and explore – there's lots to do!'

'Dorrie – who could resist you? I'll ask Ross – or, better still, wait awhile and ask him yourself – he'll be home soon.'

'No. You ask him. I – I must dash off now. It takes me ages to get ready. Will you ring me tomorrow, Sarah, and let me know? I'll probably go down on Thursday or Friday.' She made a hasty escape, speeding back to Maida Vale in the cream Ferrari, half-excited, half-fearful at what she had set in motion.

Ross came home and found his house filled, it seemed, with a lingering impression of Dorrie. He could smell her scent faintly in the air, even, he fancied, see the imprint of her slim body on the cushions of his chair. A scarf of scarlet silk lay on the floor beside it, a splash of bright colour like a talisman or token, and he picked it up and tugged it through his fingers, his face dark and angry as Sarah spoke to him.

'*No!*' he said, violently, almost before she had finished.

'But – Ross!' Sarah's eyes were childishly startled at his vehemence, 'Why not?'

'Because if I want my children to go to the country, I'll take them myself. We don't need Dorrie St James, or anyone else.'

'Darling! Why do you dislike her so much? She's not nearly as hard and shallow as you think! You should see her with the children – even Tom fell for her today!'

'*Et tu, Brute!*' Ross muttered, wryly. 'Yes, I know. She should charm snakes. But I still say no.'

'It was only for a couple of days,' Sarah said, her voice already taking on the wistfulness of a loser. 'She was going to take the children riding and exploring. It's lovely country round Ash Friars.'

Ben and Beatrice, coming soft-footed down the stairs to kiss their father, heard Sarah's words and burst into the room, whooping with delight. '*Mummy!* Do you mean it? Has Dorrie really asked us to stay? Oh, when? Can we go? Say yes, Dad!'

Above his children's excited clamour, Ross's eyes met Sarah's and conceded defeat.

It had been the most perfect few days, Ben Cavallo thought. From the ecstasy of the drive down in Dorrie's Ferrari – imagine a girl being able to drive like that! – it had all been exactly right. The huge house with its rambling corridors and the mysterious attic full of oddments from the past and dusty, shrouded furniture, the gardens, park and paddocks surrounding the house, merging into woodland where there was a lake with an island: the home farm where he, Ben Cavallo, had actually milked a cow and fed the pigs and hens. And of course, Dorrie. His only unrealized wish, it seemed to Ben, was that Dorrie might be chased by an enraged bull, which Ben would fight off, armed only with a hazel switch and the powerful authority of hand and voice. Or – or she might come to him with tears in her eyes and say that the family fortunes had somehow been irretrievably lost, and then Ben would find a secret passage with a treasure horde and save the day. He sighed gustily. Being eight years old was a handicap when you were in love.

Dorrie heard him sigh, as they leaned over the paddock fence, watching Beatrice promenading, slowly and with infinite pride, on Dorrie's old pony, Bracken. She put a hand companionably on his shoulder. 'Are you getting bored, old chap? Fed up with country life? I expect your mother will be here soon.'

'Oh, no! I'm not bored!' Ben said, fervently, 'I'm sorry it's nearly over, that's all. I wish we could have stayed for ages. It's super.'

'You can come again,' Dorrie said, wishing she might give him a hug, but not wanting to offend eight-year-old male pride, 'and next time you can stay longer. Keep your heels down, Bea! That's right!'

For Dorrie, too, they had been special days. Days in which she had felt that she was a child again, but with the companionship of other children that she had missed in her early years. She had forgotten, or never known, the charm of dressing-up games with old clothes discovered in the attic, the joy of playing explorers in the woods and kicking through deep carpets of beech leaves. They had poled the old punt across the lake to the tiny island in the middle where a crumbling stone duck-house had become Crusoe's cabin, or the stockade from Treasure Island. They had had their tea with Nanny Harding in the nursery

159

which had never been so gay and laughter-filled in all Dorrie's childhood.

None of the county had intruded on them, for Dorrie had told no one that she was at home, and she and the children had lain low when they heard the hunt streaming across the frosty fields to draw the Home Farm coverts. Her mother had been Joint Master and never missed a meet, and Dorrie usually went out when she was at home. There was something in the wild note of the horn and the hell-for-leather gallop across country that appealed to her, though she had never taken much pleasure in the killing of the fox, and found herself agreeing guiltily with Beatrice that it 'wasn't fair'.

They had been enchanted days, days out of time, and Dorrie felt a sort of melancholy come over her spirits as though they would never come again. Soon Sarah would arrive. They would have lunch and chat for a while, and then Dorrie would be alone again, on the outside of a family that had come to mean so much.

At last, Beatrice had had enough, and, lowering herself gingerly from Bracken's plump back, she begged Dorrie for a jumping exhibition.

'Just to show me how it's done,' she said. 'It'll be like our own Horse of the Year Show!'

'Especially when I come flying off and land at your feet!' Dorrie grinned, 'That'll be a real thrill for you!'

But she wasn't really afraid of falling, as she mounted the bay gelding that she had ridden for the last three years. After her mother's death on the hunting field, Dorrie had been terrified at the thought of riding, let alone jumping, but in the bleakness of her misery and the anguish of feeling that her mother had died without ever really caring for her, she had set herself, not merely to ride and jump, but to do it better and more bravely than anyone else. Partly she had succeeded. If she had been single-minded enough to achieve that extra degree of concentration needed, she would have been unbeatable, but, somehow, because she was Dorrie St James and didn't give a damn, even riding became an accomplishment to be shrugged at and cast aside for long periods of time.

She was good, though. Even Beatrice's and Ben's untutored eyes could appreciate the grace and fluidity of movement as girl and horse went round the paddock like one creature. The gelding, Hentzau, was a genius at jumping, never refusing, and taking off with impeccable timing, as though he was bound for the moon. He had the breeding and the ability to be an international show-jumper, but, like Dorrie, every so often he would lose concentration or seem to become bored, and deliberately knock every fence with a trailing hind hoof. But today he gave a world class exhibition, flying over the hurdles as though they had been six feet high and seeming to be inspired by the shrill cheers of the children. Ben, who had always considered riding to be rather sissy, gazed enraptured at Dorrie's flying figure and wondered if he could possibly take private lessons and then amaze everyone with his skill and daring.

Dorrie, coming full-tilt down the paddock for a final soaring leap, saw the Cavallos' BMW coming up the long drive from the main gates and raised a hand to greet Sarah as she arrived. Hentzau took the hurdle like a champion, and Dorrie pulled up and dismounted, laughing and bowing to her young audience. Then the laughter died, and the colour ebbed from her face and flowed painfully back again. It was not Sarah, but Ross Cavallo who was getting out of the car. She swallowed, tried and failed to speak, and her hand moving convulsively on the

161

reins made Hentzau snort and toss his head so that she was able to turn and soothe him, patting his nose with a hand that shook.

The children were leaping about their father, both talking at once, trying to cram everything they had done into one long, involved sentence. He bent his dark head, listening to them, smiling faintly, until Dorrie approached leading her horse and he looked up.

'Sarah's not very well, I'm afraid,' he said, rather formally, 'so I came instead.'

'What's wrong with Mummy?' Beatrice asked anxiously, and Ross tousled her hair gently, his hand resting on her thin child's neck.

'Don't worry, pet – it's nothing serious. But I told her to stay in bed today.'

'I'm sorry – about Sarah,' Dorrie said, 'but you needn't have rushed down to fetch them today – they could have stayed longer.'

'Thank you. They have to go back to school tomorrow. And I'm sure you've had quite enough.'

'No – I've loved having them,' Dorrie said, miserably. Why did they have to talk like strangers? Why did he have to speak to her in that cool, detached way, hardly glancing at her?

'You'll have lunch?' she said, 'I expect it's almost ready.'

He hesitated, on the point of refusing, then, with a slight inclination of the head, 'Thank you,' he said, 'it's very kind of you.'

'Dorrie – can we put the horses away?' Beatrice asked, importantly. Dorrie glanced over at the house and saw Lambert the groom, outside the stable-yard.

'Of course. Get Sid to give you a hand. And you can

162

get a couple of apples from Mrs Duffy if you go to the kitchen door.'

Beatrice and Ben, visibly swollen with pride, led Hentzau and Bracken the pony carefully the couple of hundred yards to the stables where Lambert, grinning cheerfully, instructed them in the use of the dandy brush.

'Would you – would you like to come in?' Dorrie felt stiff and awkward. What a fool she was being – what a fool love was making of her. If it had been Jack Larcombe or Tariq el Said, she would not have been at a loss for words. She never had to think before she spoke, and there were few people who could say they had had the better of a verbal exchange with her, but this quiet man with the dark, strained-looking eyes had reduced her to the conversational level of an adolescent.

They walked back to the house, side by side, but a couple of feet apart, and Ross made some appropriate comment on the Elizabethan architecture and the beauty of the mellow stone. There were shallow steps to the porch, where the huge oak door stood open in most weathers, and inside there was grey stone and a couple of pairs of antlers, an indefinable smell of dog and boots and antiquity. Floss, the old spaniel, looked up from her slumbers as they came past, and thumped her tail briefly in greeting.

There was a vast reception room, a sort of Great Hall, with much oak panelling and bookshelves and even, Ross was amused to see, a suit of armour standing in an alcove.

'One of your ancestors, I suppose,' he said to Dorrie, breaking the silence between them, and was relieved to see the strained expression on her face lighten.

'I'm afraid not,' she said. 'In fact, I bought it in a junk shop in Twickenham and I don't think it dates back much before the nineteenth century. My father was furious with

163

me, but I told him he couldn't have a stately home without at least one suit of armour. Now he's got quite fond of it, and calls it Sir Tinplate.'

There was a huge fireplace, surmounted by armorial bearings carved in stone, where what looked like a small tree was smouldering, but the room was fairly chilly.

'We don't sit in here,' Dorrie said, 'there are far too many draughts. Through here.'

She opened a door and preceded him into a smaller room where the panelling was white-painted and the chairs and curtains were a pale William Morris print in green and cream. It was warm, with a bright log fire burning and the south-facing windows catching the late morning sun.

'Do sit down,' Dorrie said. 'Will you have some sherry before lunch?'

He did not sit, but turned to stare out of the window, hands in pockets. He was not looking at her, but he could still see her in his mind, with her golden hair tied back in a knot for riding, her sweater of scarlet cashmere outlining her bosom, which was full without being heavy, and her fawn jodhpurs emphasizing the long, slender line of her legs. His face was expressionless, but Ross Cavallo was cursing himself for having come.

'Ross?' She used his name for the first time, her voice hesitant. The children would be in soon, then they would have lunch and say goodbye, still as strangers. She felt she could not bear it. 'Ross – why did you come?'

For a moment she thought he would not answer. He stared out of the window at the wooded hills and green fields that lay placidly beneath the autumn sun. In the silence, the crackling of the logs on the hearth seemed suddenly loud, and a robin sang a brief snatch of melody outside the window. He turned at last and faced her, meeting her eyes for the first time, and as she saw the hunger in his expression, Dorrie's heart began to pound heavily.

'I came because I had to,' he said, slowly, 'because Sarah wasn't well and asked me to. I came because I couldn't stay away. That's what you wanted to hear, isn't it?'

'No,' Dorrie whispered. 'No. I know you won't believe me – but – I don't want you to be unhappy, Ross. And – I like Sarah, and the children. I couldn't bear to hurt them. I know you think I'm hard as nails . . .'

'Oh, Dorrie – I wish you were. If you could have stayed as you seemed when I first met you, I'd have been safe. It was only when I saw the lost child beneath the tough exterior that I – that I – '

'Yes?'

'No – don't make me say it. We won't speak of it any more. I was a fool to come, I suppose – but I shall soon be gone. Shall we go and find the children?'

'Yes – no – I – ' She half-turned as if to go, her hands making a little blind gesture of defeat and despair, and Ross felt his heart contract with an almost physical pain.

'Wait – don't go,' he said softly, and, stepping forward, he took her deliberately into his arms and held her, close-wrapped, against himself, his cheek resting on her hair. 'Dear, dearest Dorrie,' he whispered, 'don't be sad and hurt. You must understand – it's not that I don't – don't want you – but – I can't cheat Sarah. She's had so much terrible misery in her life – and yet she's come through it with no bitterness, nothing twisted about her. I love her, Dorrie – she's my wife and the mother of my children – and at the moment she's not well. How could I risk hurting her?'

Her face against his chest, Dorrie nodded dumbly, not

165

trusting herself to speak. She knew that everything he said was true, and that if Sarah and the children were hurt, she and Ross would end up hating and despising each other. She knew and accepted it – but at the same time she wanted to stay there, in the sweet comfort of his arms for ever.

'And at the same time,' Ross went on, 'I won't cheat you either, Dorrie. You deserve more than a half-life of snatched embraces. You need a husband and children of your own, and I won't have you hanging about waiting for me to leave Sarah. It won't happen, my dear – ever. God knows why I was such an idiot as to come near you today – but it won't happen again if I can help it. Do you understand?'

She nodded again, pressing herself closer to him, her arms tightening round him, and as she turned her face up to him, he could see the thick gold lashes of her closed eyes were damp with held-back tears.

'Oh, God,' Ross said. He bent his head and kissed her, softly, gently, tasting the sweet, salt velvet of the lovely mouth, feeling her lips part beneath his own, her tongue twining with his in a tantalizing imitation of the act of love.

It was a moment that seemed both endless and instant. Neither of them knew how long they stood there, crushed against each other, their embrace as desperate a leave-taking as though the world was to end. All thought and reason were suspended so that there seemed to be only their two bodies, aware of each other in every tingling cell.

The children's voices, and their footsteps on the polished oak floor of the next room awakened them from a sort of trance. With a gasp Dorrie freed herself and turned away, and when Beatrice and Ben came in, she was pouring sherry, the bottle clinking against the edge of the crystal glass and wine spilling unheeded on the marquetry tulip-wood table.

Lunch-time conversation was conducted only with the aid of the children, and neither of the adults was able to do much justice to Mrs Duffy's excellent meal. Even afterwards, when they were alone again, Beatrice and Ben having gone to fetch their cases and to bid a last farewell to the horses, their talk over the coffee was of impersonal things. They avoided intimacy as though they had awakened old wounds in each other.

Ross lit another cigarette and inhaled the smoke deeply. He tapped ash off the end and stared at the glowing tip, frowning in concentration.

'You're a friend of Johnny Pacelli, aren't you?' he asked abruptly.

'I know him.' Dorrie's voice was defensive, as though she suspected a rebuke.

Ross smiled briefly. 'It's only that he seems to have been losing a lot of money lately – I wondered if he could afford it.'

'I don't know. I would have said not, because he's always whingeing about not getting a fair deal from his record company. There was talk of him suing them, or his manager or something. I don't know – I don't see him a lot, you know.'

'Good. I can't stand the fellow.'

'Ross – you can't – ' she stopped, biting her lip, and he crushed his half-smoked cigarette into the ashtray with a savage movement.

'I know. I can't dictate to you who you go out with. I've no right. Don't worry – I'm not going to start interfering in your love affairs – that would take more bloody cheek than even I am capable of.'

167

He spoke bitterly, and she didn't answer, sitting in silence until the children returned.

They were exuberant in their thanks, begging her to come and see them as soon as she got back to town, and hugging her as though she were a beloved elder sister. She and Ross did not shake hands, did not even speak. 'Goodbye' would have been too painful.

Dorrie had planned to stay at Ash Friars for a week or two, but that evening, when Lady Susan Ascham called on her about the Hunt Ball, having got wind of her presence, she was nowhere to be found. The empty rooms, made emptier by Ross's brief presence, had proved too much for her and she had gone back to London.

6

'Cy! You must get rid of Waldo-Horlicks for the weekend. I want to go to Paris, and you must come, too.'

'Sorry, kiddo! This weekend is spoken for! Ask one of your raunchy male friends – I'm sure any of them would be delighted.'

'Oh – don't be dreary! What can you be doing that's more fun than going to Paris? I'm treating you, you nit!'

'Still sorry, I'm afraid. Dorrie – when will you realize that airily saying "I'll pay!" doesn't automatically solve all problems? This weekend I'm going to Greenham Common. We're joining hands round the perimeter fence.'

'Oh, bloody useful that'll be!' Dorrie said, resentfully, 'Then you're going to sing "Ring a Roses" I expect?'

'Don't be cheap, Dorrie,' Cy said, peering in the mirror as she applied make-up to her eyes. 'If there was any other way of expressing what we feel is right, we'd do it. What would you do?'

'Oh, don't ask me,' Dorrie said, irritably, kicking a pair of shoes across the room, 'Blow up the whole bloody Government, I suppose.'

'You would,' Cy said, flicking a brush at her hair. 'Why do I always look like something from the Battersea Dog's Home? But the point is, it has to be a peaceful demonstration, you twerp. Anyway – why this sudden urge to fly off to Paris – I thought your sex-life seemed rather varied and interesting at the moment, with Arab princes and what not?'

'Oh, screw the Arab princes,' Dorrie said, 'and you too, Cy. I hope you get raped by the entire US air force.'

'I should be so lucky,' Cy said, but Dorrie had gone, flinging into her room and slamming the door.

Cy stared at her own reflection in the mirror, owl-eyed with astonishment. 'Curiouser and curiouser,' she murmured.

After a moment, she went and tapped on Dorrie's door, then opened it. Dorrie was lying on her bed, not weeping, but with an expression of such clenched misery that Cy was alarmed.

'Dorrie? Listen – I have to dash, or I'll be late for work – we'll work something out about the weekend. Don't worry, kid. I suppose you wouldn't like to come to Greenham with me?'

'All right,' Dorrie said, listlessly, and to Cy's surprise, 'I might as well. It'll be an experience, I suppose.'

It was a bleak day. The icy November wind whipped a thin rain across Greenham Common and into the faces of the women huddled there. Some of them had been there all night, dozing in makeshift tents except when they were wakened by sudden raids. Then they had to stumble sleepily on to the public footpaths from which they could not, by law, be evicted. Any tents or possessions left would be smashed or taken away, and when this happened the women mostly said nothing, some of them looking as apathetic as women in concentration camps, and only the occasional cry of "Bastard!" cutting through the night air, thin and eerie as an owl's cry.

Cy and Dorrie had come on a coach with forty-four other women. Dorrie had wanted to drive down, but Cy had insisted that that would be contrary to the whole spirit of the thing.

'Besides,' she added, practically, 'you don't realize how much hatred the Peace Movement arouses. You wouldn't want your lovely car smashed up, would you?'

'Aren't you exaggerating a bit? I don't see people like Lady Olga Maitland kicking in the headlights with their bovver boots. Never mind – we shall join the proletariat for the day, comrade Cy, if that's what you want. Am I allowed Brie in my sandwiches, or must it be Spam?'

It was all so bloody futile, Dorrie thought crossly, pulling the collar of her old Burberry closer round her neck. And, since she was sure that she was the only person present to think so, it made her feel even more of a fraud and an outsider. They were hanging around, waiting for everyone to turn up. There were a few sporadic outbursts of singing, and some thin cheers when Bruce Kent put in an appearance. There was a police presence, but, for the moment at least, they were keeping a low profile and nothing exciting seemed likely to happen. Was this how governments were toppled, Dorrie wondered, by dogged, rain-soaked crowds standing in quiet ranks to protest? It would not be Dorrie's way. She would have a lot more of what the Americans called pazazz. She would make the bomb-makers sit up and sweat. She would – a woman beside her was offering her a thermos cup of coffee.

'Thanks,' Dorrie said. 'Is it always as slow-moving as this?'

'Mm,' the woman smiled, showing crooked teeth in a plump, cheerful face, 'It's like what they used to say about the trenches – something like ninety-nine per cent boredom and one per cent sheer bloody terror! Your first time here, is it? My name's Sally Peters.'

'Hallo. I'm Dorrie. You're an old inhabitant, I gather?'

'Oh, yes. I've been coming for three years now. I used

to camp a lot, but the old man was getting a bit fed up, so I just come odd weekends. Specially now I'm expecting.' She patted the curve of her stomach and grinned again at Dorrie, 'You married?'

'No.'

'Sensible girl – hang on to your freedom while you can! My Terry's always grumbling – says it's a waste of time and so on. He can be a right pain. But I tell him, if no one does anything, well, we might as well be extinct already, d'you know what I mean? Oh, sod it – here come some of those Rage people. Turn your back or start singing or something – they soon get fed up.'

A little way along the perimeter fence, a small knot of people was moving slowly towards them. The central figure was a woman of about thirty in well-cut tweeds, who was using a loud-hailer with an unpractised hand to direct her plummy accents at the crowd. A man was holding an umbrella over her expensively coiffed head.

'And you really are a disgrace to our sex,' Dorrie heard, as the group came nearer, interspersed with odd whoops and whines from the loud-hailer. 'You are making the most ghastly mess of our environment, and I really don't see why we, the residents, should have to put up with you. Some of you must have husbands and children – your place is with them, not making a nuisance of yourselves and costing the rate-payers . . . *Dorrie St James!*' Her last words, coming in a loud shriek over the amplifier, made dozens of women peer curiously. Dorrie stared blandly and wiggled her fingers in salute. 'Hi, Chloe. What a lovely surprise! Have you had any lessons on that thing or are you playing it by ear?'

Chloe Pemberton fumbled hastily to turn off her loud-hailer.

'Dorrie – what on *earth* are you doing here?' she said,

breathlessly, 'I mean – is it a joke or something?' Chloe's lack of humour was so legendary that she was always mortally afraid of missing the point, and her constant query was 'Is it a joke?'

Dorrie grinned nastily. 'I bet you'll say that when you're being blown sky-high, Chloe: "I say – is this some sort of joke?" No, actually, it's not a joke. But you are, rather, with your little band of Storm-troopers and your exhortations. Why don't you go home and do some more macramé work for the next Conservative bazaar?'

'Well really, Dorrie – I don't know what Sir Anthony would think of this – I mean, these people are hardly your class, are they? Some of them – ' she lowered her voice dramatically, 'some of them are *lesbians*!'

'You're speaking from your own personal experience are you, Chloe, my dear old dyke?'

'*Dorrie!* How dare you! You're disgusting!'

'So are you. Now fuck off.' Dorrie turned her back, shoved her hands in her pockets and began to whistle piercingly, and the women on either side of her giggled. Chloe went scarlet and made gobbling noises in her throat, then retired in confusion, followed by ironic cheers. Dorrie felt a bit ashamed. It was so easy to score points off Chloe that it was a bit like baby-bashing. Besides, the woman was only acting according to her beliefs, which was more than Dorrie could claim to be doing. She stopped whistling and sighed, half-inclined to go home. Her jeans were damp and clammy and she had no idea where Cy had got to. What a lunatic scheme it had been. If she hadn't been feeling so bloody miserable about Ross, she would never have agreed to come. Still, at least when Sarah had rung to invite her for Sunday lunch, Dorrie had been able to claim a prior engagement.

There was no way she was going to be drawn into the circle of the Cavallo family again.

'Come on,' Sally Peters said, 'we're joining hands now.'

Obediently, Dorrie moved forward to the wire fence and linked her hands with the hundreds of other women that surrounded it. Someone started singing 'We Shall Overcome', and the sound swelled up, rose and fell on the bitter, unresponsive air.

Dorrie was suddenly, ridiculously moved and swallowed fiercely at the lump in her throat. She felt for a moment that she was part of something that was greater than all these individual ordinary women, a sort of communal spirit that must have moved people like the suffragettes. Then Sally Peters said, 'Right, give me a leg-up, Dorrie! This is where I make my final gesture!'

'What the hell are you doing?'

The pregnant woman was clawing at the mesh of the fence, clambering awkwardly up it like some odd species of mammal.

'I'm climbing over the top,' she gasped, 'I shan't be back for a while, so I'll give them something to remember Sally Peters!'

'Don't be such a bloody fool,' Dorrie said, 'You'll hurt yourself!'

Quite a number of other women were scrambling up the fence with varying degrees of success, and the police, who had been only a brooding presence in the background, moved forward.

'Come on down, Sally,' Dorrie urged, 'the police are coming.'

'Not much further. If I can just reach the top . . .' she was gasping for breath and straining upwards as though it was a mountain she was climbing. A policeman came up.

174

He looked young and his expression was a mixture of boredom and nervousness.

'Come on, out of that,' he said, laconically. Sally reached the top and hung there, her swollen body heavy. She put a hand through the wire to support her weight and panted for a moment. 'All right, I'm coming.'

'Well, look sharp, then!' The policeman reached out and tugged at one of the woman's legs and she shrieked, her other leg kicking out for a foothold and catching the man's helmet so that it slipped sideways on his head.

'You stupid bitch!' he shouted, grabbing her by the legs and pulling violently, and Sally's shriek became a scream of pain as her hand, caught in the wire fence, twisted, and the wrist broke. For a moment she struggled, trying to ease the pain, her body ungainly, jerking like a puppet, then she fainted, her hand was wrenched free and she fell heavily at Dorrie's feet.

'You sodding *bastard*!' Dorrie shouted. She hit the policeman in the face as hard as she could, aware in an odd flash of surprise that she had skinned her knuckles badly against his teeth. As he turned on her, his face contorted with anger and pain, she followed up her advantage by kneeing him in the groin. He doubled up, clutching himself and Dorrie regarded him with satisfaction. 'And I hope your balls turn black and blue and drop off,' she said. Some of the other women had gathered round Sally Peters and seemed to be administering first aid. There was nothing Dorrie could do there, except get in the way. She decided she had had enough. It had been a stupid, useless day, and part of the stupidity was she hadn't even brought enough money to take a train or a taxi home. She would have to wait for the special coach with Cy. Hunching her shoulders against the rain and pulling down the brim of her ancient trilby, Dorrie set off to hitch back to London, but she had only taken half a dozen strides before a loud male voice in her ear said, 'Hey! You!'

'Fuck off,' Dorrie said, not even looking round.

'You're under arrest.'

'Oh, shit,' said Dorrie.

The magistrates' court was a mixture of Gothic chill and modern strip-lighting. Dorrie, feeling grubby, jaded and resentful after a night in police cells, blinked under the fluorescent glare as she was ushered into the dock by a policewoman. Her case was one of the last of the morning, after batches of peace women had been dealt with and summarily fined or sent to prison, and she had been furious, as she waited in the ante-room, to see her father's solicitor approaching her.

'What are you doing here?' she muttered angrily, as Mr Strasek of Strasek and Whitby, picked his way towards her, dainty as a cat.

'Good morning, Miss St James – I'll be brief because we haven't much time. A pity you didn't contact us yesterday – your friend, Miss Coram, was unable to get in touch with your father until this morning. However, we'll see what we can do.'

'You can bugger off, if you like,' Dorrie said, sprawling back on the bench with her feet stuck out in front of her and her hands in her pockets. The policewoman beside her tutted in reproof. 'I mean it – I didn't contact you because I don't want anyone, and when I see bloody Cy again I'll wring her neck.'

Mr Strasek smiled pleasantly. He looked like a cat, and like a cat was always unsurprised.

'Miss St James,' he said, 'you must realize the seriousness of this charge – assaulting a police officer – you could be sent to prison.'

'He wasn't a police officer – he was a member of the SS – and he attacked a pregnant woman and probably broke her wrist. If they want me to say sorry for kicking him in the crutch, I'll spit in their eyes. So you can take your brief, dear Mr Strasek, and shove it . . .'

The solicitor's face was still bland as he made a few notes. 'Fortunately for you, my dear young lady, I am acting on your father's instructions, not yours. I should like you to plead "Not Guilty", and I will endeavour, in the limited time available, and without a hope of calling witnesses, to make a case for you.'

He had extracted a few grudging details from Dorrie and taken his leave, still calmly smiling, and now here he was, popping up in court like a bloody Jack-in-the-box, and claiming to represent her. She took the oath in a sullen monotone, glowering about her and noticing with irritated boredom that the magistrate, one Colonel de Freitas, was a friend of her father. He looked as bored as she did and was obviously miles away, not even bothering to look up at her, his thin face bent over a complicated doodle in front of him.

The police prosecutor was speaking: 'Is your name Dorian Caroline Victoria de l'Isle St James?' he intoned, stumbling a bit, and the Colonel's baldish head came up as though jerked by string.

'Yes,' Dorrie said, wondering where they'd dredged that lot up.

'And do you reside at No. 4, Petrie Mansions, Randolph Gardens, London NW6, and also at Ash Friars Manor, Lower Poltenay, Devon?'

'Yes.' Old de Freitas was regarding her with something like alarm.

'It is alleged that on the twelfth of November, you did . . .' he droned on, cataloguing Dorrie's crime of striking the poor defenceless policeman, and getting into slight difficulties when describing where she had hurt him the most. There was only one witness, the policeman himself, and Dorrie noticed with regret that he was walking quite normally. His upper lip, however, was undoubtedly swollen, although, on the whole, Dorrie thought perhaps her bruised and skinned knuckles had come off the worst. The prosecutor was quoting her words in a flat, dispassionate voice, 'And then the accused remarked, Your Honour, "I hope your balls turn black and blue and drop off."'

De Freitas was seen to close his eyes briefly. Dorrie felt an inappropriate desire to giggle.

Strasek got up then, urbane and unhurried. He had done a lot of work in the short time available, and was able to give details of Sally Peters's injury and the fact that she had been admitted to hospital the night before and had given birth to a premature child. Obviously a major scandal was brewing. His client, a susceptible and tender-hearted girl, who had come to Greenham Common for the first time at the instigation of a friend, had been panic-stricken and horrified, and had struck out in the heat of the moment. He asked the court to take into account his client's previously good character, her extreme youth and so on and so forth.

Colonel de Freitas summed up, quietly and rapidly, without meeting Dorrie's eyes. He told her what a serious offence assaulting a police officer was, and what a disgrace it was that a member of such an old and respected family should bring her name into such disrepute, and should behave in such an unladylike way. He then fined her five hundred pounds and bound her over to keep the peace. The usher asked the court to rise, and de Freitas made his escape while Strasek came over to Dorrie purring quietly.

178

'I think I got you off quite lightly,' he said, offering Dorrie his hand, which she ignored.

'That's what you're paid for, isn't it?' she said, turning away and pushing through the people by the door. There were photographers outside, and somebody from the *Sun* shouted, 'Hey, Dorrie! Give us a smile!' She would have been tempted to give him a rude sign instead if she hadn't been sure that was just what he wanted. A woman from the *Guardian* approached and asked her if she would be continuing to support the Greenham women, and would she care to do an in-depth interview with Polly Toynbee? Dorrie gave a blunt 'No' to both queries, and continued to push her way out, cameras flashing and whirring on all sides.

'Dorian!'

With a feeling of heart-felt relief, she saw the tall figure of her father, and felt an absurd desire to burst into tears and fling herself at him. He took her firmly by the arm and piloted her out of the crowd, parrying the reporters with an ease and urbanity born of long practice, as he opened the passenger door of his Rolls and ushered Dorrie inside.

'Sir Anthony – can you tell us please what your feelings are about your daughter's activities?' called a young woman reporter with earnest horn-rims.

'I think they have been greatly exaggerated, my dear,' Sir Anthony said, and, raising his hat politely, he got into the car and drove off.

'Thanks, Dad,' Dorrie said, in a small voice, huddling down in the seat. Then neither of them spoke again for a few miles, until Dorrie noticed the direction they were taking.

'You're going the wrong way.'

'No. I'm going home.'

'But . . .' Dorrie subsided. Her father was a kind and indulgent man, but she knew that particular set of the jaw well enough not to argue. Besides, a few days in the quiet of Ash Friars would not be unwelcome. She felt weary and bruised in spirit by the events of the last days. She would retire and lick her wounds, take the dogs for walks, ride Hentzau, perhaps do some hunting. With a sudden relief that the ordering of her life had been taken out of her hands, and weary from the wakeful night in the police cells, her eyes closed and, lulled by the soft purr of the engine, she fell asleep.

Sir Anthony glanced at his only child and drew a breath that was almost a sigh. What a wayward creature she was. And yet, he supposed the fault had been with himself and with Antonia – Dorian had been indulged too much, without having the real, caring attention she had needed. For himself, he had always loved the little girl, but his wife had been such a demanding partner, needing, or seeming to need, his mind, body and soul in full measure, twenty-four hours a day. She had seen Dorian, he knew, only as an accessory to her own beauty, or another perfect accomplishment by the lovely Antonia St James. And he – yes, he had to admit it, even though it was a bitter admission, he had allowed her to get away with it, besotted as he had been by her. Even now, six years after her death, he sometimes woke in the night aching for the feel of her long, smooth limbs entwined with his, her generous breasts warm against his body. Sir Anthony allowed himself a brief, wry smile as he thought how astonished Dorian would be if she knew what human feelings were harboured in her father's breast. In common with most of her generation she would think that physical passion was out of place, even unseemly, at the age of sixty, and she certainly knew nothing of the discreet little

180

pied-à-terre in Chelsea where her father visited a quiet, dignified woman of forty-two and was comforted in the flesh, if not the spirit.

There was much that they did not know about each other, Sir Anthony reflected, for they both had an inner core of secrecy, although Dorian hid hers beneath a façade of brashness and vivacity, while his was at the centre of a reserved though urbane exterior. But he did love her, and very deeply, this child-woman who lay sleeping at his side, her full mouth parted a little, her eyes with faint shadows beneath the thick, gold lashes. As he glanced down again, he saw her lips move as though silently calling someone's name, and then her mouth curved downwards as though, still sleeping, she wept.

They stopped for coffee and sandwiches at a pub near Taunton, and by three o'clock they were driving through the village of Lower Poltenay and turning into the long driveway that led to Ash Friars. The banked rhododendrons and azaleas on either side of the drive were dark and forbidding in the early November twilight. Even her beloved Ash Friars looked grey and ghost-ridden and Dorrie wished she had refused to come.

'Why on earth did we come down?' she said, grumpily, shivering as she got out of the warmth of the car into the chilly afternoon, 'You know it's absolute hell at this time of year.'

'We came,' Sir Anthony said, taking her arm and guiding her firmly towards the main door, 'because I thought perhaps it was time to remind you of one or two things. Let's start here.'

They stopped just outside the porch and he directed her gaze upward with a firm hand beneath her chin, to the family arms, carved in the lichened stone above the threshold.

'"Amor et Servitium" – "Love and Service",' said Sir Anthony, 'Does it mean anything to you, Dorian?'

'I do my best,' Dorrie said, lightly.

'Don't be flippant, my dear,' Sir Anthony's voice was wintry, 'At best, it's childish. That motto was adopted by the St James family in the reign of Henry the Seventh – as I need hardly tell you. For the past five hundred years we have upheld a tradition of love and service to our country. St James men have fought – against the Armada, against Napoleon, in the Crimea – your own grandfather was killed in the First World War, and I myself, as you know, served in the Second.'

Dorrie hunched her shoulders against the wind, looking rebellious.

'I know all that, Daddy. Look – can't we continue this trip down memory lane inside? It's bl – it's *rather* cold.'

Sir Anthony opened the door just as Ramsden the butler hurried towards it.

'Sir Anthony – Miss St James – you're a little earlier than we anticipated, sir. There's a good fire in the small drawing room – would you care for some tea there?'

'Thank you, Ramsden. That would be splendid. How are you? Well, I hope?'

'Yes, indeed, Sir Anthony.' Ramsden helped his employer with hat and coat as smoothly and adroitly as though he had worked in a men's outfitters, which in fact, he once had. 'And I trust you and Miss Dorian are in your usual good health?'

He was so smooth, Dorrie thought, shrugging out of the old Burberry before Ramsden could help her, so very polished that, if you tried to scratch the dapper, immaculately groomed surface, your fingers would slip off as though from gleaming plastic. She smiled sweetly at the man and wondered how he would react if she said,

'Ramsden, I'm randy as hell!' She wouldn't mind betting that his face would not flicker. He was only about thirty, but he seemed to have as much hot blood as a robot.

Ramsden took Dorrie's coat, and behind his impassive exterior, he observed as closely as possible the curve of her full breasts beneath her jumper and the round taut-ness of the buttocks beneath her jeans. A tasty bit of stuff, all right, was Miss Dorrie, and he wouldn't mind giving her one – but he had seen one or two colleagues tempted in that way, and they'd had their marching orders pretty quickly. This place was too cushy to jeopardize. He'd stick to his fantasies and the cosy embraces of Tom Priddle's daughter in the village. He opened doors and saw Sir Anthony and Dorrie installed beside the fire in the small drawing-room, then went to arrange about tea. When he had gone, Sir Anthony returned to the attack.

'What I am trying to say, Dorian, is – '

'I *know* what you're trying to say, Daddy – I'm not a fool. Noblesse oblige and all that crap – sorry, rubbish . . .'

Dorrie flung herself off her chair and knelt by the hearth, poking vigorously at the fire until a shower of sparks roared up the chimney.

'You'll set the chimney on fire,' Sir Anthony remarked calmly. 'Yes, I know it's fashionable to sneer and to think that serving one's country is a silly, out-moded idea. But it is an idea that has kept Britain great for many hundred years, and the lack of it is, I feel, at the root of some of our present troubles.'

'Oh, Lord. I'm not going to start a political argument. I *could* say that those women at Greenham Common were serving their country more whole-heartedly than the self-seeking politicians you support, but . . .'

'No doubt you could. And no doubt in some cases you

would be right. I'm not talking about that. I'm talking about the way you, the representative of our family, have behaved. Attacking a policeman and using language I should scarcely expect to hear from a docker. You can mock, Dorian, but – look at this, for example – ' He indicated a water-colour of a middle-aged Queen Victoria, with the inscription by Her Majesty, 'To my good friend Hilary St James, in recognition of his services to his country.' 'You see, my dear – no matter what you say, people like us *matter*. What we say and do is noted, not just by monarchs and nobles but by the ordinary man in the street. You, especially – I don't have to flatter you, you know you're an exceptionally good-looking young woman, and you have what I believe is called charisma. Your example is no doubt followed by countless young women who read about your doings in newspapers and magazines. What do you suppose the headlines in the popular press will say tomorrow?'

Dorrie's head was bowed, her tangle of bright hair hiding the expression on her face.

'I'm sorry, Father,' she whispered, 'I know I've been a disappointment to you . . .'

'No . . .' Sir Anthony reached out a hand to caress his daughter's hair, then withdrew it, too much inhibited by public school, army and breeding to tell her how dearly he loved her.

There was a discreet rattle from the tea-trolley outside the door.

'I don't want any tea,' Dorrie said, in a muffled voice, 'I'm going up to see Nanny Harding.'

She pushed past Ramsden and the tea-trolley and took the polished oak stairs two at a time, then ran along the broad, panelled corridor to the nursery wing which was now a self-contained flat for Nanny Harding. She had been Lady Antonia's nanny, and then Dorrie's, as much a part of the family as if she had been born into it, and she looked up from her quiet cup of tea with love and welcome in her face as Dorrie burst into the room.

'Oh, Nanny,' Dorrie cried, just as though she were six years old again and had fallen off her pony, 'Oh, Nanny – I'm so miserable . . .'

'There, there, lovey,' Nanny Harding stretched out her arms, wincing a little because they had got very rheumaticky, 'there, there, my pet. Come and tell Nanny all about it.'

The *Sun* headline was as bad as Dorrie had expected. Beside a front-page photo of herself looking, she thought, like a street-walking Cindy doll, was the caption ' "I hope they drop off!" says playgirl Dorrie!'

She didn't bother to read the rest, but returned his paper to Lambert, who received it with a sympathetic grin.

'For God's sake, don't let my father see that, Sid!'

'Don't worry, Miss Dorrie! I should forget about 'un, my dear! 'Twon't be long till 'tis all forgotten. Why don't you take old Hentzau out – he'm grown fat and lazy. Time you come back, Sir Anthony'll've forgotten the morning paper, like as not. I'll get 'un tacked up for 'ee.'

'Okay, Sid. Though I don't think he'll forget it in a hurry – even if *The Times* is too polite to mention it. I shall have to keep a very low profile for quite a few weeks, I think.'

7

November blew away on a gust of icy wind; the Christmas lights were turned on by an American soap-opera star; and the streets of London were filled with frantic shoppers. In the House of Commons, Members were beginning to think about the Christmas recess, and the Whips were sometimes hard-pressed to keep enough Members on hand to make up a quorum. The Prime Minister's popularity was on the wane again, and there was talk of an early General Election. Jack Larcombe was present at the Commons on most days, but his private life now occupied rather more of his thoughts than his public one, and though he spoke on several occasions and to quite good effect, and was a member of a Select Committee, he was conscious that the fire in his belly was fuelled more by Natasha Troy's lovemaking than by his former desire to serve his fellow-man. Not that Natasha tried to distract him from his work – on the contrary, it seemed as though she was possessed of a driving ambition for him, and sometimes she would want to sit and discuss the doings of the House when all Jack wanted to do was to go to bed. He was not in love with Natasha. He was in love, as much as ever, with Dorrie St James, and on the few occasions that she summoned him, he abandoned Natasha with absolutely no compunction. But, there was no doubt, the quiet little secretary was the best lay he had ever had. She was amazingly erotic, unendingly inventive in bed and out of it, although her sexuality was generally concealed beneath her tailored suits and her owlish glasses, at least when she was at work. Sometimes, however, especially if she thought Jack's interest in her was flagging, she deliberately sought to arouse him at work.

Once, sitting demurely beside him, apparently intent on her shorthand notebook, she took his hand and guided it beneath the severely cut skirt, and he found that she was wearing stockings, suspender belt and nothing more, and, as he explored the swelling, throbbing folds with his fingers, she reached out and unzipped his trousers, stroking and rubbing at his penis until it rose in a tense pillar and Jack groaned aloud.

'Oh, God – Natasha – what are you doing? What if someone comes?'

She smiled, seeming to find the thought stimulating rather than otherwise, and, getting up, she went calmly to the door of the office and locked it, then returned to him, her eyes greedily on his jutting erection. 'No one will come,' she said, quietly.

Jack felt ashamed. He was an MP, he told himself, elected by his constituents to represent them in Parliament, and not to use an office in the House of Commons for this frantic rutting. It was not adult or seemly – it was not even to be dignified by the name of lovemaking – it was a simple and basic gratification of the senses at its most animal level.

'No, Natasha,' he muttered, as she coolly pulled her skirt above her hips and he saw the white tops of her thighs above the stockings and, beneath the black silk of her suspender belt, the densely curling pubic hair and the moist pinkness of her vulva.

'Yes, Jack. Why not, Jack? I missed you last night.' She unfastened the front of her blouse and released her small, sharp-nippled breasts from their confinement, then, straddling his knees, she came down upon him very slowly, grasping his hard penis in her hand and guiding it into the slippery tight heat of her vagina. Jack gasped, bending forward and taking her breast in his mouth, sucking and teasing at the nipple until she, too, lost her calm, erotic enjoyment and moaned with ecstasy, driving herself down upon him as though she would impale herself. He grasped at her buttocks almost savagely, working her eager body up and down on himself mercilessly and without pause, and not much caring whether she obtained any pleasure or not. But, as always, the tumultuous spasm of her orgasm came at the very moment of his own ejaculation, her legs tightening convulsively around him as she muffled her exultant cry in his shoulder, lest any sound should echo down the august corridors of the Mother of Parliaments.

After a few moments, Jack pushed her away, disgusted with himself and with her, and feeling that he had reverted to the uncouth farm boy that he had thought was left far behind him. Natasha, calm and satisfied as a cream-fed cat, appeared not to notice his mood. She fetched a box of large, practical tissues from her bag and gave him a handful, cleaning herself neatly and without embarrassment before she unlocked the door again. Two minutes later it opened, and the Shadow Agricultural Minister, Henry Greaves, put his head round with a question about dairy production. He noticed the way Larcombe flushed and stammered, but put it down to the shyness of the new Member. The mousey little secretary was so much a part of the furniture that he did not notice her at all.

When Greaves had gone, Jack looked over at Natasha, now busy at her typewriter, and scowled.

'Look here, Natasha – in future we keep our private lives for after work. I mean – if we'd been caught then, I'd probably have been asked to resign – a lifetime's

188

struggle wasted for a – a quick screw! It doesn't bear thinking about.'

If Natasha was annoyed or resentful, she didn't show it. 'I'm sorry, Jack,' she murmured, 'Really – it won't happen again. I just – wanted you rather badly.'

His face softened and he bent over her shoulder and kissed the smooth top of her head. Her face was still a little flushed, he noticed, and she had fastened one of her blouse buttons in the wrong hole. This tiny imperfection in her usually immaculate exterior made Natasha seem suddenly rather touching and vulnerable to Jack.

'Tonight,' he said, gently, 'we'll go out for a meal, shall we? And then to the Olympus, if you like?'

'Oh, yes – thank you! That'd be lovely!' Natasha's face was radiant as a child's so that she looked almost pretty.

'And after that,' Jack said softly, 'we'll have the night together – in comfort.'

He had to leave shortly after, for a sitting of his Committee, which was investigating the administration of drugs to farm animals and the possible effect on human beings. Natasha finished her typing methodically, tidied the desk and prepared to return to the 'Pool'. She looked forward to the evening with mixed feelings. First, the meal. She would have liked to eat somewhere smart and trendy, with nouvelle cuisine or Greek or Italian, somewhere like Inigo Jones or Gavvers. But Jack – she shuddered slightly – he thought dining in style was a sitdown at the nearest Pizza parlour. Still – her role was not to educate his tastes – except his sexual ones – and she made herself seem always quiet and submissive except when they were in bed. The contrast was all the more piquant. As for the Olympus – she was a little concerned about that. So far Jack had only gambled quite small amounts, and she could tell from his tension and the tiny beads of sweat on his fresh complexion that he hated the thought of losing. And yet, he went back again and again, always to the Olympus, and Natasha wondered whether it was the gambling fever that had infected him, or if he simply went there in case Dorrie St James was there. Oh, yes, Natasha knew about Dorrie. She had guessed from Jack's face and voice the first time she heard him speaking on the phone to the girl, and when Dorrie had spoken to them at the Olympus, it was as obvious as though he was a fourteen-year-old boy, blushing and trembling in the throes of calf-love. Shrugging contemptuously, Natasha turned her thoughts to the final part of the evening's entertainment. Now that was something she looked forward to. Her tongue darted out and moistened her small, pale mouth as she contemplated it. Not that Jack Larcombe was the world's greatest lover – in fact, if it were not for Natasha's inventiveness, a quick five minutes in the missionary position would be all they ever achieved. But – she could use his body as one might use a musical instrument. It was pleasing and in its prime, the body of a countryman not yet grown soft with town living, even though the belly had begun to thicken slightly. He had broad shoulders and a smooth, solid chest, the skin tasting clean and slightly salty, strong, firm thighs and the sure hands of a man who has had much to do with animals, and the big, fleshy thrust of his penis gave Natasha more pleasure than any man she could remember. So, for the sake of that pleasure, and for her future plans, she was prepared to overlook his occasional bêtises and naïvetés, and the way his speech sometimes dropped into that irritating Somerset drawl. He was her raw material and, for Natasha Troy, approaching thirty and with unexceptional looks, the best she could hope for.

* * *

'What are you doing for Christmas, Dorrie?' Sarah Cavallo said. She had come into town for the day to do some Christmas shopping, and she and Dorrie were having coffee and pastries at Richoux in South Audley Street, surrounded by packages.

'Oh – I don't know. I haven't decided yet,' Dorrie said. 'I may go down to Ash Friars with Father, if he wants – but – it's been a bit dreary since my mother died. She used to make such a big thing about Christmas – masses of holly and stuff, a party for everyone in the village with presents off the tree, carol singers and mince pies and mulled wine – you know, all that sort of feudal thing.'

'It sounds marvellous. Don't you do that any more?'

'No. No – I can't be bothered. It would only seem like a pale imitation of Mother's Christmases, and I don't think Father would like it. He doesn't like Christmas very much now, anyway, and I think he'd be quite happy to stay in town, instead of having to keep up a sort of false bonhomie with me while we wander round Ash Friars like two ghosts of Christmas Past.'

Sarah leaned forward impulsively, her pinched-looking face suddenly animated above the dark fur of her coat: 'Come and have Christmas with *us*, Dorrie! Oh, do – the children would love it! They're always talking about you – we'd be so pleased to have you.'

Dorrie flinched and bent her head, very busily reducing a delicate pastry to crumbs with her silver cake fork. Christmas at the Cavallos'! Sitting opposite Ross at the dinner table, painfully aware of every passing expression on the beloved face, longing for, yet fearing, the slightest casual, passing touch of hand or body, the light-hearted kiss beneath the mistletoe, the eyes suddenly, helplessly seeking each other out. It was not to be borne.

'That's sweet of you, Sarah. I'd love to, but if Father

isn't keen on going to Devon, I've almost promised Tariq to join his party. He's cruising round the Caribbean – and I really am most awfully sick of British weather.'

'Oh – of course! That's marvellous – you *are* lucky!' Sarah said. 'Who wouldn't rather go on a cruise, especially at this time of year?'

I wouldn't, Dorrie said, silently. If I could wake up on Christmas morning with Ross beside me, I wouldn't want anything again as long as I live. But aloud she said, 'Yes – it will be fun. Several people I know are going. Mind you – it won't be very Christmassy – Tariq's a Muslim, I suppose, so he's not likely to be planning turkey and crackers.'

'Oh – that's a bit sad, isn't it,' Sarah said, sympathetically, 'missing all that side, I mean. I love the carols and the Christmas crib, and Midnight Mass on Christmas Eve.'

'I didn't know you were a Catholic,' Dorrie said.

'Oh, yes. I'm a convert – but Ross was brought up in the Church. His father was Italian, you know. Don't look so startled, Dorrie – we're not very holy Catholics! You look as though I was going to haul you off to confession or something!'

Dorrie forced a smile and began to gather packages together. 'Silly. I just didn't know, that's all.' And even if he was not a Catholic, she told herself fiercely, Ross would never divorce Sarah for me. It just makes it that tiny bit more impossible.

'Listen,' she said to Sarah, 'what about bringing the children to town before Christmas and I'll take them to a pantomime or something, and tea afterwards. Would they like that?'

'Would they?' Sarah smiled, 'You are sweet, Dorrie. They'd love it. I've been feeling so washed-out lately, I haven't been taking them anywhere, and all the Christmas preparations are giving me nightmares!'

'You should see a doctor,' Dorrie said, noticing suddenly how white and thin-faced Sarah was. 'Are you all right?'

'I'm fine, really. I've seen my doctor. Just old age creeping on, I expect. Come on – we'd better go. I still have to get something for Ross, and you must help me choose.'

8

The yacht 'Quaid' rocked quietly, like a gleaming white
sea bird with folded wings, its lovely lines perfectly
reflected in the blue waters of Marigot Bay. The gentle
trade wind blowing from Santa Lucia brought soft drifts
of scent from oleander, hibiscus and bougainvillea, mingled with a faint spiciness that was one of the characteris-
tics of the Caribbean.

Dorrie lounged, eyes closed, on a deck chair, blissfully
soaking up sun through skin that was already, after a
week, dark golden, in contrast with her hair that was
bleached almost silver. She wore the briefest bikini
bottom, her breasts bare and gilded by the sun till they
were like ripe, warm fruits.

Money, she reflected, was no guarantee of happiness,
but it certainly assured one of a fair amount of bodily
comfort in which to be unhappy. It had been the right
decision to join Tariq and his party for this cruise. It was
impossible to be miserable when one was surrounded by
beautiful lush scenery, the scents and sounds of the
Caribbean, the smiling black faces on the islands, the
surfeit of superb food and drink, and the continual
flattering attention from a handsome prince. London
seemed like a remote grey dream when viewed from this
technicolour brilliance, and she had made a real effort to
banish Ross Cavallo and his family from her thoughts.
Half-opening her eyes, Dorrie glanced at Tariq, dozing
beside her, slightly unfamiliar in bathing-trunks and without his 'egal', the white head-dress that he often wore

even with Western clothes. Here on his yacht, with only a select few of his usual retinue apart from the crew, the Arab seemed more relaxed and easy-going, less stiffly conscious of his wealth, his background and his position.

He was a magnificently built man, Dorrie thought, detachedly, broad-chested and slender-flanked. Almost all the other women in the party had their tongues hanging out for him, but he did not seem to have the least interest in any of them, apart from Dorrie, and that, she thought wryly, was probably because she had not succumbed to him.

Beyond Tariq, some of his other guests lounged, somnolent after a lavish lunch, some of the women completely naked.

'Does all this bare flesh offend you, Tariq?' Dorrie asked idly, 'I suppose, as a good Muslim, it must.'

He opened his eyes and turned towards her, leaning on one elbow, his dark eyes travelling the length of her body.

'Offend? No – I have seen too much of it. Most of it is neither more offensive nor exciting than the meat in a butcher's shop. But – when the flesh is *your* flesh, my dear, and is like a gilded lotus flower, then I find it very disturbing indeed.'

His white teeth glinted, contrasting with the blackness of his beard, and Dorrie grinned back at him, liking him more than she had in the past.

'I'm sorry I've been disturbing Your Highness,' she murmured, 'Perhaps if I were to put on a – what do you call those long white things?'

'A thaub? They are worn only by men. As an Arabian woman, you would wear an "abbaya" – a black covering over your dress, and of course, a "ghishwa" or veil – but I am afraid, Dorrie, that you would still contrive to look erotic even in these garments.'

'Thank you – if that's meant as a compliment! But I don't mean to tease you. Why should I?'

'Why indeed?' Tariq said, dryly. 'Would you like a drink?'

'Mm – thank you. How pig-like I'm getting. Lying around, guzzling and swilling drink – I shall be fat as a cow by the time we go home.'

Tariq stretched out his hand and ran it lightly over the line of her flat, golden stomach. 'I think not,' he said, quietly, and his hand moved almost imperceptibly down to where her bikini covered little more than her pubic hair. Dorrie fastened her fingers firmly but good-humouredly over his wrist.

'Just imagine I'm wearing my abbaya, Tariq, dear,' she said, 'even if it is invisible.'

He laughed, not at all put out, and clapped his hands for a servant who came immediately gliding up and served them swiftly with Margaritas.

'Tariq, mon cher,' called one of the women, a French-woman with undoubted chic, but boney shoulders and, Dorrie thought, a tendency to lesbianism. Her name was Estelle de Gondeville. 'Are we making a little visit to the shore this evening? What do you say, hein?'

'As you wish,' Tariq shrugged. 'I am at the disposal of all of you. What would you like to do, Dorrie?'

Dorrie took a sip of Margarita to hide her smile as half a dozen pairs of inimical eyes turned in her direction. Really, it was too stupid. Here were all these women, almost a harem, all of them panting for Tariq to make love to them, continually being referred to Dorrie when there was anything to be decided. And Dorrie would not have shed a tear if Tariq el Said, his yacht and all his oil-wells were spirited out of sight as in an Arabian Nights' story. She wondered briefly if Tariq had invited these women to demonstrate how attractive he was to the opposite sex. He certainly had not invited any competitive men. There was Tubby Dorset, unappetizing as his plump flesh reddened and peeled, an adolescent-looking Viscount who spent his time either drunk or stoned, a top jockey, whose riding Dorrie admired, but whose conversation was as meagre and underdeveloped as his stringy little body, a gossip columnist from the *Echo*, who looked as though he were being poisoned by his own venom, and two or three nonentities, lesser known disc jockeys and so on.

'Well,' Dorrie drawled, sipping some more, 'really, Tariq – your barman must give me the recipe for these Margaritas – they're superb. Yes – let's go ashore. There's supposed to be a good night-club at Soufrière, isn't there?'

'"Le Magot Rouge"?' Tariq said. 'Yes – we might go there. Who else would like to come? I will arrange transport.'

In the end, the whole party of a dozen went ashore, a little time after the brief violence of the tropical sunset had painted the sky rose and purple and orange and faded swiftly into night. A big motor-launch brought them to the landing-stage and three Cadillacs waited to whisk them away to Soufrière.

The night was warm, scented, loud with the noise of frogs and cicadas, and the party from the 'Quaid' was scented also, and at least as loud.

'Tonight you are more beautiful than ever, Dorrie,' Tariq said, softly, sitting with her in the leading car. There was only the chauffeur with them: the other guests had had to pack themselves into the remaining two cars as best they could.

'You're too kind,' Dorrie murmured. She fluttered her

thick eyelashes mockingly, and moved a fraction further away from him. 'Too hot for physical contact,' she explained, 'at any rate for cold-blooded Northerners like me.'

'Nothing will make me believe you are cold-blooded,' he said. 'I feel there are fires within you that only I could arouse – will you not permit me?'

'No, Tariq. I am sometimes tempted by you, I admit it freely, but, on the whole, I don't choose to become yet another in your long line of conquests.'

'No – you would never be just "another", I promise. Have I not shown you how much I care for you? You must know you have my heart in your keeping?'

Dorrie laughed aloud, causing the black driver to look round at her, grinning. 'Tariq! You've been reading Barbara Cartland, I swear it! Oh, God – you really are the limit!'

Tariq frowned. He did not enjoy being laughed at, especially by Dorrie. And what was so exquisitely funny, anyway? What did the woman want? He had tried the open, straightforward, physical approach, and he had tried to overwhelm her with romantic words and gifts. She was a maddening creature and he would have her, one way or another, he swore it by the beard of Allah.

'I'm sorry, Tariq – that was rude of me to laugh!' She came close to him again, with a soft rustle of silk and put a hand through his arm, 'But – you know it's not your heart that you're worrying about, my prince, but only, if I may say so, the Imperial cock. God help any woman who really loves you – you'd trade her in for a string of camels as soon as look at her!'

'Not you, Dorrie – not you!' He believed, as he spoke, that it was true. There had never been any woman who had roused him so continually. He thought about her, and about the act of possessing her so often, that his usual pleasures were becoming tasteless as the desert sand, and other women's bodies as exciting as his grandmother's. Tonight Dorrie was so cool and lovely, the cream silk Givenchy gown she wore clinging to her breasts and leaving her shoulders smooth and bare. The necklace that he had given her to welcome her on board was round her throat, a glittering circlet of green fire, and her only other ornament was the gilt of her hair, coiled in a shining coronet about her small head and seeming to reflect light in the dim interior of the car. As he watched her, she put up her hand to touch the jewels.

'I'm wearing your emeralds, you see. And they're very lovely. I just think, if they were an investment, that you'd get a better return for your money elsewhere.'

Tariq reached for and grasped her shoulders, his fingers hard against the bare flesh. 'Again I tell you, foolish one, that money is nothing to me – it is dust! I do not try to bribe you or to buy you – only to show you a little of my feelings for you – only a little!'

'You're all heart,' Dorrie drawled. 'Would you mind not grabbing me so hard? I bruise easily.'

He let her go, and almost flung himself away from her, arms folded, brows drawn down in a black frown. Dorrie shrugged. If Tariq wanted to sulk, she couldn't have cared less. But by the time they reached the little French town of Soufrière, she had relented, and set herself to charm him back to good humour. Santa Lucia was too idyllic to be spoilt by quarrels, she thought, solemnly feeding Tariq a prawn from her plate as a peace-offering. They were having dinner in a palm-thatched restaurant beneath the stars, where the waiters were French and the seafood was exquisite, and Tariq had again arranged that he and Dorrie were at a table for two, a little way away from the

199

rest of the party, even though he was still annoyed with her. He took the prawn she fed him, catching her hand in his own and gently taking the tips of her fingers into his mouth. She shivered involuntarily, and he saw, his eyes hot and intent on her face.

'Ah – you want me – you know you do!' he whispered. 'You were made for love, Dorrie – and nobody can love a woman more skilfully than an Arab!'

'Have another prawn,' said Dorrie.

Later, at the 'Magot Rouge', they danced to a steel band and drank cocktails, piled with tropical fruit and liberally laced with rum. Voices grew louder and laughter more frequent, and most faces were flushed and perspiring. Neville Jameson, the gossip columnist, asked Dorrie to dance, and steered her skilfully amongst the bobbing, swaying couples, his pale, hatchet face showing no sign of all the alcohol he had consumed.

'You were wearing a look of unutterable contempt, Dorrie my darling!' he said, 'You must cultivate a more bland exterior.'

'Why? As a rule it doesn't matter to me if people know what I think.'

'Ah – the arrogance of youth! And of wealth! If you were a poor, aging journalist like me, you would have to hide your feelings.'

Dorrie laughed. 'I wouldn't call your column in the *Echo* hiding your feelings.'

'You wouldn't? But I only hint and allude – whispering deliciously of scandal! If I put my real feelings down, my editor would blue-pencil the lot, I assure you!'

'Really? You don't care much for the rich and titled, then?'

'My dear! Strictly entre nous, I think they should all be sterilized without anaesthetic, stripped naked and turned

200

out into the world. That not being part of the general scheme of things, I allow them to provide me with a comfortable living.'

The band swung into a cha-cha rhythm and Jameson's hand on her bare back was dry and cool, like snakeskin. Dorrie shivered suddenly and he pulled her a little closer so that they were almost cheek to cheek and she could smell the faint, dry, asexual odour of his skin.

'I wonder why people invite you, Neville,' she said. 'I must say you wouldn't be top of my guest list.'

'Ah – that's where you would be mistaken, sweetest! I rarely bite the hand that feeds me – it's a kind of insurance. There's always plenty of material amongst the guests. Par exemple – that rather foul old hag, de Gondeville. She pretends to be attracted to our friend Tariq – but did you know she had her hand discreetly under the dress of the Mainwaring child a little earlier?'

'Oh – shut up! If you want to rummage in the cesspits of humanity, just keep it to yourself! You're disgusting.'

'But – so is life, don't you think? My dear – if you only realized, copulating and eating are the two main pleasures of the rich – well, and the poor, I suppose, but their tastes are, of necessity, simpler. Some of my best stories are too, too bizarre, even for the *Echo*. Did I ever tell you about Lord Dunwoody and the Irish wolfhound?'

'No – and don't bother. You're such a poisonous man, Neville, that I think you've poisoned yourself, too. There *are* decent, normal people in the world, but you're just too twisted to notice.'

'Sweet!' Jameson's pale lips stretched into a thin smile and he squeezed Dorrie against himself, 'You are so naïve, my precious, that you might be six years old! I suppose you wouldn't care to sleep with me? It would be deliciously like paedophilia!'

'Thank you, but no.' Dorrie disengaged herself, 'You probably dip your prick in venom as well.'

She went back to Tariq, who was watching her moodily, sipping at the rum drink which was forbidden him by his religion. He never danced.

'What was Jameson talking about?'

'Nothing. I can't stand him – he's like a poisonous lizard. Let's go back to the yacht, shall we?'

Tariq shrugged. 'As you wish. The others appear to be enjoying themselves – they can come later.'

They went back to the Cadillac where the driver dozed, his hat over his eyes, and woke cheerfully at Tariq's summons.

The streets of Soufrière were crowded with tourists and residents, late as it was, and, as they passed a little white-washed church, Dorrie saw a stream of people coming out and remembered that it was Christmas Eve. She had not really forgotten, of course. She had presents already wrapped up in her cabin on board the 'Quaid', and there was an improbable silver Christmas tree sparkling in the main salon. But the sunshine and blue water had made Christmas seem far away, and it was only the sight of these worshippers, coming smiling from Midnight Mass and the Christ-child newly born, that made her realize. 'I love Midnight Mass on Christmas Eve,' Sarah Cavallo had said. Were they there now – Sarah with her sweet, pale, Madonna-like face, the children, Ben and Beatrice, Ross . . . ? A lump came into Dorrie's throat and she blinked back sudden tears. 'Happy Christmas, Ross,' she said, silently.

'You are very quiet, Dorrie,' Tariq said, 'Are you tired?'

'Yes – no, I'm not.' She knew she would not sleep easily. She wanted to be weary enough to fall into her bed and not to think about Ross Cavallo for a second. 'Can we walk on the beach a little before we go back to the yacht? I'd like some fresh air and exercise.'

'You English! It is a fetish with you, is it not? You take exercise as a sort of medicine, whether you wish to or not, whereas to us Arabs, it is a part of life – something that happens naturally.'

'Nonsense – there's nothing very natural about your way of life, Tariq. Your ancestors might have galloped about the desert on camels – but you probably don't know one end of a camel from the other.'

He grinned. 'I still take my exercise in a more enjoyable way, however.'

They stopped the car at La Toc beach, not far from Marigot Bay, and wandered on to the sand which glittered white under the moon. Dorrie took off her shoes, enjoying the silky warmth of the sand beneath her bare feet. The moon bobbed like a silver balloon above the calm waters of the Caribbean, and the palm-leaves were etched like cut-outs of black paper against the midnight velvet of the sky. In the background the night-time noises of the tropical rain-forest blended with the moist sweetness of a thousand flowers. It was an idyllic spot, Dorrie thought, so why could she not enjoy it, and enjoy the company of the man at her side, who was handsome, rich, attentive, intelligent? There was no answer to that, except that he was not Ross Cavallo.

She reached out and took Tariq's hand, looking up into the dark, inscrutable face. 'Tell me what sort of life you lead when you're at home in Saudi?' she said, 'You never say much about yourself.'

He glanced down at her, surprised. 'I did not suppose it would interest you. What can I tell you? The life I lead in Saudi is a very simple one – a very traditional one. I belong to the House of Saud – my grandfather was Abdul Aziz, and my father was Saif el Said. We have a palace in Riyadh, and I have a – well, it is a large house nearby. When I am at home, I visit my friends, sometimes we go hunting together.'

'Hunting?'

'Yes – with falcons. You would enjoy that, Dorrie. We have two types – the shahin and the al hur. The first is very fast, but the al hur is much bigger and stronger. We hunt bustard with them – it is a very ancient sport, very skilled. Sometimes, too, we hunt gazelle with dogs.'

He fell silent. Dorrie tried to imagine life as a desert prince. The contrast between the hardy, spartan days before oil and the present affluence must be strange, even for a prince.

'Go on,' she said, 'tell me some more. What do you eat? What entertainment do you have? And what about your women? Are they still as repressed, and still kept separate from the men?'

He laughed and kissed her hand. 'Enough. How can I describe something that you have never seen? I am not a poet. You must come and see for yourself.'

'Yes. Perhaps I will,' Dorrie said, idly.

Tariq stopped and turned her to face him. 'Would you? Would you come to Riyadh with me? Dorrie – would you, perhaps, be my wife?'

'What? Tariq – you must be mad! Are you joking?'

'No – never! I would not joke! Dorrie – I must have you, I have sworn it by Allah. You will be happy with me, I promise you.'

His dark eyes were glittering with excitement in the moonlight, and Dorrie could feel his hands trembling on her arms.

'Tariq,' she said, uneasily, 'I don't want to marry

204

anyone. I'm only nineteen. And – and your way of life is so different.'

'A man and a woman who love – that is the same all over the world, is it not? And I do love you, Dorrie – do you understand? You have bewitched me.'

She turned her head away from him and stared out to sea. 'I'm sorry, Tariq. You're a lot nicer than I thought – but I don't love you, I'm afraid. Let's go back to the yacht.'

In her cabin, which was as large, and infinitely more luxurious than many first-class hotel rooms, Dorrie undressed and showered, then lay naked on the big, comfortable bed in the dark, watching the moon's slow descent to the waiting waters of the Caribbean. She thought of Tariq and his extraordinary proposal – marriage was the last thing she would have expected him to suggest. Her lips twitched as she pictured herself as an Arabian princess – and how would Sir Anthony react to a tribe of Bedouin grandchildren? In this way, she kept the image of Ross at bay until at last, rocked gently by the soft swell of the ocean, and a little numb with all the rum cocktails, she slept.

And fell at once into an ecstatic dream in which she lay in Ross's arms, held like a child and conscious only of loving and of being loved. Then, from this simple, almost spiritual state of being, she became conscious of their two bodies, and the pleasure that they were giving each other. With a vividness she had never before experienced in a dream, she felt his mouth warm at her breasts, very soft and gentle, seeming to surround each tingling nipple with a ring of fire, an aureole of flame. Then his mouth and his hands were moving further, gently exploring, touching her body inch by inch until her breath quickened and she moaned his name softly. With the sound, she came awake, sure for an instant that he was with her, her whole body quivering with the ecstasy she had felt, her pulses racing with the expectation of receiving him inside her. Then, as she woke fully, she gave a cry compounded both of fear and disappointment, as she realized that it was Tariq beside her – Tariq, naked and strong and potent, Tariq whose greedy tongue and hands had laved and stroked and sucked at her sleeping body until she was roused almost to the point where she could not resist him. Almost. It was only the sweet, already-fading dream of Ross that gave her the strength to control her trembling body and to push violently at Tariq's shoulders.

'No!' she hissed, her finger-nails digging into him till he drew in his breath with a gasp. Without a word, he grasped her arms and lay on top of her, pushing her legs apart with his own.

'Don't be stupid,' he whispered, 'Don't struggle so much – you won't enjoy it if you fight.'

Real panic swept Dorrie. My God – he was actually going to rape her! She could feel his penis, thick and heavy between her legs and he was gradually inching it towards her vagina, hampered by his grasp on her arms. He was sucking at her breasts again, but now the sensation seemed to make her flesh cringe. She could hardly bear his touch, and she twisted and writhed beneath him.

'Get off me! Get off me, you bastard!'

'Hush – I love you – it is all right – let me, Dorrie – you know you want it – you're only pretending,' he panted, 'Let me – I felt you opening to me like a flower – don't fight . . .' He was trying to soothe her with his voice as though she were a half-tamed falcon, sure that she would succumb to the urgent cravings of her flesh.

Suddenly she lay quite still, and he thought he had won, and released his grip on her wrists in order to grasp his

206

penis with one hand and push it into her, and in that moment, with a violent thrust of her legs against him, Dorrie managed to push herself away from him and to roll off the bed. She stood shivering, despite the heat of the tropical night, her arms wrapped round her body, furiously, incoherently angry.

'You bastard!' she gasped, 'You bloody demented rapist! Who the hell do you think you are, coming in here and attacking me as though – as though you owned me?'

He did not reply. She could see him in the moonlight, sprawled across the bed, his penis still erect, his eyes glittering darkly as he watched her.

'Get out of here,' Dorrie said, 'and if you come near me again I swear I'll scream till the whole bloody lot of your friends come running. Now get out.'

He went, still silent, and a black fury in his heart. What he had felt was the beginning of real love for Dorrie, was transformed into nothing more than a burning desire to possess, to punish, to humiliate as he himself, a royal prince, grandson of Abdul Aziz, had been humiliated. Without pausing, almost without thinking, he went into the cabin of one of the other women, a minor television starlet who had been sending him 'come-on' signals for days. She woke from a semi-drunken sleep and hardly had time to be aware of who was in her room before he was on her like a wild, crazy beast, pushing wide her legs with impatient hands and thrusting inside her with no preliminaries, his mouth savage on her breasts, his whole powerful body battering at hers which was luckily anaesthetized and relaxed with drink, until, panting and sobbing, he reached a violent climax. Then, without a word or a caress, he withdrew himself and left the woman alone, aching, bruised and resentful. 'Do you come here often?' she murmured to the unresponsive air, 'Arab bastard!'

207

Christmas Day was a day of brooding atmospheres and tension on board the 'Quaid', and Neville Jameson's pale, clever eyes flickered from face to face as he entertained himself with delicious surmise about what had been going on. He began mentally to compose a vitriolic piece about Dorrie which would stop just this side of libel. A hint – he was so good at hinting, that she had spent the entire cruise spreading her legs for every Tom, Dick and – yes, Harriet, why not? – would be lapped up with the corn-flakes and orange juice in a million British homes. They did like a bit of smut with their breakfasts.

Dorrie spent the morning swimming and diving in the transparent waters of the bay, dozing in the shade of the palm-trees on the hot, white sand when she was tired, and talking to some of the islanders. They swarmed round the pretty white lady, plying her with cotton sun-dresses, straw hats, dressed dolls and mountains of exotic fruit. Dorrie, smiling lazily, bought something from everyone and instructed a boat-man to ferry it all over to the yacht. Then she spread out her towel on the hot sand and indicated that she was going to sleep. She did sleep for an hour, limp and relaxed after the tension that had kept her awake for most of the night, and when she woke she felt fresh and in a more forgiving mood. Poor old Tariq – it was not his fault, really. If she had been in love with him, his reception would have been different – or even if she had not been in love with Ross, because she admitted that her flesh, at least, had been stirred and excited by Tariq's caresses. She decided in the true spirit of Christmas to forgive and forget, and swam back to the yacht for Christmas dinner.

There was turkey and plum pudding, mince pies and crackers, the latter containing gew-gaws and personal jewellery worth about a hundred pounds each. Dorrie, who had not spoken to Tariq all day, raised her glass to him and smiled. He inclined his head and raised his glass in return and Dorrie thought that everything was as it had been. She disliked scenes and atmospheres and, although she was often quick-tempered, she was just as quick to forgive an injury. But she did not understand the mind of Tariq el Said. Beneath the impassive politeness of his exterior, his desire for vengeance was hot and strong. For the only time in his life he had shown weakness to a woman. He had exposed his heart and offered it to her and she had spat upon it. Never again would he make himself vulnerable. One day, Dorrie would suffer for what she had done, but, in the meantime, one must be civilized. One must smile and be polite and wait – wait with the patience of the desert dweller.

After dinner, presents were exchanged – expensive presents chosen mainly for ostentation rather than with any real thought for the recipient.

Dorrie gave Tariq half-a-dozen St Laurent shirts, some silk, some Sea Island cotton, all discreetly monogrammed, and he received them with polite thanks, raising her hand to his lips with regal condescension. He hesitated a moment, then. The present he had intended for Dorrie, lying with the others on the table next to the silver Christmas tree was not, he thought now, suitable for the woman who had insulted him. Then he shrugged. It was a priceless gift, but what was price to him? Let the woman have it – she would see he was no niggardly prince.

Dorrie stared wordlessly at the contents of her package. It was an Arabian head-dress, embroidered with large and beautiful pearls and hung with gold coins, most of them antique and some of them dating back to the Renaissance, a prince's ransom to hang from a princess's head.

'It is an Arab wedding head-dress,' Tariq said, watching her face. 'It has been in my family for many generations and each generation has added to it.'

'But – Tariq! You can't give me a family treasure like this – I – I can't accept it!'

'I want you to have it, nevertheless,' he said, frowning suddenly, autocratic, not to be gainsaid.

The others gathered round with exclamations indicating their various emotions of admiration, envy and amusement.

'Oh, do try it on, Dorrie, darling – it's simply *you*!' drawled Neville Jameson, his eyes alight with malice, and Anya Mower, the woman whom Tariq had raped the previous night and ignored all day, added her urgings: 'Yes, *do*, Dorrie – it's just *too* mediaeval for words!'

Rather unwillingly, Dorrie placed the close-fitting head-dress over her loose hair. The coins lay flat on her forehead, their gold no brighter than the thick lashes of her eyes. She had the look of some goddess of ancient times, a mixture of the voluptuous and the ethereal, with her high cheek-bones emphasized by the close-fitting head-dress, and her direct blue gaze contrasting with the sensual droop of her full mouth. The Egyptian Isis, perhaps, the moon goddess, or Aphrodite, newly risen from the waves, golden as summer. There was silence for an instant, an acknowledgment of rare and unusual beauty, and then Dorrie, going over to where Tariq sat a little aloof, bent and kissed him gently on the lips.

'Thank you, Tariq dear,' she said, 'It is the most beautiful present.'

'You'd better watch it, Dorrie,' Anya said, acidly, 'You'll probably find that putting it on and kissing His Highness makes you number ten wife!'

That night the 'Quaid' sailed for Barbados, and after

that for a fortnight it dawdled leisurely about the Caribbean, stopping at Grenada, Martinique, Guadeloupe, Antigua, an odyssey of pleasure through calm waters and lush green islands, but, for the rest of the cruise, Tariq el Said did not go to Dorrie's cabin, nor speak intimately to her again.

9

For Ross and Sarah Cavallo, it had been a quiet family Christmas. Sarah had worked hard preparing all the traditional food, and by Christmas Eve she had been white with exhaustion.

'For God's sake,' Ross said, tired and irritable himself, 'what on earth is the point of working yourself into the ground like this? Does everything *have* to be home-made? Surely we can afford to buy a few things from Harrods or Fortnum's – it won't exactly poison us, you know.'

Sarah's eyes filled with tears, and she turned away, her throat aching miserably, unable to reply. Ross, contrite, put his arms round her and kissed the top of her head.

'Darling, darling – don't cry! I'm only being a pig. But – I hate to see you worn out like this – no wonder – ' he stopped, but Sarah knew what he had nearly said: 'No wonder you're too worn out and tensed up for love-making.' He didn't understand that it was because she was denying him her body that she wanted to show him in other ways how much she loved him. And it was not exhaustion that made her tense – he should know that. Dr Colley had told them both that it was her mind that was knotting the muscles of her body and causing the pain, the dull, nagging pain that was never any better. They slept in separate beds now. It was better like that, because in the big bed that they had shared for the whole of their marriage, Sarah was continually reminded of Ross's physical need for her. Once, since she had been to the doctor's, she had turned to him, offering herself, and

212

he had begun to make love to her, gently and slowly. But, after a minute, watching her face and seeing the spasm of fear and pain that she could not control, he had withdrawn, kissing her lightly on the cheek and turning to his own side of the bed.

'Not again, darling,' he had said, quietly, 'Not till you're better. I want a wife, not a human sacrifice.'

There was tension between them, inevitably. Ross's face was leaner and grimmer and he spent more time at the casino. He drank a little more and smoked heavily. It was not just Sarah, although his enforced celibacy added to the strain. It was Dorrie. He found himself thinking about her all the time. Even when his mind was on casino business, he found that she was never far away from his thoughts. It was, he told himself, a ridiculous and undignified state for a grown man to get into, rather like catching measles at an advanced age, but it was none the less painful for all that. It would have been better, more loyal to Sarah, perhaps, if he had made love to Dorrie at the beginning, treating her like the high-class whore she had sometimes appeared to be. One quick fuck and she would have been forgotten. But now she had got into his blood-stream, insidious as a tsetse fly, and he wondered if he would ever recover. If he had not been so preoccupied, he would have given more time to considering his growing uneasiness about the relationship between Khalid and Pacelli and what was happening in the casino. Pacelli was always there, and always with vast amounts of money, although Ross knew from Beatrice that it was six months since Pacelli had had a hit record and, in fact, his place in her affections had already been taken by a young man with a bald head and ring through his nose who went by a name like Boo Bluechick.

It was always cash. Sometimes he gambled it all away

213

with careless abandon. Other times he scarcely bet a hundred pounds, and then he would ask to change his chips back into a cheque, usually saying that he was going on somewhere and didn't want to carry a lot of money. That he was on drugs, Ross was sure. The distinctive smell of hash was common enough, but often Pacelli's dilated pupils and trembling hands spoke of something stronger. Ross wondered if he were dealing in drugs, and thought it probable. He would have spoken to Khalid about it, except that the casino owner seemed to be on close terms with Pacelli. Not that there was much love lost – Khalid had referred to him more than once in Ross's hearing as 'that singing prick', but a couple of times he had seen them conversing together with an unsmiling intentness that made him wonder. Still – it was his job to run the casino efficiently and at a profit, to make sure that the gaming laws and the licensing laws were obeyed, and to keep the punters happy. He was doing all those things, and the complexities of his private life kept him too preoccupied to worry much about little punks like Johnny Pacelli. Khalid seemed quite happy with the profits that the Olympus was making, and gave Ross a fat Christmas bonus.

'I'm very pleased, Ross,' he said, 'You're doing a good job, boy! I tell you what – I'm going to do something for you – I'm going to send you to Vegas for a while, to our casino there! How'd you like that? A great experience, huh?'

Ross was puzzled rather than pleased. It might well be a great experience, although Vegas would not be his top choice of places to live. Still, the kids could see something of the States, and perhaps the change would be good for Sarah. What he could not understand was why, when the

214

Olympus was doing so well under his management, Khalid should want to send him away?

'Thank you, Mr Khalid,' he said, 'I'm sure it will be an experience. When did you want me to go?'

'Oh – I dunno. Soon. Spring, I guess, eh? If that's okay by you and your wife?'

'I'll talk to Sarah about it. She hasn't been very well lately.'

'There you are then, Ross, boy! You take her to the States. Great climate in Vegas – she's gonna feel better in no time! You give her my best respects, eh? She's a real classy lady is Mrs Cavallo!'

The next day a huge basket of exotic fruit arrived from Harrods for Sarah, with a label scrawled with Giovanni Khalid's name. Sarah was delighted and the children rapturous, but Ross stared, frowning, at the sumptuous basket. 'Beware of Greeks bearing gifts,' he said.

'Darling – what do you mean? Anyway, Mr Khalid's an Arab-Italian, and I think it was very charming of him.'

'Very. Only why does a black-hearted bastard have to be charming? He usually has a motive, only I can't think what it is at the moment.'

'You old grouch! You just have a suspicious nature! Have a peach, and give Mr Khalid a kiss from me!'

Ross's mother came down from Inverness to join them for Christmas. Maire McDonnell Cavallo was a slim, upright woman with the far-seeing light-blue eyes of the Highlander and an aureole of shining white hair.

She took one swift look at her son when he met her at King's Cross and said, 'What's wrong, Ross?'

'Now, Mother,' he said, grinning faintly as he stowed her bags in the BMW, 'don't start doing your fey Highland lady bit so soon.'

'Dear laddie, I don't have to be fey to see how thin your face is. Are they working you too hard at that place?'

The casino was always 'that place' to her. She had a deep-rooted dislike of what she called 'robbing dens of iniquity' and declared they gave her 'the scunners'. She was, however, like Sarah, deeply interested in the doings of the famous, and would question Ross about various celebrities, saying, 'And what like of a person is yon pop-star' or film-star, or TV personality, listening with the absorption of a child to his answer. But she was not to be put off in her pursuit of the reason for Ross's lack of spirits and was only satisfied when he told her that Sarah hadn't been well and he was worried about her.

'Mitchy me, lassie!' she said, when she saw her daughter-in-law, 'You're like a bone! And yellow as my duster! You should see your doctor – get him to give you a tonic or some such thing. You were always a fine, sonsy lass, Sarah – it doesna just suit you to be so peely-wally. You see your doctor, lassie!'

'I've seen him, Maire – it's nothing to worry about,' Sarah said, flushing slightly, but smiling at the same time as she always did at her mother-in-law's rich Doric vocabulary.

'What – yon Collie fellow?' Maire said scornfully. 'I wouldna trust him to tell me if I was alive or deid! I have a good friend practising medicine in London – she and I were at school together. You go and see Janet McFarlane – I bet she'll put you right! She's a grand, kind lassie and knows her job – not like yon saw-bones! I mind when I was here once and went to see him – what an auld wifie he was!'

'He's very good,' Sarah said, defensively, 'and I've known him a long time . . .'

But in her mind, the idea of going to see this Dr

216

McFarlane took root. Stupidly, she had not thought of a sympathetic lady doctor. It had been the idea of a man poking about her insides that had made her freeze with terror. And the pain was really quite bad now, with her intermittently by day and by night. She couldn't go on consuming scores of aspirin and expecting Ross to live like a monk. Something would have to be done.

Before Maire went back to Inverness, Sarah had Janet McFarlane's address in her handbag and had half-promised her mother-in-law to contact the doctor.

'Mind you do, now,' Maire said, patting Sarah's cheek with a gloved hand, 'I want my bonny Sarah back – not some wittrich, nae-weel crater!'

One day early in January, Ross got up around midday to find Sarah flushed and indignant over an article in that day's *Echo*.

'It's that Neville Jameson,' she said, 'and it's about Dorrie – it's obvious. Oh – he must be the most horrible man – he's hinting absolutely vile things about her – I wonder if she could sue? Listen to this . . .'

'I'm not the least bit interested,' Ross said, reaching for coffee, 'and I don't know why you get that scurrilous rag – especially if you find it so offensive.'

Sarah was silenced, but later on Ross bought a copy of the *Echo* on his way to work and read Jameson's column in his office, his mouth grim with angry distaste. Was this Dorrie that was being portrayed to the prurient masses? Was this the golden girl he dreamed of so often, this shameless, decadent Queen of Whores that the man Jameson's pen was depicting. Surely these were lies – and yet – the fellow would hardly dare if there were not some truth in it. Suddenly Ross crushed the paper in his fist and hurled it at his waste-basket. What did it matter? Dorrie could sleep with who the hell she wanted, as long as she stayed out of his life – and out of his dreams.

But it seemed as though some perverse Fate was determined to throw Dorrie in his path. He found that Sarah and the children, learning that Dorrie was back in London, were planning to invite her over to Kew.

'Why the hell do you have to do that?' Ross demanded, and his family stared at him with startled eyes at his savage tone, even Thomas giving a crow of surprise.

'Oh, Ross – what's the matter with you? We're asking Dorrie because we like her! And look how good she's been to the children,' Sarah said, reproachfully.

'Well, let her do her Lady Bountiful act when I'm not around,' Ross said.

'I *like* Dorrie,' Ben said, bravely, scowling at his father and preparing to defend his idol. 'She's not soppy like a lot of girls – she can drive a car and swear just like a boy! *And* she's pretty!' he finished, blushing scarlet. Ross smiled at his son, painfully aware that his own heart was even more vulnerable than the little boy's.

'That's all right, Ben – you don't have to stand up to me about your friend. I just hope you don't copy her swearing, that's all.'

'Gosh, no, Dad! I wouldn't do it in front of you and Mum, anyway!'

So it was only when Ross was sure to be out that Sarah invited Dorrie to visit them or went into town to Dorrie's flat, and the unlikely friendship between the two dissimilar women gradually deepened, until it seemed natural that Sarah should ask Dorrie to accompany her when at last she made up her mind to see Dr McFarlane.

'I'm such a funk – I might run away at the last minute if you're not there to shove me!' she confided.

'Of course I'll come,' Dorrie said. 'When is it?'

'Oh – in a couple of days. Dr McFarlane's very booked up, but when she knew I was Maire's daughter-in-law, she said she'd rearrange something and ring me back. Can I let you know?'

'Sure – any time will be okay. Just give me a ring, and I'll come a-running.'

But when Sarah rang, it was Cy who answered the phone and told her Dorrie was out.

'Oh – could you give her a message, please, Cy? Just that my appointment's at eleven tomorrow morning.'

Cy noted the message in her small, neat handwriting on the pad by the phone, but Dorrie, coming in late and slightly drunk did not see it, and Cy had left for work long before she got up in the morning. It was the telephone shrilling insistently at ten that finally woke Dorrie. The bell on the extension by her bed was switched off, and by the time the noise from the other one had penetrated her sleep, the caller had hung up.

'Hell,' muttered Dorrie, snuggling down and trying to recapture sleep. But it was useless – she was wide awake. She got up and had a shower, taking a long time over it and turning the water to its hottest, then she wandered into the kitchen and made coffee. It was not till after half past ten that she came across Cy's note and swore with annoyance. That must have been Sarah ringing before – why on earth had she not woken more quickly? Or why had Cy not left the message in a more prominent position? Now Sarah would think she wasn't coming. Hastily Dorrie pulled on clothes and shot out of the flat, yelling for Perks to bring her car round as soon as the lift doors opened. He didn't move.

'Don't you remember, Miss? You asked me to book it in for a service – they came for it this morning.'

'Oh, *shit*! Call me a taxi – no, don't bother, the tube

219

will be just as quick.' She took a flying leap down the steps and pelted for Maida Vale tube station, almost jumping up and down on the platform with impatience as she waited for a train. Half-way there, changing at Hammersmith for the District Line to Kew, she realized a taxi would have been quicker, and when she emerged from Kew Gardens station at last, it was to an almost black sky and a torrential downpour. Doggedly she began to trot down Kew Gardens Road, and within ten minutes she had arrived at the Cavallos' house, drenched and too late.

Ross, wearing a dark silk Sulka dressing gown, opened the door at last to her frenzied knocking and ringing.

Lotte was out for the day and Tom slept cherubically in his cot. When he saw who it was, he stood motionless, one hand still on the door, staring. Dorrie stared back at him. She had not seen him since November when he came to Ash Friars and she had half-hoped that the real Ross Cavallo, when she saw him in the flesh again, would be an anti-climax, a disappointment, even, after her vivid dreams of him.

But he was there, now, in front of her, as tall and broad-shouldered as she had remembered, the dark face with its brooding eyes and its half grim, half tender mouth, as beloved as ever.

The hunger wrenched at her heart as painfully as before, and she stood with the rain darkening her hair and plastering it to her head, running off her nose and down her unmade-up face, simply looking at him.

He recovered his composure first of all. 'Sarah's gone,' he said, 'She took a taxi. She wouldn't let me go with her.'

'Oh – I'm sorry – I was going with her, but I didn't get her message in time . . .' Dorrie said, speaking almost inaudibly for the pulse pounding in her throat.

He smiled without amusement. 'I shouldn't worry. Your friends must get used to your casual little ways.'

She flushed painfully, sketched a sort of farewell with one hand and turned to go.

'Wait.' He should have steeled himself and hardened his heart – but it was impossible to see that bedraggled, waif-like figure turn dejectedly away in the rain and to stand silent.

'You'd better come in and dry yourself,' he said, curtly. 'I'll make you a cup of coffee and run you to the tube.'

Not looking at him, she came inside obediently, carefully avoiding the least contact as she passed him. He closed the door, shutting out the noise of the heavy rain, and they were suddenly aware of the quiet intimacy of the house.

'Let me take your coat – it's drenched. You'd better take your shoes off as well.'

She handed him the soaked and ancient Burberry which had been the first garment that came to hand in her hasty dash, and kicked off her wet sneakers.

'Very suitable for a wet winter morning,' Ross commented dryly, trying to keep his mind from the image of her slender feet, tanned and straight-toed as a child's. 'Your T-shirt's wet as well. Go and dry your hair in the bathroom and I'll find you something to wear.'

She went in front of him up the stairs and into the bathroom where she stripped off her wet jeans and T-shirt and wrapped herself in a big bath-towel, rubbing her wet hair with another. She knew she should not have come in to the Cavallos' house. Rain or no rain, when she saw Ross, she should have turned round and kept on walking. But now – the sweetness of being near him was too precious for her not to savour every second of it – just to hear his voice, even to know he was in the same house, was pure, unalloyed delight. She rubbed herself with the warm towel, the healthy tan of her skin tingling and glowing again, and when Ross tapped at the door with dry clothes in his hands, it was not a bedraggled waif who opened it, but a goddess of living flesh, warm, vital and golden, her bare shoulders gleaming above the white of the towel, her eyes startlingly blue in the tawny beauty of her face.

'Dorrie?' he whispered.

She did not answer, but he saw her throat move as she swallowed convulsively. He dropped the clothes he was carrying to the floor and his hands reached slowly out to her shoulders. At his touch she shuddered, trembled, her breath coming in a soft, ecstatic sigh. Wordlessly, he pulled her into his arms and bent his head to kiss her, a slow, sweet kiss that quickened the blood till it beat fast and urgently in their two bodies. The towel that she had been clutching to herself fell between them as her arms went round his neck, and he was holding her sweet nakedness in his arms, assailed by an overpowering temptation that he knew had at last defeated him.

He lifted her, feeling how light and supple she was in his arms, and carried her into the spare bedroom that he was occupying, laying her tenderly down on the bed. For a moment, releasing himself from her arms, he sat beside her, looking down into her face, his eyes filled with blind hunger and with a tormented pain.

'You know I want you,' he whispered, 'I've wanted you so long, Dorrie – '

She nodded, not trusting herself to speak, and her hand sought his and clung to it.

'But, Dorrie – I can't cheat you. I love Sarah – I always will do, and I can't offer you anything.'

Dorrie moistened her lips with her tongue and when

222

she spoke her voice shook slightly, 'Just this once, Ross – just love me this one time – I promise I won't be a nuisance to you . . .'

He closed his eyes briefly, at that moment hating himself for what he was doing to this girl and to Sarah, and then Dorrie's hand reached out, almost shyly to his cheek, her fingers touched and traced the firm line of his lips and slid softly over his chest, and it was too late to think of anything but the desire which mounted in him like a tidal wave. He shrugged off his robe and lay beside her on the bed, and their hands touched, explored, caressed each other with a delight and pleasure that was quite free of lust. Softly he cupped her breasts in his hands, glorying in their ripe fullness, and he bent to taste them for the first time, the nipples sweet and firm in his mouth, her flesh warm and yielding.

Dorrie moaned softly. The feel of his mouth at her breasts was unbearable bliss, an agony of delight that sent ripples of fire pulsing down her body. Then, slowly, with the most infinite sensual pleasure, he covered the golden curve of her belly with kisses, and then the soft, silk skin on the inside of her thighs, and she drew in her breath sharply and ecstatically as she felt his lips gently caress the most intimate part of her, his tongue softly, rhythmically touching the sensitive clitoris until she felt that all the pleasure she had ever felt was concentrated in that point of melting fire, and the world seemed to stagger and whirl on its axis. She wanted it to go on for ever, and at the same time, with a cry that echoed round the quiet room, her orgasm rushed through her like a volcanic eruption, shaking her whole body and leaving it bathed in bliss.

He came into her then, gently and expertly, feeling the tightness of her young vagina closing about him with such an uprush of heady joy that he had to lie still upon her for a second, lest he came at once like a raw schoolboy. Then he moved on into her body, claiming it for his own, and he had not noticed her sharp intake of breath as he entered her, nor her odd maladroitness.

'Dorrie,' he whispered, his face against her neck, 'Beloved . . .' And he thrust into her again and yet again, each time with a mounting ecstasy that was stronger than anything he had ever experienced, and reaching a climax that left him spent, collapsed like a drowned man in the quiet lagoon beyond the reefs of passion.

Time went swiftly past, or stood still – it was impossible to say which, as they lay silently together, their bodies entwined on the edge of sleep. The sheer physical relief of the love-making after his long celibacy was such balm to Ross's frayed and over-stretched nerves that he felt only blissful euphoria, into which no painful thoughts could intrude.

Dorrie lay still, afraid almost to breathe, lest she broke the spell that still bound them. The feeling of Ross's body against her own filled her with such happiness that she wanted, without any conscious blasphemy, to give thanks to that vague, far-off God she had prayed to as a child. She felt that she had tasted Paradise in the arms of this man that she loved so much, so entirely, and she knew that, whatever happened, she could never love any other man in the same way.

The sound of a taxi drawing up outside was like a sudden electric shock. In an instant, as the vision of Sarah's white, agonized face flashed into his mind, all the sweetness and bliss of their love-making faded from Ross's consciousness and he knew only that he had betrayed his wife and that Dorrie had been a partner in that betrayal. There was no beauty left in the encounter at that moment, only a sordid rutting for the gratification of the senses, and his face was so savage as he pulled on his robe that Dorrie shrank from him. She could sense the imminent destruction of the most important thing in her life and she was powerless to prevent it.

'Get up!' Ross said, sharply, taking her arm and pulling her from the bed, 'Go and get dressed – then come down. Hurry!' He almost pushed her from the room in front of him, his self-loathing so great that it included Dorrie as well, and in that agonizing moment he hated her.

He went downstairs and opened the front door as Sarah came up the steps. 'Hullo, darling – you weren't very long!' His voice seemed strained and artificial but Sarah did not seem to notice. She was pale, but scarcely more so than usual, and her dark brows were contracted in a look of painful preoccupation. She came past Ross, into the big hallway and stood looking about her as though she had never seen it before.

'By the way,' Ross said, quickly, 'Dorrie did come, after all – she had your message late. She – she got soaking wet, so I sent her upstairs to change.'

'Yes . . .' Sarah seemed hardly to hear him, 'Oh – yes, I knew she would come if she could. She's kind . . . Is there any coffee?'

They went into the kitchen, and Sarah perched on a stool, her elbows on the table and her hands cupping her chin. She still had the remote look of a sleepwalker about her.

'What did Dr McFarlane say?'

Ross switched on the percolator, grateful to be doing something that enabled him to avoid Sarah's eyes.

'She said – ' her voice was flat and without emotion, 'she's going to send me to Hammersmith Hospital for some tests – but – I'm sorry Ross – she's pretty sure that I have cervical cancer.'

The word had been spoken. It hung sombrely in the air in the warm, pretty kitchen, and the clock echoed it, the noise of the percolator seemed to repeat it, it sank slowly into Ross's brain and tightened round his heart in a cold iron band.

'Cancer?'

She nodded, her eyes now searching for his and fastening on them in mute appeal.

The door opened then, and Dorrie came in, wearing the jeans and sweater of Sarah's that Ross had given her.

'Hallo, Sarah – I'm sorry I missed you,' she said, sounding nervous and shy. Sarah looked round, her smile warm and unforced.

'Dorrie! Come and have coffee!'

'No! No – I won't stay. I must – oh! How did you get on at the doctor's?'

'Fine! Just fine – I'll tell you all about it another time if gynaecological delvings don't make you queasy!'

'No. Good – I'm – glad it's all right. I must dash now, or – I'll be late . . .'

To Ross, she looked as guilty as if she had been caught naked in bed, with her flushed face and tousled hair, her mouth, to his eyes, still swollen with his kisses. He went over to her, almost hustling her out of the kitchen, handing her the still-wet Burberry, scarcely seeing her except as an intruder, the instrument of his betrayal. She was Lilith, Jezebel, Delilah, all the wanton women that men have blamed for their weaknesses since time began. He opened the front door, not looking at her.

'Ross?' she whispered, sensing his feelings but hardly able to believe that their joy in each other was to end so abruptly. She put a hand out hesitantly to touch his arm, and he flinched away from her.

'Just go,' he said, curtly, 'Quickly.' Then he closed the door, shutting her out.

Before going back to Sarah, he went quickly upstairs to erase any traces of occupancy from the spare bedroom. He could still smell Dorrie's perfume like a ghost of herself, and suddenly his heart contracted with pain as he remembered her frightened, beseeching face and his own brusqueness. She was normally so tough, so independent and invulnerable that he was only beginning to realize the tender child that lay beneath. He bent to straighten the crumpled coverlet and paused, staring down at it. He remembered now that sharp gasp of pain as he had thrust into her. He remembered how oddly inexpert and unpractised her love-making had been. The worldly-wise, the brash, the experienced Dorrie St James, the golden girl whom everyone believed had had countless lovers, had, after all, been a virgin.

He went down to Sarah again and took her in his arms to comfort and reassure her, and she suddenly clung to him and wept with the abandon of a child, the last tears he saw her shed for a long time.

'Oh, Ross – hold me. I'm so frightened . . .'

'Hush – darling, don't cry – thousands of women get better – you know they do. They've made fantastic advances in medicine – it's not nearly so serious as it used to be . . .' He went on talking, reassuring, bringing out all the platitudes as though it was nothing more than a severe toothache that Sarah was suffering from. And at last she raised her face from his chest and gave him a tremulous smile.

'You know, darling – isn't it silly? – when Dr McFarlane

first told me, I thought, "Thank God it's not something in my mind that's all screwed up!"'

'That stupid bastard, Colley!' Ross said, savagely, 'I could kill the bungling, incompetent fool . . .'

'No – don't say that. I should have gone for a test long ago . . . but . . .' She shrugged, accepting the harsh legacy of her past with resignation. 'Anyway – as you said, darling – they do marvels today, and Dr McFarlane seems very able. She won't waste any time. I've to go to Hammersmith tomorrow morning. Just – don't tell the children, will you? Or anyone – not just yet. It – it may not be so serious – it'd be silly to worry anyone.'

It was still raining steadily. Hardly aware of her direction, Dorrie turned on to Kew Bridge and began walking back towards town. She stared straight in front of her, her face set and white, splashing through deep puddles as though she didn't see them. She felt as though she had been lifted to the gates of Paradise, allowed one brief glimpse, and then hurled down. Was this Hell? If so, Hell did not burn. It was cold and grey, and the other inhabitants were dim ghosts, hurrying past, too intent on their own sorrows to care about anyone else. Tears began to trickle down Dorrie's face, mingling with the rain and she rubbed them away, hating the self-pity that had brought them. Then the tears turned to anger and self-contempt. Was she to bawl like a spoilt kid and think life was over, just because of Ross Cavallo? He had been honest with her – there was none of that 'my wife doesn't understand me' stuff. And she had wanted him – wanted him to be the first, offering him her inviolate body as a free gift, asking nothing in return. But – to have turned from her so abruptly and coldly afterwards, as though what they had shared had been worthless or shameful – ah, that had been cruel.

With a quick, impulsive gesture, she pushed back the wet hair from her face and shouted for a passing taxi to take her home. Not bothering to take off her soaking clothes, she stood dripping on to the carpet as she dialled the number of the Hilton.

'His Royal Highness returned to Riyadh some days ago.'

Dorrie bit her lip. She returned the receiver to its rest and stood thinking for a moment, her brows drawn together in a faint frown. Then she picked up the phone once more and dialled. In a calm, unhurried voice she booked a first-class air ticket to Riyadh, then, stripping off her wet things, she showered and began to pack. Into the Vuitton cases went the dresses and suits, jeans and evening gowns with their expensive designer labels, and on top, carefully wrapped in a swathe of tissue, went the Arabian wedding head-dress.

PART TWO
Riyadh

10

Muhna crouched in the dimly lit ante-room. It had Western-style chairs, but she preferred, had always preferred, sitting on a cushion on the floor in the traditional manner. She liked all things to be traditional and as they had been since time immemorial. When she was fourteen, her father had arranged her marriage with Prince Tariq el Said, and there had been no thought in Muhna's mind of disobedience. Many of her friends, it was true, had become modern and Westernized. 'Choose your own husband!' they had said. 'Do not let your parents dictate to you!' But Muhna had only smiled shyly and shaken her head. Did not Allah create men to be in charge of women? Besides, it was a great honour for her family that she should be chosen as the first wife of the Prince. And such a Prince as Tariq el Said! Truly it could be said that he would make any woman happy. And Muhna had been happy for ten years now, and had borne her husband two fine sons and three female children. Even when her beloved husband had taken another wife two years before, Muhna had been kind to fourteen-year-old Fatima, and had told her many private things that pleased their husband. She had not been angry with the girl, even when Tariq had stayed away from her own bed for several weeks. It was all the will of Allah.

But this new marriage! This joining together of East and West, of the yellow-haired woman with the Arab Prince – that was surely as contrary to the teachings of the prophet as the mating of a falcon with a bustard. The woman had come, some days since, quite alone and

233

unaccompanied by any father, brother or uncle to negotiate the marriage settlement. She came to offer herself in marriage to the Prince – so his mother, old Ahira, had told Muhna, shaking her head and rolling her eyes in horror at the impropriety of it all; and with her face naked for all men to see. Ahira had tried to speak to her son, for she was an old and wise woman and her word was venerated. But he, Tariq el Said, had replied harshly, telling his mother not to meddle in his affairs. He had said, so Ahira told Muhna, 'Mother, I have sworn by Allah to have this woman and Allah has sent her to me. His will be done!'

And so today there had been the wedding – a shameful affair with none of the bride's relations present – and the bride had worn the traditional head-dress on her strange yellow hair, and a morta'isha, the heavy gold and jewelled necklace with pendants hanging almost to knee-level. She had worn traditional Bedu wedding garments and the bridal chamber was strewn with herbs and perfumes in the age-old manner. It was hung with embroidered satin and velvet and curtains put round the bed where the bride and groom were to sleep, lest anyone enter the room, for it is shameful to be seen. The yellow-haired one had acquiesced in all – she seemed to be quiet and her face was not joyful, but when, after the feasting and merry-making was done and they wished to carry her to her husband wrapped up in a priceless carpet in the old Bedu manner, she became angry and refused. Muhna did not understand English, but Ahira spoke it, and she said that the new wife had spoken bad words and said she would not be trussed like a chicken.

Ahira was not pleased, for she came of an ancient Qatari family and was related to Sheikh Khalifa bin Hamad al-Thani, and it was because of her that the Prince's household was run in the ancient and traditional way. Other women in modern Saudi might become West-ernized and disobey the teachings of Koran and Sunna, but the house of el Said was very strictly Wahhabite and followed the word of Allah and of Muhammad, his prophet.

The Prince had gone in to his new bride, and his wives and mother, with some of the women of the household, had waited in the ante-room. They waited a long time, to hear the bride cry out and weep, for then it is known that she is intact, and all is well. But the yellow-haired one did not cry out – she made no sound at all, of joy or sorrow, and after a time Ahira and the others had gone away, shaking their heads and predicting no good outcome of this marriage. But Muhna had stayed, shivering a little in the cold air from the desert that blew through the unglazed window slit, for this was an old part of the building. She waited with patience and she heard the Prince take the woman four times, for he was a man of great power, a prince among men, but still the woman was silent. And at last, Muhna thought that Tariq el Said must have discovered that the woman was not pure and that the mark of maidenhood was not on the sheets, for she heard him say one English word, very loud and in an angry voice, and there was the noise of a sharp blow. Then he came out of the dim ante-room, striding past Muhna as though he did not see her, and disappearing to his own quarters. And Muhna heard weeping at last, very quiet and muffled, and she smiled, and went to bed.

The air in the wedding-chamber smelt musty and heavy with the scent of over-sweet perfume and herbs. For a while Dorrie lay still, glad at least to be left alone and to relax her aching body. Four times Tariq el Said had made love – no, that was not the right phrase. The Anglo-Saxon word was the only possible one. Four times he had driven into her with the power and the apparent indifference of a hammer-drill, as though he had saved all the months of frustrated waiting and meant her to pay for them in one night. There had been no preliminaries, no love-play. He had stripped her naked and gazed at her body, and his face had never seemed so predatory. She had been prepared to simulate passion or even affection, knowing that the self she was offering to Tariq could never wholly be his, either physically or spiritually. But the near-rape had taken her by surprise. Never before had she felt so strongly that she was a mere chattel – what Cy would call a 'sex-object', and that her feelings and responses were of such little importance. Looking up into the bearded face of this stranger who was her husband, as he lay heavily upon her, Dorrie could see no tenderness in his eyes – no recognition even, only a blaze of triumph as though he had cut down an enemy with his sword. The engorged penis that he had shoved into her with such savagery felt more like machinery than human flesh, a mechanical piston that thrust and thrust, faster and faster, generating no pleasure but only a sick realization that sex could be Paradise with one man and Hell with another. She bit her lip, willing herself only to endure and not to cry out, to deny him the pleasure of knowing that she suffered. Because she recognized the expression on Tariq's face. It was too late, but she knew that it was called revenge. At last, with a grunt, he had finished, and she felt the trickling semen with a feeling of relief that she could sleep at last. But he did not move or speak, and after a few moments the soft limpness inside her thickened and hardened once more, swelling until it seemed to fill her whole belly, and once again she endured the dull misery of thrusting flesh, and again, and yet again, until the world seemed one nightmare of scarlet and black and she felt that she had never hated anything as much as she hated that bearded face that hung over her, the eyes blank with lust.

When he had finally finished, his last ejaculation seeming fully as potent as the first, and had rolled off her, Dorrie turned on her side, too exhausted to do more than long for sleep. After a moment, she was conscious of Tariq kneeling beside her, motionless, and she half-turned to see what he was doing.

There was a lamp in the wedding-chamber, a horrible Western electric lamp which changed colour like a firework display. By its light, Tariq was intently studying the sheets, and, as Dorrie turned, he put a hand on her buttocks and shoved her violently away so that he could see where she had lain.

'What is it?' Dorrie whispered, tiredly, and then recoiled at the face he turned to her. She had shamed him, and shame was something that Tariq el Said would never forgive.

'Whore!' he shouted, and before she knew what he was doing, he had struck her a heavy, open-handed blow on the side of the face.

Morning came and the sun shot from the rim of the desert like a pouncing lion, reflecting from the glittering, shifting dunes with colours of bleached gold and peach and brick-dust, and from the sleek and gleaming high-rise buildings of modern Riyadh. The humidity was near eighty degrees, the heat as unexpected as a blow to the head, and Dorrie began to realize that the thick curtains that shrouded most of the rooms in a Victorian gloom had a very practical purpose.

She waited in her room for what seemed a long time, that first morning. She was suddenly afraid of this alien land and its people, whose politeness and impassivity could conceal a face of primitive brutality. She told herself

237

that she was being a fool. She had never feared Tariq el Said before, or any other man, and if, as seemed likely, she had made a stupid mistake with her impulsive decision to have a new and different life far from Ross Cavallo, why, then she could pack her bags and take the next plane back to London. There was no need to stay here and be treated like some mediaeval princess. The distant, amplified voice of the muezzin, calling the faithful to prayer, brought her to the window. The palace of Tariq el Said was outside Riyadh, separated from it by a rippling expanse of sand, whose extent was difficult to judge. It might be a long hot walk if Tariq wanted to be awkward and refuse to let her have a car to the airport. But, surely, he would not want her to stay? He must be as eager to be rid of her as she of him.

There was a modern bathroom next to the bedroom, with a gleaming pink suite and thick towels, although the water from the gold-plated taps was tepid and a little rusty-looking. Dorrie took a bath, lingering in the cool water and letting it lap soothingly against the tender ache of her genitals. When she came out, she found a tray with coffee, hard-boiled eggs, dates and Arab bread on a low table, and she ate hungrily, although the coffee was strongly flavoured with cardamom and almost unpalatable.

The bath and the food gave her strength and courage, and she looked at her situation as dispassionately as possible. She had been a stupid, impulsive fool, as usual, but her mistake was not irreversible – in Arab countries, she was sure, divorce was quite simple. She would speak to Tariq about it straight away.

Only her toilet things, nightwear and a silk wrapper had been brought to the wedding-chamber. Her other clothes and luggage were still in the guest room she had occupied before the marriage ceremony. Still a little confused about the layout of the palace, which was a complex of different buildings within a compound, with courtyards and gardens between them, she eventually found her way to the room, encountering only a couple of servants on the way, who bowed shyly and scuttled aside.

Another servant girl was in the room, and with her was Ahira, the fierce-looking old lady who was Tariq's mother. Dorrie's luggage was spread out on the floor, her clothes being held up by the serving girl for Ahira's inspection, and placed in one of two piles, one already very much larger than the other.

Dorrie paused in the doorway and stared at them and Ahira glanced over without any change in the expression on her face.

'Good morning,' Dorrie said, calmly, 'May I ask what you are doing with my clothes?'

Ahira spoke a few guttural words to the girl, who stopped delving and stood with hands clasped and eyes downcast.

'These clothes – ' Ahira indicated the larger pile with one bony hand, 'they are not suitable for a Saudi princess. They must go. You will have new clothes – proper clothes. And you will wear the abbaya over your dress and, if you go out, you will wear the ghishwa or the batula over your face.'

Dorrie felt an insane desire to laugh. Could this be happening to Dorrie St James? An old Arab lady instructing her on how she was to dress?

'I'm sorry,' she said, as gently as she could, 'but I'm afraid I must ask you to leave my clothes alone. I shall wear what I choose.'

Ahira did not answer. She took a step nearer to Dorrie and struck her on the cheek, a light, stinging slap.

'You will learn respect, daughter,' she said, in her halting English, 'and you will not bring shame on the house of el Said with your Western garments. You are my son's wife – but only his third wife – you will be humble and respectful at all times.'

Dorrie was almost incoherent with rage. To be hit by Tariq had been bad enough, but at least he had the excuse of his anger at finding she was not a virgin. But for this autocratic old bitch to strike her with that detached air of correcting a wayward child – it was not to be borne.

'This is ridiculous!' she said, 'It's the twentieth century, for God's sake! Where's Tariq – I want to speak to him!'

'He will not come at your bidding! He is not one of your Western husbands who follow their wife's will as though they were calves!' Ahira said, with pride. 'He has gone out hunting – he will return when he wishes. And when he does return, disobedient one, he will chastise you if you do not do as I, Ahira, say. Do you not know that many of these clothes are "haram" – that is, forbidden by Islam? Not many years past, the Mutawain, the religious police, would have beaten your bare legs with sticks if you went out in these short dresses. It is not seemly, no – and you are part of this family now, and will bear my son's children, Inshallah.'

She gestured to the servant girl, who picked up the pile of rejected clothing and hurried out, ducking her head as she passed Dorrie. Then Ahira turned to go.

'Come,' she said, rather more gently, 'I do not wish to be discourteous to a stranger. It is hard for you to learn our ways. Come – I will show you where you are to live, in the women's quarters.'

The room she took Dorrie to was furnished with bed, wardrobe, dressing-table and so forth, all in European style, but ugly and heavy. This part of the palace was of more modern construction and the windows were glazed and curtained, fastened tightly against the daytime heat. It was also air-conditioned, almost to the point of chilliness, and Dorrie shivered in her thin silk robe.

240

'You see,' Ahira said, not without satisfaction, 'your Western garments are not best for Saudi. Here – put this dress on – it will become you, and you will please my son.'

'I couldn't give a shit about your son,' Dorrie thought, but as there seemed little alternative, she dressed in the long, shapeless gown which was a rather ugly light mauve colour with a turquoise motif and thick embroidery encrusted on the bodice.

'So! Good, good – you will be a good wife, I know! There – you are comely now, – let your hair be loose – ah! what a colour, like the sun!' crooned Ahira, obviously determined to be pleasant. 'Come now – we will sit for a while in the women's "diwan", and you shall tell me and Muhna and Fatima about your life.'

The diwan was a long, low room overlooking a court-yard where a fountain played and a carefully tended lawn and lemon and acacia trees provided a welcome patch of green after the glare of desert sand and white stucco.

The floor to ceiling arched windows had elaborate fretted stonework embellishing them, and led out on to a balustraded terrace. The effect was of simplicity and elegance, rather marred by the ugly, Western chairs and sofas that stood against the walls and the electric lamps with eccentric bases and garish shades of multi-coloured glass. There were knick-knacks, ornaments and curiosities everywhere – jewel boxes with twirling ballerinas, ciga-rette boxes with mechanical birds that picked up cigarettes in their beaks and inevitably broke fifty per cent of them, animal ornaments in all colours and sizes, from small, gaudy elephants to gigantic pink plush rabbits and, on the walls, a few hideous paintings of large-eyed children from the Place Pigalle, and a blown-up photograph of an Alpine scene.

Ahira indicated the room with pride, 'You will feel at home here, will you not? You see how modern we are?'

The two young women in the room, who were seated on cushions on the floor, looked up as Dorrie and Ahira came in, and the younger one smiled timidly. Dorrie knew that they were Muhna and Fatima, Tariq's other wives, although she had not known of their existence until the wedding feast the day before, and this was the first time she had seen them unveiled. Muhna was a strong-faced young woman who could have been anything from twenty-five to thirty. She stared at Dorrie without smiling, and there was something like contempt in her large, dark eyes. The other girl was much younger, in her mid-teens, with a sweet, timid face and huge kohl-rimmed eyes like those of a gazelle. She rose from her cross-legged position in a graceful movement and came forward to greet Dorrie.

'Welcome, my sister,' she said, in English. 'We are happy you have come, Muhna and me. Muhna speaks no English, but she wishes me to greet you.'

Dorrie doubted that, looking at the cold eyes of the older woman, but she smiled at her in as friendly a fashion as possible.

'Yes – these are your sisters now,' said Ahira. 'You must all live together in harmony and not disturb my son's peace with squabbling. He is a good man, Alham-d'ullillah, but he is not patient with noisy women.'

Fatima took Dorrie's hand, and began to lead her round the big room, full of naïve pride in the possessions of the family.

'It's all very modern,' Dorrie said, carefully, 'don't you have any traditional Arabian things – furniture, or bedouin rugs or anything?'

'Oh, *no*!' Fatima laughed, 'We have had enough of old things! We have been a poor country for too long – we don't wish to be reminded of our hard past!'

More cardamom-flavoured coffee was brought in, on a heavy silver tray, and Fatima chattered on, pausing sometimes to translate to the unresponsive Muhna and evidently enjoying her importance. Ahira stayed for a while, making an occasional dry comment, then she left the daughters-in-law to their own devices, and there was a lightening of the atmosphere, as though an autocratic teacher had left a classroom.

Dorrie wandered over to the long windows and looked out. 'The garden's pretty,' she commented, idly, 'Do you ever sit there, or is it against some law or other?'

'Oh, no!' Fatima giggled. 'No law – that is our garden! But – it is too hot just now – we will go out later in the afternoon, if you would like, and sit in the shade.'

'Sitting again? Don't you ever get any exercise, like riding or sport?'

Fatima shook her head, a little abashed that her new sister might despise them. 'We have television,' she offered, 'it is very good. Sometimes there are BBC programmes – also very good, but many bits are taken out by the censors.'

'It sounds exciting,' Dorrie said, and wondered if one easily went mad from boredom. A few days of this and she might even welcome Tariq into her bed just by way of breaking the monotony.

Lunch-time came and the four women ate in the room by themselves, waited on by female servants. They squatted on the floor around a large mat, which one was supposed to pull over one's knees before feeding from huge, communal silver platters with one's right hand. There were vast quantities of food – piles of fresh Australian steaks, kebabs of veal and chicken, salads, bread, dates, fruit and yogurt. Dorrie noticed that Muhna, as she sat down, puffed a little, and was a good deal overweight beneath her loose gown. No wonder, with three large

243

meals a day and no exercise. There had been boxes of confectionery in the diwan as well, slightly sticky with heat despite the air-conditioning, from which Muhna and Fatima had helped themselves constantly, wiping their fingers fastidiously on the Kleenex that was so prevalent that Dorrie half-expected to see it flying from flag-poles. Even two weeks of this, and she would look like Michelin-man, Dorrie told herself, trying to eat sparingly of the tit-bits that Fatima was piling on to the rice in front of her. Her decision to leave Tariq enabled her to go through the day with equanimity, and she felt so tired that she was able to enjoy the lazy afternoon sitting in the shade of the courtyard garden amongst the flowers, drinking fresh-pressed lemonade or Coca-Cola, and listening, half-dozing, to the fountain and Fatima vying in their quiet chatter. It was only for a little while – a short unpleasant-ness with Tariq and she would be on her way back to London. In the meantime, this odd, mediaeval life was strange enough to be savoured as an experience, if nothing else.

The evening meal came, with another abundance of food, and Tariq still had not been near his wives, the old or the new. Dorrie, keeping her voice as humble and respectful as possible, asked Ahira if the Prince was back from his day's hunting.

'Aye!' said Ahira, shortly, through a mouthful of rice flavoured with spices and dried lemons.

'Well – may I speak to him, please?' Dorrie pursued meekly, longing to tip the food platter over her mother-in-law's venerable head.

Ahira munched and mumbled, her bony jaws working vigorously as she reached out a hand for another tit-bit.

'He is tired,' she said, at last, 'I expect he will wish to sleep.'

Dorrie held on to her temper with both hands. 'I only

want to speak to him for a few minutes. Would you please see His Highness and crave the favour of an audience?'

Ahira chuckled, missing the irony of Dorrie's tone. Come, this was better! The yellow-haired one was learning humility quickly. She might make a good wife after all. Let her speak with Tariq – it was right that he should sow the seed of his loins in her now, while his passion was still strong. That was the way to make lusty boy children. She finished her meal at leisure and rose to her feet. 'Wait!' she said.

A short while later she came back to the diwan. 'You may come now,' and, as Dorrie made to follow her, 'Wait! First your face must be covered – put this batula over it.'

She handed Dorrie the beak-shaped face-mask. Dorrie took it, but did not put it over her face and Ahira stared at her impassively.

'I am only going to speak to my husband! Surely I don't have to hide my face for that? Good heavens above – in Riyadh, most of the women had their faces uncovered!'

'Pah!' Ahira spat, 'They have been led astray by dogs and infidels. In this house we follow the old ways, the ways taught to us by Muhammad bin Abdul Wahhub, praise be to Allah, Lord of the Worlds. Hurry. If you wish to speak to my son, you will cover your face – there are other men who might see you.'

With an ill grace Dorrie obeyed, and followed Ahira through a maze of apparently random corridors, rooms and courtyards. She could feel her irritation mounting as she was instructed to wait in an ante-room until Tariq was ready to see her. Also in the ante-room were several of Tariq's entourage who had been with him in London, but for all the recognition they gave Dorrie, she might as well have been invisible. Ahira disappeared again, leaving Dorrie fuming and kicking her heels in the small, crowded room. She would not have waited to be told to go in, except that a large, impassive bodyguard blocked the door. There was nothing to do but sit on one of the big, cream-cushioned sofas that lined the wall, and wait.

After ten minutes, she thought that Tariq was probably trying to humiliate her a little more, to show her that her place here in the palace was very far beneath him. What, she wondered, had she done to make his feelings for her change to this near-hatred? The man she had felt she was beginning to know and like, despite his sometimes uncontrollable passions, when they were cruising in the Caribbean, seemed to have donned a new personality when he put on his Arab-style thaub, gutra and ageel. Well, she was not going to sit here in these ridiculous garments like a bundle of forgotten laundry. She rose to her feet, and one or two of the men glanced incuriously at her, as she turned to go through the arched doorway by which she had entered. As she did so, shuffling footsteps sounded along the corridor and a moment later a man confronted her. He was somewhere in his mid-twenties, though he could have been either much younger or much older. Thick-set, and with a soft fleshiness unusual in an Arab male, his hair grew low over his forehead, his nose was formless as though it had been badly broken and left unset, his mouth was loose and wet, a thin string of spittle hanging perpetually from one side, and his eyes had the unfocused dullness of the deranged. Dorrie stepped quickly to one side to let him pass, but as she did, he too side-stepped, his mouth opening and curving upwards into the mockery of a smile. Dorrie stood still, hoping that he would pass her and let her escape, but, instead, he brought his face near to hers, crouching and peering up at her with an expression of ludicrous glee. Dorrie tried not to shrink back, but there was a dreadful rank odour from the man, compounded of sweat, urine, spices and some

246

sweet, cloying perfume. She glanced round for aid to the other men in the room, but there was no help there. One of them picked up the newspaper *Al Riyadh* with studied indifference, and became absorbed. Others conversed together and one or two grinned openly, enjoying the Englishwoman's discomfiture.

'Excuse me,' Dorrie said, quietly, 'will you let me pass?'

Grinning still, he put his hand out and took a loose tress of her hair in his fingers, muttering something incomprehensible below his breath. Dorrie felt her heart begin to beat uncomfortably. Were these men going to sit by and watch while this lunatic mauled her? Sharply, she pushed his hand away, and said, 'No! Don't touch!' Then to the other men, all now watching with interest, she said, 'Tell him to let me pass. You – what's your name, Khalife, isn't it? You know who I am – make this man go away!'

Khalife, whom Dorrie knew spoke English perfectly well, shuffled and looked embarrassed, muttering in Arabic and spreading his hands in a gesture of helplessness. The idiot, excited by the feel of the silky hair in his hand, babbled louder and louder and pushed against Dorrie, forcing her back against the wall with his body until she was nearly retching with disgust and fear.

'Hammad!'

At the sound of Tariq's voice, the man shrank back, cowering away from Dorrie and emitting a pitiful howling sound. He crouched on the floor, his arms protecting his head, as though in anticipation of a blow, then, still on his haunches, scuttled as rapidly as a crab through the archway. His shuffling footsteps could be heard limping quickly away, then there was silence.

'Well,' Dorrie said, trying to control her breathing and clenching her hands to stop them trembling, 'what a charming household you have, my dear! Any other little surprises in store for me?'

He did not answer, merely turned and preceded her into the inner room and Dorrie had perforce to follow him. She closed the door behind her.

This inner room was an office, with a big desk, telephones, a telex, even a computer. It was carpeted in pale grey and the upholstered chairs were dark red, the only splash of colour against the unadorned whiteness of the walls. Tariq was in thaub and head-dress, but it was Dorrie, in her enveloping dress with the black abbaya and the face-mask, who felt out of place. She tore the mask off and flung it on the ground. Tariq watched her, impassively, sitting behind his desk with his hands folded calmly before him.

'Good gracious!' Dorrie said, 'we're back in the twentieth century are we? I was beginning to think I'd got into a time warp.'

'Yes – you despise us, do you not?' Tariq said, 'Our ancient traditions and culture, our religion – they are all stupid in your eyes. Do you think I do not know that, Dorrie? That I was tolerated for my wealth but laughed at by you British because I am a dirty, oil-rich Arab?'

'Don't be bloody ridiculous!'

'No – I am not ridiculous! It is you Westerners with your corrupt ideas, your godless society, your fornication and adultery who are ridiculous!'

'My, oh my! Puritanism is alive and well – correct me if I'm wrong, old son, but I seem to remember a fair amount of fornicating and corruption that you did yourself when you were away from home. Besides – I certainly never despised you. At one time I was beginning to like you – otherwise I would hardly have come out here to marry you, would I?'

'You came to hide your shame,' Tariq said, curtly. Dorrie laughed.

'Oh, grow up, for God's sake! Compared with most English girls I'm whiter than white. We don't set such a premium on virgo intacta, you know – we're rather more interested in things like being kind and considerate to one's wife, and not raping her like a mad dog.'

Tariq flushed darkly. The epithet was one of the most insulting one could offer an Arab. He half rose from behind his desk, but Dorrie was continuing.

'Anyway – there's no point in us wrangling about the virtues of our different cultures. Let's call it quits, shall we? The mistake was mine, in thinking that you cared for me in anything other than a purely physical way, and in not realizing that I could not possibly fit in with your way of life. I believe a divorce is quite a speedy procedure in Saudi – perhaps you would arrange it? And while we're here in your up-to-date office, maybe you could arrange my flight home.'

For the first time since the wedding ceremony, Dorrie saw Tariq smile. It was a smile of genuine amusement which she answered uncertainly, and it spread to his eyes, and then he put back his head and laughed.

Dorrie glowered at him, uncertain whether he was laughing at her or with relief at being so easily rid of her.

'Oh, so easy, is it not?' he said, when he could speak, wiping his eyes with a handful of Kleenex from his desk. 'It is like a dress you buy from Harrods – it does not fit, or you do not care for it – never mind, send it back! Quite simple! No, Dorrie – I'm afraid it will not be as easy as that.'

'What the hell do you mean? Stop playing games, Tariq – it's not bloody funny!' She leaned forward on his desk, her fists clenched on the immaculate blotter. Tariq smiled blandly, his eyes cold.

'Did you ever see,' he remarked, with an apparent change of subject, 'did you ever see a programme on your British television, called "Death of a Princess"? Sometime in 1980, I believe it was. It caused horror in your country and here, in Saudi, there was grave offence at the intrusion in our family affairs. The princess in question, my cousin Mishaal bint Fahd bin Muhammad, had been foolish. She had committed adultery, and our laws, as she knew, are very strict, especially for the Royal House, who are expected to set a good example of purity and chastity. Are you following me, my dear?'

'Are you trying to threaten me, Tariq?'

'No – merely to point out that what to you is an insignificant lapse, is here an offence actually punishable by death. Yes, my gazelle. Believe it or not, I could have your pretty golden head struck off your shoulders, quite legally.'

'Why bother? I can just as easily remove my head and my body too, as they're so offensive to you. Divorce me or not, as you please – I'm in no hurry to remarry. I just want to shake the desert sand from my feet as fast as I can.'

'Perhaps. But you will not.'

'Really? Just try and stop me!'

'Now you are being childish, Dorrie. Consider – I have your passport for a start.'

'Oh – Ahira pinched that as well, did she, the thieving old witch. Well, I expect I can get another at the British Embassy.'

'And if you do? Do you think my family is powerless? We *rule* this Kingdom, foolish one. You will not be allowed to leave.'

Dorrie licked lips that had suddenly gone dry.

'Tariq – don't be unreasonable. You don't really want me here – you don't care for me. Let me go.'

'No. I am afraid that that is really not possible. It is true that I do not love you – you have deceived me and I will not forget that. But – it would be shameful for me to let you go – you must see that, surely? It would be like admitting I had made a mistake. No – you will stay. You will learn to be submissive and obedient – a perfect Saudi wife. You will respect me and my mother and your sister wives. It should be an interesting experiment.'

The blood pounded in Dorrie's ears till she felt she was suffocating in the depths of a nightmare. It could not be true – not really happening to her – she would wake in a moment and that dark, bearded face would only be a hateful memory.

'You *bastard*!' she screamed suddenly, launching herself at him with her hands outstretched to claw the mocking smile from his lips.

Something cool and sweet-smelling was being stroked gently on to her aching back, smarting where the skin was broken. Dorrie groaned and twisted her head round. Fatima smiled timidly, squatting beside her on the floor with a pot of ointment at her side.

'Are you very sore, my poor sister?' she whispered.

'Am I – oh, shit!' Dorrie tried to sit up and found all her muscles were stiff and aching.

'No – lie still. Do not move yet. I will soothe it for you.'

She wanted to shout and scream, to yell like a fish-wife and call Tariq el Said the filthiest names she could think of. She wanted to run through the palace, naked as she was, till she found him, and drive a dagger right into his heart. Instead, as Fatima stroked her throbbing back with a small soft hand like a child's, and murmured gently to her, Dorrie found herself choking back tears.

'What the hell *is* that stuff, anyway?' she said, gruffly,

swallowing hard, 'Pounded camel dung and rose petals, I suppose.'

'Oh, *no*!' Fatima said, giggling, 'Only Nivea cream – it was all I could find. But it is cool and soothing, is it not?'

'Sure. Soothe away.' Dorrie closed her eyes.

She had been beaten. Tied up like a dog and beaten with a whip. Ten lashes, from her shoulders to her waist, and they had hurt more than anything she could remember in her life. And then, when it stopped at last, and they had untied her, she had fallen to the floor, half-fainting, and Tariq had raped her, matter-of-factly and immediately. With the strength of hatred, and oblivious of the weals on her back, she had fought him off, her body clenched against him, fists and feet struggling to injure him. He had enjoyed that, all right. Oh, boy – that had been a mistake. She had heard his breath coming quickly with excitement as he forced her legs apart, and he had hardly managed to get inside her before he ejaculated. She would not struggle again. Next time she would put up as much of a fight as a slab of wet fish. See how he liked that. At least she had not cried. Screams and oaths, yes – but she had not given him the satisfaction of her tears. It was only now, with Fatima being kind and sympathetic . . .

'Our husband,' Dorrie said, 'is a bastard.' Then she wept.

After a while, when her tears had stopped and she felt only a dull tiredness, she said to Fatima, 'Does that often happen?'

'What – a beating? Oh, no, sister! Never before, either to Muhna or to me. Our husband is a good and kind man – you must have made him very angry!'

She looked at Dorrie with something like awe, 'But you are from the West, and you do not yet know our ways. It will be better soon.'

'I'm a fast learner,' Dorrie said, wryly. She got gingerly into a crouching position and, wincing, stood up and reached for her wrap. 'Fatima – tell me who that creature is – Ahmed or something – he looks as though he's completely crazy.'

'Hammad? He is the half-brother of our husband. Yes – he is mad,' Fatima said, matter-of-factly.

'Well, why isn't he in a mental hospital?'

Fatima's brow furrowed, 'Please? A hospital? Oh, no – he is quite well. He is not sick, only mad.'

'Yes, I know – but that means his brain is sick. He should be looked after by doctors and nurses.'

'No – it is the will of Allah. It is our duty to care for people like Hammad. Also, he does no harm. He is happy, thanks be to God.'

'He might well be – but I wasn't very happy when he tried to maul me.'

'Maul? Oh – he touched you? Yes, Hammad likes pretty things. But he would never harm you. You see – we have very strong family feeling here in Saudi. Our old people, our people who are ill in the head like Hammad – we like to take care of them, and not to shut them up as you do in Britain. Don't worry about poor Hammad – he never comes to the women's quarters.'

'Hammad's the least of my worries. But, potty or not, if he lays a finger on me, I'll knee him in the crutch.'

'Please? You must help make my English good – what is "knee in the crutch"?'

Dorrie giggled. 'Ouch – that hurts. One thing's for sure, Fatima – you're going to have the most interesting vocabulary of any Arab lady!'

Early next morning, when Dorrie got up, she stood for a long time at her window, staring out towards Riyadh. It looked so modern, with its towering concrete buildings, its new houses springing up all around it, and yet here, separated by a stretch of sand, she was a prisoner in an environment that was almost mediaeval. It was impossible – she had come of her own free will, and she would leave by it. If Tariq el Said thought she could be beaten into submission, he could think again. She would damn well walk across the desert – it couldn't be more than three miles. But, before she went, she would ring the airport from Tariq's office, and book a flight.

It was very early. The palace was still sleeping and there were only a few servants moving noiselessly about. Dorrie had dressed in Arab garments and veiled her face with a ghishwa, the thin silk Arab veil, in order to escape notice, and she made her way without hindrance to the part of the palace where Tariq had his office. No one stopped her or spoke to her, no harsh voice called her peremptorily back, and the office was open and unattended. There was even a card by the telephone with instructions in several languages for the use of visitors, and numbers, including that of the airport. It was as though everything was being made easy. She dialled the number, heard it ring, was answered and transferred to someone who spoke perfect English. Yes, indeed, there was a flight to London that afternoon, arriving at Heathrow at 15.30 hours. First class, certainly madam. What name?

'Dorrie St James.' As she spoke, she was methodically pulling out the drawers of Tariq's desk. Her passport would probably be there. He would think her too cowed to come searching for it. There was a brief pause on the other end of the line. Then, 'Excuse me, Miss St James, but – do you have your exit visa in order?'

'My exit visa? No – how do I get it?'

'Oh – through the usual channels, you know. It need not take too long. You are a guest of Prince Tariq el Said, are you not? He will be able to arrange it for you.'

254

'I see. Thank you,' Dorrie said, dully.

'Not at all. Shall I wait to confirm that flight until you call back, then?'

She replaced the receiver without bothering to reply, half-expecting to hear Tariq's mocking laughter behind her, and stood motionless for a few moments, the fingers of one hand drumming a light tattoo on the desk.

She returned to her room and put a few essentials into a small handbag. She would have liked to change into jeans or something less encumbering than the voluminous Arab dress, but Ahira had, of course, removed anything of that nature. The sun was well up by now, but still all was quiet, as though the palace was held in an enchanted sleep while she made her escape. Luckily, it was almost all on one storey, with the exception of the two-storey central 'majlis' for the reception and entertainment of guests, so she was able to open her bedroom window, hitch up her skirts and jump to the ground quite easily. It was all so simple, so unmelodramatic, that she nearly giggled, reminded suddenly of the Enid Blyton books of her youth. 'Five Escape from the Harem,' she thought, grinning. Then she picked up her bag, directed a vulgar gesture at the shuttered windows of the palace, and trudged off towards Riyadh. If she could get to the British Embassy, she would be all right, she was sure. Her father's name carried a lot of weight in diplomatic circles – they would get her out, somehow, even if they had to smuggle her out in the diplomatic bag. Let them worry about that. The main thing was to concentrate on getting there. She would pretend she was a child again, walking on the beach with her father. Saunton Sands – that long, quiet stretch of beach, with its white sand backed by grassy dunes, the sea-birds wheeling and mewing above, a salt breeze combing your hair into tangles and your six-year-old self leaping and springing as though youth filled your veins with fizzy lemonade.

But this was not Saunton. This was the desert, Arabia Deserta, and the sea was nearly a hundred miles away. Before she had been walking for ten minutes, sweat was pouring off every inch of her body, soaking the thick cotton dress and making her back sting with pain. She was stiff and sore, weakened by the beating she had had, unable to hurry, or to do anything more than trudge doggedly on. She had a silk scarf, an elegant Hermès square in her bag, and she put it over her head, but the sun beat through it as though she was being struck on the head with a brass hammer. Her mouth was already dry – what an idiot, not to bring water with her. Still, she would not panic or go back – she could actually see Riyadh, quivering on the horizon mirage-like, in a haze. As she stood resting for a moment and looked towards her goal, a plane took off, twinkling briefly in the still blue air like a silver insect, before it veered and settled on its course to the west, the sound of its engine coming faintly to Dorrie's ears.

Her head was aching now, so that each footstep seemed to jar all the way up to her skull. The road was rough and dusty, pot-holed and unpleasant to walk on, and the sand, though softer, filled her shoes and was like struggling through treacle. She had never been so hot. She felt as though the blood would boil as it pounded in her brain, and a dizzy nausea kept rising in her and making her stagger. Her back was on fire as though each lash was being reapplied with a hot iron. Why had she not waited until she felt stronger? Why had she not been better prepared? She should have stolen one of Tariq's cars – she could have been in Riyadh in ten minutes. She looked back at the palace. She seemed to have covered a pitifully small distance, and Riyadh looked as far away as ever. There was the faint noise of a motor, and a car came out of the main gate of the palace. There was no cover – the scrubby thorn trees would not hide her. With an angry sob of despair, she began to run, the blistering air filling her lungs like a furnace blast, and within a few steps, the pain in her back seemed to rush up like a fountain to the pain in her head and combine in a whirlpool of darkness that swallowed her up and crumpled her into the dust.

She was beaten again. And, a week later when she tried once more, at night, she was brought back and beaten again. Shortly after that, Dorrie made a discovery that prevented her from trying again, at least for the moment. She was pregnant.

11

Dorrie shifted uncomfortably on the deep, upholstered chair. There was an ache in the small of her back and she felt suddenly irritable, as though the last two weeks of her pregnancy were equal in length to the first eight and a half months. Fatima and Muhna were mesmerized by a soap-opera on the television, so bland and inoffensive that it sent Dorrie to sleep every time she watched it, despite, or perhaps because of, the fact that she now understood a little of the language. She poured herself a drink of orange juice and reached for one of the little saffron cakes called 'al ogeili'. She had developed a liking – almost a craving – for the cardamom and saffron flavoured cakes and sweets since her pregnancy, but, as she ate, a twinge of uncomfortable indigestion made her think that she had better start cutting down on sweet things if she was ever to see eight and a half stones on the scales again.

Fatima, too, was pregnant, about four months gone, and Muhna had had an early miscarriage which had left her more grim-faced than before and more antagonistic towards Dorrie. Tariq was away, visiting the gaming tables of Monte Carlo. He had laughed when Dorrie asked politely to be allowed to accompany him.

'Oh, no, my sweet pearl!' he had said, derisively, 'For your condition is too delicate and fragile. You must not travel.'

'Are you trying to drive me mad?' Dorrie had asked, in a low voice, 'Keeping me shut in this place – I can't stand it! You let Muhna and Fatima go out – they're always

258

being taken to the souk and to the supermarket. Fatima even said you were going to take her to London. Why not me?'

He laughed again. 'Does one take a half-tamed falcon and let it fly free? No, my dear! You know what we do? When we have a new, wild bird, we sew its eyelids together at first with fine thread – we allow it to see nothing. It is very angry – it tries to bite the string that ties its leg, and to scratch and bite its master – it would fly away if it could. And so would you, my little shahin – I read it in your eyes. You must be tied till you are tame.'

'Have I tried to run away again? Am I not tame enough? If I promise not to try to escape?'

He shook his head. 'No. You would break your promise, I'm afraid. You would argue that it was made "under duress" – is that not the phrase? Believe me, my dear – it is not that I find you very desirable at the moment, now you are grown heavy with child. When I make love to you, you are as responsive as a camel – you do not try to please me at all. And your eyes never soften to me – it is uncomfortable to read hatred in them while we are love-making. But – ' he shrugged, 'you are carrying my child. Another son, I hope. So, you must remain – for the time being, at least.'

It was this faint hope of an end to her captivity that helped Dorrie endure the long hot months of pregnancy. And now, there were only two weeks to go, perhaps three if the child was late as some first pregnancies were. She stirred restlessly and got up from her seat with difficulty. What an undignified business it was, this child-bearing. It would be different if one loved the father, perhaps, and looked forward to the birth. As it was, Tariq was welcome to the poor little bastard when it did arrive. He could get a wet-nurse in and add the child to his growing collection, as long as he gave her her freedom.

She wandered out into the courtyard garden, cool and pleasant now, with its fountain splashing and reflecting the moonlight, and the scent of roses and jasmine faint and sweet. It reminded her poignantly of the garden at Ash Friars and how lovely it would be on a mild October evening. There would still be a few tobacco flowers in bloom, perhaps, and late roses in the sunken garden. Her father liked to sit there in the evening sometimes, on the stone bench by the carp pool, smoking his pipe reflectively. Perhaps he was there now. Perhaps thinking of her. She had written to him, and he had replied, as kind and uncritical as ever, although she knew he had been distressed at her hasty marriage to Tariq. Her own letter was censored — she was not allowed to write anything of which Tariq did not approve — and, besides, she would have hated to make her father worry about her any more than he did already.

For that reason she had discouraged him when he suggested coming out to visit her, and she had told no one about the baby. They would only be horrified when she abandoned the brat. They would not understand.

She sat down heavily on the marble edge of the fountain, wondering how soon after the baby was born Tariq might let her go. Perhaps she would be home for Christmas. How marvellous a quiet, traditional Christmas at Ash Friars would be — she would never complain of boredom there again.

The indigestion was worse. She would have to ask Fatima for something. Curse this child — and its father. She hated the whole miserable business of pregnancy — the silly physical discomforts, the clumsiness of a body that had always been so limber and healthy that she had been almost unaware of it. She was well, she knew, and the young female doctor who came to see her every week was pleased with her, and quite happy that she should

260

have her child at the palace in accordance with Tariq's wishes.

'But – I want to have my baby in the hospital! Suppose anything goes wrong?' Dorrie had demanded. She didn't give a damn if the brat was born alive or dead or three-headed, but if she could get into the hospital she might be able to get away from there to the Embassy.

But the doctor, a vivacious, unveiled and apparently emancipated young woman, had only laughed.

'Now, now, Princess! That is foolish talk! I am quite sure you will have no trouble at all. You are very fit and healthy, and the baby is big – already you can feel how big he is! Your husband wishes you to have him at the palace – and I do not see why you may not!'

'Listen,' Dorrie had said, 'please try and help me – I am virtually a prisoner here . . .'

Ahira had come in then, gliding quietly over the tiled floor in her slippered feet as though she had been listening at the door. She had exchanged a few sentences in Arabic with the doctor, who smiled kindly at Dorrie.

'Yes, it is true. You are a little nervous, a little frightened. It must be strange for you, coming from England.' She had begun packing up her bag. 'I know, believe me, because I have been to England – to Leeds, to do part of my training. Do you know it?'

'No.'

'Ah – well it is very different from Riyadh. I will leave a prescription for a soothing medicine to calm your nerves.'

After that, Ahira was always present when the doctor came, and her vigilance had not relaxed since Tariq had left: she seemed to watch Dorrie constantly, even though her alien daughter-in-law was subdued and quiet and rarely left the women's quarters.

It was not only the watchful eye of Ahira that kept

Dorrie to her room, or the women's diwan and courtyard. It was a fear of encountering Hammad, the mad half-brother. She had never forgotten the feeling of horrified repugnance he had aroused in her when he had pushed his plump, malodorous body against hers, and, with her solitude, the incident had preyed on her mind to an extent that was quite foreign to her nature. Once, coming back to her room after an afternoon in the garden, she had smelt a rank smell and some of her underwear had been taken from a drawer and dropped on the floor. Shuddering, she had destroyed it. Another time, she had woken in the night and heard a noise – a sort of snuffling grunt like some nocturnal animal. She had turned on the light and yelled for a servant and heard limping footsteps shuffle away. After that, she had her bed moved into Fatima's room.

They had become good friends, she and Fatima, different as they were. The shy, dark-eyed girl came from a poor Qatari family, although her mother had been well-born and claimed to be one of the Al al Sheikh – the descendants of the Prophet. Her father had been a pearl fisher, a nokhatha or captain, with two small fishing boats, moderately prosperous until the advent of Japanese cultured pearls knocked the bottom out of the market. Things were better now – the Government took good care of its people, but there had been hard times before the oil came. Many had starved, and Fatima had been brought up with a reverent respect for the wealthy and particularly for the man who had deigned to marry her and give her a life of ease and comfort. So, although she had grown to love Dorrie, her 'sister-wife' as she called her, she would never do or say anything against the honour of her dear husband, not even deliver a letter to the British Embassy when Dorrie asked her to.

'I dare not – I must not!' she had pleaded, her dark

eyes tear-filled, 'Our husband would be so angry – he would divorce me, Dorrie, and send me in shame back to my family. Oh – do not ask me! Indeed, I would do anything to please you, dearest sister! I would cut off my right hand and give it to you . . .'

'And what the hell would I want with your sodding hand, you idiot!' Dorrie had stormed. 'Oh, forget it. I shouldn't have asked. Never mind – I suppose it's what you call the will of Allah. Perhaps I'll die in childbirth and solve all my problems.'

'Oh – Dorrie, no!' Fatima had burst into tears at the pathetic picture and it had taken Dorrie an hour to quieten her down, and then Ahira had taken her to task for upsetting Fatima in her delicate condition.

'What about my delicate condition?' Dorrie had said, 'No one gives a bugger about that!' and Ahira, who was gradually learning all the Western swear words, had slapped her sharply on the cheek. Dorrie thought she had never hated anyone, even Tariq, as much as she hated her old witch of a mother-in-law.

She was in the diwan now, squatting in front of the television with the others, and she glanced sharply round as Dorrie came in from the garden and leaned against one of the stucco pillars that flanked the doorway.

'Fatima,' Dorrie said, 'have you got something for indigestion? I've got such a pain.'

Fatima jumped willingly to her feet, even though the television programme was her favourite. She loved chemists' shops and never passed one without buying something, with the result that she had a remedy for every known ailment that flesh is heir to, and a few more besides.

'Of course!' she said, 'Only one minute and I will find something very good. I will . . .'

She paused as Dorrie suddenly gasped and clutched at

263

the pillar. A feeling as though a giant fist had slowly closed on her swollen belly made her stare at Fatima with something like fear. A second later, she felt a sudden gush of liquid from her vagina as her waters broke. The clenching fist tightened, then gradually relaxed its grip, and Dorrie, still clutching the pillar and staring wide-eyed at Fatima, felt her teeth beginning to chatter.

Ahira glanced at the pool on the tiled floor and rose unhurriedly to her feet. 'Your time is upon you early, my daughter,' she said, in her flat, unemotional voice. 'Come.'

Dorrie got a grip on herself. Now that the pain had gone it was easier – not that it had been unbearable, it was nothing compared to being whipped, but – it was such an unknown sensation, outside all experience, like being touched on a part of the body you had not known existed.

'Will you call Doctor Aziz, Ahira?' she said, calmly, 'Unless you think it would be quicker for a car to take me to hospital.'

Ahira shook her head. 'I will telephone. Come with me.'

Dorrie opened her mouth to argue and clamped it shut again as another contraction, stronger than before, made her gasp. Surely they shouldn't be coming as quickly? Why had she not read more about childbirth? Or listened attentively to the enthralled conversations between cousins and friends sharing the intimate details of their confinements? Idiot! she told herself. How many mares have you seen in foal? None of them read it up before-hand – it was a perfectly natural process and nothing to be afraid of. Besides, Dr Aziz seemed quite competent and she would be here in ten minutes. When the contrac-tion was over, she followed Ahira, and made to go into her own room, but the old woman took her arm in a skinny claw.

'No – not there. Come – there is a room prepared.'

The room she took Dorrie into was gloomy. An old-fashioned kerosene lamp, which Ahira lit, was the only illumination, and the bed was a plain mattress on the floor.

'What on earth? This is no good – I'll go to my own room, Ahira. Good God – there isn't even an electric light – how the devil is Doctor Aziz going to manage, poking about in the dark?'

'You stay here,' Ahira said, firmly, 'until Doctor Aziz comes. It is better.'

She planted herself in the doorway and, short of wrestling with the wiry little creature, Dorrie saw that she would have to stay where she was. Another contraction had started and she needed all her concentration to cope with it.

'Just go and ring the doctor. Quickly,' she panted, 'I'll stay here, damn you – till she comes anyway.'

Ahira stood watching for a moment longer until Dorrie sank down on the mattress and lay on her side, her knees drawn up as far as possible, then she nodded, satisfied, and went leisurely away.

When Doctor Aziz comes, Dorrie thought, she will see that I am moved to another room. She is a modern, twentieth-century doctor. Oh, God – let her come *soon*. I won't be afraid – I can bear this – it isn't really a pain, it's only the uterus contracting to push the baby out. Oh, shit, oh, hell – oh, *God*, it's hurting! I want to yell – I won't yell, Ahira's probably waiting for the screams. She hates me. Let the doctor come. Please God, let the doctor come and I'll believe in You, I promise. Oh, God – it hurts, it hurts.

The contractions sharpened, deepened, came in rhythmic waves. In between them, her mind wandered in a dream world and she imagined that her body was a pendulum with a swollen dragging weight on the end. It swung slowly back and forth between fire and darkness, and the fire was agony, and the darkness relief.

When Ahira returned, she could not tell if it was minutes or hours later. 'Is the doctor coming?' she whispered, and the old woman nodded and smiled, the bobbing shadows that the lamp made across her face giving her a macabre, witch-like aspect. She squatted down by the mattress and pulled up Dorrie's dress, pushing at the mound of her belly and nodding, her withered mouth working as though she mumbled to herself.

'It will not be long,' she said, 'Do not be afraid.'

She lit some incense in a burner and the heavy sweetness mingled with the smell of kerosene, making Dorrie's head swim. Then the old woman squatted on her haunches again, and began to sing a weird, tuneless chant beneath her breath.

Suddenly Dorrie half sat up, staring at her mother-in-law, 'You didn't ring the doctor, did you? Doctor Aziz isn't coming!'

'Lie down, foolish one!' Ahira pushed at her shoulder, 'Think you that I cannot bring my son's son into the world? The doctor woman is only a girl herself – has not yet borne children – how can she know what to do? It is modern foolishness.'

Dorrie struggled to get up, but the old woman held her shoulders down with unexpected strength, and the contractions were merging into one long agony.

'Fatima!' Dorrie cried out, her voice sounding shrill and cracked, 'Fatima, help me!'

Ahira watched her impassively, hardly bothering to turn her head, even when Fatima's swift, light footsteps were heard approaching.

'Oh, Dorrie! Poor sister-wife! Is it hurting much? Would you like to hold my hand?'

Dorrie began to cry tears of helpless rage. 'Fatima – she – Ahira – she won't call the doctor! She wants me to die!'

Fatima's childish mouth half-opened, and her eyes widened. She crouched down by Dorrie and took her hand.

'No – no, you must not say such things! The doctor will be here soon, will she not, Ahira?'

Ahira sniffed and bent forward to prod at Dorrie's belly again.

'Be silent, Fatima. You are a child who knows nothing. Go back to the diwan.'

'You see?' Dorrie panted, 'she wants me to die! Ring the doctor, Fatima – please! *Please!*'

Fatima rose slowly to her feet, still holding Dorrie's hand. Her face was troubled. 'Is it true, my mother? Have you not spoken to Doctor Aziz?'

Ahira's voice was like the hiss of a snake. 'Return to the diwan, insolent one, or I shall have you beaten, and my son will divorce you and send you back to your dog-eating miserable parents in disgrace.'

Dorrie could feel Fatima's small hand trembling in her own, but she stood very straight, and her voice was firm as she said, 'And if you do send me back, my parents would rather that I was divorced than that I turned away from a suffering human being. So, do what you will, Ahira. I am going to send for the doctor.'

Ahira shrugged. 'So – the little gazelle turns into a tiger? As you wish, child – send for the doctor. At any rate, she will be too late. This prince is impatient to enter the world.'

The pain was almost unbearable now, and with the heat and the incense, Dorrie felt herself losing consciousness. She felt her legs being pushed apart and a hand groping into her vagina, but she was too weary and pain-racked to

267

protest, and she could only moan faintly as another long contraction seemed to tear her body in half.

'Ross,' she whispered, half-conscious, 'Ross – where are you?' The misery of his loss to her, and the hopelessness of her love seemed to become a tangible thing, part of the pain, and she suddenly hated them all – all these dark-faced strangers and their alien God who had deserted her. And, more than anything, she hated this monstrous child fathered on her without love, who was destroying her in his struggle to enter the world. She felt an irresistible urge to expel the creature from her body, and she began panting to push it from her with the last of her strength.

She was dimly aware of Ahira's voice muttering beside her, words of gruff encouragement and exhortation, but she did not heed it. Her whole being was concentrated on ridding herself of this hated burden. She was dying, she was sure of that, dying in this stuffy, foreign room with no one near her except a malevolent witch with bony fingers that probed and hurt. The world was a black cloud lit by forks of scarlet lightning and she would be glad to leave it – but first she would void this monster from her body.

She heard Ahira mutter, 'Gently, gently, my daughter, wait one second,' but she would not wait. With a final thrust that tore the skin of her vagina and seemed to rip through her like a jagged knife, the child was born, its body slithering into the world with such a feeling of relief that Dorrie tried to shout with joy, her dry throat producing only a faint sob.

'Here, daughter! Do you not wish to see the son you have borne?' Ahira said. She tied and cut the cord as she spoke, but Dorrie, her eyes closed, only shook her head weakly. 'Drown the little bastard,' she whispered. Ahira grunted, held the child up by its heels, its tiny arms flailing the air, and it had begun to yell even before she smacked it. At the sound Dorrie's eyes flew open and she stared in astonishment. Her thoughts were suddenly so confused and disorientated that she thought she must be going mad. It was as though, all through her pregnancy and the labour itself, she had refused to think of what she carried as a human being. And now it was here, separate from her body, a complete entity, crying out and waving its arms as Ahira held it upside down, a triumphant grin cracking her toothless face.

'Give it to me!' Dorrie demanded. She half sat up, and held out her arms for the child, some strange, fierce emotion suddenly gripping her. Ahira, grinning still, handed the child carefully to its mother.

'A fine son, a fine prince,' she said, 'and safely delivered, eh? Old Ahira is not such a green fool, eh? Now – be still. The afterbirth is not yet delivered.'

Dorrie held her son in her arms and looked at him. Like a traveller from some distant bourne, he was stained and weary, and his newly opened eyes gazed at her, full of ancient, not-yet-forgotten wisdom. His skin was a delicate flushed pink and he had a down of fine dark hair on his head. His eyes were the inky-blue of most new babies and there was something, some indefinable cast of feature, or some expression that reminded Dorrie vividly of another time, another place. A quiet, firelit room, a baby in her arms, her own violent, overwhelming desire to bear a son to Ross Cavallo . . . She gazed down into the eyes of her son and began to laugh softly.

'What – you are pleased now? Aye – you should thank Allah for your safe delivery! And Ahira, too, perhaps! Now – lie down and put your legs apart and up – so. I will stop the bleeding and make your womb close again.'

A moment later, Dorrie cried out with pain as something like hot cinders was put into her tender, bleeding vagina.

'My God! What the hell are you *doing*?' she cried, and at that moment the doctor hurried in, bag in hand, flustered and apologetic.

'My dear Princess! I am so sorry – I was certainly not expecting you to be early – two weeks is it not? It was some minutes before Princess Fatima was able to reach me – and now, it seems I was not needed after all! Perhaps I could see the baby? Princess Ahira – could you ask for hot water for me to wash this young chap!'

Ahira, supplanted, scowled. 'In my time we did not bathe the baby the first day. This modern nonsense! I will bring fenugreek and camel milk for the girl – it is good for bringing milk.'

'If she does,' Dorrie said, as Ahira disappeared, 'I shall empty it over her.'

Doctor Aziz smiled briefly. 'I will try to discourage her – but you know what these old women are like. They will not accept the modern medicine. Well, this young man seems fine and healthy. You can hold him while I have a look at you. You must have had a very short labour – you are fortunate.'

Dorrie lay back, her baby in her arms, and opened her legs once more, resignedly. 'What has the old witch done, down there?' she said. 'It felt as though she was cauterizing me with a red-hot poker.'

She could see the young doctor's dark, intent face bent over her, and she saw the sudden frown and the sharply indrawn breath, heard the quiet murmur of anger.

'What is it, doctor?'

'It's all right. Do not distress yourself, my dear Princess. It is fortunate that I came. You are, I'm afraid, the victim of ignorance. Your mother-in-law has put hot salt in your vagina. It is – or was – a common enough practice, done to stop bleeding and close the cervix. The fact that it causes acute pain and sometimes makes the cervix seal up

270

altogether is apparently immaterial. I am afraid you will think that we Arabs are living in the Dark Ages – but believe me, it is not the sort of thing I learned in Leeds.'

Dorrie smiled wanly, 'I don't suppose it is. And I suppose Ahira was only trying to help. I thought she was trying to finish me off.'

Dr Aziz smiled uncomprehendingly. 'Now – we must stitch a little, I am afraid. Where on earth is that hot water? Perhaps you would like to suckle the baby, Princess? It is a good idea to do it quite soon.'

With a hand that shook a little, Dorrie unbuttoned the high front of her dress and exposed her breasts. The baby, feeling the warmth and softness against his cheek, turned his head eagerly, his mouth opening as he sought the nipple, his hand spreading, starfish-like, with ecstacy as he found it.

Dorrie felt the warmth of the little mouth and the strong tugging as her son sucked vigorously, and she tightened her arms round him. This was the monster that she had hated, this the child whose life or death had not mattered to her, whom she had been ready to cast aside so that she could escape from the palace and from Tariq. This was the child – a child conceived not in hatred, but in love. Her son – her son and Ross Cavallo's.

12

Ross woke suddenly. His heart was beating heavily and he was sweating. Still half-awake, he sat up and stared towards the faintly lit window.

'What is it, darling?' Sarah, wide awake, reached out to touch him gently. They were sharing a bed again since Sarah's illness was diagnosed. 'Were you dreaming?'

He shook his head to clear it, passed his hand over his eyes. 'I thought . . . someone was calling me.'

'Silly. You're getting obsessed with that stupid casino – you can't have a night off without them ringing you up. Don't start dreaming about it, too!'

'I wasn't . . .' He lay down again, kissing her lightly as he did. 'Sorry I woke you, darling.'

'I was awake.'

'Are you all right? Do you want anything?'

'Fine. Perfect. Dr McFarlane's very pleased with the way I've responded to treatment. Poor patient darling – poor monk! Soon I'll be able to be a real wife to you again, I promise.'

'I know. Don't worry. I'm having a very torrid affair with Leila in the meantime.'

Sarah giggled. 'Now I know you're desperate! Thank goodness your secretary is fat and fifty. Now, if it was someone like Dorrie St James . . .'

Ross grunted non-committally, kept his muscles from stiffening with a great effort and turned on his side as though preparing to sleep.

'I wonder how Dorrie is,' Sarah pursued, quietly. 'I

often think of her, and wonder if she's happy with her Prince.'

'Sure to be,' Ross said, shortly, 'He's rich and handsome – what more could a girl want?'

'Love,' Sarah said, snuggling against him, 'I hope she's got it. I'll write to her again – she didn't answer my last letter.'

'Shall we go to sleep?' Ross enquired, 'or shall we discuss a few more of your waifs and strays?'

'Sorry!' Sarah, contrite, fell silent, and was asleep quite soon, but Ross lay and stared into the darkness. It had been of Dorrie that he had been dreaming – she had been in a dark room, in pain, and calling him to help her, and he had been transfixed, powerless to move or speak. The memory of her agonized voice calling his name made him sweat, and he lay for hours trying to throw off the vividness of the dream, and trying not to think of Dorrie and the constant longing to hold her in his arms.

Tariq had returned. He had been away for the whole of Ramadan, in Monte Carlo, London and Las Vegas, gambling away the millions that his oil revenues gained for him faster than he could lose it. He had taken women when he needed them and had scarcely given a thought to his three wives in Riyadh. Even Dorrie – when he remembered how obsessed by her he had been, only a year before, he smiled to himself. There had never been another woman whom he had lusted over and desired so passionately, but he was a man to whom the pursuit was all – it was the spinning of the roulette wheel that excited him, the possibility of winning or losing rather than the result, and it was the same with women. While his conquest was uncertain – which was rare – his interest was at its height, but, once he had possessed someone physically, they lost much of their power to arouse him. Dorrie

273

had been different, in a way – more beautiful than most, to begin with, and he had never made her submit her will to his. But – in the end he had grown tired of her continual defiance. She had ceased to struggle and fight when he made love to her, but lay like a dead thing, limp and inert. There was no pleasure in it. And then, as her slender body, that had once reminded him of a lily, grew swollen and distorted with pregnancy, the last of his desire died away.

He returned to Riyadh having made up his mind to give the woman her freedom. There was no point, after all, in keeping her, since he no longer desired her, and she might corrupt the impressionable Fatima with her Western ways. Also, there was a new woman in Tariq's life – a woman whom he wished to invite to the palace as his guest. He had met her at the Cannes film festival and she called herself an actress, but her talents lay elsewhere. Her name was Nicole Montalban and she had improbably red hair and was unbelievably skilled in the most bizarre and erotic bedroom arts. Tariq was not thinking of making her his wife – he would never make that mistake again – but, as a long-term house-guest she was a most appetizing prospect. But not with Dorrie in residence. Nicole was neither intelligent nor refined – Tariq could easily imagine how Dorrie's caustic tongue would flay the French woman without mercy. And an angry or humiliated mistress was not good in bed. So – Dorrie must go.

He summoned her – not to his private room, or even to his office, but to the huge, impersonal majlis, or public reception room at the centre of the palace, and ordered her to bring his son with her.

He sat on a carved, Western-style chair to receive her, although he preferred when at home to sit on the floor-cushions, and when she came in he motioned her to take a seat beside him. She did not sit, but stood before him, her child in her arms, her eyes downcast, more subdued and submissive-seeming than he had ever seen her. She was thinner, too, he noticed, and her skin was pale, with none of the golden, healthy glow that had enhanced it when he first knew her. He made her wait in silence for a few moments, relishing the subjection of this once-proud creature, before he spoke.

'Are you well, Dorrie? Has your health been good since the child was born?'

'Yes – yes, perfectly . . .' she murmured, her eyes lowered so that she looked at her son rather than her husband.

'Give me the child, then! Let me see my new son!' He held out his hands for the baby. Dorrie hesitated, her arms tightening round the child, and Tariq scowled.

'At once, woman! Do you think I am not used to handling children? Give him here!'

Reluctantly, Dorrie passed the baby to Tariq, and he held the boy up at arm's length and stared at him.

'He is not much like either of us,' he commented.

'Oh – it's hard to tell at that age, don't you think?' Dorrie said, quickly. 'He has your dark hair and eyes. Your mother thinks he looks like your Uncle Faid.'

He grunted, 'Perhaps,' and placed the boy on his knee, in the crook of one arm. He did it competently, as he was used to handling babies and, in fact, was a kind and indulgent father, but Dorrie irritated him by her anxious expression, as though she was afraid he would drop the child, so he did not allow any tenderness to show. 'You have called him Sultan, as I instructed?' he said, and she nodded, then said, diffidently, 'I – I thought, perhaps, if you wouldn't mind – could he be called St James as well?'

Tariq considered, pursing his lips, but he was not ill-pleased to name his son after a branch of the British aristocracy.

'Yes,' he said, at length, 'Yes, I believe I can agree to that. And now, Dorrie – it is time to discuss your future.'

He paused again, enjoying the suddenly strained attention in those blue eyes.

'I find,' he went on, 'that we are quite – what do you say? – quite incompatible. You will agree, I expect. I therefore propose to divorce you and send you back to England as swiftly as possible.'

An expression of incredulous joy spread over Dorrie's face, lightening it in an instant to the beauty that still gave him a slight pang of regret.

'Tariq! Do you mean it? That I can go?'

He shrugged. 'Of course. Why not? We are civilized people, are we not?'

'Yes. Thank you. How – how soon?'

'When you will. As soon as you wish. Tell me when you want to leave and I will arrange a flight and your exit visa.'

'Any time – as – as quickly as you can, please. Thank you. What about Sultan? Will he need innoculations, do you know?'

'Sultan?' Tariq's black eyebrows rose in assumed puzzlement, 'Why should he need innoculations? My son stays here with me, of course.'

It was interesting to see the colour drain from the woman's face, leaving it the same shade as the marble pillars behind her. She took a step towards him, holding out her arms, and he could see her lips trembling as she moistened them with her tongue.

'No . . .' she whispered, 'please, Tariq – don't be cruel. Let me have my baby . . .'

'My son remains with me,' Tariq said, firmly, 'He is a Saudi prince. Do not worry – he will be well looked after.'

'Are you – is this just a game? A trick you're playing

on me, to see me beg you for something? All right – I don't care! Look!'

She dropped to her knees and put her forehead on the ground at his feet. Look, Tariq – I beg you, as a humble favour, to let me have my son – please! What can it matter to you? You have other sons – and daughters. In the name of God – or Allah, or whatever you like to call Him – don't do this to me! Don't be so harsh – I'm sorry if I haven't been what you wanted in a wife – it was my fault, I admit it. You can sleep with me again, if you want to, and I'll make it up to you – do anything you want . . .'

He considered this for a moment, then shook his head. 'I no longer desire you, Dorrie. It is too late. Now, I am busy – I do not wish to discuss the matter further. Have the goodness to prepare to leave.'

He rose to his feet, the baby in his arms, about to hand the child back to its mother, and Dorrie, her face suddenly flushing crimson with murderous rage, lost all reason.

'*No!*' she screamed, '*No* – you can't have him! He's mine – he's mine – and you're not even his father!'

A pool of silence seemed to widen about them as the words echoed in the vast hall, a silence that was broken by Tariq's harsh breathing as he stepped forward and gripped Dorrie's shoulder in one hand.

'*What?* Not his father? Have you shamed me yet again, woman? Made me a laughing-stock amongst my people? Then watch – thus perish all infidels and unbelievers!'

He took the baby by its heels and it woke and howled with fright as Tariq swung its head towards the unyielding marble. Dorrie screamed, a terrible sound that reminded Tariq of a mare he had once had, who had her belly ripped out by a tiger, and he missed his aim, the moment of blind rage passed, and he could not do it. He pushed the child roughly into Dorrie's arms, and she subsided to the floor, cradling him, and began to sob, deep, racking sobs, with her eyes closed and the tears pouring down her face.

'It was a lie,' she whispered at last. 'I was lying to you, Tariq. I'm sorry.'

'Go!' he snarled, shaken by the scene, and wanting to be rid of her. 'Get out and pack your clothes. The child remains – and whether he is a true son of my loins or not, he will be brought up as Prince Sultan el Said.'

Dorrie rose to her feet. She felt old, old and tired. 'I'm not going,' she said, quietly, 'I don't care if you divorce me – I'm staying with my son.'

'You fool!' Tariq said, 'You stubborn fool – how dare you defy me? Do you want to be whipped again?'

'I don't care. Whip me if you want – I'm not going.' She turned and left him, and Tariq sat on for a few moments in his high, throne-like chair, his fingers drumming angrily on the arm. Then his face cleared, the dark, Mephistophelean features creased upwards into a smile, and Tariq el Said began to laugh.

Dorrie was not surprised to be woken in the night by someone entering her room. She had expected Tariq's revenge to take the form of sexual abuse, and if that was the price she had to pay for remaining with her son, she was prepared to pay it.

The room was pitch dark, the windows heavily curtained and shuttered against the day-time heat and the freezing night, and it was impossible to see more than a stealthy movement. Dorrie had already decided that, for Sultan's sake, she would at least simulate desire for Tariq, so that he would feel more conciliatory towards her. She leaned over and switched on the bedside lamp. Tariq was there, an odd expression of suppressed excitement on his face, and, behind him, half-cowering, his loose, wet mouth twisted into a dog-like grin, the mad half-brother, Hammad.

'What's *he* doing here?' Dorrie sat up in bed, pulling the sheet round her bare shoulders, keeping her voice low so that she would not wake the baby, sleeping peacefully in the little ante-room. She had a sick feeling that Tariq had brought the creature here to watch his love-making, in order to humiliate her. It was just the sort of twisted thing he would think of.

'Well, my dear wife,' Tariq said, softly, 'as I told you earlier, I no longer desire you. But that is a shame for you – so I have brought someone who does. Someone who likes you very much.'

'No!' Dorrie whispered, 'Oh, God – Tariq – please! You couldn't be so cruel – so wicked . . .'

Tariq grinned. 'You wish to stay here? You must be prepared – often – to be kind to my dear little half-brother! Hammad!' He spoke a few guttural words of Arabic, and Hammad shuffled forward, his eyes flickering from Tariq's face to Dorrie's, like a dog who sees a tempting bone but is afraid of a beating if he grabs it.

'Go on!' Tariq said, 'Go on, good boy!' He laughed. 'I believe you would say in the West, "he thinks it's Christmas!"'

Dorrie looked frantically about her for a weapon, and her hand closed on a bottle of mineral water by the bed. 'Don't dare let him near me,' she gasped, 'I'll kill him, and you, I swear it!'

Tariq grabbed her wrist with a swift movement and bent it painfully back until the bottle fell harmlessly on the floor.

'Bastard!' Dorrie spat, and raked the nails of her other hand across his face.

He slapped her so hard that she felt her teeth bite into her tongue, and the salt blood in her mouth, but he was not angry – in fact, he laughed. 'So – I wondered how long the she-wolf would keep her gentle dove's plumage! Good – it is more enjoyable when the woman is lively. Hammad! Come!'

Tariq held Dorrie's shoulders down on to the bed without effort, and Hammad inched forward, snuffling and uttering little grunts and whimpers. Timidly, he pulled the sheet from Dorrie, and at first, he seemed quite content to stand gazing stupidly, a vacant smile on his face, until at a sharp command from Tariq, he fumbled at the thin silk nightdress Dorrie wore and pulled it up over her shoulders.

Dorrie spoke to him in Arabic, putting all the cold authority she could into her voice, 'Don't you dare touch me! Go away – do you hear? Go away!'

Hammad paused, whining a little in his throat, his eyes on Tariq. Tariq jerked his head. 'Hurry.'

Clumsily, Hammad pulled off his thaub, and the stench of his naked body was strong in the room. He was fat and pot-bellied, black, rank hair clustering over his chest and round his groin. He stank of excrement, onions, sweat and perfume and Dorrie felt her stomach begin to heave as he came near her.

'Ah, see!' Tariq murmured, 'See how he grows! What a man the little brother has become! He will make you so happy, my dear!'

Hammad climbed on to the bed and pushed Dorrie's legs apart, too excited now to be frightened any longer, drooling and uttering short, inarticulate cries.

Dorrie stared up at Tariq's impassive face. 'How could you do this?' she whispered, 'I hope you burn in hell. I hope . . .' she broke off with a moan as Hammad drove his penis violently into her.

* * *

It was over. They had gone, and Dorrie dragged herself from her bed and into the bathroom where she vomited until she was empty and exhausted. Then she ran a bath of water as hot as she could bear it, scrubbed herself, emptied the bath, filled it again, scrubbed again, full of a sick loathing which extended even to the body that she felt would never be clean again. It was nearly dawn – the dawn of another day which Tariq had promised would bring Hammad to her bed again.

Dorrie got dressed in one of her few remaining Western dresses, and picked up the sleeping Sultan from his cot. She stifled the desire to kiss him, or hold him once more to her breast. Walking like an automaton, her face a mask cut from white paper, she went to Fatima's room.

Fatima, herself heavy with child, woke and smiled sleepily at Dorrie, 'What is it, sister-wife?'

'Fatima – I have to go. Tariq is divorcing me . . .'

The girl sat up, rubbing her eyes, 'But – this is what you wanted, is it not? I am happy for you, for I know you long for your own people – but I am sad to lose my dear sister.'

'Fatima – ' Dorrie felt her throat closing up, swallowed, struggled and spoke again. 'He won't let me take Sultan. I have to leave him.'

'Oh! Dorrie!' Fatima gave a little wail of sympathy.

'No – don't – I'll only start blubbering. Fatima – will you take care of him for me? Will you have him as – as your own child – and look after him – I – I love him so very much, you see, and . . .'

'Yes. *Yes*, I promise you – I will love him as my own – I already do – oh, Dorrie!'

They were both weeping now, clinging together with the sleeping baby between them, their tears dropping on the dark, unconscious head like a baptism.

PART THREE
London

13

Another Christmas came and flew past like a swift, tinsel bird. Again Ash Friars stood empty except for the staff, for Dorrie was back in her Maida Vale flat, and Sir Anthony did not care to go alone to Devon. He was worried about his daughter. The ill-advised marriage had been a foolish mistake – that had been evident from the start, and he could only be relieved that it was over, despite the unpleasant publicity and the wild speculations of the gutter press. But – this was not his daughter who had returned from Saudi. This thin, white-faced woman with the strained, almost desperate look in her shadowed blue eyes, was hardly recognizable as his golden Dorian. She was drinking, too, he was sure. Once or twice he had telephoned and her voice had been slurred, hardly coherent. And she was out every night, at parties, her name continually in the gossip columns linked with one man after another, usually of an unsavoury reputation.

He had tried to talk to her, to understand just what it was that had happened over the last year to change her so much, but her face took on a shuttered look and she only shrugged and turned his questions aside with a brittle laugh.

'Daddy – I don't ever want to talk about it, okay? Let's just forget I was ever away – that's all I want to do. Have another drink and cheer up! You've got your loving daughter back – a confirmed bachelor girl now – to look after you in your old age.'

He had smiled at that, and suggested mildly that of

course she would marry again: 'You had better, my dear. I would like a grandson to live at Ash Friars one day.'

He saw the sudden expression of pain on Dorrie's face, but a moment later she had turned away and was refilling her glass with Scotch, so her father concluded that her experience of married love was such that it had put her off the whole idea of sex and child-bearing. A shame – but with the right man it would all be overcome. Dorrie, however, seemed to be hell-bent on only mixing with the wrong men. She appeared to be estranged from all the decent people she had ever known. Cy Coram, of whom Sir Anthony had initially disapproved, but whom he had come to like and respect, had gone, shortly after Dorrie married, to work with Waldo in a kibbutz. The young MP, Larcombe, whom Dorrie had once seemed interested in, was never mentioned by her. And there was that other woman, a pleasant, sweet-faced girl, an unlikely friend for Dorrie – what was her name? Sir Anthony had had lunch with her and Dorrie at the Gay Hussar once, and had met her again at Dorrie's flat. She had been a kind person, someone who would perhaps be able to help Dorrie more than he could. Cavallo, that was it, Sarah Cavallo.

'Do you never see that friend of yours, Mrs – Cavallo? – nowadays, my dear?' he asked, casually. 'That nice woman whose children you took down to Ash Friars?'

'Sarah? No – No, I haven't seen her since I came back. She wrote to me once or twice when I was in Saudi. I must phone her or something . . .' But they both knew that she would not. Sir Anthony sighed. Perhaps it was only a reaction to the restricted life Dorrie had led for the last year, all this drinking and the wild parties. He had gathered that it had been restricted when he had asked Dorrie about Riyadh and she had told him that she had driven through it twice, once going and once coming

286

back. 'Oh, yes, Father,' she had said, with a wry smile, 'I have been leading a cloistered life – almost nun-like, with a few notable exceptions.'

But he continued to worry about her and the company she was keeping and when, in February, she narrowly missed arrest when police raided a party and found quantities of cocaine and heroin, Sir Anthony wrote to Sarah Cavallo and asked if she would try and see Dorrie.

'As a very elderly parent,' he wrote, 'I am acutely conscious of the generation gap, and that Dorian must find it difficult to confide in me, perhaps because she feels that I would be shocked. It is hard for children to believe their parents were ever warmed by the fires of youth! But my daughter has always spoken so affectionately of you, Mrs Cavallo, that I feel you may succeed where I have failed, and may persuade Dorian that her present way of life is only doing her harm. Do forgive me for imposing on you in this way – as a parent yourself, you will understand my deep concern.'

Sarah wrote a note to Dorrie and received no reply and, at the beginning of March, after a few fruitless attempts, managed to reach her on the telephone.

'Dorrie? It's Sarah.'

'Oh.'

Unbidden, a line from some half-forgotten poem she had learned at school came into her mind, something about 'the joy of an old wound waking'. She had ignored Sarah's letter because she had been afraid even to think of Ross Cavallo. She had wanted to blot the memory of him from her thoughts, drown it with drink, deafen the persistent sound of his voice beneath the harsh clangour of disco music. And with it, the memory of his son, her little Sultan, far away from her now, as lost to her as though he had died.

With an effort, she forced herself to say, 'Hallo, Sarah. How are you?'

'Well – not exactly bounding with health. In bed today, as a matter of fact. I wondered if you'd like to come out and visit me. It'd be a corporal work of mercy, you know.'

'I'd love to – I can't today, though – I have a heavy date. Soon, I will. I'm sorry you're not well – what's the trouble?'

'Oh – just some bug. I'm not infectious. Do come soon – I need cheering up.'

'Of course. How are the kids?'

'Fine. They've been longing to see you ever since they knew you were back. Dorrie – I was so sad things didn't work out for you. You must feel a bit sore.'

'No. I'm okay. Look – I have to go, Sarah – but I will try and come out to Kew soon.'

Dorrie replaced the receiver, her hand trembling. She would have liked to see Sarah but she could not bear the thought of being in Ross's house again, passing the room where they had made love – where their son had been conceived. At the thought, she felt tears welling in her eyes and she fought them back, clasping her empty arms around her thin body and rocking back and forth in an agony of despair. 'My baby,' she whispered, 'I want my baby.' She reached once more for the Scotch bottle, poured half a tumbler full and drank it down, the glass clattering against her teeth and spilling down her clothes until, in an access of self-disgust, she hurled it crashing against the wall and collapsed, sobbing, on to the carpet, her golden hair tangled and whisky-soaked.

She did not go to Kew, and it was nearly a month later that Sarah rang again.

'Dorrie?' Her voice was scarcely more than a whisper, almost unrecognizable, 'It's me – Sarah.'

'Oh – hallo, Sarah. I'm sorry – I'm sorry I haven't been

out yet. I keep meaning to . . . You sound very faint – have you got a sore throat or something?'

'Something. Dorrie – please come and see me – now, tonight.' The voice faded away as though exhausted, then came again with desperate urgency. '*Please*, Dorrie!'

The line went dead, and Dorrie stood for a moment with the receiver in her hand, frowning. How unlike Sarah, that hoarse, imperious summons. And how hard to ignore. She would have to go, if Sarah wanted to see her that urgently – she owed her that much at least, even if it would be painful. Slowly, she went and showered, dressed more carefully than she had been doing, brushed her hair and rinsed as much as she could of the taste of Scotch from her mouth. Then, before she left, she rang the casino and asked to speak to Mr Cavallo

'He's in his office. Hold the line – who shall I say is calling?'

Dorrie hung up. At least she would not bump into Ross.

The door of the house on Kew Green was opened by Lotte Behrens, the Cavallos' German au pair. She greeted Dorrie politely and stood back to let her inside.

'Mrs Cavallo's room – you know which one?' she enquired.

'Yes – why, is she still in bed ill?'

The German girl looked at her as though she did not understand and Dorrie tried again in her scanty German, '*Frau Cavallo – sie ist doch krank*?'

'*Ja* – you do not know? She is very ill. She has been in hospital for three weeks, but then – ' Lotte shrugged, 'she wished very much to be at home. They cannot do more, I think. She has a nurse.'

'What do you mean? Are you sure? What's the matter with her?'

'You do not know?' the German girl said again, infuriatingly, 'She has the cancer. *Ja*. It is very bad. The children, Beatrice and Ben – they are with their grandmother. I stay to look after Thomas and to cook, *ja*?'

'No one told me,' Dorrie muttered, stupidly. She felt she had been hit in the solar plexus.

'No – well, Mrs Cavallo – she thought she was getting better. It seemed so until before Christmas and then – *ach, der Lieber Gott*! – very quickly she became quite ill again. She is a brave lady. She does not complain.'

'Oh, God.' Dorrie put a hand on the carved newel post at the foot of the stairs. There was a copper bowl of spring flowers on a table beside it, scyllas and narcissi and little yellow irises, bright and fresh with their promise of new life and hope after the winter. She felt that her legs had been stuffed with cotton wool.

'You go up,' Lotte was saying, encouragingly, 'I must go back to the kitchen – I have left Thomas in his highchair. Come, when you have seen Mrs Cavallo, and I will give you coffee and *küchen*.'

The stairs were of infinite length. Dorrie mounted them slowly, holding on to the banisters. She could not have known, she told herself – she had kept away for Sarah's sake as much as for anyone's – and now it was nearly too late. Sarah had wanted to see her, and she, Dorrie, had failed her, as she had failed so many people. Slowly, she opened the bedroom door.

The curtains were drawn, although the sky outside was still the pale amethyst blue of a spring evening, and a bedside light was the only illumination. The small figure in the bed was so still that Dorrie thought at first she was asleep, but then, as she closed the door gently, Sarah turned her head and smiled at her.

I mustn't cry, Dorrie thought. I mustn't let her see the shock on my face. I must be natural and cheerful.

'Hallo, you old malingerer,' she said, sitting by the bed and taking Sarah's hands in hers, and she was hardly even aware of the tears which had begun to slip helplessly down her face.

'Don't cry, Dorrie, dear,' Sarah said, putting her wasted hand up and feebly wiping Dorrie's cheeks, 'There's nothing to cry about any more.'

'Oh – Sarah! Why didn't I come before? I'm so sorry – I –'

'Hush! I know. I know why you didn't come, dear. I understood.'

Dorrie could only stare at her, her eyes straining wide with a terrified appeal, her cheeks flushing a dull, shamed scarlet.

'You fell in love with Ross, didn't you? Oh – don't be ashamed, Dorrie. How could I be cross – I love him, too – I'm just surprised every woman he meets doesn't fall for him.'

'How did you know?' Dorrie could not meet her eyes, and her fingers nervously pleated the edge of the bedspread.

'Oh, dear – I'd have to be a fool! You were so afraid of meeting him! Unlike you, Dorrie!'

'I'm so sorry – so ashamed . . .' it was the merest whisper.

Sarah sighed, closing her eyes for a moment. 'Silly. Don't be. You didn't do anything wrong. You tried to keep away as much as possible – I loved you for that, Dorrie. I don't think I could have done it . . .'

'Don't! *Don't!*' This was a refinement of torture, to have the woman you had injured praising you for your strength of character. Dorrie wanted to kneel down by the bed and blurt out her confession, to hear Sarah say she was forgiven. But she could not do it. She would have to live with the secret for the rest of her life.

'Dorrie – ' she felt Sarah's hand gently touching her bowed head, 'Dorrie – I – I don't want to know if – if Ross felt . . .' She stopped, took a deep breath, and continued, stroking Dorrie's hair, 'He's been so marvellous, this last year – so loving and kind, and – I know it's been hard for him. If he thought of you – well, he's only human, and you're so beautiful.'

'Oh, Sarah – you know Ross loves only you! Dorrie said, desperately, 'He told me once that – that to him you were the loveliest woman in the world.'

Sarah closed her eyes, her lashes wet with tears. 'Thank you,' she whispered, 'I wondered sometimes – I didn't want him to be unhappy . . .'

'He loves you,' Dorrie repeated.

Sarah suddenly took a sharp breath. She drew up her knees and turned away from Dorrie so that the younger girl would not see the agony on her face.

'Please . . .' the word was only a stifled groan.

'What is it? What can I do? Oh, God, Sarah – where the hell's the nurse?'

'No . . .' Sarah reached out a hand as if she were drowning, and Dorrie took it and held it, vividly reminded of another scene in another dimly lit room, when Fatima had held her hand. After a moment, during which she clutched at Dorrie's hand until it was aching, Sarah turned again, letting out her breath in a long sigh, and smiled wanly.

'Sorry,' she said, 'did I hurt you?'

'Sarah . . .' Dorrie shook her head, 'is the pain so bad – is there nothing you can take?'

'Yes – pills, over there. In the bottle.'

'How many?'

'About twenty.'

Dorrie looked up from pouring water and Sarah smiled crookedly.

'No – it's all right. I shan't ask you to help me out. Would you, though? If I said I couldn't bear it any more? Would you help me, Dorrie?'

'*No* – God – how could I? Was that what you wanted me for? I couldn't do it, Sarah – you know I couldn't.'

'Don't worry. I know. Here – give me two capsules – you can see the dose on the bottle if you don't trust me. Thanks.'

She half sat up in bed, and, as the covering fell away, Dorrie could see how terribly emaciated Sarah had become, with the bones of her shoulders and chest standing out through the transparent skin. Her once thick, glossy curls were only a thin covering on her head, which looked small and doll-like against the white pillow, and her face was yellow and shrunken. There were purple marks beneath her eyes and her lower lip was raw where she had bitten into it in her pain. Only her eyes still seemed alive, bright with affection as she looked at Dorrie.

'Cheer up!' she said, 'Don't look so woe-begone. Tell me some of your news.'

Dorrie made a helpless gesture. 'I don't know . . . oh, Sarah – why you? I can think of a thousand people who deserve it more . . .'

'That's sweet of you, Dorrie – but why not me? Anyway, Catholics are supposed to believe that suffering is good for the soul. It knocks a few years off purgatory, you know.'

She glanced up at the crucifix that hung on the wall beside her bed, and smiled as though the person on it was an old and valued friend, then her eyes closed and she lay still and quiet for a while, only the constant pain playing over her features like the movement of water in a quiet pool.

Presently, without opening her eyes, she murmured,

'You've never had a baby, Dorrie, so perhaps you won't know what I'm talking about – but – this is – rather like having a baby. Only all I'm giving birth to is pain and death.'

Dorrie could not answer. Sarah's pain was so real and palpable, and yet, even in its presence, she wanted to blurt out all her own troubles, to tell Sarah about the horrors of her life in Saudi, and how she sometimes woke in the night with the memory of Sultan's eager little mouth and hands at her breast, and wept. Sarah would understand and comfort her, even in the middle of her own pain, but Dorrie was silent.

After a moment, Sarah opened her eyes again. 'Now it's me who's being woe-begone and morbid. The nurse will be giving me my morphine soon and I'll get all fuzzy and won't be able to talk any more. How lovely you look, Dorrie! You're thinner – but you're more beautiful than ever, I think. Stand up and let me see properly what you're wearing. Oh – lovely! Let me guess – Chanel? Jean Varon? Turn round!'

Dorrie turned obediently to show off the chic cream cashmere two-piece. Her father had taken her to Paris for a weekend at the New Year and had spent a great deal of money at some of the top fashion houses in his pleasure at having his daughter back.

'Yes – it's Chanel. Father's choice, as you might guess! But nice, all the same, after a year of ghastly baggy dresses, to show the world that you still have legs.' She sat down again and swung them as she spoke, long and slim, her feet encased in cream kid high-heels.

Sarah smiled, 'It *is* nice to see you again, Dorrie. I'm sure it's done me good. What a pity Bea and Ben aren't here – they'd have loved to see you.'

'I'll come again,' Dorrie said, 'Really – I promise.'

'I know. Go and see Tom before you go – I bet you

won't recognize him! He toddles around everywhere and says heaps of things!'

'Yes, I will. And – Bea and Ben can come down to Ash Friars for a while, if you like.'

'Soon. Thank you. Perhaps when – oh, God, Dorrie, this is going to sound maudlin, and I expect we're both going to start howling, but – it's silly. Some things have to be said, and planned for, just as if I were going on a journey. Listen. After I – ' she stopped, took a deep breath, started again firmly, 'after I'm dead – there, I've said it – will you, sort of keep an eye on – on them all? On the kids – and – and on – '

'Sarah! Don't! Please don't! What are you asking me to do?' Dorrie's face was suddenly contorted with weeping.

'I know, hush, I know! Don't cry, dear!'

But Dorrie was on her knees by the bed, her head against Sarah's thin shoulder, sobbing like a child.

'Now then, Miss! What are you doing, upsetting my patient?' The nurse had come in, silent and swift-footed despite her bulk, and was regarding Dorrie with disapproval, 'I shall have to ask you to leave, in any case. It's time for Mrs Cavallo's injection.'

Dorrie scrambled to her feet, wiping tears away clumsily with the flat of her hand. She tried and failed to summon a smile to take leave of Sarah, but Sarah smiled up at her, her eyes quite calm and unafraid despite the pain.

'Goodbye, dear. Don't be too sad – I'm not. And – please, Dorrie – remember what I asked you?'

Dorrie nodded and turned away, her throat aching too much for words. She went downstairs and let herself out, unable to bear the thought of Lotte's chatter, or of seeing Tom and being reminded so painfully of the little son she had lost.

Sarah lay passively awaiting the injection that would bring her relief, watching Nurse Woodward at her deft preparations.

'Nurse?'

'Yes, my dear?' Despite a lifetime of professional non-involvement, Amy Woodward had been unable to help a feeling of warmth and admiration towards this young woman who bore her sufferings so courageously.

'Nurse – answer me honestly. I want to know. How much longer have I got?'

'Honestly – it's hard to tell. The human body is an odd mechanism – sometimes those that look the most fragile are the ones that endure.'

Sarah sighed, holding out her thin arm for the injection. 'I know it's wrong,' she said, in a low voice, 'but I – I just want it to be all over. I – can bear the pain, even when it's bad. But I can't stand the – the sort of reflection of it in the faces of people I care about. Do you know what I mean, Nurse?'

Nurse Woodward nodded, 'It's hard,' she said, gruffly, 'I know that.'

'It's Ross, mostly, that I mind about,' Sarah went on, 'it's this dreadful, long-drawn-out leave-taking – it's so awful for him. I wish it could be over, and he could remake his life. It's destroying him, this constant watching of my pain . . .'

Her voice was getting slower, dreamier, presently she would sleep. The nurse tidied away the empty morphine ampoule and the disposable hypodermic, and blinked fiercely once or twice. When she spoke, her voice was not altogether steady.

'Don't you worry, my dear,' she said, quietly, 'we won't let it go on too long. Don't you worry.'

Sarah drifted on the edge of sleep. From downstairs, Lotte's voice came faintly up to her, singing some German nonsense rhyme about '*Im Pompei : Wir fahren nach America und du gehst mit . . .*' Tom's delighted crows of laughter floated up the stairs to his dying mother.

14

It had been an unpleasant session in the Commons. Jack Larcombe, driving back to his Bayswater flat, felt a prickle of sweat at his hairline as he recalled it for the tenth time. He had risen to make a point – a telling point, and rather well-phrased, about the cuts in the real value of Child Benefit, and had himself come under swingeing attack from some Tory MPs who evidently knew as much about his private life as he did. It had been embarrassing, and had done the image of the Labour Party little good, as Neil Kinnock had not failed to point out to him afterwards. 'I know it's bloody unfair, boy,' he had said, 'but, you see – we have to be above reproach – at least as far as expensive vices like gambling go!'

It had been humiliating, as well as hurtful, to see the controlled annoyance in Kinnock's face. Jack admired the man, and had hoped to impress him with his abilities. Fat chance now, when he was labelled as a dissolute gambler. He would *have* to stay away from the casino – his savings had gone and he had a three-thousand-pound overdraft. But how on earth could he get out of debt if it were not for the chance of a really big win at the tables? There always *was* that chance – Jack had seen people win ten thousand with one spin of the wheel. He had also seen them lose hundreds of thousands, but that was because they were fools, who didn't know when to stop. He hesitated a moment, making a right-hand signal to turn down Leinster Mews and Natasha, then veered back into his original lane again, to a chorus of hoots and imprecations. No, tonight he did not want Natasha. Her love-making was inventive and often exciting, and more than catered for Jack's sexual appetites, but there were times when her avidity reminded him uncomfortably of a female spider, and he wondered if he were going to be sucked dry.

He stopped once, to buy fish and chips. He would have a quiet bachelor evening, and drink a can or two of beer in front of the telly with his feet up. And on Monday, he would show Neil Kinnock what a sober and industrious fellow he could be. No more dissipation.

There was a message from Natasha on his Ansaphone, asking him to ring as soon as he got in. He hesitated a moment, one hand on the receiver, then shrugged. She could wait a little longer. He put his supper in the oven on a low gas and went and had a long hot shower, consciously relaxing himself, and telling himself that it was not too late for reform, that he was, basically, the same honest, zealous countryman who had been returned from Brendon less than two years before. The telephone rang while he was still in the shower, stopped, and rang again, and he cursed mildly and wrapped a towel round his waist. Natasha would have to realize that she did not own him, that there were times when he wanted to pig it on his own, rather than spend an evening of gourmet food and sex with her. But the voice that spoke his name when he lifted the receiver was not Natasha's, and his heart had begun to thump heavily even before his brain had formulated the name.

'Dorrie!'

'Yes. Hallo, Jack – how are you?'

She was as casual as though they had met the day before, and he felt the familiar irritation rising in him, struggling to keep his voice as off-hand as hers.

'I'm fine. It's lovely to hear from you – I didn't know you were even in England.' It was a lie, of course – every small item of news about Dorrie had been read and remembered.

'Yes. It didn't work out – my marriage – but I don't want to talk about it. Listen – are you free this weekend? I'm going down to Ash Friars, and I thought you might like to come.'

'Well – I – ' his heart had speeded up its beat again. 'It's a bit short notice – I'm not sure. What is it – a house party?'

'God – no! Perish the thought. Just you and me.'

Jack moistened his lips, swallowed and hoped she had not heard. It sounded incredibly as though Dorrie was propositioning him. He couldn't believe it, and had to remind himself how many times before he had expected to end up in bed with her, and how many times he had been disappointed.

'Okay,' he said, cautiously, 'that sounds great. What time do you want to leave?'

'Well – it'll take me about thirty minutes to get to your place. I'll pick you up in an hour.'

Jack started laughing. 'Dorrie – you're incredible!'

'Why – what's wrong?'

'Nothing. Only, do you mind if I bring my fish and chips with me?'

'Sure – as long as you don't get grease on the upholstery.'

'Whose upholstery?' he asked, and they were both laughing as she rang off.

'You idiot!' Jack said to himself as he shaved, 'You bloody, blithering idiot!' But his reflection grinned back at him, quite unabashed.

She was at the door, as she had said, in an hour and Jack was ready and waiting. After some thought, he had dressed in a Hardy Amies sports jacket and slacks. Natasha had chosen them for him and laughed at him wincing over the price. 'You may be a Labour MP,' she said, but you must realize that jeans and duffel coats, all that sort of thing is out. People expect you to look smart. And the grey flecks match your eyes exactly, darling! Besides, £150 for a jacket is nothing, really!'

Jack remembered, with a rueful smile, the rough, grey jackets and trousers he had worn to school, and the humiliation he had suffered when other, older boys had pointed out that they were the clothes their mothers had donated to jumble sales. But even then, as a small boy, his hurt and anger had seemed part of something greater – he had wanted to redress the wrongs of all the down-trodden poor.

Perhaps he was growing up at last, he told himself. He was beginning to realize that in this world it was every man for himself and, by a process of natural selection, those who couldn't cope went under. Besides – he was no ascetic, and there was no point in pretending he was. The good life that he had sampled since he started earning a decent salary had come to mean a lot to him. Of course, he would still fight for people's rights, for a better deal for the old and sick, but surely to God he didn't have to live like a bloody monk while he did it?

He relaxed into the comfort of Dorrie's Daytona, watching her profile as she negotiated the traffic. She was more beautiful than ever, he thought, with the last vestiges of childish roundness fined away from her face. There were faint, delicate hollows at her temples and cheekbones and the soft curve of her mouth seemed to have more sadness in it than boredom. They had not spoken much, and Jack was content to watch her assured handling of the powerful car, which he found, in an odd way, to be very sexually arousing. She had said nothing intimate to him – had not offered him so much as a light kiss or a handshake when they met, and now, apart from

300

an occasional desultory remark, she seemed content to drive in silence, her face remote and thoughtful. Why on earth, then, had she invited him?

Because I am not afraid of you, Dorrie could have answered him. You are not a cruel or depraved man like Tariq, and I can hold you at bay or bring you closer with a word or a look. Because I want to be at home, at Ash Friars, and yet I can't face the thought of being there alone. I want to get away from London and away from Sarah Cavallo dying by inches in a quiet, pretty room. I want to get away from any chance of seeing Ross, because – oh, because he might look at me and think I wish Sarah dead. I can't bear that he should ever think that. And, in a way, her death will come between us even more than her life did, because I cannot, will not profit by it.

They were at Lower Poltenay by ten-thirty, driving through the quiet village with the snarl of the Ferrari's engine echoing back from the thatched roofs and white-washed walls, and from the ice-cream-coloured façades of the new bungalows. It was a clear, soft evening in May, the light not long gone from a cloudless sky, and the car's headlamps picked out the pink and crimson glory of the rhododendrons and azaleas on either side of the long, curving drive that led to the Manor.

Jack was impressed into silence. The place was so huge – so solid, with such an air of generations of wealth about it. The Pettits' place was nothing compared to this – a mere shack! He felt, all at once, as though Dorrie was very remote from him, as far out of his sphere as if he were still simply the son of a farm labourer.

'Come on!' Dorrie said, impatiently, but smiling at him, 'Come inside and let's see if we can rustle up something to eat – I'm starving! The guided tour isn't till tomorrow.'

He picked up their bags and followed her, wishing that he felt suave and self-assured, and sure that the dapper manservant or butler or whatever he was, who met them in the big, echoing hall, could see right through the Hardy Amies sports jacket to the runny-nosed little farm boy beneath.

'Hallo, Ramsden,' Dorrie said, casually, 'Nice to see you again. Are you married yet, or still playing the field?'

'No, Miss – not married yet,' Ramsden said, stiffly. Bloody cheeky tart – what business was it of hers? 'We've put Mr Larcombe in the yellow room, Miss – will that be satisfactory?'

'Fine. Jack – this is Ramsden, our butler. Don't let the Jeeves-like manner fool you – he's a randy little goat underneath, or so I've been reliably informed.'

The men looked at each other embarrassed. Jack was not sure whether one shook hands with the butler – or whether that would be condescending. He compromised with a sketchy salute. Dorrie smiled, a shade ironically.

'Come on, Jack – we'll raid the kitchen.'

'I can fetch anything you would like, Miss Dorian,' Ramsden said. 'Mrs Duffy, I know, has prepared a cold supper.'

'Good – we'll have it in the kitchen. Now, don't fuss and get all grace and favourish, Ramsden, there's a dear. We shan't disturb anyone. You can take the bags up and then go to bed. Whose, I do not ask.' She grinned again, then took Jack's arm and led him by way of a broad, stone-flagged passage to the kitchen.

'Why did you have to needle that poor chap?' Jack said, frowning. 'You shouldn't do that – he can't answer back, you know.'

'I dunno. Just bitchy, I suppose. Also – he *is* a randy little goat – he may not be able to answer back, but I've intercepted a few glances that have been as good as a quick feel.'

Jack winced. 'Dorrie – how can you be so vulgar?'

She laughed, leaning back against the enormous Aga, her face mocking. 'Dear Jack! Haven't you discovered yet, the upper classes *are* vulgar! Mainly because they don't give a fuck what anyone thinks of them! It's your social-climbing middle classes who feel they have to watch their Ps and Qs and be fraightfully naice! Oh, there are a few ladies and gentlemen still around – my father, for instance, but on the whole, we're a decadent lot.'

There was no one else in the vast, quarry-tiled kitchen. The windows were big and mullioned, with stone sills, and a black beam as big as a tree supported the chimney-breast above the Aga, but, apart from these evidences of great age, the place was any modern cook's dream, with a gas hob and electric oven, a microwave, dish-washer, mixer and food-processor, enough equipment to provide a banquet.

Dorrie poked about in the fridge, which was big enough to step into, and produced salads, a cold game pie, a mousse of smoked salmon.

'You don't mind pigging it in here, do you?' she said, and Jack glanced at her with a suspicion that she was being sarcastic, but her face was quite guileless as she filled the coffee percolator.

'It's a palace,' he said, simply, and was surprised when Dorrie came over and kissed him warmly on the mouth.

'Sometimes you're very nice!' and then, as he made to pull her into a closer embrace, she laughed. 'Not tonight, Master Jack! I'm too tired to fight.'

'Do you have to fight?'

'No.' She looked at him thoughtfully, 'No – perhaps not.'

Jack was, ridiculously, too excited to sleep well, and the first early shout of birdsong brought him awake, just as though he had not spent most of his life in the country.

The window was open, and he pushed aside the elegant

sprigged curtains that matched the wallpaper, and leaned out. It was a beautiful morning. There was a wash of pearly mist, spangled with spiders' webs, across the broad stretch of lawn, and the flowerbeds were bright with wall-flowers, tulips and forget-me-nots. A ha-ha led to the park, dotted with oak and beech, and he could see deer grazing quietly, seeming to float on the mist like quaint, anchored ships. Away to the left, folding park and gardens in its centuries-old embrace, Poltenay Forest stretched, with its unspoilt reaches of mature hardwoods, its floor carpeted now with bluebells and smelling of spring and youth.

Jack breathed the sweet air, his hands on the warm stone of the window-sill. What a place! What a beautiful place! He suddenly ached with a hunger to possess it.

Quickly he got dressed in the slacks he had worn the night before, and an open-necked shirt. It was not yet six o'clock, so he hoped he would avoid any servants if he went out and wandered in the grounds. There was no one about when he went downstairs, though he could hear faint noises from the kitchen, as though the Aga was being riddled, and he let himself out of the front door, which had an enormous key like that of a church, with a feeling of stealth. An old spaniel, asleep in a basket in the stone porch, rose stiffly, wagging its tail, sniffing and peering up at him with filmy eyes. When he went out, she followed him, trotting companionably at his heels, and he stooped and fondled the silky, golden ears, rather touched at the offer of friendship.

'You're a nice old girl, aren't you?' he murmured, 'and you can do the honours and show me round. I'm afraid I don't know your name.'

For a while he wandered in the garden, skirting the smooth-cut lawns with a sense of trespass, but enjoying all the same the beauty of the flowers, perfuming the air, as the sun rose and turned the mist to opal.

The deer in the park raised their heads as he jumped down from the ha-ha, and moved off unhurriedly, but he skirted them and made for the woods, where it was quiet with the listening peace of a great cathedral, and birdsong echoed and rang in counterpoint to the soft murmur of the beech leaves.

Underfoot, a prodigal carpet of bluebells, late primroses and delicate wood-sorrel grew amongst mosses and the fine, thin grass of the forest floor, and his quiet progress startled a grey squirrel which bounded to safety, its tail frisking impudently behind it.

He sat down under a tree, and the spaniel lay across his feet, sighing gently and watching him with one half-open eye. A little way off, the triumphant shout of a cuckoo made him suddenly remember his boyhood, and days like these when he had escaped from the daily reminder of poverty, and wandered in the woods, drinking in the pleasure of peace and beauty. Sometimes, as he got older, there would be a girl with him, lying on her back amongst the bracken. But that was a different pleasure. Recalling it, though, made him think of Dorrie, and he got up, stretched and began to make his way back to the house.

There was a girl in jeans and T-shirt sweeping out the porch as he approached, and she smiled at him in a friendly way. 'Morning, sir! Were you looking for Miss Dorrie? She's round at the stables, I think. Oh, there you are, Floss, you silly old girl! I was wondering where you'd got to!'

Jack went round the side of the house where the girl had indicated, by way of a lavender-edged path, and found himself in a cobbled yard lined with loose-boxes. One door stood half-open, and he went and looked in and saw Dorrie with her arms round the neck of a big, bay gelding.

'Hi!' she said.

'Hallo. I'm jealous – who's my rival?'

'His name's Hentzau and I haven't seen him for over a year. I wish I could believe he'd missed me.'

'Oh, he has, Miss! I can vouch for that!'

The voice, seeming to emanate from a chestnut pony in the next stall, made Jack start. Why hadn't Dorrie warned him there was someone there, before he'd said – what had he said? Something bloody stupid. He nodded to the grinning young man who emerged from the next stall, dandy brush in hand. 'Yes – went right off his feed, he did, Miss!'

'Rubbish – he's fat as a pig! He's been eating his head off and had no exercise at all!'

'No, Miss! Muscle, that is! He's in beautiful condition!'

'Oh, bugger off, Sid!' Dorrie said, but laughing, 'You've put on weight, too.'

'Got meself married, Miss, that's why. Me missus is what you might call a dab hand at the old treacle puddens!'

'Oh, yes? Who is she? Someone local?'

'Yeah. Sylvie Palfrey, as was. 'Er Dad used to be blacksmith, years agone.'

'I know. Well, congratulations. And tell Sylvie to back-pedal on the treacle puddings or you'll break poor Hentzau's back!'

Lambert nodded, grinning again, and went off across the yard, whistling cheerfully. Dorrie gave a final pat to the big horse then squeezed past him and joined Jack at the stable door.

She was wearing jeans and a checked shirt, her hair caught up in a knot from which fronds were already escaping, her face free from make-up. There was a faint, clean scent about her as she stood close to Jack, a mixture of soap and hay and warm, sweet flesh.

Impulsively, he put his arm round her and hugged her, and for a moment, to his delight, she rested against him, before she pulled gently away.

'Don't frighten the horses!' she said. 'Besides – I want my breakfast. All that talk of treacle pudding's made me ravenous.'

They ate in a small, sunny room that led off the main hall. It was no bigger than an average dining-room and Jack wondered what happened when there were large numbers of guests, but was afraid to expose his ignorance by asking. Dorrie answered his thought as though he had voiced it. 'One of the advantages of a great big house like this, is that there are rooms of all shapes and sizes for every occasion. Father and I always eat in here when we're on our own – but there's a huge room with a mahogany sideboard, silver chafing dishes and all. Very impressive and ugly. I hope you prefer this.'

'Of course. You know me – overawed by the slightest display of wealth and power. I'd be happier in the kitchen, really.'

Dorrie made a face at him. 'We can always give you a crust to gnaw on in the stables, if it'd make you comfortable. We're quite used to eccentric guests.'

The breakfast was excellent, but without ostentation: fruit juice and cereal, several kinds of toast, and scrambled eggs with bacon.

'What?' Jack murmured, 'No kedgeree or devilled kidneys? Another illusion crumbles.'

'Shame. And unfortunately there's no one in the stocks this week and the mad relative who's usually shut up in the tower is away for the weekend. However – we do have a nursery, and my old nanny will keep you enthralled

307

for hours with tales of my youthful adventures. What would you like to do today?'

'If I answer honestly, will you promise not to hit me?'

'You're incorrigible. Are all MPs as randy as you? Perhaps it's best not to know. Now, behave – and tell me if you'd like to ride?'

She had refrained from asking if he *could* ride, he noticed, with a sort of delicacy of which she was occasionally capable.

'Yes. That'd be great. Can we take a picnic or something?'

'Okay, but if you're expecting "Déjeuner sur l'herbe" I warn you it's still too cold for me to take my clothes off! Have you finished? I'll go and get Mrs Duffy to pack up some lunch.'

They rode for miles, Dorrie on Hentzau and Jack on a well-mannered grey which was Sir Anthony's mount. He had not ridden for years, and was hard-pushed to conceal the stiffness of his aching limbs when they dismounted for their picnic. There was a curious innocence about that day, which matched the perfection of the spring weather, and Jack never thought of it in later years without a feeling of nostalgic sweetness. It was as though they were children together, he and Dorrie, as though the resentful, impoverished little boy that he had been, and the spoiled, lonely little girl that she had been, were reborn into a new golden childhood. And the feeling lasted throughout dinner and into the evening, when they played Scrabble, Dorrie cheating shamelessly, in the pretty green and white drawing-room. It lasted, in fact, until the telephone rang.

'It's for you, Miss Dorrie,' Ramsden said, 'A Mrs Cavallo. Will you take it in here?'

'Sarah? No – I'll come to the hall. Pour yourself a drink, Jack – I won't be long.'

'But the voice that responded to her 'Hallo, Sarah?'

was a Scottish one. 'No, my dear – it's not Sarah. It's her mother-in-law, Maire Cavallo. It's – I'm ringing because – Sarah asked me to, and your father said I'd find you at your home. Och – this is very hard . . .' There was a sudden tremor in the lilting accent, 'My dear – this is to let you know that Sarah died last night. She wanted me to ring you . . . are you still there?'

'Yes,' Dorrie's mouth felt cold, as though she was going to faint. She clenched the receiver in her hand, and for a moment a terrible anger rose up in her at the unfairness of life. Only for a moment, and then the anger broke in a wave of unhappiness.

'She – I only saw her a week ago,' she whispered, 'I didn't think . . .'

'None of us did, lassie. And of course, you go on hoping till the end. But – at least she's free of pain, now. She had a deal of suffering at the end, and it was terrible to see. But she spoke of you – she said I was to tell you not to forget what she'd asked. That was all.'

'Oh.' It was the merest breath of sound.

'Aye. The funeral's to be on Wednesday, at St Winefride's here in Kew – but only very quiet, just family.'

The gentle, kind voice spoke on for a few minutes, and Dorrie supposed later that she must have answered, but she could never recall what they had said. When Maire Cavallo had hung up, Dorrie did not rejoin Jack. She wanted to be quite alone and quite silent, and she went to her room and locked the door.

It was the room she had occupied since childhood, still scattered with some of the books and toys that had been her companions then – the 'Narnia' books, and 'Wind in the Willows', some of Rider Haggard and a few pony books; a crumple-faced Teddy bear and a paper-weight that made a snow-storm, all familiar and friendly. But tonight something else was added. The ghost of Sarah Cavallo, thin, dark-eyed, insistent.

'Please, Dorrie – keep an eye on them . . .'

She meant, please take my place. How simple – even the wife whom she had helped Ross to cheat, was conveniently removed, and, what was more, had practically bequeathed her husband to Dorrie with her dying breath. How easy, just to wait a while till the first shock of her death was over, and then, with gentle sympathy, perhaps through the children, to be gradually accepted into the heart of the family. How simple – how easy – how utterly and finally impossible.

Jack went to bed with the familiar feeling of hurt and resentment against Dorrie burning in his throat like gall. He had sat on in the drawing-room, waiting for her to return to him, and for the marvellous, easy-going, companionable day to continue to its close. But – he might have expected it. She had done it to him every time – first the big build-up, then the crash landing. He sat on, poured himself another drink, flicked through *Horse and Hound* and wished he had never come to Ash Friars. If it had been possible, he would have left straight away, and he did consider walking down to the village and trying to get a bed in the local pub. But, on reflection, it seemed that he would probably end up feeling even more of a fool than ever, having to encounter the politely surprised stare of the landlord, whom he had met earlier when he and Dorrie had a drink on their way home. At half past ten he went up to bed, encountering Ramsden on his way across the hall, and sure that he read contempt in the man's smile, and polite, 'Goodnight, sir.'

In bed, he lay unsleeping, the sweet air and the night sounds that reached him through the open window contributing to his fury. This peace, this sweet, untainted air from the acres of private ground – this was what wealth and privilege bought you. All this, and the power not to care what anyone thought of you, the knowledge that whatever you did to people, there would always be plenty of sycophantic boot-lickers ready to take their place. Well, Jack Larcombe would not be one of them. This was the last time Dorrie would make a fool of him. Tomorrow morning he would take a taxi to the nearest station, which was Exeter, and go back to town.

It was nearly two before he fell asleep, and he had slept for only minutes before he was awakened by the door of his room softly opening.

'Jack?' It was a barely audible whisper, 'Jack, are you asleep?'

He raised himself on one elbow, suddenly wide awake. She was standing in the doorway with one hand still on the handle, but when she saw his movement, she closed the door and came over to him.

'Jack?' she was standing next to the bed now, her voice sounding hesitant, almost timid. 'Jack – I'm lonely – and cold. Move over, will you?'

To his incredulous delight, she slid into the bed and into his arms and he felt the warmth of her body through the thin silk nightdress that she wore, pressed unbelievably close to him. Her arms were round his neck and her face pressed against him, and he suddenly realized from her breathing and the trembling of her body that she was crying.

'What is it, darling? What's wrong – tell me. Don't cry . . .' He kissed her hair and folded her close against him, conscious of his own strength and of the slender fragility of her body beside his.

'One of my friends died – someone I – I cared for a lot,' Dorrie whispered. 'Don't talk – just hold me, Jack.'

For a while he held her, the dizzying sweetness of her perfume in his nostrils, the warm softness of her full

311

breasts against his naked chest, and, inevitably, he felt the heat of his loins and the erection rising urgently between them.

'Dorrie,' he groaned, 'if you go away now . . .'

She drew a deep, unsteady breath. 'No – it's all right, Jack. I shan't stop you this time. Poor old fellow – you've waited a long time.' Her hand slid softly down his chest and belly and caressed his tense penis, stroking and gently pulling, and her mouth sought his in the darkness, offering its sweetness with a childish lack of passion that made Jack feel he was the first man she had ever kissed.

In a fever of excitement, he pulled the thin silk night-gown from her shoulders and she wriggled out of it and kicked it from her, then his head was at her breast as he fondled and sucked the nipples and felt them gradually hardening. Her body was so perfect, so sweet – he would, in one sense, have been glad to spend the night in the gentle exploration of it, hardly able to believe that it was here, at last, naked in his arms. But the clamouring in his loins would brook no delay, and it was all he could do to wait for the act of possessing her.

'Gently . . .' she whispered, as he lay on top of her, and he felt her grow suddenly rigid as if with fear.

'Hush – it's all right – I won't hurt you, darling – ever, ever . . .'

With infinite care, he eased himself into her, at the same time rubbing and stroking the softness of her clitoris with gentle fingers and gradually he felt her relax beneath him and her body responding to his own.

'Dorrie! Dorrie!' Over and over again he whispered her name, blinded, deafened by his passion, all his senses concentrated on that one centre of unbearable ecstasy. He tried to hold back as long as he could, but he was as powerless against the overwhelming climax as though it had been a tidal wave that picked him up, thrust him before it deep into her body and left him panting, groaning, only gradually aware of his surroundings again.

Her hand was stroking his hair, gently and detachedly, and her voice was quiet and calm as she said, 'I suppose you realize you'll have to marry me now.'

'Don't tease me, Dorrie,' he mumbled, his head still pillowed against her breasts, 'not when I've just been in Paradise.'

'Have you, Jack dear?' she said, softly, 'I'm so glad. But I wasn't teasing. Could you marry me?'

With an exclamation, he leaned out of bed and switched on the light so that he could see her face. She stared up at him from the pillow, the blonde hair spread like a halo, the blue eyes quiet and unteasing, but with a look of strain about them.

'Do you really mean it? It's not a joke?'

She forced a smile. 'Jack – this is unflattering. Do I have to make a formal proposal? I got the impression – correct me if I'm wrong – that you found me not unpleasing!'

There was a small glint of laughter in her eyes now.

Jack was speechless. Absurdly, he felt tears pricking at his eyes and he sat up on the edge of the bed and covered his face with his hands for a moment, trying to steady himself.

Dorrie was touched. She looked at the broad, fair-skinned back, the shoulders bowed with overwhelming emotion, and put a hand out to him, feeling a pang of tenderness and sorrow for him.

'Dear Jack!' How easy it was – and, in a way, how sweet to make someone happy. He would be a good, kind husband. She was fond of him and, in time, if she tried hard, a sort of love would grow in her heart. There would be children – fair, sturdy sons with nothing about them to remind her of the first-born, and their life together would be contented and cheerful. He loved her so much – surely that would be enough?

He turned at last, sliding down to kneel beside the bed and take her hand in his. He kissed the palm of it gently, and when he raised his head, Dorrie saw his face was transformed by love. 'Don't!' she wanted to cry, 'Oh, Jack – don't be so vulnerable.'

'I promise I'll make you happy, Dorrie,' he whispered, 'I love you so very much.'

'I know.' She did not say she loved him – she could not bring herself to lie to him – not now, not yet.

She leaned forward and kissed him tenderly on the lips. 'I must go back to my room now – I'm a respectable engaged lady, and we don't want the servants talking, do we?'

'Don't go!' He got into bed, put his arms round her again, 'Let me make love to you again.'

'No!' Her voice was sharp and she seemed to flinch away, then, more quietly, 'No, Jack – not tonight – I – I'm tired, and a bit shaken . . . I want to adjust gradually. I'll see you in the morning.'

She kissed him again and, unwillingly, he let her go, watching with covetous eyes as her slim, naked body bent to retrieve her nightdress. Then, with a half-mocking smile which seemed to change this new, gentler stranger into the Dorrie he had known before, she was gone.

'Natasha – this is very difficult for me . . .'

Why was it that at moments of emotional stress, trite words and phrases were the only ones that sprang to one's lips? Of course, there had never been any engagement between Natasha and himself. It had been an adult relationship, thoroughly enjoyable on a purely physical plane, but with no emotional ties whatsoever. It should have been quite simple to explain to her that he was now engaged to Dorrie, and would not be seeing her again, but – damn it, she wasn't giving him any help, just sitting there on her sofa in the red silk dressing-gown he had once given her, her face expressionless, looking paler than usual and quite plain without any make-up. Why the hell couldn't she say, 'Of course, Jack, I understand,' instead of leaving him to flounder like this. He half-turned from her and picked up a small Meissen figurine from her mantelpiece, examining it minutely. Natasha had always liked collecting things whose value she expected to appreciate.

'I'm engaged,' he blurted out, at last, 'to Dorrie St James. So you see, we'd better not see each other any more, I'm afraid.'

She stared at him, still without speaking, and Jack felt himself reddening and found himself blundering on, 'It's not that I haven't – that it hasn't been a – a marvellous relationship – and – and I think you're a wonderful girl and that you'll make some man a terrific wife . . .'

She suddenly laughed, a harsh, shocking sound that made him stop and stare at her.

'Oh, bloody wonderful!' she said, her mouth twisted with scorn, 'I wondered when you'd trot that one out! Why not tell the truth, Jack, my darling? Why not say, "Look here, Natasha, you've been very convenient for a quick fuck when I felt like it, but you're no good as a wife for an ambitious little prick like me." That's what you mean, isn't it?'

'Be quiet!' He suddenly felt nothing but distaste for her. The memory of their love-making seemed to him bestial, compared with the sweet innocence that he had shared with Dorrie. When he remembered some of the things Natasha had done, that she had made him do, he felt revolted.

'I can't help it if you're upset Natasha. I'm, sorry, but

there it is. I never pretended we were going to get married or anything . . .'

'Oh, no. It was all very adult – you haven't used that word yet, Jack. And I quite understand you preferring the delectable Dorrie St James – not forgetting her even more delectable millions. In fact, Jack, my precious, I feel almost sorry for you, having to call it off! I do hope Cartier's haven't started making the ring yet?'

'Don't be bloody stupid! Why the hell should I call it off. You certainly can't make me.'

'I can't?' For a moment longer she regarded him, her eyes glittering with dislike. 'I can't . . . Daddy?'

'What?' he whispered.

'Oh – I think you understood. Let me put it more plainly. I'm up the spout, in the club, have a bun in the oven, I am with child, in the family way, carrying – in a word, pregnant.'

'I don't believe you,' he said, his voice uncertain.

'Ah. I thought you might not. I didn't believe it myself at first. So, I have here a medical certificate from my doctor, confirming it. You may ring him up, if you wish – he has my permission to discuss it with you.'

'You must – that is, I'll pay to have it aborted, of course. Any hospital you like – the best.'

'You're too good. But, you know, I don't think I want an abortion. Besides – didn't you speak out against abortions of convenience in the House only a few weeks ago? I seem to remember typing your speech. For shame, Mr Larcombe – you must practise what you preach.'

He felt a damp stickiness in his palm and looked down at the Meissen figurine, broken in half, and the welling cut on his hand.

'All right, Natasha,' he said, trying to speak calmly, 'I suppose you want money. How much will it take?'

316

Smiling, she shook her head. 'No. I want you. I want us to get married.'

'And if I refuse?'

'You would be foolish. The press would make a lovely story of it – especially the Tory papers.'

'You wouldn't do that.'

'Try me. There are precedents.'

'What – the Keays girl? I doubt if it did her much good. Besides, Parkinson was married.'

'Yes – and got a certain amount of sympathy for returning to his wife. Do you think you would? Getting your secretary pregnant then leaving her in the lurch while you marry a rich girl?'

'You bitch! You bloody, scheming little bitch!' He smashed the remains of the Meissen statuette against the wall and lurched towards her, suddenly drunk with rage. His hands were on her throat, and if she had screamed or struggled, he believed he would have choked the life out of her. But she just went on staring at him out of those cool, cat-like eyes.

'Get your hands off me, you fool,' she said in a low voice. 'You've used me – now it's your turn to be used. You're going to marry me, Jack Larcombe, whether you like it or not.'

'Natasha!' he said, desperately, 'don't! Don't make me! How can a marriage like that ever work? Do you want me to hate you?'

'I don't give a twopenny fuck, my dear! You need never come near my bed again, as far as I'm concerned. But, I'll tell you one thing. You need a woman like me, Jack, if you're not to be a complete also-ran. Without me, in five years you'll be a fat failure who's out of a job. With me, you can be rich and perhaps powerful as well.'

'Who cares? I don't want to be rich and powerful –

317

don't you understand? I love Dorrie – *love* her! I'll never love any other woman . . .'

'Oh, don't be such a provincial bore! You talk like a women's magazine. And you know what, Jack? You can't be honest even with yourself. If Dorrie St James was a shop girl, you might screw her a few times – but it's the St James millions you're so set on marrying, my dear! Well – not to worry. We'll make a nice little pile of our own. And for a start, you can go and see Humphrey Manville-Walker. He has a couple of very useful directorships he can offer you. I'm afraid I confided in him that we were thinking of marrying, and he was extremely helpful. You're seeing him in the morning. Oh – and Jack! Keep away from the gaming tables in future, my lad. You and me, we're going places – respectably!'

Jack stared at her, his heart filled with a black, sickening despair. There seemed no point in struggling against her any more – the whole thing had a bleak, everyday air of truth about it, quite different from the golden exhilaration of the last twenty-four hours when he had seemed to float a little way above the ground. Natasha returned his stare unflinchingly, then her gaze softened a little.

'Ah – come on, Jack dear! Don't be so miserable – it won't be all bad. Haven't we had some lovely times in bed together?'

His anger and the threat of physical violence had made her suddenly randy. She felt her nipples rub against the soft roughness of her silk gown and a tingling warmth in her genitals as they engorged and moistened in readiness. Reaching out, she took his hand and guided it between her legs.

'Leave me alone, Natasha – for God's sake,' he snarled, but he did not pull his hand away.

'You see – I still want you – can you feel? I still love you, Jack,' she whispered, and she moved his quiescent

318

fingers, rubbing and stroking them against her clitoris, her breathing quickening as she did so. 'Jack – please – do it to me once more – even if you never fuck me again – ' she groaned, and he felt his traitorous organ swelling and thickening despite himself. Without a word, he tore off most of his clothes and pulled her down to the floor, thrusting himself between her open legs, his penis forcing into her like a battering-ram. There was no finesse, it was semi-rape, and not much pleasure in it; the heat of the gas-fire was scorching one of her shoulders and a tiny piece of broken china dug painfully into her buttocks, but, beneath the jerking, panting body of her future husband, Natasha Troy smiled.

Giulio Verga was a small, spare man with gold-rimmed spectacles and an unconvincingly luxuriant toupee. He dressed in dark, three-piece suits from Savile Row, spoke quietly, collected Renaissance art, and the words 'hood' or 'mobster' would have been the last anyone would have used to describe him. He looked more like a successful lawyer, but in fact he was one of the most powerful *capi mafiosi* operating from Las Vegas.

He sat at his ease in Giovanni Khalid's penthouse apartment in Mayfair, his manicured hands folded on his lap, his thin lips composed and expressionless, a glass of fresh-squeezed orange juice at his elbow. He neither smoked nor drank, and had no use for personal adornment, despite the sobriquet 'Jewels' or 'The Jewel' that was often applied to him, and his only personal indulgence was his art collection. He was supposed to have a wife somewhere, but no one had ever seen her, and he showed no interest in sex of any description. He was, in fact, the antithesis of his partner Khalid, who was deeply interested in anything that he could eat, drink or screw, and who sat opposite him now, a fat cigar dropping ash down his

Turnbull and Asser silk shirt, his second bourbon and water of the morning half-empty.

Between the two of them, on a chair which he felt had been deliberately chosen to be absurdly low, sat Johnny Pacelli, his thin, jeans-clad legs sticking out in front of him, his Adam's apple bobbing above the neck of his tailored T-shirt as he swallowed convulsively. He was sweating.

As the prolonged silence continued in the room, Pacelli's eyes darted from one man to the other, his habitual drooping-eyed expression replaced by one of staring fright. Finally, like a cornered rat, he burst out: 'I don't have to take no shit from you!'

Verga's face did not move a muscle, but Khalid's bulky frame shook with silent laughter. He took the cigar from his mouth.

'What's that, Johnny? The title of your latest hit? Or – no, I was forgetting. You haven't had one of those for a long time, have you? The record companies get a bit fed up with being loused about by junkie singers who never turn up when they're supposed to. You don't have to take no shit? You're full of shit, Pacelli – and you'll take all we can throw at you.'

Verga cleared his throat with a soft rasping noise and Khalid was silent, eyeing his partner respectfully.

Verga placed his elbows on the arms of his chair and steepled his fingers below his chin, gazing at Pacelli contemplatively.

'Now, Mr Pacelli,' he said, as though no one else had spoken, 'it seems you've made one or two little errors of judgement . . .'

'Errors of judgement, my ass!' Khalid growled, 'he's come near to screwing up the whole operation. If he didn't walk up to Cavallo and tell him the Olympus was used for laundering money, he may as well have.'

'Well – hell! Why can't you get one of your own people in as manager,' Pacelli whined. 'Why have Cavallo there at all?'

Khalid got to his feet with a speed surprising in a man of his bulk, and grasped Pacelli by the front of his T-shirt. '*Because* he's clean, you punk!' he said, softly, administering a stinging slap to the side of Pacelli's head, '*Because* he has no record, and he's always dealt straight. This ain't Vegas, you know, you junkie hophead – we can only square a certain per cent of the law, and the rest will crucify us if we get caught. But they know Cavallo ain't crooked – he ain't never been suspected. What's more, punk' (another back-handed smack to Pacelli's face), 'what's more, *I* trust him. He ain't never going to rip me off, you know what I mean? I put a mobster in there and pretty soon he gets ideas about lining his pockets. But Cavallo – as long as he thinks it's a legit operation, he just does his job like he's supposed to.'

Once again Verga spoke. 'Am I to understand, Giovanni, that this Cavallo now suspects the Olympus operation?'

'Hell – I don't know how much he knows, Jewel. A while back, he said something to me about Pacelli bringing in a lot of money. I told Pacelli never to come in and do it under Cavallo's nose – but the stupid prick had to screw it up of course, not just once, but a dozen times. Cavallo may be straight, but he ain't no fool. It's only with his wife dying and all that, that's put it out of his mind – for the moment.'

Verga pursed his lips, frowned slightly, took a small sip of orange juice and patted his mouth delicately with a clean handkerchief.

'I believe you mentioned, Giovanni, the possibility of sending this Mr Cavallo to Vegas?'

'Yeah – we talked about it – I was going to send him a

year past, but, like I said, his wife took sick and she just died a couple of weeks back, so I figured he had enough on his mind not to worry about Pacelli or the casino.'

'His wife has just died, you say? And was it a happy marriage?'

'Yeah. Sure. Never knew him play around.'

'Then, this would seem an opportune moment for Mr Cavallo to visit Las Vegas. A change of scene, eh? And let us not forget, Giovanni, that a grieving man is – let us say vulnerable? No man is without a weakness, is that not so? And this Cavallo is no exception. You see what you can do, eh, Giovanni? And perhaps Mr Pacelli could help us, yes? Then we can put this little misunderstanding, this unpleasantness, behind us.'

'Sure – of course I'll help. Anything you like, Mr Verga,' Pacelli said, eagerly. 'I'd really be pleased to set Cavallo up – I hate his guts!'

'Get out now, Johnny,' Khalid said, softly. 'Blow, before I forget I'm a gentleman and put my foot up your ass.'

Pacelli stumbled awkwardly to his feet and stood hesitating. Khalid turned obsidian eyes on him, slowly and unblinkingly. 'Well?'

'What about the – you know, the smack?'

'Pacelli,' Khalid said, as though he was tired, 'like I said, you're full of shit. You don't want to go pumping more into yourself.'

'But – ' Pacelli's voice was thin and frightened, 'please, Giovanni – you – you know I've got to have it! I – I'll get the shakes – I'll – '

'Blow,' Khalid said. 'Maybe tomorrow. Or even the next day. Perhaps you'll remember to do like I say in future – if you want your fix regular, that is.'

* * *

322

Pacelli went back to his hotel suite and the girl he was currently living with. She jumped up as he came in, hollow eyes glittering in her thin, unwashed face.

'Did you get it?'

'The hell I did!' he snarled, pushing past her to get into the bathroom.

'*What?* Why not? God, Johnny – you know I need it bad – what am I going to do?'

'Shut up!' Still smarting from Khalid's blows, Pacelli swiped the girl across the face and she staggered and nearly fell, beginning to cry in a dreary, helpless way. 'Shut up, you stupid bitch! You think I don't need it, too? All I want is you whining and nagging at me.'

'I'm sorry, Johnny, really I am – it's only that I need a fix so bad. If I can only get myself together, I can make a comeback – I know I can – and we can make that record together we talked about. You know, Johnny? You haven't forgotten?'

Pacelli unzipped and relieved himself, not bothering to flush the lavatory afterwards. The bathroom stank, and the hotel staff were beginning to complain about the filthy mess the couple made, and the smell of pot that hung about the room.

'Comeback?' he said. 'You make a comeback? Have you looked in a mirror lately? The only comeback you'll make is in a horror movie.'

'Screw you,' she muttered. 'You don't look so hot yourself. And when did you last make a disc – let alone have a hit?'

'You're the one that'll have a hit if you don't fucking button your lip,' he said. 'Now just shut it and let me think.'

He threw himself down on the bed and rolled himself a reefer with hands that shook violently. The girl picked up a grubby hairbrush and wandered over to the mirror where she made a few ineffectual passes at her matted hair. Soon her hand dropped to her side and she stared at her face vacantly for a while, as though a dull amazement had penetrated her fogged brain that a cheeky, vivacious teenager called Linda Watson, famous overnight as 'Glitter' with one hit record to her credit, could have changed so rapidly into this haggard woman, used, abused, disillusioned. She was nineteen years old.

Presently, she took the hairbrush in both hands, as though it were a microphone and, raising it to her mouth, she began to murmur the words of her hit record: 'Tomorrow when I want you, will you be here? Tomorrow when I need you, will you love me?'

'Stop that fucking caterwauling,' Pacelli said, violently. He shied an ashtray at her, which struck her a glancing blow on the shoulder and made her yelp with pain. 'How can I fucking *think*!' he complained, sitting on the edge of the bed and gripping at his long black hair with his hands as though he would pull ideas out of his head. 'They want to get at Cavallo – find a chink – God damn it, the guy can't be so fucking pure he never wants to screw or . . . wait a minute . . .'

'What is it, Johnny? Have you thought of a way to get some smack?' Unwisely, she hurried over and bent down, putting her face near his. He shoved his palm into it, so that she fell backwards on to the carpet and sat there staring ludicrously up at him.

'You stink like a wrestler's crutch. Keep away from me, can't you, or I'll throw you out for good. I just thought of something might interest Khalid.'

He grabbed the receiver, misdialled, dialled again, and then spoke, his voice quietening into obsequiousness, 'Mr Khalid? Sorry to disturb you, but – what? Oh – it's Johnny. Yeah, Johnny Pacelli. I just remembered something – you know, what we were saying about Cavallo? I

324

remembered something that might help. What? Oh, yeah, sorry. It's this – Bob Haley, at the casino, told me once he thought there could be something going on between Cavallo and Dorrie St James. I said it was bullshit, but he said, no, but, like he didn't know if Cavallo was actually screwing her but, something – I dunno. It might help, though, eh? Yeah – I just wanted to let you know. And – Mr Khalid? About the smack? If you could just let me have even one fix? Sure – yes, I'll be here all day.' He hung up.

'He's going to ring back. He said maybe.'

'Maybe what? One fix for you, you mean?'

Linda wriggled out of reach across the carpet, then got to her feet and went into the bathroom, locking the door behind her. She had a bottle of amphetamines hidden in the cistern, and Pacelli could go screw himself before she would let him have any.

PART FOUR
Las Vegas

15

When the invitation came, Dorrie had tossed it to one side, after the initial shock, half joy, half fear, of seeing the Olympus Casino's elaborate letter-head at the top. But then she had realized it was only one of those standard publicity letters, sent out to dozens of well-heeled members. It was the usual thing, a first-class, luxury trip to Las Vegas, all expenses paid, to stay at the Olympus's sister casino-hotel, the Golden Nevada. What was known in the trade as a 'junket'. Why she had been asked, Dorrie could not imagine. She was rich, with the solid richness of land and inherited wealth, but she had never gambled heavily, and for more than a year had not set foot in the Olympus. She shrugged and put the letter out of her head, so that Giovanni Khalid's phone call a week later took her by surprise.

'Miss St James – Dorrie? This is Giovanni Khalid. How are you, my dear?'

'I'm well, thank you, Mr Khalid,' she answered, slightly puzzled. 'What can I do for you?'

'Ah, my dear! I rang to see if you were considering our little holiday jaunt to Vegas! It would be delightful if you would! The very best of service, of course! May I tell you, I have reserved our most beautiful rooms, the Pompadour Suite – just in case you were thinking of . . . no other rooms would do justice to your beauty, my dear! You will be our guest of honour . . .'

'Hold on a minute, Mr Khalid! You know, I think you must be mistaking me for someone else. I hardly ever gamble at all . . .'

'Mistake you? You are being facetious – how could one mistake the most lovely woman in London? And who mentioned gambling?'

'Oh, sorry – silly of me! I just got the impression that was what people mainly did in Las Vegas.'

'But – my dear! Las Vegas is a glittering exciting international city, and the Golden Nevada is a terrific hotel! We get all the movie stars there, believe me! Let me tell you, Sinatra is coming to sing – and I would be so pleased to introduce you!'

Dorrie yawned slightly. 'Pardon me while I swoon,' she said, dryly. 'Look, Mr Khalid, I have to go now. I can't say the idea grabs me, but if I change my mind I'll let you know. Will that do?'

'You are a very gracious lady. I do hope we will have the pleasure of your company. Goodbye, now, – or, *arrivederci*!'

Cy had returned from her kibbutz, her hands roughened from peeling potatoes and her heart a little sore from leaving Waldo shacked up with a nice Jewish girl. She raised her eyebrows at Dorrie in mute enquiry.

'Oh, nothing. Only that human crocodile Mr Khalid from the Olympus. He wants me to go on an all-expenses-paid trip to Las Vegas – of all places. Why, I can't imagine. I'm not what I believe they call a "high-roller"!'

'Publicity, I expect,' Cy said. 'You're a name, and I suppose you'd attract other punters. Why don't you go, Dorrie?'

'To Las *Vegas*?'

'Anywhere. You need a holiday – you look really wishy-washy.'

'Thanks, my friend. Anyway, I can take a holiday anywhere – it doesn't have to be Las Vegas.'

'But you won't, will you? You'll just drift around town, drinking too much and feeling miserable. Why not have a change of scene? I mean, you don't have to stay put in Vegas, do you? You can wander about for a while, get a new slant on life. Buy some new clothes for the trip!'

'You make me sound a real empty-head. What if I just don't want to go?'

'It's up to you, honey-chile. I'd go like a shot – it's such a bloody awful summer we're having here. At least you can guarantee you'll be warm.'

And, at last, she had rung Khalid and accepted his invitation, hardly knowing why she did so, except that it was something to do. Jack Larcombe's sudden withdrawal from their short-lived engagement had taken her aback, but she had not been devastated. It would probably have been a mistake for both of them, and when she saw the announcement of his engagement to Miss Natasha Troy, only daughter of the late Colonel Harry Troy, she sent him a friendly note of congratulation, to which he did not reply. But, she reflected, having lost the man she loved, the man she had married and the man she was engaged to, in little more that a year, did leave one at something of a loose end. The frenetic activity of a gambling city might give her something to do other than brood on her own problems.

It was hot, that much was certain. She had hardly arrived at the airport, which had so many fruit machines it almost qualified for the title 'casino' itself, and had been whisked into a limousine, before she had forgotten the chill grey skies of a damp English summer. Even Dorrie, who adored the sun and could bask for hours, found herself grateful for the icy coolness of the air-conditioning in the car.

There were about fifty of them on the junket, some of whom Dorrie knew, and all of whom were at least millionaires. The luggage alone was worth thousands of pounds, and the labels in the women's frocks were like a roll-call of Paris fashion houses.

Stella and Harry Fielding were there, considerably richer these days, since Harry had done some quiet arms deals with anonymous men in the Middle East; and Johnny Pacelli, who came and sat beside Dorrie on the flight out, quieter and less bombastic than she remembered him, thinner, and with the long black hair receding a little at the temples.

'How are things with you, Johnny?' she asked, only mildly interested.

'Great!' he answered. 'Terrific! I've got a month's engagement at the Nevada, and then I might go on to the Starlight Room at the Desert Inn. Things are really buzzing, Dorrie!'

'I'm glad.' She wondered if she could open her paperback and read without interruption, or whether it would be kinder to just pretend to fall asleep. And why, anyway, did she feel she had to be kind to a conceited jerk like Pacelli, whom she had never, after a brief, initial attraction, liked at all? Only because the expression of confident arrogance had somehow turned to the haunted look of a frightened little man. Despite the money that he was supposed to have been flashing around, Dorrie knew he hadn't had a record in the charts for a long time, and she was pretty sure of the reason. If Pacelli wasn't main-lining heroin, she would have been very surprised. So she put up with his meandering, self-centred conversation on the flight out, and repressed a faint sigh of irritation when he climbed into the limousine beside her.

Las Vegas was exactly as she had imagined it would be, a sort of Disneyland for adults, garish, tawdry, glittering, a bright paste jewel on the rocky desert wastes of Nevada. Along Fremont Street, known as Glitter Gulch, were the basic casinos, the 'sawdust joints' – bright, vulgar, and with an eternal, restless cacophony of noise from the thousands of slot machines and the games of roulette, blackjack, craps, poker, chuck-a-luck, faro, bingo, keno – in fact, any game which man could devise for taking money off his fellow man.

Along the other main street of Vegas, 'The Strip', sprawled the luxury hotel-casinos, the Tropicana, the Sands, the Riviera, the Flamingo, the Golden Nevada, all built in styles which could be described as 'Ranch Rococo' or 'Miami Baroque', all with expensively maintained lawns and flowerbeds and turquoise pools where guests could cool off before getting back to the action.

Dorrie cursed herself mildly for having come, and made up her mind to stay one night and then to take off for somewhere more congenial. She had a friend at Lake Tahoe she could look up – at least the air would be fresher there, not like this desert heat that reminded her so painfully of Riyadh.

Beside her, Pacelli leaned forward and stared out, his eyes flickering with excitement. 'It's great, isn't it?' he said to Dorrie, then, as though conscious of naïveté, he added, 'You'll have a good time here, kid. I'll show you around – where the best action is . . .'

'Thanks, Johnny, but it's not really my scene. I thought I'd take off and visit some friends. I told Khalid I was no gambler.'

Pacelli's jaw dropped comically, 'But – gee, Dorrie – you have to stay in Vegas! I mean – Khalid would be mad!'

Dorrie scowled at him suddenly. Who did the jerk think he was? '*Have* to stay?' she said, coolly. 'I don't think so. As for Khalid – I don't give a shit about him.'

'You're making a big mistake, Dorrie, believe me!' Pacelli said, putting his hand on her arm and speaking earnestly. She shook him off.

'Don't talk like a twenties gangster, Johnny. It doesn't suit you.'

The limousine drew up in front of the Golden Nevada, and Khalid was there in the huge, marble-pillared foyer, amongst the golden mosaic-lined fountains with their spouting dolphins and chaste maidens, the banks of tropical plants and flowers. He came forward to greet his guests, his arms out-stretched expansively, a warm smile of welcome on his lips, and the English visitors stood around a little awkwardly, forced smiles on their faces, even the wealthiest of them rather stunned by the scale of their surroundings. It was like being in a huge, vulgarly elaborate cathedral, dedicated to money, and they would have liked to slip discreetly away to their rooms, make a quick change of garments and personality, and be absorbed into the anonymous crowd of gamblers. But Mr Khalid was making a fulsome speech of welcome and assuring them that their slightest wish had only to be murmured before being granted. At last he had finished. The bell-hops took the luggage and led the guests away. Champagne waited in their rooms. Vegas took them into her sleazy embrace.

'Miss St James! My dear – how wonderful that you were able to come!'

Khalid put a hand on each of Dorrie's shoulders and to her disgust, brushed her cheeks with his rubbery lips. She murmured something conventional, and Pacelli, who was still at her heels like a sheep-dog, blurted out, 'She says she's not staying, Mr Khalid! She says she's going visiting friends. I said you'd be mad, but . . .'

Dorrie suppressed a shiver as Khalid's eyes went suddenly cold, and she realized that he was not just a rather boring, faintly comical fat man, but it was at Pacelli that the implacable gaze was directed.

'I expect you'd like to see your room, Johnny?' Without

looking round, he snapped his fingers and a bell-hop ran forward and grabbed Pacelli's bags. Pacelli's prominent Adam's apple jerked as he swallowed nervously. 'Sure. Sure. I'll – er – I'll see you later, Dorrie – Mr Khalid . . .' He followed the bell-hop over to the elevators, looking back once or twice over his shoulder.

'So, already you think of leaving us, my dear?' Khalid put a fatherly arm round her shoulder and began walking her towards the elevator. Her luggage had vanished already. 'We must try and make you change your mind, yes? I think you will have a good time here, trust me! We are all so pleased to see you – and you will find the Golden Nevada is full of delightful surprises!'

The Pompadour Suite was the first of them. Mr Khalid, genially chatting, accompanied her inside. It was so vast that Dorrie thought it would be like sleeping in Wembley Stadium, and the enormous bed had brocaded curtains of blue and gold hanging from elaborate gilded bosses on the wall at its head. Underfoot, the carpet was so deep one almost needed snow-shoes to walk on it, and the furnishings were either genuine Louis Quatorze or excellent reproductions.

'Everything is genuine,' Khalid said, watching her face. 'Everything is French, antique – perhaps not all strictly in period, but – you must allow us Yanks a little latitude, yes? The Watteau and the Fragonard – delightful, are they not? And the Degas ballet dancers – a little modern, but so delicate and feminine – I had to put it in here!'

'I'm stunned with admiration, Mr Khalid,' Dorrie said, solemnly. 'Your hotel makes our country house look like wattle and daub!'

'Ah – you tease me! I know better! But, if you like it, I am delighted. Now – I will leave you, my dear. You will wish to rest after the journey. Would you do me the honour of dining with me a little later? I should like to show you round personally.'

Dorrie agreed, though inwardly reluctant to have Khalid's company any longer than was necessary. When he had gone, she stripped off the silk jersey shift she had travelled in, and dropped it to the floor, then poured herself a glass of the complimentary champagne which stood in a silver ice-bucket, and wandered about, barefoot and naked, examining the priceless furnishings of the room.

The bathroom was almost as large and certainly as luxurious, with a sunken bath, a jacuzzi, and everything possible gold-plated. The towels rivalled the carpet in thickness and softness and there were essences, bath-oils, soaps enough to stock a beauty parlour, as well as miniature bottles of 'Joy', 'Chanel No. 5' and 'Arpège'. Dorrie grinned and poured more champagne, then took a long, relaxing bath. Afterwards, it being evident that glamour and ostentation were the order of the day, she dressed for dinner in an exotic gown that the Emmanuels had made for her. It was in silk chiffon of a deep rose colour, the underskirt embroidered with silver and caught up with tiny velvet roses. It was an extravagant dream of a dress – really quite unsuitable for anything but a grand ball, but Dorrie was sure Mr Khalid would approve. She brushed her newly-washed hair, and contemplated ringing for the hair-stylist, but decided she couldn't be bothered with someone fussing over her, and left it loose, a shining silver-gilt frame for her face, then, adding a ruby and pearl choker and ear-studs and a white fox stole in traditional Hollywood style, she sallied forth for her date with Mr Khalid, grinning ironically at her reflection as she did.

The dinner, like the rest of the Golden Nevada, was opulent, luxurious, more than a little vulgar. To Dorrie's mild relief, she did not dine tête-à-tête with Khalid, but with four other people as well, including a newspaper magnate whom she knew slightly and a film actress who always played rather intellectual heroines but now revealed herself to be without two original thoughts to rub together. Bored, and slightly cross, sickened by the effusive compliments as much as by the over-rich food, Dorrie ate sparingly and drank a lot more champagne than she should have.

Khalid was as genial as ever, but she felt his eyes on her, watchfully, and there was an air of suppressed excitement about him that was irritating. He seemed, despite his urbanity, to be almost eager for the meal to be over and to show her the casino and Dorrie reflected that if he thought she was going to start wildly gambling and filling his coffers with St James money, he was in for a disappointment.

The casino proper was a vast hall with dozens of gaming tables, and a broad corridor with over six hundred one-armed bandits. Little old ladies with eyes that could have stared down the barrel of a Colt, pumped the handles as though they had been condemned to it as a sort of purgatory, and with as much enjoyment, and the people who were seated round the tables playing roulette, craps or blackjack, wore expressions of such ferocious intensity that they made the punters at home in the Olympus look like a Teddy Bears' picnic.

'You never been to Vegas before, eh?' Khalid said, watching her. 'No? Well I tell you, this part of the Casino – it's big, the biggest and best in Vegas, but I suppose you could say it's like any other joint here. But we got something different – something real classy that I just dreamed up. A sorta private club for the real high-rollers, you know? It's real classy, yes? Run on English lines. I thought maybe even French croupiers, but – well, that could be too much. Come – I show you. In here. I got this Englishman from back home organizing it . . .'

He opened a door marked 'Private' revealing a room which, though large, seemed almost intimate compared with the main casino. Its walls were oak-panelled, and gilt-framed oil-paintings of hunting scenes ornamented them. There were six roulette tables and two of blackjack and, as the door swung closed behind them, it was almost quiet.

No warning bells had rung in Dorrie's brain, no sixth sense had alerted her, and even though she had glanced idly at the tuxedo-clad back of the tall man standing nearby, it was only when Khalid spoke his name that her heart seemed to stop and she thought she would faint.

'Ross!' Khalid said. 'C'mon over here! I want you to meet an old friend.'

He turned and saw her, and she felt the colour flame into her face and ebb away. The fumes of the champagne she had drunk suddenly made her head whirl and she felt deathly sick. His face, though – she saw his face clearly in the whirling kaleidoscope of colour that threatened to tip her into unconsciousness, and it was quite still, quite quiet, not a flicker of expression to show her that he had ever given her a single thought since that day in Kew when they had made love.

He must think that she had followed him here deliberately, to force herself upon him. That she could hardly wait for Sarah to die before she came chasing him halfway round the world. A terrible sense of shame swept over Dorrie. She felt unclean, a leper, a whore. She wanted the lush carpeted floor to open beneath her and let her disappear for ever. And she knew that in another moment she was going to throw up.

'Excuse me,' she muttered to Khalid, and turned, pushing past him, out of the door marked 'Private' and into the noisy casino, nearly running, half-blind with tears of anger and shame, amongst the intent gamblers, who did not look round even when she jostled them in her headlong flight.

Safe in her room, she flung herself on her bed, but the tears would not fall from her burning eyes and the sickness had been replaced by a dreadful giddiness that turned the elaborate bed into a lurching, swooping sailing ship. She moaned, pressing her hands on to her burning cheeks and across her eyes, trying to shut out the memory of those dark eyes and the shame of what he must think of her. After a time the dizziness receded, but the sense of shame was worse than ever. She got up, her lovely dress crumpled and limp, and poured herself more champagne. A fresh bottle had been placed in the room while she was at dinner. She drank it, gulping it down as though it was water, glass after glass, some of it spilling on to the crushed silk of her dress, trying desperately to achieve oblivion.

But it was still far from her when the knock came at the door. Part of her mind was still crystal clear and as alert to its surroundings as a wild creature in a trap. Only her lips were numb and refused to form any words, and her legs were too shaky to allow her to get up. She sat on the bed, silent and mesmerized, as the knock came again and the handle began to turn.

He came into her room and closed the door behind him.

'Why did you run away?' he said, quietly.

Dorrie stared at him, miserably. Her lips moved and she bit the lower one to stop it trembling. Her mouth felt so numb, she was sure she would not be able to speak.

''Shamed,' she blurted out at last. 'Thought you'd . . .' she could not manage the words for what she had felt.

339

'Didn't know you were here,' she finished sadly, wondering if he believed her.

'I know,' he said, 'I could see it was a shock to you, as it was to me. I'm sorry.'

He was *sorry*! He wasn't angry, or despising or hating her – just sorry. She got up off the bed and took a step towards him, trying to focus her eyes on the expression on his face. Was it cool, or amused, distant or friendly? The carpet billowed treacherously beneath her feet and she staggered and was aware of him coming nearer.

'What's the matter?'

'I'm drunk,' she whispered, and passed out in his arms.

He picked her up and held her against his chest, looking down at her unconscious face. It had changed since he last saw it, no longer the face of a lovely, impudent child, but a woman's face, thinner, with faint shadows beneath the eyes, and sadness in the soft curve of the mouth. What had happened to her in the last year, Ross wondered, after her precipitate marriage to el Said? He had thought of her so often, and with such feelings of remorse, knowing why she had fled to Saudi and to what had obviously been an unhappy partnership, and in the last months of Sarah's illness, when she had been in such pain, every thought of Dorrie had been a guilty one.

And then, that soft May evening, when Sarah's last breath had fluttered from her as quietly as the cherry blossoms were falling from the trees in Kew Gardens, and he had held her in his arms and looked down at her peaceful dead face; then, his heart had seemed to turn to stone within him and he had felt as though he would never feel any emotion ever again.

Khalid's instruction that he was to go to Las Vegas to organize this private club within the casino had been a welcome one. He wanted to get away from London and all the people who knew him, away from the glances of

340

sympathy, both open and covert, and the kindly meant offers of help. He could not even comfort the children, feeling himself so far down in an abyss of grief and depression that even they kept away from him, clinging to their grandmother as the only rock in their suddenly uncertain world.

She was staying at Kew with them now, while Ross was away, tenderly piecing their lives together with loving care and canny Scots good sense. They were his family, the closest people to him in the world, and he would have died for them without a word of protest, but still his heart seemed numb, no tenderness in it for any living soul.

Until tonight. Until he had turned and seen Dorrie standing there in her rose-red dress, her lovely hair like an aureole about her face, her cheeks flushed and her eyes wide with shock. Then something had melted painfully inside him, and, as soon as he could, he followed her to her room as if drawn by some blind instinct which he could not deny.

He put her gently down on the bed, removing her shoes and the crumpled dress and covering her slender body with the silken bed-spread, then he sat nearby on a chair, watching her face as she slept.

Once or twice she twitched and whimpered in her sleep like a puppy, and once she cried his name softly and he saw tears dampen her thick golden eyelashes.

'Hush – I'm here,' he murmured, taking her hand in his.

The night wore slowly on, and he sat at her bedside, awake and watchful, just as he had sat for many nights beside Sarah as her life ebbed so painfully away. But this was no dying woman, it was Dorrie, who had always seemed to him the epitome of healthy life, resilient even in the depths of sorrow. Why, then, did his heart ache for her? Was it the suddenly fragile appearance of her face, like a brave spring flower whose petals are so vulnerable to harsh winds? Was it the knowledge that she had been a virgin when he had thought her promiscuous? She had often been in his thoughts, but the words he had used to himself in connection with her had been words like attraction, or 'physical desire', words of the flesh alone, and never 'love'.

Love was what he had felt for Sarah, something that had grown warmer and more enduring over the years of their marriage, not this adolescent passion for a girl almost young enough to be his daughter, no matter how lovely she was, or how she made his pulses hammer as though he was a boy again. Love? He asked himself, watching her sleeping face, was it possible that he loved this woman? It was so foolhardy to fall in love with someone – the most reckless sort of gambling anyone could imagine. Loving people made you defenceless; the beloved was a hostage to Fortune and Fortune was unkind. Safer to leave your heart where it was, buried in a quiet churchyard with Sarah, and to make up your mind never to love again . . .

She woke at last, her eyes opening and fastening on his with a dreamy, sweet expression, before realization widened them and she sat up with a gasp.

'It's all right – you've been asleep,' he reassured her, and, as she remembered, she flushed painfully.

'Dead drunk, you mean,' she muttered. 'I'm sorry – you must be disgusted. Thank you for staying, but there was no need. I shall be quite safe – and it's a condition I'm used to, anyway.'

He raised his eyebrows. 'Really? You used to try and make me think you were a whore – now I'm to believe you're a lush as well, am I?'

She shrugged, circling her knees with her arms, looking away from him.

'Believe what you like,' she said, her voice sulky, and he felt the old familiar irritation rising in him. The urge to administer a sharp smack on her bottom. 'Well,' he stood up, 'I'm sorry if you feel I've intruded. I'll go now . . .'

She looked up at him suddenly, defiantly. 'I suppose you think I followed you here? That I came on purpose?'

'No.'

'Well – I didn't. I *didn't*! I thought Las Vegas would be a long way away from you. If you must know, I came because I was afraid I'd make a fool of myself – throw myself at you or something.'

'That would have been dreadful,' he agreed, gravely.

She glowered at him suspiciously. 'I *never* butt in where I'm not wanted.'

'Who said you weren't wanted?'

His eyes were still mocking, still amused, but there was tenderness in them as well. He sat down beside her on the bed and took her hand in his, examining it minutely as though he had never seen it before.

'Dorrie,' he said, soberly, 'since I met you, there has scarcely been a day when I haven't thought of you – haven't wanted you . . . even, God forgive me, when Sarah was dying. Even though I felt I was betraying her – I couldn't help wanting you.'

He heard her catch her breath, then she bent her head and touched her lips to his hand in a fleeting kiss. 'Thank you for telling me,' she whispered. She wanted his love more than anything in the world, but it was something to know that he had wanted her.

'For God's sake – don't thank me,' he said, roughly, unable to bear the thought of her gratitude. He took hold of her shoulders, as though he was going to shake her, and then with a sigh that was almost a groan, he pulled her into his arms.

She put her head against his chest, clutching him, holding him to her fiercely. If this was a dream, that Ross was beside her, his body warm against hers, then she never wanted to wake again into the cold reality of life without him.

For a few moments, they were quite silent, her face against his chest, his cheek against the soft perfume of her hair as he cradled her like a child.

'You've grown thinner,' he said, quietly. 'Have you been very unhappy?'

She nodded, mutely, then after a moment he felt her arms tighten on him. 'It was my baby, Ross,' she whispered, scarcely audibly, 'It wasn't his . . . it was mine – yours and mine . . . He was so little – I loved him so much – and – and I had to leave him . . .' All at once the floodgates of the terrible grief that had been kept firmly closed for so many months were opened, and Dorrie wept. The words and phrases of her sorrow came to Ross between the sobs and, as he pieced them together, his heart ached for her. All alone she had borne his child, and had suffered for it and had it torn from her and he was helpless to do more than hold her and stroke the hair from her wet cheeks and kiss the tears from her eyes. At last her weeping lessened and she lay more quietly in his arms, only an occasional sob still shaking her body.

'Darling,' Ross said, 'we'll get him back – I promise you. We'll get our baby back again, somehow.' And, because she loved him, she believed him and was comforted for the first time since she had left Riyadh.

'Oh, Ross,' she whispered, tremulously. 'I love you so much . . .' She raised her lips to him and he bent his head and covered her sweet mouth with his own in a long kiss that held as much tenderness as passion.

At last, he raised his head and they regarded each other, unsmiling. He drew an unsteady breath.

'Dorrie . . .'

His hands were on her slim, bare shoulders, as he held her a little away from himself. 'You're so beautiful . . .'

'Stay with me, Ross. Don't leave me again – not tonight – please?' she said softly, her eyes warm with an invitation that was unmistakable, and he could feel his body begin to respond to it. But – it was too soon, too sudden – and the opulent room had seen too many loveless couplings – there was a feeling of depravity which had soaked into its very fabric. Slowly, he shook his head, then, seeing the hurt in her eyes, he took her closely into his arms again.

'Of course I want to make love to you. It's only . . .'

'I know. It's too soon. That was – clumsy of me – I'm sorry.'

'Don't be. It's not that. It's – I don't know if I can make you understand. I want to – to rediscover you, Dorrie. Since we met there's been such a lot of resentment and frustration and – guilt, I suppose. I want to put it all behind us, and start again – do you know what I'm talking about?'

'Yes, of course, but . . .'

'And this place – it's Khalid's. It stinks of money and greed and tawdry, passing pleasures. I want to make love to you somewhere else – somewhere the air is clean.'

She smiled at him, with such an uprush of relieved happiness that she would have agreed with delight if he had suggested they make love on the moon.

'We'll go to Lake Tahoe,' she said, simply. 'My friend, Judy Berringer has a house there. Can you take a couple of days off?'

He smiled back at her, 'I expect so. They owe me a few. Will your friend mind?'

'Not Judy. She's the best type of American – and she loves visitors. She's expecting me to go and see her, anyway – one extra won't throw her.'

'Well – give her a ring in the morning. I'll see Khalid about time off. Now, I'm going to leave you to your drunken slumbers. How do you manage to have a sweet mouth and clear eyes when you've drunk enough to launch the Q.E.2?' He bent and kissed her again on the lips. 'Sweet. Goodnight.'

Six storeys above them, Khalid grunted as the door closed behind Cavallo. He lit another Havana, then reached for the telephone at his side.

'Hallo?' Verga's voice was always the same, crisp and alert, never, no matter what hour of the day or night you called him, fuzzy with sleep.

'Jewels? Looks as though Johnny was right – there *is* something there. But he's pussy-footing around – thinks the Golden Nevada ain't good enough to screw the broad in, or something. He's fixing to take her to Tahoe. What do you think?'

'By all means,' Verga said, smoothly. 'Let him have a few days off. He has to come back to work, and by that time he will have formed a pleasant new habit and no doubt have lost some of his inhibitions.'

Khalid laughed with a silent wheeze, the end of his Havana already damp and bitten. 'Right on, Jewels! We let them go off and do some rehearsing for the big picture, eh?'

'Exactly.'

16

The alpine meadow lay like a green jewel against the darkness of pine and cedar, and the still, deep-blue sky arched above, enclosing them in quiet warmth. A small stream bubbled across the meadow, full of icy, melted snow from the Sierras, and its banks were speckled with bright flowers – gentians, Indian paintbrush, leopard lilies. There were no trippers about, not a building in sight – this was back-packing country, and they had walked five miles from Judy Berringer's luxurious chalet to find this perfect and idyllic spot, bringing a picnic with them.

They had arrived the previous evening, welcomed enthusiastically by Judy, who reminded Ross of a big, clean, friendly dog, white-toothed and affectionate. She was separated from her husband and lived cheerfully alone with her four bouncy children, supported by an enormous income from the family ranch near San Francisco, and entertained by a constant stream of visitors, all of whom she greeted with the same overwhelming hospitality.

The chalet was big, but it had seemed crowded and noisy, and, although their rooms were near to each other, they had slept chastely apart. It was almost as though they felt that making love would commit them to something irrevocable. They craved solitude, and here, in this Eden-like mountain meadow, they found it.

Judy had had her cook prepare them a vast lunch, although Dorrie had protested that they were only going for a hike, and not crossing the Sierra Nevada to the coast.

'It'll give you an appetite,' Judy said, cryptically and with a grin. 'It always makes me hungry. Walking, I mean.'

'Oh, really?' Dorrie said, dryly, 'Well, with all this weight of food to carry, we probably won't get further than the end of your yard.'

They had not spoken much all morning – had hardly touched in fact. Only occasionally their hands brushed, or their eyes met briefly, but when they emerged from the trees into the quiet flower-strewn meadow, they stopped with one accord, as though it was a place they knew, that they had been searching for, and found.

They spread out their lunch on the stream bank and ate, watching the sun dancing on the surface of the clear waters and the swift rising of the speckled trout after mayflies. Neither of them ate much – there was an expectancy in the air, a waiting hush that made them unaware of hunger or thirst, or anything but a quickening pulse and a growing, aching longing.

Dorrie put down a piece of chicken untasted.

'How beautiful it is,' she murmured, and Ross, seeing the blue of sky and water and the gold of sunlight reflected in her eyes and hair, reached out and turned her face towards his. There was a mute question and response as their eyes met, and then he was gently, unhurriedly, unbuttoning the loose white shirt she wore over her shorts, until her breasts and shoulders were bare, golden under the sun, unfastening her shorts and sliding them off, his hands lingering over the smooth curve of buttock and belly, touching lightly on the dense golden tangle over the mound of Venus.

Her breathing had quickened, and she lay in the spangled grass like a new-made Eve, her legs a little apart

348

and her full breasts rising and falling, the nipples already hardening into sensitivity as she looked up into his eyes.

'I love you, Ross.'

He reached out and traced a gentle line down from her throat to the tip of her breast, then on, down her slim rib-cage, over the flat smoothness of her stomach to the swelling warmth between her legs, cupped in his caressing hand. And, quite suddenly, he was able to say, with no sense of betrayal, and as though he was only voicing what he had known for a long time. 'I love you, too.'

Then his clothes, too, were quickly off, and they lay in each other's arms, filled with unbearable delight, entwined together, each giving and receiving kisses and caresses with a gradually increasing excitement until the moment when he gently parted her thighs and entered her.

For a moment they lay still. Dorrie thought that never in her life would she be able to experience greater happiness than she felt now as she lay with the man she loved, feeling him filling her body utterly and perfectly. Then they moved together in slow, sensual rhythm, an ecstasy of the flesh that made the world grow dim and far away, a love-making as unselfconscious and full of newly discovered delight as if the little meadow was indeed Eden.

Dorrie felt the electric tingling of approaching orgasm sweep through her brain and all her limbs to the centre of her body, the source of all the aching pleasure, and she cried out as a long convulsion of pure joy tossed her to its crest like a tidal wave, unresisting and weeping with happiness.

Ross, holding back until he was sure of her pleasure, abandoned himself to his climax, his orgasm as violent and ecstatic as hers, and it was a long time before either of them spoke, as they lay in the crushed scent of wild flowers and clean, sweet earth.

At last, 'You have an ant crawling up your cheek,' Dorrie murmured.

'Mm.' Ross didn't move.

Dorrie, watching his face as she gently brushed away the invader, saw how all the tension and grimness had been smoothed out, and how the firm-lipped mouth had softened into humour and tenderness.

Was it true, she wondered, did he really love her? Or had the words been spoken in the excitement of love-making – a mere convention?

As though he read her thoughts, his eyes opened and he raised himself on one elbow, looking down at her with a half-smile. He took a golden frond of her hair between his fingers and put it to his lips.

'I do love you, you know, Dorrie,' he said, very quietly. 'Perhaps I shouldn't be saying it, or feeling it, only three months after Sarah's death. It doesn't mean I didn't love her – you know I did. But – I can't help it. It's a fact of life. I love you.'

'Oh, Ross . . .' She could not find the words for everything that was in her heart. 'I love you' was used and misused, but it was all she could say, over and over again, as she covered his face with kisses.

Presently they got up and bathed in the icy chill of the little brook, laughing and splashing each other like children, and while they were thus engaged, Mr and Mrs Alvin Schumacher, teachers from Idaho back-packing through the Sierras, emerged from the forest and stared, affronted.

Ross and Dorrie didn't see them at first, and it was only Mrs Schumacher's bawled indignation that made them look round, startled.

'People like you should be operated on! It's indecent!

Defiling God's beautiful countryside! Cover yourselves up, you – you hippies!' She yelled across the meadow before turning and stomping back into the trees with her large, sensibly booted feet, her Bermuda-clad behind quivering with outrage. Her husband, on the pretext of re-lacing his hiking boot, paused for another long gaze at Dorrie's golden beauty – a picture that stayed in his mind till his dying day – then ran stumbling after his unlovely partner.

The two hippies climbed, still laughing, to the bank, and lay shamelessly in the sun to dry.

'I'm absolutely starving!' Dorrie announced suddenly, and giggled. 'Judy said I would be!'

'A very astute lady,' Ross agreed. 'Bring out the provisions again – we must keep our strength up.'

All the reserve and the tentative circling around each other, was gone. As they ate, they talked, and let each other in to the most secret places of their lives. Dorrie told Ross of her childhood and her lovely, vivacious mother; how much she had loved and admired her, and how Antonia had never seemed to have time for more than a brief word or a pat on the head for her daughter.

And Ross found himself without effort breaking his habitual reserve and talking about his father, who had been an Italian prisoner of war, working on the McDonnell farm near Inverness. How he had returned to Scotland after his repatriation to marry Maire McDonnell and father a son, but had pined for Italy amongst the misty mountains and had returned to his native land, where he died some ten years later without seeing his wife and son again. There was still a slight bitterness in Ross's voice and eyes as he spoke, remembering the struggle his mother had had to bring him up, and how his own hopes of university had been destroyed by the necessity of earning a living as soon as possible. But – perhaps he was simply growing older, or mellowing with the years, or maybe it was just his new-found happiness that made him suddenly feel able to bid farewell to that dim, half-remembered shade from his childhood, with an understanding that all men have their weaknesses, and that strength comes only from recognizing that.

As the shadows lengthened and the westering sun painted their meadow with broad strokes of enamelled gold, they began to walk slowly back toward Tahoe, hand in hand, in a state of dreamy rapture.

Judy, practising baseball with her sons beneath the spreading cedars of the garden above Emerald Bay, grinned as she saw them approach.

'I see you finished all your lunch!' she yelled, when they were still fifty feet away.

'Gee, Mom! How can you tell?' Nine-year-old Sam Junior was obviously impressed by his mother's psychic powers, especially when Dorrie, blushing, admitted that they had.

'Well, I hope you have an appetite for dinner,' Judy said. 'Cook's night off, and I'm fixing tacos.'

'Oh, boy! Mom's tacos are great! You folks'll love 'em!' Sam yelled jubilantly, turning an involuntary cartwheel on the grass and then leaping about in imitation of a deranged chimp, scratching himself and chattering.

'That kid is just gross!' Twelve-year-old Felix flopped at his mother's feet with an expression of disdain. 'I mean, really, Mom – he's so *embarrassing*!'

'Don't be embarrassed!' Ross said, grinning. 'That's just the sort of thing my son Ben does. I'm quite used to it! Hey – weren't you going to show me your fossil collection?'

'Sure thing – I mean, yes, *sir*!' Felix jumped up and led the way eagerly indoors, delighted to find someone who didn't scream with boredom at the mention of his fossils.

Dorrie and Judy followed more slowly, pausing on the wide verandah to admire the sunset that banded the western sky with pink and lilac, a skein of Canada geese obligingly adding their visual impact at just the right moment.

Judy came into Dorrie's room and sat on the bed while her friend stripped off and showered.

'I like Ross, very much,' she said. 'Easily the best guy you've had. Are you going to marry him?'

'I don't know. He – he hasn't asked me. He only lost his wife in May, you know.'

'Sure. But he loves you – a blind man could pick up the vibrations!'

Dorrie smiled. 'He says he does. And – I love him, Judy. Ever since I met him.'

A slightly wistful look crept for a moment into Judy's big, grey eyes. 'Keep him, then, honey. It's worth working at. Despite Women's Lib and all the rest of it, it's a lonesome thing being a girl on her own.'

'You're lonely, Judy?' Dorrie sat down by her friend and put an arm round her. 'But – you're always so – so full of fun – always doing something with crowds of friends.' Judy pulled a face, half-comic. 'We all play games, don't we? Just remember what I said, kiddo! If you find the man – and I mean *the* man, not just any old Tom, Dick or Harry for a quick roll in the hay – stick with him! All the money in the world's no substitute!'

'Landsakes, honey-chile!' Dorrie said, 'I declare they'll make a preacher out of you yet!' She skipped out of the way as Judy aimed a smack at her bare bottom, then stood in front of the long mirror, towelling herself, gazing at her reflection with an abstracted frown.

'It worries me a bit, though, Judy,' she said.

'What does?'

'Well – commitment, I suppose. To someone you don't

353

really know all that well. Do you understand what I mean? You find someone, you fall in love with them – and they could be Al Capone or Jack the Ripper for all you know.'

'So? If you love them, you love them. You don't make conditions, or ask for a warranty. Besides – I don't see Ross as a hoodlum or a murderer. What's bugging you? The Italian name or the Vegas connection?'

'Neither. Not really. Nothing's bugging me – in fact, the trouble is, I'm so deliriously happy I can't believe there isn't a big black fly in the ointment somewhere. By the way – you won't mind if Ross moves in with me tonight, will you?'

'Of course not, hon! Just don't tell the kids – I'm raising them to be God-fearin' and clean-livin'.'

'Hallelujah!'

Dorrie dressed for the evening in a long, Liberty-print dress that she'd had for a couple of years. The demure, tucked bodice with its fastening of tiny buttons and the long gathered skirt, emphasized the curve of her breasts, and the colours of grey and lilac and misty blue were a perfect foil for her gleaming hair. The material was a soft, fine wool, infinitely touchable, as Ross found when she came down for dinner and sought him out on the verandah where he was sipping one of Judy's famous Martinis.

She came into his arms and raised her lips to his, smiling.

'You beautiful creature,' he said. 'You've got no right to look so lovely when I wanted to concentrate on Judy's tacos!'

'Well – what about you? When you look at me like that, my whole tummy turns over – and that's no good for digestion, either!'

'You mean, I make you sick?'

'Yes – with love!' She pressed closer to him with a little

wriggling motion of her hips, smiling up at him teasingly, and was rewarded by his quickly indrawn breath.

'Hey!' he said, softly, 'I know Judy's a very liberal-minded lady, but I think she would frown on her guests rolling about the verandah before dinner.'

'Later, then,' Dorrie said. 'Ross – will you – will you come and sleep with me tonight? Really sleep, I mean, all night through so that we wake up together?'

There was something in the request that touched Ross, and he bent to kiss her cheek, breathing in the sweet, sunwarmed scent of her.

'Of course,' he said.

They moved a little apart as Judy came out, grinning at them indulgently. 'Are you ready to eat, if I may mention anything so mundane? Come along – my kids are only house-trained up to a point – another five minutes and they'll devour everything!'

They sat down with Judy and the four children and ate an enormous meal of tacos and salad followed by pecan pie and whipped cream and gallons of excellent coffee, then, despite the fact that they were all full to bursting, the children insisted on popping a panful of corn, and they sat around the wood fire, talking and occasionally munching, until bedtime. Fourteen-year-old Francesca, who was a quiet, talented girl with her mother's big, grey eyes, played her guitar softly in a corner, a gentle thread of sound that stitched the velvet quiet of the evening, and Joe, the four-year-old baby of the family, climbed on to Dorrie's knee and nestled there, dozing, a podgy thumb in his mouth.

Ross watched Dorrie's face as she held the sleepy child, and saw the sadness that drooped her soft, lovely mouth. With a pang of guilt, he realized that he had hardly thought, since Dorrie had confided in him, of the child – the little son who was his and Dorrie's, far away in

Riyadh. He was like a child in a story – not quite real, not a creature of flesh and blood. Whereas his own children – he corrected himself – his children by Sarah, were brought individually and painfully to mind by the proximity of the Berringer family. He wondered if little Tom would have forgotten him by the time he got home. He was just beginning to chatter – mostly nonsense, but the word 'Daddy' was used frequently and triumphantly.

And Ben, who had borne his mother's death with such a resolute, stern face, but whom Ross had discovered sobbing like the smallest baby in the privacy of his room – did he feel doubly abandoned now, with his father gone? Beatrice, too, with her delicate, pansy-eyed face, Sarah's face in miniature – was she missing him, secretly reproaching him for leaving them to their grief, as though their mourning was a separate thing from his own? He made up his mind to ask Khalid to send him back to London as soon as possible. After all, he had done what he was supposed to do here, and it was nothing that any of a dozen American managers could not have done. He was sick of the false glitter of Las Vegas – at least in London he could escape from the casino back to sanity and reality – in Vegas there was no such escape.

They went to bed early. Dorrie felt unaccountably shy at sharing her room with a man. It was ridiculous – but, even when she had been married, Tariq had never spent a whole night with her. Now she felt girlish and awkward as she undressed and climbed into bed. Ross stood for a moment looking down at her before he got in beside her, and beneath the scrutiny of his dark eyes, warm with the promise of passion, she felt a deep blush rising in her cheeks.

'Did I tell you,' he said, 'that I love you very much?'

They made love with a joy and a pleasure in each other's bodies that made them want to go on and on all night, and when the soft dawn breeze woke them as it lifted the curtains at the open windows, they made love again.

'If we go on like this,' Ross said, 'I shall be an old man in six months time.'

'Nonsense,' Dorrie protested. 'It's good for you!'

She got up and showered, then came back, towel-wrapped, to the bedside to dry herself and Ross, watching as she patted and rubbed at damp golden breasts and thighs, felt the resurgence in his loins and grinned up at her.

'What?' She pulled the bedcover back from him, 'Good God! You're insatiable!'

'I am? Try me!' He pulled her back into bed with a deft scoop of one arm and began to lightly kiss and caress her bare damp body. First her neck, her cheeks, her lips, shoulders, breasts, every inch lovingly explored, the tingling tip of each breast surrounded and surmounted with warm kisses, until they were sending electric signals through her whole body, and his mouth moved on across the softness of her belly to the tender, paler skin on the inside of her sun-tanned thighs and, as he felt her whole body quivering with arousal, to the soft, receptive folds of vulva and clitoris. Dorrie moaned with passion and delight, abandoning herself completely to the love-making that was like the discovery of a new dimension, or suddenly finding that she could fly, and the sudden rush of orgasm shook her almost into unconsciousness. Was this, she wondered drowsily, floating in that delicious state between waking and sleeping, what the French called 'the little death'?

They spent the day wandering about, exploring Tahoe's sandy and pebbly beaches, dazed and drunk with love. They played baseball with the children, and ate too much of Judy's delicious food, and the next day Ross had to return to Vegas.

Appropriately, the sky was grey when they got up early to catch the plane, and Dorrie felt as sulky as a child who has to leave a party early.

'I don't see why you have to go,' she said, crossly, sitting on the edge of the bed and brushing her hair. 'You could easily stay another few days.'

'I have a living to earn,' Ross said, lightly. 'I'm not one of your landed gentry, you know.'

'Don't be silly. You know I've got heaps of money – enough for both of us . . .' She stopped abruptly as she saw the expression on his face.

'Don't ever say that again, Dorrie,' he said, softly. 'Do you think I'm some sort of bloody gigolo? Whatever happens, I shan't touch a penny of your money. Ever. Do you understand?'

'I understand, all right. But it's such a sodding stupid old-fashioned idea . . .'

'My darling Dorrie – if you attack your lovely hair with that brush, you'll soon be quite bald, and then I shall abandon you. Now get a move on – we have a plane to catch.'

He saw the mutinous scowl on her face and grinned to himself. He had felt sure that the sweet, pliant Dorrie of the last few days would not last for ever. He was not quite sure which of them he loved most.

They flew back to Vegas, and Dorrie felt unaccountably depressed as she saw once again the ring of encircling mountains and the miles of desert, bare of everything except sage-brush, coyotes and rabbits.

Three days later Khalid had what he wanted. He ran the video again, watching the absorbed and unrestrained love-making without a flicker of voyeuristic pleasure on his face. His own taste was for very young boys, though he took care not to advertise the fact. A pity, really, that Cavallo did not have more eccentric tastes – it was always easier to get to a man through his perversions. Still – there were really some very nice shots there – very intimate, very uninhibited. Not the sort of thing, for example, that a man would like his mother to see, or his kids, or even, if he was suddenly out of a job, his prospective employer.

Dorrie was not enjoying Vegas. As some wag had once said, there are only three things to do in Las Vegas, and two of them are drinking and gambling. She had little taste for either of them, and the hours Ross could snatch from work, even though she knew he was going short of sleep, seemed painfully few. She longed to be back in England – to be at Ash Friars with him and the children, exploring the woods and lanes and exorcizing the ghost of the lonely little girl who had once wandered there. If only Ross were not so pig-headed, he could hand in his notice to Khalid and be free. But she knew he wouldn't, and, secretly, illogically, she knew she would not have felt quite the same about him if he had eagerly agreed to live on her money.

He had already asked Khalid if he could return to England, and the casino owner had agreed, but non-committally, refusing to give an exact date and implying that the final decision rested with Giulio Verga rather than himself.

Dorrie spent her days at the pool-side of the Golden Nevada, very occasionally playing a little roulette or blackjack, or buying the most vulgar and tacky souvenirs she could find to present to Ross when he came to her room.

Every night there was a show, with one or more famous

names, and Khalid always made a point of introducing
her to the ones she didn't already know, even though she
told him frankly that movie stars were the most self-
centred, boring company she knew. Johnny Pacelli,
despite his bragging, only rated second billing in any
show, and that only when Khalid couldn't get anyone
else. Whatever was destroying the singer, Dorrie thought,
was doing so very quickly. His voice, once quite powerful
and melodious, had a harsh note to it now, and a habit of
cracking on the high notes. The Vegas audiences were not
critical – anywhere else, Pacelli would have been hooted
off the stage. Dorrie couldn't help feeling sorry for him –
he had always been such a bombastic, conceited fellow
that his humiliation was all the greater and, oddly, she
found herself liking him more when she saw the fear of
failure in his eyes, than she had at the height of his
success.

When Sinatra appeared one night at the Golden
Nevada, Khalid brought him over to Dorrie's table, and
she chatted to him for a while, faintly amused at the
envious glances from the other women. The man had a
lot of easy charm, and an attractive air of assurance that
came from a lifetime of adulation, but Dorrie was not
vulnerable.

Pacelli was, however. She could see him hovering in
the background, and then suddenly finding the nerve to
come forward and introduce himself.

'Hi, Frank! I'm Johnny Pacelli – I've been an admirer
of yours for many years . . .'

The big star did not reply. He raised his glass and took
a thoughtful sip and Dorrie saw that the famous blue eyes
were quite cold. With a sure instinct that had kept him at
the top for years, Sinatra could smell a loser.

'Hey, Johnny. Do us a favour,' Khalid said, softly,
then, as Pacelli turned eagerly towards him, 'Fuck off.'

Witnessing Pacelli's humiliation was more painful than Dorrie liked. She excused herself and followed him from the room, stopping him as he slouched past the craps tables in the main casino.

'Johnny? I haven't seen you much this trip. Why don't you have dinner with me to tomorrow night?'

He tried to compose his features into a Brando-esque sneer, but Dorrie saw to her horror that his eyes were filled with tears.

'That no-good shit-head,' he muttered. 'He's jealous of me, you know, 'cause I'm on the way up.' And then, illogically, 'He'd've talked to me, too, if Khalid hadn't butted in. Two-bit crook – I'll get even with him!'

'Don't be silly, Johnny. You won't do yourself any good talking like that. Tomorrow night – okay? Pick me up in my room about eight.'

'Yeah. Sure,' he said, moodily, and so absently that Dorrie was sure he'd forget and kicked herself for having bothered with the little jerk. That was the trouble with being happily in love – it made you feel like a character from 'The Sound of Music', wanting to spread sweetness and light everywhere.

And she was happy – yes, completely happy, except . . . there had been no talk of the future between them. There was love-making, ecstatic and satisfying, every night, and precious hours spent in each other's company, their love seeming to grow tangibly, putting out tendrils to bind them together, but Ross had never mentioned marriage to her and she sometimes woke in the night when he wasn't there and wondered, panic-stricken, if the whole thing was just a transitory affair and like the spring-blossoming flowers in the Nevada desert – brilliant, swift-blooming and quick to die. Nothing seemed permanent about Las Vegas – the four-storey-high neon signs and the million glittering lights were like those of a fair-ground, gaudy and transient, and the people passing through had stepped out of their own lives into another dimension. The excitement and glitter kept them in a state of febrile gaiety for a few days, and then they left, usually a lot poorer, to be succeeded by the next wave, rushing lemming-like for the fruit-machines and the gaming tables.

The next day, tentatively, she voiced her thoughts to Ross, as they strolled together down the Strip, breathing the hot, dry desert air.

'Do you feel as though we're – oh, sort of unconnected with time here? As though nothing here has anything to do with the world outside?'

Ross stopped and looked down at her, taking her chin in one hand and turning her face up towards his.

'What are you trying to tell me, Dorrie? That when we leave we go our separate ways? Is that what you have in mind?'

'*No* – oh, no, of course not! I just thought you – I mean, you haven't said – I mean – oh, damn it to hell, Ross, you know what I mean!' she finished angrily. Why did he have to deliberately misunderstand? He really infuriated her sometimes.

He grinned, his teeth very white against the deep tan of his face, and pinched her cheek gently. Then, taking her hand in his, he began walking slowly on.

'You see,' he said, thoughtfully, 'I haven't been thinking about the future too much, because the present has been enough. Just holding you, loving you, having you near, is so incredible, I'm taking time to adjust. We oldies aren't so adaptable as you kids, you know!'

'Don't *say* that,' she said, fiercely. 'You're not old – anyway, I'm nearly twenty-one.'

'*That* old?' he exclaimed, horrified. 'How well you've worn, Grandma! No – don't hit me in public – if we brawl we'll both be arrested. This is a very respectable city. Listen, chuckle-head, if you will only let me express myself without interrupting every ten words – all I want to say is – I love you, and I can't imagine a future without you.'

It was not enough, but Dorrie supposed it would have to do. What exactly did he mean? A continuation of their love affair, with him visiting her flat, occasional weekends together? Could she bear to live that sort of life? It would be frustrating and unfulfilling – but if it was what Ross wanted, at least for the moment, she would put up with it. Pride would not allow her to ask if he might marry her one day. After all, she had done her best to build up an image of a free-loving emancipated girl with no hang-ups about marriage or permanent relationships – and now she was stuck with it.

'Good Lord!' Ross said, 'Look at this!'

'This' was a wedding chapel, one of the hundreds in Las Vegas, called the 'Golden Memories Wedding Chapel'. There was an electric sign in the window that proclaimed that Mrs Peggy Cleaver was open twenty-four hours a day to perform immediate ceremonies. Further signs intimated that flowers, gowns, rings, portraits and gifts were available.

'Do they provide brides and grooms as well, for single people?' Ross wondered. 'Come on – we must take a look!'

'No – Ross! Don't be silly! You can't just wander in like that!'

'Says who?'

He pushed open the door and pulled her firmly into what looked like a cross between a gift shop and a funeral parlour. Display cases of rings and dresses, corsages and bouquets, lined the walls of the outer room, while an arched doorway in neo-plastic Gothic was labelled 'Wedding Chapel', and recorded organ music blared plaintively in the background.

At a large desk which held a cash register lurking behind an ornate floral arrangement, sat Mrs Cleaver herself, according to the name-plate in front of her. She wore petunia polyester and a great deal of sparkling jewellery and was engaged in painting her nails to match her outfit. Scarcely raising her eyes as they came in, she began in a rapid monotone, 'Well, congratulations to the two of you, the lovely bride and the handsome bridegroom, and what's it to be, folks? This is a special occasion, a big day in your lives, nothing tacky or cheapjack, you've sure come to the right place, we have the loveliest selection of gowns and rings in all of Vegas. Our special Golden Ceremony, including flowers, lucky mascots, Parisian-designed gown hire, rings and witnesses, is only two hundred and fifty dollars and that includes everything.'

'Yes – it all sounds very nice,' Ross said, pleasantly, 'but there's a small ceremony we have to perform first.'

Mrs Peggy Cleaver looked up, faintly suspicious at the English accent, her heavily painted eyes behind glitter-framed glasses as hard as any of the collectors', who went to retrieve bad debts from defaulting gamblers.

'Ross!' Dorrie didn't know whether to laugh or be cross, 'What's got into you?'

'Miss St James,' he said, formally, 'would you do me the honour of becoming my wife?'

Dorrie's cheeks flushed crimson, and she bit her lip, glowering at him resentfully. 'Don't make sodding stupid jokes,' she muttered, pulling her hand away from his.

'My dear girl! Do I have to go down on one knee? Won't you let me make an honest woman of you?'

She stared up at him, dubiously, while Mrs Cleaver

gaped at them, flapping her varnished nails absently as she did so.

'Ross,' Dorrie said, 'if you *are* trying to be funny – I'll kill you.'

'Does that mean yes? Excuse me, Mrs Cleaver – I must just kiss my bride-to-be.'

He bent and kissed her softly on the mouth, and, as she met his eyes she saw he was no longer smiling, and there was an expression that made her heart lurch and turn over.

'Darling . . .' she whispered, 'Oh, darling – I love you so much . . .' She put her arms round his neck and hugged him to her.

Mrs Cleaver yawned slightly. She had seen it all a million times before.

'Whenever you folks are ready,' she drawled.

'Oh, Ross – here? In this place?' Dorrie said, suddenly aware of her surroundings.

'Mm – I see what you mean. Though it would have been something to tell our grandchildren.'

He turned to the desk. 'Well, Mrs Cleaver – we've had a great deal of discussion, and we're very tempted to use your charming facilities. But, you know, an awful lot of people are going to be disappointed if we don't get married in Westminster Abbey. So, I'm afraid we must regretfully decline your special Golden Ceremony. Perhaps next time? Thank you. Good afternoon.'

Mrs Cleaver stared after them, her mouth open and her hand arrested in mid-flap. Westminster Abbey? Had he been putting her on? But that Prince – what was his name? – one of them, anyway – she'd read somewhere that he loved practical jokes. And the girl – she looked as though she could be a princess, yes, sir! Suddenly excited, she reached for the phone. 'Hey, Myra! You'll never guess who I just had in here!'

Outside, the afternoon sun struck hot on their backs after the air-conditioning of the Wedding Chapel. Dorrie smiled and then began to laugh helplessly. 'Did you see her face, you dreadful man?' she gasped, when she could speak at all, 'What on earth did you do it for?'

'I wanted to ask you to marry me – and it seemed an appropriate place. If you'd turned me down flatly I could have made a joke of it.'

'Oh, you idiot!' she said, softly, 'Don't you know yet that I love you? I want to spend the rest of my life with you, and if it means getting married in an instant wedding chapel by a black widow spider – that's okay by me!'

'No,' he said, 'we'll do it properly at home. I want the children to be there, and – '

'The children? Will they want to? I mean – I know they liked me, as a sort of big sister. But – as a mother? Ross – let's wait a few months – let them get used to me. I don't want them to hate me.'

'They couldn't hate you, sweetheart. But we'll wait till whenever you want. As long as you don't run off anywhere and leave me.'

'How could I?' She slipped her arm through his, and he could feel the softness of her breast against him. He turned and began heading back the way they had come.

'Where are you going?'

'Darling – I'm a bit inhibited about making love on the pavement, but if I don't get you back to your room and get your clothes off in ten minutes, that's exactly what I'm going to do.'

When Ross left her, to get ready for work, Dorrie lay in bed for a while longer, full of drowsy peace, her whole body warm and relaxed and fulfilled, and her mind, too, at rest. Ross loved her and wanted to marry her. The last faint little shadow was gone from between them and there was nothing but love and trust. They would go back to

England, and she would somehow persuade Ross to leave gaming. When the time was right – when the children were happy about accepting her – then they would be married, perhaps at the little church in Lower Poltenay, and maybe they could all live at Ash Friars. She was sure she could persuade her father to agree to that. The children would love it there – they could ride and explore and picnic. There were good schools in the area – she wouldn't ever send them away. And perhaps – oh, God she hardly dared hope – but, there *were* firms who specialized in snatching back abducted children. For a price, surely one of them could get Sultan back for her? They could all be together then – a family together, living in peace and happiness. Smiling, she dozed again.

By eight o'clock she was dressed, and waiting for Pacelli to show up. She had put on a silvery, smooth-wrapped dress of silk organza cloque from Fendi's in Sloane Street, making an effort to look her best, for the sake of poor old Johnny's bruised ego. She had spent a while in the beauty parlour, having her hair dressed into an elegant chignon that made the carriage of her head seem even prouder than usual, and, knowing Johnny loved ostentation, she added a diamond bracelet, earrings and choker.

By half-past eight she was irritable and by a quarter to nine she was furious and hungry. Pacelli would never change, she told herself – a cornered, desperate, sick rat was still a rat, and she had been a fool to bother about him. She didn't feel like going down to the restaurant – it would be easier to call room-service and have them send something up. She reached for the phone just as there was a knock at the door.

Pacelli was there, but the sarcastic greeting died on Dorrie's lips as he staggered and almost fell against her.

'Come inside, Johnny,' she said, quite gently. He was drunk, of course – and probably drugged as well – but he was such a pathetic figure that the disgust she felt was inevitably mixed with pity.

'Sit down.' She gave him a slight push and he sank into the depths of a squashy, brocade-covered chair. The white tuxedo he was wearing was slightly crumpled and there was a stain on one lapel. 'Shall I send for some coffee?'

'No – I'm fine. Just great. A bit tired, that's all.' His speech was slurred, and his eyes looked sore and red-rimmed as he tried to focus them on Dorrie.

'You people don't realize,' he said, ' – hard work being a star. Groupies . . . recording dates . . . appearances . . . tiring.' He closed his eyes for a moment and Dorrie was afraid he was going to pass out. She called room-service and ordered coffee, and was at the door to receive it when the waiter arrived. It wouldn't do Johnny any good for anyone to see him like this.

'Here – wake up, Johnny – drink some coffee.'

She managed to get him to take a sip or two of coffee, though he spilled some down the front of his frilled shirt, his mouth loose and shaking. Dorrie, kneeling beside the chair, noticed how yellow and slack his skin had become over the last year, and how emaciated he was.

'Oh, Johnny,' she said, quietly, not even sure if he was fully conscious, 'what a fool you're being! You're ruining your life – and your career, too. Can't you try and kick the habit – go to a clinic or something?'

All the pretence seemed to vanish from Pacelli. 'Too late,' he muttered. 'Nothing nobody can do.'

'Don't talk nonsense. After all, Khalid offered you a chance, singing here. What if it wasn't top of the bill? You could've done really well, Johnny – and, like an idiot, you're blowing it. I could shake you. You can't expect Khalid to employ someone who's either dead drunk or mainlining heroin.'

Pacelli pushed the cup away and lay back in the chair, his eyes closed. A sort of smile twisted his mouth.

'You dumb kid,' he whispered. 'You're a nice kid – but, boy! Are you dumb! Who d'you think got me on to drugs in the first place? Who do you think supplies me with smack?'

'Not *Khalid*?'

'Shock, horror. Yeah – nice, fat smiley Mr Khalid. He started me off, real slow and careful – just the odd reefer to help me relax – a couple of years ago when I was just a dumb kid, even dumber than you. Then, when I'd get tired, sometimes there'd be speed – amphis, you know. Then coke-sniffing – like everyone does, quite harmless. Finally, the big H – and here I am, one pathetic little junkie, courtesy of Giovanni Khalid.'

'I – I didn't know . . .' Dorrie was stunned, staring at Pacelli's pinched, dissipated face as though she'd never seen it before. He opened his eyes, and they looked brighter now, lit up by a sudden malice.

'There's a lot you don't know, baby. You think Khalid and Verga make their money from casinos, right? Sure, they're money-spinners, but the real money comes from other things – drugs, mainly, and prostitution. The casinos are a front, that's all – used for laundering the big money – and suckers like me are used to help them. Till we make a few cock-ups, that is.'

Still she stared at him, not wanting to believe him. He was drunk, doped. She forced a laugh.

'You've been watching "The Godfather" Johnny . . .'

'"The Godfather"? Believe me, kid – Marlon Brando gave the Mafia a cosy, warm-hearted image compared with the real thing. You just don't know, kid – you really don't know.'

'No, I don't. But – Ross would. He *works* for Khalid, for God's sake. He wouldn't – '

'No? Cavallo gets a good screw – and I'm not talking about you. He knows when to button his lip and look the other way.'

'I don't believe you,' Dorrie whispered, 'You're lying . . .'

'Sure, I'm lying. Just 'cos the guy's laying you doesn't make him a fucking saint. But – have it your way, honey. Only, don't say I didn't warn you.'

With difficulty he pulled himself to his feet and stood looking down at Dorrie where she was still knelt by the armchair.

'I should go home, kid, if I were you,' he said, 'back to the stately home. Don't leave it too late like I did. Sorry about the dinner date – I'll see you around, okay?'

She didn't answer, and, long after the door had closed behind him, she stared at it, her eyes shadowed by a frown of painful intensity. She couldn't believe what Pacelli had told her – or, at least, if there was some truth in what he said about Khalid and Verga, it was ridiculous to suppose that Ross was involved. Something like that – it was so foreign to his nature – it would make nonsense of her feelings for him. It would mean that the man she had loved did not exist, except in her imagination.

After a time she stood up, realizing from her cramped limbs that she had been in the same position for a long time. She poured herself some of the lukewarm coffee, but she no longer felt hungry. Her appetite was gone.

It couldn't be true. She wanted to run to Ross and demand his assurance that he knew nothing about it. But – would he be angry with her, that she had doubted him? Oh, surely Pacelli was just being vindictive. He had never liked Ross, and perhaps he was jealous as well, now that Ross was obviously Dorrie's lover. That was it – it was only a jealous invention.

She made up her mind to go and confront Pacelli. She

370

had been taken aback too much to question him, but she would easily catch the little jerk out in a couple of contradictions. She would make him admit he had been lying.

Pacelli's room was on the same floor as her own, as were all the British who had come over on the London junket, and the place was deserted at this time of the evening, with everyone down at the tables. The vast, deep-carpeted corridor was empty and silent, so that the noise as Dorrie went towards Room 358 stopped her in her tracks. It was not a very loud noise – no louder than a champagne bottle being opened, but it was sharp and sudden and the silence seemed to enclose it with a complete finality.

For no reason at all, Dorrie felt her heart begin to beat very fast and heavily, and her legs shook as she hurried to Pacelli's door.

'Johnny? Johnny – it's me – are you all right?'

She hammered on the door and it swung open, slowly and noiselessly. Pacelli was sitting opposite the door as though waiting to greet her. He was sitting in a relaxed pose with his left hand in his lap and his right hand hanging down by the side of his chair. In his right hand was a gun, and most of the top of his head was missing.

'Johnny? *Johnny?*' It was her own voice that Dorrie heard, repeating the dead man's name over and over again, and she actually took a step forward, her hand going out in a fumbling gesture as though there was some way she could help him be whole again. Then her shocked brain finally took in the horror of the scene in front of her, photographed in minute detail the shattered head, the blood that still trickled slowly into the staring dead eyes, and with a strangled gasp, she turned and fled.

Back in her own room, she was wretchedly sick, her empty stomach heaving with disgust and terror, and when at last she stood up and splashed cold water on her face, she saw that her cheeks were grey beneath their tan.

There was only one thing she craved and that was the comfort of Ross's arms. He would know what to do. He would make the horror disappear. With hands that shook, she lifted the receiver of the telephone, shuddering again as that awful vivid picture came into sharp focus in her brain once more – the shattered head, the bloodstained white tuxedo, the right hand trailing on the floor with the gun still in it. The right hand.

Very slowly and carefully she replaced the receiver. She had dated Johnny Pacelli for several months, off and on. She knew quite well he was left-handed. Pacelli had been killed, and his murderer or murderers had still been in the room, or in the bathroom, when she had opened the door.

He had been killed – why? Because he knew too much? Because he was beginning to be dangerous, blabbing about what he knew to other people? Had someone heard what he had told her, and was that why he had been killed almost immediately?

That meant that what Pacelli had said was true. The Golden Nevada and the Olympus were only respectable fronts to conceal the most vicious of criminals – and if that were true, then it was surely also true that Ross Cavallo was involved.

With a blind, panic-stricken instinct for flight, Dorrie threw clothes into suitcases, stuffing them carelessly in, shoes on top of designer gowns, powder spilling, jewellery flung anywhere. She rang for a bell-hop to take her bags down, and was at the desk checking out in ten minutes, bound for the airport and the first flight out of Vegas, no matter where it was going.

Ten minutes later Cavallo had his first break of the evening and took the elevator to the second floor to see

Dorrie. He knew she had been dining with Pacelli, and why, although he thought her sympathy for the little pain in the ass was misplaced, but he had noticed that the reserved table in the dining-room had not been used. Perhaps Pacelli was drunk and was making a nuisance of himself.

He knocked on Dorrie's door, and, when there was no reply, tried Pacelli's. For long seconds he stood in the doorway, staring, his face devoid of all expression. Then he went into the room. 'You poor little bastard,' he said, softly, picking up the phone.

'Mr Khalid? Cavallo. I'm in Pacelli's room. It looks as though he's shot himself.'

Within an hour, everything had been discreetly cleared away. There was very little mess – the armchair had absorbed the bullet and most of the blood, and that very evening Room 358 was occupied again. There were not many questions from the police. Suicide was not that common in Vegas these days, but it happened, and when the victim was some junkie with no known relatives, it was best to get it all sorted out as fast as possible. No one wanted trouble in Las Vegas – it was, as Ross had remarked, a very respectable city.

It was nearly midnight when Ross had finished giving a statement to the police. He had done so as concisely and matter-of-factly as possible – there was little enough to tell, after all, but all the time part of his mind was thinking about Dorrie and wondering where she was. Had she known about Pacelli's suicide? His door had been open, and she might have gone to investigate if he hadn't turned up for their dinner date. Or had she simply waited a while, and then gone off somewhere by herself? When he was free and back in his own room, he tried to ring her, but the girl at the desk said, 'I'm sorry, Mr Cavallo – Miss St James checked out earlier this evening.'

'Checked out? What do you mean? Are you sure?'

'Yes, sir. About ten o'clock. She took a taxi to the airport, sir.'

'Thank you.'

The desk clerk hung up, but Ross stared at the receiver as though he still expected it to connect him with Dorrie. It was just impossible that she would have walked out, without even seeing or speaking to him. He toyed with the idea of a kidnapping – but the girl had been quite clear that Dorrie had left alone. Had she perhaps got cold feet, now that the subject of marriage had come up? He dismissed that idea as well. Someone as straightforward as he knew Dorrie to be, would have talked about it with him. Something, then, had happened since he left her at six o'clock that evening, to make her act so out-of-character, and the only thing it could have been was Pacelli's suicide.

Ross stood up, and poured himself a shot of bourbon from the drinks cabinet in his room. He had cut down on smoking a lot the last year, but he lit a cigarette now and drew the smoke deeply into his lungs, frowning with concentration. Why had Dorrie fled so precipitately from Pacelli's suicide? She had dated the guy, certainly, and his exit had been messy and horrific – far more violent than one would have expected from the little creep – still, that was not reason enough for Dorrie to run. Why had she not called him? She knew she could reach him in an emergency, so why had she run from him as well, as though he was somehow connected with the horror? Suicide was horrible, of course, and shocking – but not, surely, frightening? Not like murder.

Ross ground his cigarette slowly out on an ashtray and reached for another, while he went over in his mind every detail of Pacelli's death as he had seen it. Could it have been murder? There had been no signs of a struggle – if

Pacelli had been killed, it had been by someone he knew quite well. And – he was a drug addict, obviously on the way out as far as his career went. People like that were high on the potential suicide list, although it had to be admitted that their way out was normally by an overdose. Besides – what reason would anyone have for killing Pacelli? No one could profit by his death – he was broke, without possessions. The only motive might be that he was a nuisance to someone, an irritating, superfluous nuisance, buzzing around like a fly who has been on the dungheap and is intent on spreading the dirt.

Cavallo sat by his window, motionless, only his hand moving occasionally as he put his cigarette to his lips or lit another. He watched the glittering neon of Vegas, sparkling in the crisp night air of the desert, and the headlamps of hundreds of cars still driving up the Strip, though it was nearly one A.M. As he watched, he tried to piece together all the little things about Pacelli that had caused him uneasiness in the past two years, but which he, absorbed in his own affairs and, later, in his grief, had pushed to the back of his mind.

It seemed so obvious now, what had been going on, and he had been a fool not to see it. Fifteen years in gaming, and he had acted like a greenhorn, shoving suspicion aside, not wanting to know, shrugging even when Sandy McNeil had said, 'Johnny Southpaw was in again with a great wad of notes. Took most of it out again in a cheque, though.'

Laundering money. The most obvious illegal use to which a casino could be put. And the manager had let it go on under his nose, as though he didn't give a shit, as long as his hands were clean. And how clean were they now, now that a man was dead, whether it was suicide or not? Poor old Johnny Southpaw – that was what McNeil, ex-boxer, had called him because he was left-handed.

And, of course, a left-handed man did not shoot himself with his right hand.

Heavily, Cavallo got to his feet. He crushed out his final cigarette and, leaving his room, took the elevator to the ninth floor and Giovanni Khalid's suite. He hardly knew what drove him, unless it was the knowledge that Pacelli had been murdered, and that Dorrie, aware of this, had somehow felt that he was involved in the whole dirty business. Of course, it would seem like that. He was, after all, Khalid's right-hand man. Filled, suddenly, with a cold, murderous rage, that made him recklessly ignore the possible danger to himself, he hammered on Khalid's door, wanting only to confront the man, to tell him to take his job and stuff it, Ross Cavallo was not going to be a dumb puppet any longer.

The door was opened by Tony, one of the heavies that Khalid employed as a collector. A huge man with an impassive, almost thoughtful face and hands that a demolition gang could have used, he was very successful in persuading people to pay up, even though gaming debts were not legally collectable in the US.

He recognized Ross and stepped aside, a jerk of his massive head serving as an invitation to enter.

Khalid was there, comfortable and at ease, with his glass of bourbon and water, his damp, chewed Havana smouldering at his lips, talking to his friend and colleague, Mr Verga, who sat very straight in his immaculate three-piece suit as though he had just come from a business meeting.

Khalid looked up as Ross came in, an expression of friendly welcome on his face. 'Ross! Come in, boy – have a drink! I was just telling Jewels – Mr Verga – about this sad business. Poor old Pacelli – we both used to admire his singing, eh? But I figured he was depressed – how about you, Ross? Did it seem that way to you?'

'No. He may have been depressed. But that wasn't what killed him. He was murdered.'

The black, shining eyes didn't flicker, nor the cigar give the smallest jerk of surprise. 'Murdered? No – you're way off beam there, Ross! Hell – the gun was still in his hand.'

'Yes. His right hand. Pacelli was left-handed, Mr Khalid – you should have known that.'

Was it imagination, or had a tiny spark of rage ignited somewhere deep in those unblinking eyes?

'Why would anyone want to murder Pacelli, Ross?' It was not an idle question. Khalid really wanted to know how much he knew, and Verga, too, leaned slightly forward, his thin, dry-looking fingers steepled beneath his chin.

Ross answered steadily. He knew by now that he could be signing his own death warrant by this impulsive confrontation, but he felt as though he couldn't care less. 'I think he died because he couldn't keep his mouth shut. I realize now what his job was, and also that he was getting to be too much of an addict to be reliable. Perhaps he said something to someone. What does it matter?'

'Ross,' Khalid said, gently, 'I've always said you were a real smart guy . . .'

'Oh, yes – too smart for words. I let it all happen right under my nose – you must have loved me!'

'Sure – I've always been fond of you, Ross – I always treated you like a son, eh? Now this business – this suicide of Pacelli's – let's call it suicide, eh? We're grown men, for God's sake. Like you say, what does it matter? A punk like Pacelli – one more, one less. They're ten a penny. But a man like you, Ross – a man with brains! You could go a long way in our organization. You're no fool, and you're no whinger – Mr Verga agrees with me that there's a place for you.'

There was a momentary pause. Khalid and Verga both

377

regarded Cavallo with genuine interest. Sure, they held all the cards, and even if Cavallo went to the police, there was not much chance of his accusations being taken seriously. Mr Verga had some close friends in very high places. But it was kind of amusing to see how someone like Cavallo reacted. He sat facing them, his big frame quite relaxed and his face unreadable.

'Mr Khalid,' he said, quietly, 'and you, too, Mr Verga – a man died tonight. Not much of a man – in fact, a bit of a jerk. But a man, all the same. I happen to believe that only God Almighty has the right to rub people out when he gets fed up with them. On these grounds, I must ask you to take your job, and any other you might offer me, and stuff it as far up your ass as it will go. Do I make myself clear?'

Khalid listened politely, a slight smile on his face. They could have been discussing a new duty roster for the casino, or next year's profit plan. His cigar had gone out and he fiddled messily with clippers and matches, flapping a hand as Ross half-rose from his chair.

'Wait, Ross, hold on!' He puffed busily, and Verga interrupted, speaking for the first time.

'Yes, Mr Cavallo. One moment.'

His voice was as thin and dry as himself, a lawyer's voice, but it had a sharp note of authority in it that made Ross pause and glance at the man.

'Mr Cavallo – my friend Giovanni has spoken highly of you. You have been a conscientious and hard-working employee and, as far as we know, an honest one – no skimming, no hustling, no rip-offs. So far, so good. But now, Mr Cavallo – now you're making a mistake – you're being foolish. I do not wish to make threats – to remind you that the desert is large and empty and that people disappear without trace, not only in Vegas, but all over America. That would be stating the obvious. But what you perhaps do not realize is that our organization is more than a group of businessmen. It is a vast family, joined by ties of blood and loyalty. One of our cardinal rules is that an offence received by one of our members must be considered an offence to the entire society and must be avenged at any cost. You're an intelligent man, Mr Cavallo, you follow me. I am quite sure.'

Cavallo followed him. It meant that, if he went to the police, and if, by any remote chance Khalid and Verga ended up behind bars, Ross Cavallo would not live long. No matter where in the world he went, sooner or later there would be an unfortunate accident. If he accused them of murder, he might as well go out and throw himself under a bus.

Khalid, watching Cavallo's grim, unmoved face, chuckled suddenly.

'Of course he follows! Eh, Ross? We understand each other, no? But – hey, I almost forgot, old fool that I am! I almost forgot the home movies!'

Ross stared at him. Had the old devil flipped his lid? But both Khalid and Verga looked quite normal – friendly, even, and Khalid was nodding to Tony.

At the other side of the vast, luxurious room there was a giant TV screen set into the wall behind velvet curtains that matched the ones at the windows. At Khalid's signal, Tony dimmed the lights and set a video in motion, his movements unusually deft for such a big man.

After five seconds, Cavallo realized what he was watching. Every intimate moment that he and Dorrie had spent making love in her room, every tender embrace, every loving, passionate, exciting, uninhibited thing they had done to each other had been watched and recorded by Khalid. At that moment of blind fury it would not have mattered if the man had had a gun trained on him.

'You *bastard*!' Cavallo launched himself through the

gloom, knocking a table and glasses flying, and his fist slammed into Khalid's face. The impetus made him stumble and nearly lose his footing, and by the time he had regained it, the lights were up and Tony and another heavy, who had appeared from nowhere, were on him, their fists thudding against him like pile-drivers.

He had one satisfying glimpse of Khalid's face, the mouth bloody and full of shattered cigar, and he was briefly aware of Verga's quiet voice saying, 'Tony! Bernard! Not on the face, please,' and then the world narrowed down to a confusion of pain and struggle. It was impossible to win, of course, against men who had taken classes in brutality and graduated *cum laude*, and it wasn't long before he set himself simply to endure the onslaught, his mind empty of everything except the will to survive, to refuse them the satisfaction of hearing him moan or plead. It finished at last, on some signal from Verga, and the two thugs shoved him into a chair and retired to the other side of the room, where they waited, immobile, perfectly trained.

Ross, too, waited for what was to come next, conscious of a vast pain all over his body, and a sharper one every time he breathed which told him that at least one rib was probably broken. He hadn't the energy to turn his head and look at Tony and Bernard, but he knew very well that every one of the punches he had managed to land on them had been returned ten-fold.

Khalid was still dabbing his mouth and spitting out bits of Havana, and, for once, his eyes were simply inimical and malevolent, without the usual oily film of bonhomie. It was Verga who had taken on the role of spokesman, and who still sat in virtually the same position, austere and unmoved by anything that had taken place.

'Now, Mr Cavallo,' he began, as though he were

discussing a rather obscure clause in a legal document, 'I hope you are ready to be sensible and co-operative.'

Ross was silent.

'Because, you see, we hold all the cards. You know, of course, that in the long term, the punter cannot win against the casino. The casino always has the edge. It is the same here. As you have seen, we have very intimate photographs of you and Miss St James. Nothing wrong, of course – she is a lovely woman, and – in this day and age – ' he shrugged slightly, 'Still, they might cause you a lot of embarrassment in some quarters – and Miss St James as well. Secondly, you have just received a fairly severe beating – would you like a drink, by the way? No? Not a really sadistic going-over, by any means, I think you will agree? No torture – we are civilized men. Just the sort of thrashing you might get if you entered the ring against a couple of heavy-weights. So what? you might say. You are a fit man, a strong man, and in a few days your body will forget the bruises. But – I must ask you, Mr Cavallo – supposing it was your children that had to suffer? Or even Miss St James? Could you bear that with as much stoicism?'

Cavallo drew a deep breath and felt the pain in his side stab through him. He looked into Verga's eyes and saw them empty of any humanity, blank, cold and dead.

'Would you do that, you bastard?' he whispered. 'Would even you stoop so low?'

Again Verga shrugged. 'Personally, I deplore violence of any description, and violence against women and children is especially abhorrent to me. But – ours is a vast organization, and there are men of all types within it, some of them, regrettably, with rather depraved sexual appetites who find young children of either sex a temptation not to be resisted.'

He paused again to let the images he had conjured up

sink into the other man's brain. Ross felt physically sick. He wanted nothing more than to destroy Verga, Khalid and their whole vast, evil empire, but he knew he might as well take up arms against the Four Horsemen of the Apocalypse.

He didn't speak, but Verga knew all the same that they had won. As always, the odds were stacked against the player. Still tenderly feeling his mouth, Khalid broke in. 'Okay, Jewels. If he squeals we take his kids, his girl – maybe even his dear old Momma, eh? But I know this guy – he's stubborn. He may try to figure a way – or he may think it's worth the risk. What I say is, he has to owe us, see? If he does – then who's going to listen to him, huh?'

Verga permitted himself a thin smile. 'Your psychology is excellent, my dear friend. Very well, Mr Cavallo – I have a generous proposition to put to you. Refuse, and you endanger the lives of all the people you care about the most.'

PART FIVE
London

17

Dorrie got back to her flat as dawn broke. August had been hot and the dark leaves of late summer were tired and dusty in the London parks, the grass trodden bare and bleached yellow, but the perfect dawn moistened and refreshed everything, bringing an illusion of spring to the city.

She was not sure what day it was, so disorientated by fatigue and misery that she could hardly remember when she had left Las Vegas on the first lap of a headlong, unpausing flight that had taken her to Miami and New York before she got a direct flight to Heathrow. And all the way, Pacelli had seemed to sit in the next seat, the top of his head a cavernous ruin, and every time her eyelids drooped with fatigue, it had seemed that he, too, slumbered, lolling towards her so that his head rested on her shoulder and she woke, sweating with fright. She had accepted countless in-flight drinks from the stewardesses – enough to make her completely unconscious, but the only effect had been to give her a pounding headache and make her eyes feel as though they'd been stuck with glass splinters.

She paid off the taxi and let herself into the flat, wondering if Cy would be up, and whether she would have anything so decadent as an aspirin. She dumped her cases. The room looked clean and tidy, unfamiliar. She opened Cy's bedroom door and looked in, and two rumpled heads raised themselves from the pillow, blinking owlishly.

'Sorry,' she said. 'Hallo, Waldo. I'm back, Cy.'

She closed the door again and stood in the middle of the sitting room, her hands clenched in the pockets of the jeans she had travelled in, staring at nothing. After a moment, Cy came out, wrapped in a towelling robe with a big 'W' monogrammed on the front, yawning and running her hands through her mop of hair.

'My God!' she said, mildly, 'You're no advertisement for the Las Vegas climate! Have you spent the whole time in debauchery and dissipation? You look like a cross between Medusa and Lady Macbeth!' Then, as Dorrie's expression of tense misery didn't lighten, Cy's voice softened and she put a hand gently on her friend's arm. 'What is it, Dorrie? When you rang last week everything was great – you sounded as though you were floating six feet off the ground. What's happened? You haven't quarrelled with Ross?'

Dorrie shook her head. 'Pacelli's dead,' she said, flatly.

'Good Lord – really? What was it, suicide or an accidental overdose?'

'No. It was supposed to be. But – Cy, he was murdered – I – I found him – and – oh, God, it was so horrible . . .'

Her control broke and she clung to Cy, sobbing and trying incoherently to explain what had happened and how she thought Ross was involved.

Waldo came out in a T-shirt and underpants, his longish straight hair hanging down each side of his solemn face, and Cy sent him briskly off to make coffee.

'The real stuff,' she called after him, 'this is no time for principles.'

When the kitchen door had closed behind Waldo, Cy pushed Dorrie firmly down into a chair and sat cross-legged on the floor beside her.

'Now, what the hell makes you believe Ross Cavallo is some sort of mobster? Did I hear properly? Pacelli told you Ross was in the know? *Pacelli?* And just because someone killed the little jerk (probably a music lover) you immediately took all his words as gospel.'

'No – Cy, it wasn't just that – I – I'm sure it was true, about Khalid getting Johnny on drugs – and I'm sure it must have been Khalid who had him killed. Cy – Ross has been working for them for years – how *can* he not be involved?'

'Dorrie,' the other girl said, with an air of patience, 'you know – you're incredibly naïve sometimes. You were born with a silver spoon in your mouth – the whole bloody canteen, in fact – and it seems beyond your comprehension that some of us have to work for a living and we're too damn glad to get a job that pays a decent wage to quibble about niceties. Okay – gaming's a dirty business. So's writing copy every day to sell products that you know probably stink – but I haven't much choice, and nor, I suspect, has Ross Cavallo.'

Dorrie was silent. She knew, from the brief, unemotional history Ross had given her, that he had gone into gaming instead of going to university so that he could bring a wage home for his mother.

'And another thing,' Cy pursued, relentlessly, 'before you wash your hands of the man without even hearing what he has to say. Has he ever been dishonest with you, or lied to you? Did he ever give you the "my wife doesn't understand me" bit, even when you were in hot pursuit of him?'

Dorrie shook her head, miserably.

'What a pity,' Cy said, conversationally, 'that your august Pa didn't kick your backside a bit more often when you were a kid. You might be a bit more sensible now, and less likely to go off at half-cock. And, apart from everything I've said, you dim-wit – if you love someone, you love them, even if they're Genghis Khan and Al

387

Capone rolled into one with a sprinkling of Rasputin. And, whatever they do, you go *on* loving them. And on.'

She looked up and grinned fondly as Waldo came in with the tray of coffee. 'Even,' she added, 'if they come back to you still hot from the arms of their Yiddisher Momma.'

Waldo smiled feebly, and shrugged. 'Oy-veh!' he said, and began to pour the coffee.

'Keep mine hot, please, Waldo, Dorrie said, drawing a deep breath, 'I'm just going to make a phone call to Las Vegas.'

She disappeared into the bedroom, but came out within a few minutes, her eyes wide and tragic.

'He's gone! He's not there – the girl just said, "Mr Cavallo has left" – she wouldn't say any more. Oh, God, Cy – you don't think they'd have – have killed him as well?'

'For crying out loud, Dorrie – sit down and have your coffee and don't be so bloody stupid. Do you think Las Vegas casinos would continue to function if they had wall-to-wall corpses? Ten to one he's on his way back to England – probably to sock you on the jaw for disappearing like that. Just wait – he'll phone you.'

'Sure he will,' Waldo agreed, cheerfully. 'Say – this tastes much better than dandelion, you know?'

Dorrie waited, tense with impatience, leaping at the phone every time it rang, and reluctant to go out anywhere. But there was no call from Ross that day or the next. The day after that, she rang the house at Kew, almost afraid that Ross would answer and would say he didn't want to see her again, but it was Lotte Behrens who spoke to her and told her that they did not expect Herr Cavallo home from Las Vegas for some time yet.

Dorrie was sick with anxiety, an ever-increasing fear that something had happened to Ross making her unable to sleep, eat, or even talk to anyone, and she prowled restlessly about the flat, eyeing the telephone and refusing to speak for more than a minute to anyone who rang her.

'Dorrie,' Cy said on the Saturday morning, 'if you don't go out for a walk or something, one of us is going to climb up the wall. You've snapped my head off three times and it's only midday.'

'Sorry, I didn't mean to. It's only because I'm so worried – oh, Cy – surely if he was all right he'd have got in touch with me?'

'Why? You walked out on him, didn't you? Is he the type to come running after you, begging for explanations?'

'No – but . . .'

' Perhaps he's visiting friends in the States, or relatives. Who knows? But one thing's for sure – you won't bring him back by pacing up and down, snarling like a caged tigress. Look – don't be a cretin. Why don't you go over to Kew and have a nice long walk in the Gardens – it's a lovely day. When you've done that, go and have a cosy visit with your prospective step-children, and if your beloved should happen to ring, which I doubt, I'll tell him where you are. How's that for a wizard wheeze?'

Dorrie frowned thoughtfully. In one way she hated leaving the flat, feeling that even if she went to the bathroom Ross might ring at that exact moment. She kept waking in the night, checking and rechecking that the extension by her bed was properly plugged in. The phone was becoming an obsession with her. And it was a warm, sunny day – the walk would clear her head and, if she could pluck up courage, it would be good to see the children again.

'Okay,' she said, at last, 'you've persuaded me. I'll go – before you send for the men in white coats.'

'Not like that, though, idiot child! D'you want to frighten everyone you meet? Your hair hasn't been brushed properly, and those jeans are nearly walking by themselves! Suppose Ross is home – d'you want him to sweep you into his arms or into the garbage can?'

'Don't fuss, Cy. If he was home he'd have called me – I know he would.' But she brushed her hair and changed into a peach-coloured cotton jacket and trousers from Biba with a white sleeveless T-shirt.

'Hmm,' Cy said, with grudging approval, 'very pretty. Don't sit – or roll – on the grass, though.' She gave Dorrie a little push towards the door, hesitated and added an uncharacteristic peck on the cheek. 'I hope you find him today, kid.'

'Thanks, Cy.'

The Ferrari, lovingly cared for and exercised by Mr Perks, responded so beautifully to her touch that she was tempted to head for the West Country and lose her problems in a wonderful rush of speed and sound. The next moment she was imagining Ross ringing the flat – Cy perhaps out for a while – and she had to stop herself slamming on the brakes and rushing back the way she had come.

She parked near the station and went into the Gardens by the gate in Richmond Road, buying a slice of veal-and-ham pie at Newens when she remembered she hadn't had any lunch. She sat on a bench by the pond and shared mouthfuls with the ducks, then wandered aimlessly through the gardens, hardly conscious of her surroundings, but dimly aware of the September warmth on her back and the rich, honeyed scent of plants and earth that had basked in the sun all summer long.

She instinctively avoided the crowded area round the Palm House and the rose gardens, and wandered along the path that leads past the Queen's Cottage, her feet noiseless on the trodden earth, then down the path running parallel with the river; the dim shadows beneath the trees and the damp smell of leaf-mould and river mud more in tune with her mood than the brightness of the late summer flowers.

She came to the place where she had met the Cavallo family, that cold winter's day, and the echo of their voices seemed still to float on the air, and Sarah's face with its expression of gentle kindness was suddenly very vivid to her. 'We're going home for tea – would you like to join us?' she had said – so warmly, so trustingly, inviting into her home a woman whose only desire had been to steal her husband. 'I'm sorry, Sarah,' Dorrie whispered, 'I didn't want to hurt you – I loved you, too.' But the ghosts were silent. Not even a faint breeze ruffled the leaves, and the only sounds were from a distant group of children running and leaping on the grass.

For an instant, seeing a thin, dark-haired boy, she thought they were Ross's children, and without thinking she took a few steps towards them, almost running, her arms outstretched. When she realized her mistake, the longing to go to his house and see Beatrice, Ben and Tom again was stronger than she could bear, and she turned and began to run across the hard-baked grass, along the paths, past the strolling groups of people who turned their heads to stare after her flying figure, out of the main gates on Kew Green, and within seconds she was standing at the Cavallos' front door, her hair a windswept mane and her face flushed with the exercise.

Beatrice opened the door to her – a Beatrice almost two years older, with a shadowy sadness lending maturity to her dark, expressive eyes, and the beginnings of roundness in her slim figure. She stared at Dorrie, her eyes widening, without saying a word, and Dorrie suddenly wondered if she had been forgotten. Then Ben, racing across the hall and pushing his head beneath his sister's arm to inspect the visitor, gave a whoop of delight.

'It's Dorrie! It's *Dorrie*! Bea – don't stand there gawping – let her in!'

He grabbed at Dorrie's hand and pulled her inside, literally dancing with glee. 'Hey, everyone! It's Dorrie!' he yelled again.

From the direction of the kitchen, Lotte Behrens appeared, a big smile on her plump, high-coloured face. Tom, trotting beside her, was not recognizable as the tiny baby she had once held in her arms – he was an independent two-year-old with a large, if idiosyncratic vocabulary.

'*Grüss Gott, Fräulein!* It is good you came,' Lotte said, extending a big, capable hand, 'I will make tea, *ja?* Ah – here is Frau Cavallo!'

For a second Dorrie's heart jolted painfully before she realized that it was Ross's mother that Lotte referred to. Of course – he had told her that his mother was looking after the children, and she had forgotten, in her usual impulsive rush, so that now she felt awkward and embarrassed, an intruder in a house where she had no place.

But the slim lady with the halo of silver hair and the far-sighted blue eyes was smiling at her and holding out her hand.

'Well, well, so this is the famous Dorrie, eh? I'm forever hearing about you – and you're just as bonny as they said! Come away in and have a cuppie of tea – we're just making it.'

She ushered Dorrie towards the big drawing room at the front of the house and Thomas trotted in front of them across the polished parquet floor. 'Dorrie!' he crowed, banging the door open with two plump fists, 'Dorrie! Dorrie, Daddy – Dorrie!'

Maire Cavallo was saying something, but Dorrie never knew what it was, although she was aware of answering at random, and Ben was tugging at her hand, pulling her into the room where Ross stood, staring at her, unsmiling.

There was a pulse beating heavily in Dorrie's throat, and she had to swallow before she could say, 'Ross? When did – when did you get home?'

'Last night,' he said, evenly, 'quite late.'

'Dad's been to America,' Ben said, proudly, 'and he brought me a baseball cap – and some *real* shark's teeth and – '

'Ben – do be quiet and let Dorrie sit down,' Beatrice said, speaking for the first time. She glanced shyly at Dorrie, but her smile was as welcoming as her mother's had been. It *is* nice to see you again, Dorrie. Gran – shall I go and help with the tea?'

'Yes, my pettie – and take my scones out now, will you? Yon Lotte always overbakes them. Sit you down, Dorrie – may I call you Dorrie? Ben tells me you're a great one with the horses?'

'*And* cars, Gran! She can drive as well as a man!'

'Will you listen to the blethering of the wee chauvinist? Away with you and help carry in the tea-things!'

'Okay!' Ben said, cheerfully, 'I say, Dorrie – you'll never guess what? We're going to Italy!'

'To Italy?' Dorrie repeated stupidly.

'Yes – not for a holiday – to live! For *good*! And we'll all have to learn to speak Italian, like "spaghetti bolognese, Signorina" and stuff like that.' He disappeared, then put his head round the door again. 'Did you know my Grandad was Italian?'

Dorrie nodded, not trusting herself to speak. She stared at Ross, her eyes begging him to explain, and his eyes were dark and unresponsive. Maire Cavallo glanced shrewdly from one to the other, then clicked her tongue impatiently.

'The bairns will likely forget about my scones in all the excitement. Will you excuse me for a wee while? Come on, Thomas.'

She left the room, closing the door firmly behind her, and for a few seconds there was silence.

'Ross?' Dorrie's voice was barely audible, 'Is it true? Are you really going to Italy?'

He nodded. 'Yes. I'm going to buy a farm – probably near Milan. My father's people came from that area.'

'But . . .' For the moment, all that she could comprehend was that he had planned a future, for himself and his family – a future which seemed to take no account of her. 'Ross – I wanted to explain – to say I was sorry – for running off – '

He shrugged. 'There's no need. I understood.'

'It was – I *found* him, Ross – I found Pacelli – it was so horrible, so frightening, that I just wanted to get away. It wasn't suicide – it was murder . . .'

'Yes.'

'And I – I – '

'And you thought perhaps I was mixed up in it. Quite understandable.'

'*No!* Oh, Ross – it wasn't that – oh, God, I wish I could make you see – '

'But I do see. And, in a way, it's true. I've been too many years in gaming not to accept being mixed up with all the dirty business. But I actually had nothing to do with Pacelli's death. I'd like you to remember that.'

'Ross!' His voice was so cool, so unemotional, as though there was an immense distance both mental and physical between them, that Dorrie felt her eyes fill with tears.

'Don't cry, Dorrie – and for God's sake, don't start feeling sorry for me. I'll survive. You're in no way committed, you know that.'

'God damn you, Ross!' As her tears spilled over, Dorrie was suddenly violently angry, 'You bloody cold-hearted bastard! You said you loved me – you said you wanted to spend your life with me – and now you're giving me the brush-off as if I was some kind of casual one-night stand! You stupid sod – you know damn well I love you! Oh – I *hate* you!' Her hands balled into fists and she almost threw herself at him.

He caught her wrists and pulled her into his arms, and Dorrie, her head against his chest, could feel him laughing.

'Which is it to be?' he murmured, 'Love or hate?' And then, as she turned her tear-stained face up to his, 'Oh, Dorrie – I thought you'd gone for good . . .'

'I'll *never* go – *never*!' she said, fiercely, hugging him to her, and he drew in his breath sharply at the pressure on his broken rib. 'What's wrong? Darling – are you hurt? What happened?'

'Nothing – only a slight accident. Nothing to worry about.'

'Ross – you've been hurt. Was it something to do with Johnny's murder?'

'Don't ask, darling. It's all over.'

'Is that why you're going away – to Italy? Ross? Answer me! Did Khalid have you beaten up? Did he threaten you?'

'In a way.' His voice sounded weary, defeated.

'My God – Ross – you can't let that cheap crook get away with it – you can't not stand up to him – '

Hearing her echo the thoughts that had gone round and round in his mind for the last few days was like a dentist's drill on a raw nerve. He gripped her shoulders, pushing her a little away from himself, his face bleak with anger.

'What the hell do you know about it? Just shut up, Dorrie! It's nothing to do with you!'

'It *is*! I love you – I can't bear you to – to – '

'To run away? I'm not running. I've just had enough of the whole dirty business, that's all. I'm going to retire and raise pigs and grow vines. Now – are you coming with me, or not?'

'Just one thing, Ross – ' her eyes were fixed on his and her voice was quiet but still unsteady, 'Ross – farming needs a lot of capital, I know that. It – oh, Ross – it's not Khalid's money, is it?'

His face had taken on that shuttered remote look again, but his eyes did not avoid hers. She willed him with all her strength to say 'No'. Even if he had said that he had no money, but was hoping to use hers, she would have felt nothing but gladness. But the silence went on and on.

'You wouldn't take my money,' she whispered, painfully. 'You wouldn't use a penny of it. But you take a bribe from that evil man for keeping your mouth shut.'

'If that's the way you see it,' he said, impassively. He would not explain. He would not deliberately frighten her by telling her that it was her own life and the lives of his children that had been the bribe, and even when she turned away from him with a little gesture of defeat, he did not call her back, but watched her go out of the room and out of his life in silence.

Somehow, she had expected it to be night outside, or at least a grey, shadowy twilight. It seemed ridiculous that the September evening sun should be shining as brightly as ever. People in summer clothes were wandering out of Kew Gardens, talking cheerfully, stopping to buy ice-creams, strolling across the Green. There seemed to be people all round her, and she felt as though she had been flayed – as though her whole body was raw with pain, and she would scream if anyone touched her. She began to hurry, crossing the main road over the Green without even hearing the squeal of brakes and the angry shouts behind her. A man put his hand on her arm and said, 'You'll get yourself killed like that, my dear!' and she looked at him with blank eyes and shook herself free. There was a quiet, residential road, tree-lined, by the little pond, and she followed it, in an instinctive search for somewhere to hide, like a hunted creature that bleeds and dies but still hurries onward. But there were people everywhere, mowing lawns, standing at their gates, calling to children, all of them, it seemed to Dorrie, staring at her curiously, as though they could read the anguish on her face and were mildly interested. She went on, as though pursued, through the quiet, leafy, dusty streets, until she came to the Catholic church, and it was such an ugly, red-brick building that she would have passed it if the name 'St Winefride and Our Lady of Loreto' had not caught her attention. Like a distant echo, she heard Maire Cavallo's soft Scottish voice saying, 'The funeral's to be here at St Winefride's.' Of course, this was Sarah's church. This was where she had come every Sunday to Mass, and very often during the week as well, on holy days and Feast days, to confession and to benediction, her whole life, even throughout her last illness, supported on the strong framework of her faith.

Even as she pushed the half-open door and went inside, Dorrie knew she was an intruder who had no place here. But at least it was somewhere quiet, and it was a place that Sarah had loved and believed in. Just as they both had loved and believed in Ross, Dorrie thought, but Sarah had been lucky. She had died without ever knowing that the man she loved did not exist.

She sat down in a pew, her hands in her pockets, and stared up defiantly at the crucified figure over the altar. How remote it was. How little concerned with her petty miseries and desires. And how infantile to expect help and comfort from carved, painted wood.

A priest, black-robed, crossed the altar, genuflected

briskly and disappeared into the sacristy, not even glancing at Dorrie, and she felt perversely irritated. He should have spoken to her, offered her religious solace, so that she could have laughed in his face.

An elderly woman came in and lit a candle in front of the statue of Our Lady of Loreto, kneeling down with her lips moving, as earnest and matter-of-fact as if she were consulting a doctor or an accountant.

Dorrie wanted to shout aloud that it was all sham and hypocrisy, that nothing good or beautiful existed, that you could love someone so deeply that it hurt with a pain that only their lips and arms could banish, and all the time that person was not the strong, the beloved demi-god that you had almost worshipped, but only a man, as weak and corruptible as any.

She glared up at the Christ figure, the drooping head and pierced side. Weak. Letting Himself be crucified for the sake of an idea. If she worshipped any God, it would be a strong God, an Old Testament God with a thunderbolt in one hand. Not a God who made himself vulnerable by loving people. Loving people was stupid – when you fell in love, you gave hostages to Fortune and you were no longer your own person. People could make you do what they wanted.

There was, it seemed to Dorrie, a long silence. The statues stared quietly into the distance, the Man on the cross was as intent on greater sorrows as before, and if God spoke, his voice was so still and small that she could not hear it.

But, slowly, silently as the dust-motes sifting down through the westering sunlight that filtered through the church windows, the idea grew in her mind that perhaps – perhaps Ross Cavallo, too, had his hostages to Fortune.

She got up after a while, and went out, shutting the

door carefully behind her, and walked back along the quiet street, not hurrying any more.

When she reached the house on the Green she paused, standing there in the gathering dusk, and looked through the drawing-room window, one hand lifted to tap on the glass.

The curtains were not yet drawn and Ross was there, sitting alone and staring at nothing, his face half in shadow so that she could not see his expression.

'Oh, God,' Dorrie thought, 'Am I being a fool again?'

For a moment, a wild impulse to turn and run took hold of her, then, as he raised his head and saw her, and all the harsh lines of his face softened in an incredulous joy, she knew all at once that it was going to be all right.

The fears and doubts and painful anxieties seemed to dissolve as though they had been a hard lump in her breast and she began to cry and laugh at the same time, her hand beating a light, impatient tattoo on the window.

'Ross! Let me in! Let me in! I've come home.'